SHADES OF THE PAST

THE THIRD BOOK OF THE DARK GODDESS

MELISSA MCSHANE

CHAPTER
ONE

A red-bellied fly buzzed high in one corner of the charter house, the buzz growing louder briefly every time it bumped against the ceiling. To Ginnevra, it looked like it was trying to find an exit, what with how intent it was on that particular corner. She watched it meander first one way, then another, relentlessly searching for a crack or hole that would let it escape this overheated, brightly-lit room that smelled of candle wax and sweat and Justicer Talliapanne's unique perfume. Even Ginnevra's highly developed sense of smell couldn't decide whether the scent was apricots or lilacs. For the most part, the scent faded into the background, but then Talliapanne would flick her hair over her shoulder, releasing another whiff, and Ginnevra's senses leaped into action, trying to pin down the elusive smell.

Ginnevra breathed shallowly through her mouth, trying to prevent another round of the guessing game, and watched the fly bob across the ceiling. Devoyenne's charter house, where legal cases were tried before a justicer, was as old as the republic, and its age showed in the heavy ceiling beams and the much-mended plaster between them, the corners still dark with soot from the torches that had lit the room hundreds of years before. The fly was a dancing dot of red against the sooty background; if Ginnevra unfocused her eyes, its flight traced a drunkard's path of crimson across the ceiling.

A loud cough drew her attention away from the fly and back to the men and women seated on the hard wooden pews. Light slanted through the clear glass windows on the western wall, heating the air further. Almost everyone on that side of the room had shifted away from the squares of sunlight, but with how hot the room already was, Ginnevra didn't think it much mattered where anyone sat. The Sezarni, the people who had occupied the Lordagne region long before the coming of the Goddess's Faith, had called this time of year "hiraldi," which in their language meant something like "days of being broiled alive." Ginnevra liked the heat of late summer, but even she had her limits, and the charter house was testing all of them.

She shifted her weight and reflected that at least she wasn't wearing her paladin's plate mail armor. Talliapanne had looked disappointed when Ginnevra had arrived at noon dressed in her usual jerkin and breeches rather than her armor, but she hadn't said anything critical, just eyed the greatsword slung across Ginnevra's shoulder and nodded politely. Since the justicer had on her own robes of office, a long-sleeved knee-length black robe over long black trousers, Ginnevra suspected Talliapanne wished she, too, could have worn something cooler.

The man standing in front of the justicers' desk sounded as if he was wrapping up his statement. Ginnevra had stopped paying attention the third time he repeated himself. If she were in charge, she'd have brought his meandering story to a halt fifteen minutes earlier. But she was in the charter house to learn, not to enforce her whims, and she was enough conscious of her lack of legal understanding not to let her impatience interfere with that learning.

She sat up straighter in her hard, uncushioned chair and wobbled as the uneven legs tipped her forward. Ginnevra had observed over the weeks she'd assisted with hearing legal matters in Devoyenne that no one in the republic believed justicers should think of themselves as special or superior to the average citizen. In practical terms, that meant no luxury for those hearing cases. Ginnevra didn't believe having a chair that didn't teeter would incline someone to consider herself superior, but, again, not her business.

Talliapanne, to her left, held a pencil with its tip hovering over the sheaf of paper on the desk in front of her. She hadn't written anything on the top sheet the whole time the man had spoken, hadn't even doodled or scrawled a shopping list. Either Talliapanne had better self-control than Ginnevra would have had in her position, or she'd actually been listening to the monologue.

"...and so I ask your ladyships' justice upon me," the man said. He'd gestured repeatedly while pleading his case, but now he clasped his hands behind his back as if he feared them escaping and regarded Ginnevra and Talliapanne with wide, intent eyes.

Talliapanne turned to Ginnevra. "Prime? What questions have you?"

Ginnevra cleared her throat and hoped she had, in fact, understood the important parts. "Sieur Roncio," she said, "just to clarify —your mare escaped its field and wandered into your neighbor's?"

Roncio's eyebrows drew together above the bridge of his nose. "Yes, as I said, Prime Cassaline."

Ginnevra glanced at Talliapanne. The justicer's expression was bland, neither critical nor encouraging. Ginnevra forged ahead anyway. "And you're suing for reparations against that neighbor, Madama Encollitano, because her stallion impregnated your mare?" She hadn't meant that to sound so much like a question.

"Even so, prime. I had an arrangement with Piero Falscane to breed her." Roncio looked increasingly confident, standing with his head thrown back. "Now I'm out the breeding fee and I'll be saddled with a foal of improper parentage."

Again Ginnevra shot a look at Talliapanne. Talliapanne nodded, the slightest motion. Well, it wasn't as if this was a matter of life or death, and delivering justice was one of a prime's duties. This one was just so obvious a verdict Ginnevra felt awkward about having to put it into words.

She sat forward in her chair, rocking it again. "Sieur Roncio," she said, "why is it Madama Encollitano's fault that *your* horse trespassed on *her* property?"

Roncio's lips thinned in a tight frown. "She lured Tansy into that field," he said. "It was on purpose to ruin me."

"I did not!" a woman seated a few pews back exclaimed, shooting to her feet. "That's a lie!"

"Madama Encollitano, you've had your say. Please be seated," Ginnevra said. "Sieur Roncio, three of your neighbors testified as to the condition of your fences. Namely, their poor condition. I would think someone concerned about the purity of his stock would care about preventing an accident such as this by keeping his prized mare well contained."

"Accident?" Roncio said. "But—"

"Yes, accident," Ginnevra said, cutting across his protest. "And I choose to believe it was an accident, sieur. Because the alternative is for me to look more closely at your mare's lineage and that of the intended stud. It would mean calculating the value of a foal born of that lineage. And it would require comparing that value to the much, much larger sum in reparations you've demanded of Madama Encollitano, who coincidentally came into a sizable inheritance only last year. That's the kind of investigation that could go on for a while, and who knows what else it might turn up?"

Roncio's jaw hung slack with astonishment. "I wouldn't," he said, swallowed, and tried again. "I wouldn't risk my breeding plan like that."

"I did say 'accident,' did I not?" Ginnevra fixed him with a direct, penetrating gaze. "Do I want to know why you leaped to 'on purpose'?"

Roncio swallowed again. "No, prime. I misspoke."

"Very well." Ginnevra sat back in her chair. "Madama Encollitano, will you join us?"

She waited for the woman to make her way down the pew and stand beside Roncio. Neither of them looked at the other. "Sieur Giuste Roncio, I judge your claim null. No reparations are due you from Madama Piettra Encollitano, and I require you to repair your fences immediately. Madama Encollitano, as this was an accident, you are not entitled to claim a stud fee from Sieur Roncio. This is my judgment as prime of the Blessed. You're both free to go."

Roncio shot a poisonous glance at Encollitano, but said nothing. Encollitano's expression was as bland and emotionless as Talliapanne's. Ginnevra guessed she would reserve her celebrating for a less public place so she wouldn't appear to be gloating.

Talliapanne rose. "This concludes today's hearings. Charter house convenes again in two days."

She turned to Ginnevra as the remaining citizens exited the room. "That was well spoken," she said. "You're becoming comfortable with the justicer's role."

"That one was too obvious, though, don't you think?"

Ginnevra ran a hand through her short hair; it came away damp with sweat. "Should I have penalized him for wasting our time?"

"The citizens of Devoyenne are entitled to have their grievances heard, regardless of what those grievances are." Talliapanne wriggled out of her justicer's robe, revealing a fine linen shirt whose appearance was marred by sweaty patches beneath the arms. "There are provisions in the law for handling repeated frivolous charges, but in general we don't try the person, we try the case. Meaning we aren't supposed to judge anything but the claim at hand."

"Even if the person clearly has no grounds for the claim?"

"Even then." Talliapanne folded her robe neatly and tucked it under her arm. "Think how much power a justicer would have if she could enforce the law according to her whim."

"I used to believe that's what justicers did," Ginnevra said. She slung her sword over her shoulder and followed Talliapanne to the door. "I mean, every city-state has its own laws, so how can a justicer know all of them? It seemed to me that it would be easier for a justicer to make her own justice."

"Most places abide by the Code of Cierallo," Talliapanne said, pushing open the charter house door. "So the law is more uniform than you'd imagine. But I'm not sure it matters to you. A paladin's justice is considered purer than temporal law, since it's rooted in the decrees of the holy city. I suppose that means you *do* have tremendous power, since it's your good sense that's at the foundation of your judgments."

"Oh, don't say that," Ginnevra groaned. "I still know so little about the law."

The street outside the charter house lay in shade at this time of the late afternoon, and a light breeze stirred the heavy, warm sea air, cooling Ginnevra slightly. Devoyenne was an old city, a trading hub since before the Faith had come to the Lordagne, but it looked young thanks to the ongoing renewal of lath and plaster buildings eroded by the salt winds that blew in off the harbor. Sturdier brick construction marked newer buildings, most of them taller than their neighbors. Ginnevra didn't find them appealing; the grayish-red bricks always looked dirty in full sunlight and mud-spotted under an overcast.

"Sometimes common sense and a desire to do what's right are more important than a strict interpretation of the law," Talliapanne said. "I hate to admit it, but more than a few times justicers have manipulated the letter of the law to suit their whim. We're all human, Prime Cassaline, and subject to our human weaknesses. Approach your judgments with humility, and I think you'll do just fine."

Ginnevra looked past Talliapanne to where the street intersected Devoyenne's main thoroughfare. Her heart lightened. "Thank you, madama, that makes me feel better," she said, though in truth it was the man at the end of the street whose appearance had cheered her. "I'll see you in two days, yes? That's the end of my time here."

"Your training progresses nicely," Talliapanne said. "I think the Blessed will have no reason to complain." She clapped Ginnevra on the shoulder and turned right down the street. Ginnevra hurried in the other direction, her sword bobbing over her shoulder in her eagerness.

She met Eodan halfway to the thoroughfare, managing not to break into a run. It wasn't as if they'd been separated more than a few hours, but an afternoon of hearing cases, not all of them interesting, made that separation feel much longer. Eodan's smile when he saw her made her feel even lighter. She closed the final distance between them and put her arms around his waist, pulling him close for a kiss. "I am so glad to see you."

Eodan's smile widened. "I thought I was tired, but you've

made all that vanish." He kissed her in return. "Shall we eat? And then take a walk on the beach? It's been a busy day for both of us."

"You have such wonderful ideas." Ginnevra hooked her left arm around his right and tugged him back the way he'd come. "I take it you treated a lot of patients."

"Word about the visiting physician has gotten around," Eodan said. "Even a big place like Devoyenne doesn't have enough physicians to meet the people's needs. But it was a good day. I only had to turn away two whose illnesses weren't something I could treat."

"I don't know if I could do that. Maintain my optimism in the face of suffering people I couldn't help." Ginnevra gripped his hand swiftly. "Oh, I forgot, you're one of nature's pessimists."

Eodan laughed. "A physician can't afford to be wholly pessimistic, or he'd never successfully treat anyone. But it's true I had to learn to accept that some things can't be fixed."

"I choose to be grateful that so many things can," Ginnevra said.

Though it was still early, not quite five o'clock in the evening, Devoyenne was coming to life, its main street thronged with citizens leaving their shops or entering taverns. Food vendors cried out, advertising their wares, and the smell of hot meat warred with the sweeter scent of honeyed dates and sugar-roasted almonds. Ginnevra breathed in the aromas, mingled with the salty bite of sea air, and the last of her tension fell away.

"I hope I'm not called away any time soon," she said. "The sea is beautiful, and Devoyenne is a friendly place." She nodded politely at someone who gawked at the sword.

"I admit to being fond of looking at the sea," Eodan said. "It's so different from my mountain home."

"And I imagine there are citizens of Devoyenne who would be awestruck by the mountains if they traveled north." Ginnevra tugged on Eodan's arm. "Let's try this place. They had those fried tomatoes a few nights ago."

The dimly-lit tavern did smell of tomatoes, as well as garlic and hot oil and balsamic vinegar. Small round tables that would barely seat four, and then only if the four were all very friendly, crowded the tap room. Few of the tables were occupied this early, and Ginnevra and Eodan took one in the corner that let them both sit with their backs to the walls. Ginnevra didn't expect to be attacked in the middle of the city, let alone taken by surprise, but she also didn't believe in taking chances.

An extremely handsome young man, his eyes bright and his smile mischievous, brought them wooden mugs that he set down without comment. Ginnevra sniffed hers; dark ale, her favorite. So someone remembered her last visit.

Eodan took a long drink from his mug and set it down with a deliberate *tock*. "When do you expect to be called on?"

"I don't know." Ginnevra shrugged and drank. "I'm nearly done with my training here, and if the Devoyenne justicers approve of me, they'll send word to the Blessed that I'm fit to be set loose on the populace. Which means more official missions on the Blessed's behalf."

"I'm looking forward to seeing what those are. Humanity is so varied and so interesting, and I like the excuse to meet new people and learn how they live."

Ginnevra took another drink. "And if they know you are a werewolf?"

Eodan chewed his lower lip in thought. "The Blessed sent that decree to the sanctuaries, explaining about the werewolves like me who turn their backs on the Bright One. She hasn't seen fit to make that decree generally known. And I think she's right. If word gets out that there are, well, good werewolves in the world, that will get people wondering about all the bad ones, or how to tell the difference. Better to introduce the idea a little at a time."

"And maybe on a less abstract level," Ginnevra said. "I mean, people get to know you, they trust you, you're not a danger, and *then* they find out you're a werewolf. It's harder to stay bigoted when it's someone you have a personal relationship with."

She leaned back so the handsome server could put a steaming plate in front of her. Fried tomatoes drizzled with oil and balsamic vinegar, cod battered and deep fried, and half a loaf of nutty brown bread—southern coastal cuisine had so much going for it. She forked up a bite of fish and blew on it to cool it. "I'll definitely miss this."

"Why haven't tomatoes made it farther north?" Eodan asked. He was already making inroads on his. "They're so delicious."

"I know very little about agriculture." Ginnevra dipped her bite of cod into the vinegar and ate it before it could drip on her breeches. "It might be too cold in the north to grow them, if they're native to places south of the Lordagne. But someone will eventually figure it out. That's how civilization works."

"It almost makes me regret—well, not regret leaving my home, because I had no choice, but I'm sorry I'm not in a position to bring the things I'm discovering to my pack." Eodan took another bite and wiped his mouth. "We adopt human inventions when we have the chance. Some human inventions, that is. The ones we can maintain without losing who we are."

Ginnevra eyed him covertly. Eodan wasn't reticent about werewolf behavior, but he rarely talked about his own history and never said anything about what had driven him away from his pack beyond the bare facts of having been at odds with those werewolves who chose to worship the Bright One. "Is that something you used to do? Bring back human things or foods?"

Eodan's gaze fixed on her, blue-eyed and fierce. "No," he said, and it was the sort of "no" that denied any possibility of a follow-up response. Ginnevra took another bite of fish to keep from blurting out any demands that he speak. His past was his own business, and she had no right to pry. She certainly had things in her past she didn't want to discuss.

She chewed, swallowed, and said, "Well, I agree with you that it's a pity tomatoes aren't more widely eaten. They're so versatile."

"I like them on pasta," Eodan said. It was such a bland response Ginnevra knew she'd done right in not pushing.

They ate in silence then, a comfortable silence Ginnevra enjoyed. Aside from one youthful fling with the neighbor's son before taking her paladin's oath, she had never had a relationship that lasted more than a few days. Paladin companies were always on the move, and maintaining a romance under those conditions was difficult. Falling in love with Eodan had changed that. The knowledge that he would be there in the morning still stunned her with its beautiful certainty. They'd been together for almost five months, and already Ginnevra had trouble remembering what life had been like before him.

The handsome server brought them a second set of mugs, and Ginnevra waved off a third. Three tankards of ale wasn't enough to get her drunk, but she wanted to enjoy the evening without being tipsy. She mopped the last drops of oil and vinegar up with a chunk of bread and sighed deeply. "I feel so satisfied," she said. "I did well hearing cases, I'm full and comfortable, and I have you. It's the perfect day."

Eodan smiled and took her hand. "Let's go for that walk on the beach, then, and make it a spectacular day."

Ginnevra rose, bringing him with her. "I want to leave my sword in our room. I don't need it bouncing over my shoulder on a romantic stroll."

They walked down the main street, which was busy now that the sun brushed the distant horizon. Pedestrians walked wide around Ginnevra and her sword regardless of the crush. Their expressions ran a spectrum from uncertainty to awe, something Ginnevra wasn't accustomed to even after five years as a paladin. Awe, maybe, but she didn't like the ones who looked fearful, as if she might attack them unprovoked or accuse them of terrible crimes. She kept her gaze focused straight ahead, nodding in a friendly way when she couldn't avoid meeting someone's eyes. The frightened ones sometimes became more nervous when they knew she'd noticed them.

The inn Ginnevra and Eodan had stayed at the past two weeks was on a side street away from the main thoroughfare, a quiet, little-trafficked street that seemed worlds away from the bustle of the busy road. Ginnevra liked how their room looked out over the stable yard, giving her a good view of her horse Dauntless. He didn't need her watching over him, and the stable yard was secure, but she enjoyed seeing him interact with the stable hands, all of whom knew the blue roan's tricks by now.

As they approached the inn's front door, someone emerged from it and stood on the stoop, looking up and down the street as if she didn't know which way to go. Her eyes met Ginnevra's. Ginnevra took a few more steps before memory struck her breathless.

For a moment, the sounds of the street vanished, and she heard in memory a voice saying *If there's anything left to say, I don't know what it is.* She almost didn't recognize the voice as her own. Then there was fire in darkness, and soot-blackened faces, and the flash of steel. Someone cried out, so loudly Ginnevra thought for a moment the sound was here, now—but it, too, was memory.

Then Eodan was saying, "Ginnevra, what's wrong?"

Ginnevra shook her head. She released Eodan's hand and

walked forward to meet the woman, who hadn't moved beyond turning to more fully face Ginnevra. She was almost as tall as Ginnevra and more heavily built, muscular rather than fat, with long dark hair pulled back from her face in a horse's tail and thin, sharply-drawn eyebrows that arched to give her a slightly astonished appearance. It had been four years, but Ginnevra recognized her instantly.

She came to a stop about five feet from the woman and said, "Filippa." She couldn't think of anything more to say that wouldn't be banal or trite or viciously accusatory.

Filippa put a hand on the hilt of the short sword she wore at her hip. "Ginna—Ginnevra," she said. "I need your help."

CHAPTER

TWO

G innevra's jaw clenched. "Do you," she said flatly. "Is this about your mad obsession? Because I told you four years ago I wanted nothing to do with it."

A muscle twitched in Filippa's cheek. "Things have changed. Please, Ginnevra. Just hear me out."

"The way you listened to me?" Ginnevra exclaimed. "Damn it, Filippa—"

"I won't make excuses. And I wouldn't have tracked you down if this weren't important." Filippa's hand closed more tightly on the sword's pommel. "This time I have proof."

Ginnevra squeezed her eyes shut. "Proof. Of what? We *failed*, Filippa. There's nothing to prove!" She opened her eyes. Filippa hadn't moved. "There's nothing you can learn that will change the past."

"That's not true," Filippa said. "Half an hour. Ten minutes, even. Give me ten minutes, and if I can't convince you, I'll walk away and you'll never see me again."

Her words stabbed at Ginnevra's heart. She hadn't seen

Filippa in four years, had managed not to think of her for most of that time, and yet the idea of never seeing her former best friend again hurt as much as it had the first time Ginnevra had walked away from her. Cursing her weakness, she said, "Fine. Ten minutes."

Filippa glanced up and down the street again, prompting Ginnevra to do the same. It wasn't as busy as the main thorough-fare, but there were still plenty of people around, and all of them were watching the paladin with poorly disguised interest. "Is there somewhere we can go for privacy?" Filippa asked.

There was no way Ginnevra would bring Filippa to her room. She hesitated. Beside her, Eodan stirred. "We can use the private parlor," he murmured.

She'd forgotten he was there. Once more, she took his hand. "That's a good idea. Thank you." She gestured with her free hand at the inn's front door. "This way."

There was a moment of darkness as Ginnevra crossed the threshold from the bright, warm sunlight of the street to the cool dimness of the entrance, and then her paladin's eyes adjusted, showing her the narrow, long corridor extending away from the front door to stairs at the far end going up. Doors flanked the front door on either side of the hall, stained dark in contrast to the pale pink plaster of the walls. The air smelled of dust and lamp oil, though the lamps burned low and the floors were clean and brightly waxed.

Ginnevra opened the left-hand door. "Sieur, would you mind giving us some privacy?" she said to the elderly man seated near the room's one window, reading a book.

The man glanced up and did a double take upon seeing the sword. "Of course, my lady, it's no problem," he said, rising from his chair. "I can—that is, anything for a paladin—"

"It will only take ten minutes," Ginnevra said. She stood aside for him to exit. The man nodded politely to Eodan and to Filippa and headed for the stairs.

Filippa followed Ginnevra into the private parlor. "I'd forgotten what that's like," she said, sounding amused. "Being the one they all make way for." Her tone was exactly as Ginnevra remembered, and it made her angry that Filippa still mattered to her on some level. She grabbed a chair and swung it around before dropping into it.

"Your ten minutes begins now," she said. "Talk."

"Can I at least be introduced to your friend?" Filippa's calm words didn't match the tension in her jaw. That she was as uncertain as Ginnevra eased Ginnevra's heart somewhat.

"This is Eodan," she said. "He's my companion. Eodan, this is Filippa Genovarde. She used to be—" A thousand possible words rushed into Ginnevra's mind. "She's an ex-paladin. We were in the same company five years ago. Our first company."

Eodan had taken a chair near Ginnevra, and he now sat leaning forward with his elbows on his knees. "A retired paladin?"

Ginnevra and Filippa exchanged glances. Filippa still looked tense, but she made no move to speak, tacitly giving Ginnevra the choice about what to say next. "Not retired," Ginnevra said. "She's no longer a paladin. She abandoned her vows and left the Faith entirely."

Filippa shifted her weight as if she wanted to object, but still she said nothing. Ginnevra immediately felt guilty and just as quickly crushed that guilt into oblivion. It didn't matter what Filippa thought she'd done; the facts were clear, and Ginnevra hadn't said anything the Commander General hadn't said, years before.

"I see," Eodan said. Ginnevra was sure he didn't, because how could he possibly understand what Filippa had done to Ginnevra by leaving? They had been sisters, once, and—Ginnevra made

17

herself breathe slowly, controlling her anger. None of that mattered.

"So, tell me why you're here," she said. "And it had better be something new."

Filippa nodded slowly. "I found evidence," she said. "Proof that we were set up. I swear it's true, Ginnevra. None of what happened was our fault. Captain Ercole didn't sell us out. Someone else set those attackers on us."

Ginnevra's breathing sped up again, and she controlled herself. "Proof?"

"Ginnevra," Eodan said, "what is she talking about?"

Ginnevra almost turned on him, snarling. She almost told him to mind his own business. But his expression was so concerned, so worried for her, it brought her to her senses in time. "Tell him," she snapped at Filippa. "You're the one who cares. Tell him about our greatest failure."

Filippa's hands closed into loose fists in her lap. "Ginna— Ginnevra and I were in the same company," she said. "Under Baranzia Ercole. We'd ridden together—do you know what that means?"

"You were partners in the company," Eodan said. "Rode together, fought as one."

"Right. We'd ridden together for a little over a year." Filippa opened one hand and rubbed her palm over the rough fabric of her breeches. "Our company had been riding the southern reaches, and we ended up in Quinizelle. The king of Quinizelle's sister was betrothed to a lord in Paese, and our company was tasked with escorting her south to her wedding. It was supposed to be simple. The route is well trafficked, and nobody's seen bandits along it since forever." She laughed, one curt, sharp sound. "Can't say that anymore."

"Just tell the story," Ginnevra said.

"Sorry. You can probably guess what happened. We were ambushed by bandits, a troop more than double the size of our company. They knew when we'd be there, and they knew our strengths. It was a massacre." Filippa drew in a deep breath and let it out slowly. "Ginnevra was badly wounded and left for dead. I suffered a head injury and fell unconscious. The bandits slaughtered the king's sister and our company and every one of the lady's retinue. And they left Captain Ercole alive and uninjured."

Eodan sat up. "I think I see what comes next."

Filippa laughed again. "Probably. The king of Quinizelle has plenty of enemies, and he decided the bandits were in the pay of one of them—and that the captain herself had been paid off to tell the bandits where to attack. Captain Ercole swore she was innocent, but the evidence against her was strong, and neither Ginnevra nor I were allowed to testify on her behalf."

"That doesn't seem fair."

Filippa shrugged. "Ginnevra was still recovering from her wounds, and I was knocked unconscious in the opening stage of the battle and saw nothing that would prove or disprove the captain's guilt. It didn't matter. Captain Ercole committed suicide when it became clear she wouldn't be exonerated. She was a proud woman, and an honorable one."

"Honorable," Ginnevra said, scowling. "She took the easy way out."

"And you think you'd have been willing to live with that smear on your reputation?" Filippa retorted. "Nobody stood up for her. Nobody believed her. You and I could have changed that, if they'd let us."

"A couple of damaged paladins whose witness was compromised because of their loyalty to a traitor," Ginnevra shot back. "Yes, I'm sure everyone would have listened to us."

"Stop," Eodan said. "I can tell this is an argument you've had before. I don't think it's getting either of you anywhere. So Captain Ercole was convicted of treason and killed herself. I assume the two of you weren't tarred with that brush?"

Filippa leaned back in her chair, no longer looking at Ginnevra. "We were considered innocent victims of the captain's treachery, fortunate survivors who didn't know any of what had happened. We were sent to a different company as soon as Ginnevra recovered."

"But you couldn't let it go," Ginnevra said.

Filippa's jaw tightened again. "Nothing about the incident felt right. The captain would never have sold us out, not for any reward. And yet someone told those bandits where to find us and how best to attack. And I..." She lowered her gaze. "I couldn't let Captain Ercole's memory be tainted."

"She was *dead*," Ginnevra said. "She'd gone where it no longer mattered what people thought of her. You were so obsessed with proving things different you forgot what it means to be a paladin."

"And what is that?" Filippa exclaimed. "Defending the innocent? Destroying the Bright One's creations? Bringing justice to those who need it? Tell me that's not what being a paladin means."

"It *means*," Ginnevra said through gritted teeth, "not dwelling on what's past and wishing things had turned out differently. That is *blasphemy*. And it's what got you stripped of your grace and your paladin's enhancements. You should have let it go, Filippa."

"I did what I believed was right," Filippa said. "And now I have proof. But I wouldn't regret my choices even if I ended up searching forever and never finding anything."

It felt like a punch to the jaw. Ginnevra blinked away tears and hoped Filippa hadn't noticed her moment of weakness. *Wouldn't regret abandoning me*, she wanted to say. Instead, she said, "Fine. You have proof. I'm still listening."

"It took years, and a lot of underworld contacts, but I tracked down the bandits who attacked the caravan." Filippa leaned forward again. "They weren't bandits. They were mercenaries, hired to destroy us. That much was true."

"But not by Captain Ercole," Eodan said. He was intent on Filippa, his brow furrowed and his eyes narrow with thought.

"No. Not by the captain. Not all the mercenaries had been around for that raid four years ago, but some of them remembered. And with a little persuasion and a touch of bribery, they gave me evidence. A noble's insignia." Filippa's eyes were alight with excitement. "They said the man who hired them was anonymous, but one of them followed him after the initial meeting and saw the insignia. He drew it for me."

She reached into her jerkin and removed a folded sheet of paper. Ginnevra took it and opened it. It had been torn from a larger sheet, and the creases were dirty as if Filippa had carried it for a long time. Sketched on it in charcoal, the lines smudged here and there, was a circle divided into four quarters. Two of the quarters were blank. The lower left quarter was filled with a zigzag pattern of chevrons; the upper right had a sketch of some kind of animal so poorly drawn Ginnevra didn't recognize it.

"The mercenaries said it was a wolf's head," Filippa said.

Despite herself, Ginnevra's interest sharpened. "Whose insignia is it?"

"I don't know yet," Filippa said. "That's why I came to you. You're a prime now—you can investigate in ways I can't. You can find the person behind the ambush and you can set history straight."

"*I* can?" Ginnevra's voice squeaked in astonishment. She cleared her throat and said, "Why would I do that? I told you,

Filippa, I don't agree with your decision. The past should stay in the past. And what would proving things different matter, anyway? It won't bring Captain Ercole back, or any of the victims of the massacre."

"Doesn't it matter to you that someone wanted to see paladins defamed?" Filippa replied. "The king of Quinizelle turned on the Faith because of our failure to protect his sister. Our reputation—not just our company, but all paladins—was tainted. You heard the whispers about how maybe we don't have the Goddess's blessing, after all. This—" She flicked the paper— "this represents a chance to restore what we lost. To prove to the world that paladins can't be bought."

Ginnevra stared at the crude drawing. Once more, memory gripped her. That had been a bad time, all those rumors. When they weren't about Ercole's motives, they'd been about why a paladin company could be destroyed so easily. As if there had been anything easy about those bandits' victory. Even with her paladin's enhancements and rapid healing, Ginnevra had been over a month recovering from her wounds, and she'd accounted for at least three bandits before they took her down. No, not an easy victory at all.

"That was four years ago," she murmured. In a louder voice, she added, "Nobody remembers what happened except you and me and maybe the Commander General and the Blessed. Nobody whispers anymore about corrupt paladins or their weakness. It was hard, damn hard, for a while, and then it was over."

She handed the paper back to Filippa. "It's over," she repeated. "I'm not going to live in the past. That's not what the Goddess teaches us. She wants us to make our future, moment by moment, not dwell on what we've lost or try to change what's happened."

Filippa tucked the paper away without looking at it, fixing her entire attention on Ginnevra. "Even if it means letting evil go unchallenged?"

"We're not talking about someone who's still out there slaughtering innocents, Filippa. And suppose you're right, and that picture leads you to someone else responsible for those deaths? All you'll do is stir up old rumors." Ginnevra stood. "I don't want anything to do with this."

Filippa looked up at her. "Then I'll do it alone."

"That's your business." Ginnevra's voice trembled, and she cursed herself. She didn't want Filippa to think she cared, because she didn't. Not one bit.

With a sigh, Filippa rose. "I'm sorry I came. I thought, maybe it's been long enough—but that's not the point, is it?"

"No. It's not," Ginnevra said. This time, her voice was steady.

Filippa nodded at Eodan. "Take care of her," she said, and walked out of the room.

Ginnevra waited for the door to close and Filippa's footsteps to fade out of earshot. Then she walked to the fireplace and stood looking at the grate, one hand gripping the mantel. The fireplace was ashy and filled with the charcoal ends of logs from an earlier, small fire, probably lit by Eodan for use in his treatments. Soon enough, the weather would turn, and winter storms blowing in off the harbor would make this fireplace a necessity for anyone using the private room. She and Eodan would be long gone by then.

She heard Eodan approach, but he didn't touch her, didn't speak. She drew in a deep breath and said, "I don't know why she came. She had to know what I'd say."

"Because you matter to her," Eodan said. "Even a stranger could see that."

"Then why didn't she listen?" Ginnevra shouted. "I *told* her. I told her the path she was on only led to excommunication. She cared more about her stupid cause than she did—" She swallowed hard against the tears that threatened to fall.

"I know I'm right about this," she finally managed. "It's not just blasphemy, it's pointless. What good would it do stirring up old wrongs? It won't bring back the dead."

"Can I ask you something you might find offensive?"

Ginnevra turned to look at him. "That's ominous. All right."

"If Filippa is right, then someone committed murder and got away with it. Isn't that the sort of crime a paladin should prosecute?"

Anger flashed through Ginnevra, but she reminded herself Eodan wasn't the enemy and replied calmly. "I know that's how it looks. But that 'evidence' Filippa has isn't much more than a theory. I'm guessing she's been looking for proof for four years and she's grasping at whatever she can find. But the trial was legitimate. Captain Ercole was guilty, however much I wanted to believe otherwise. This is just Filippa's obsession."

"I see." Eodan nodded. "But there's a part of you that doesn't believe what you just said."

Ginnevra scowled. "Yes. The weak, foolish part of me that wishes I had my sister back. That's in the past, Eodan."

Eodan sighed. He drew Ginnevra into his embrace and held her close. "I'm sorry for your pain," he whispered. "You are the strongest person I know."

"Because I could reject someone who used to be closer to me than a real sister?" Ginnevra put her arms around him and rested her head on his shoulder. "I'm not sure that makes me anything but a cast-iron bitch."

"Because your faith makes you strong." Eodan kissed her. "Let's go. We don't need to do anything but walk, and I think you need some time when no one's making demands of you."

Ginnevra nodded. "I know you're right."

SHE WOKE LATE the following morning, roused by the cries of sea birds and the smell of sausage. The morning sunlight bathed the room in liquid gold, warm and promising an even warmer day. Ginnevra rolled out of bed and crossed to look out the window. Below, a street vendor served a man at the head of a short queue a sausage slapped into a length of bread slit sideways. Ginnevra had never seen queueing before coming to Devoyenne, but she liked the innovation. So much tidier than mobbing a vendor and shoving through the crowd to get his attention.

She stretched and turned to look at Eodan, and was surprised to see him awake and looking back at her. "I guess we needed sleep," she said, and yawned. "If I weren't hungry, I'd want even more sleep."

"I should rise and ready myself for another day of treating patients," Eodan said, but he made no move to get up.

Ginnevra returned to the bed and sat on its edge. "I've nothing to occupy myself today. I hate being idle."

A knock sounded at the door. "My lady paladin?"

That sounded official. Ginnevra said, "One moment," and pulled on her shirt and breeches. Barefoot, she crossed to the door and opened it to reveal a young man dressed in the black and silver surcoat that indicated service to the Goddess. He looked a little askance at her informal appearance, but handed her a folded, sealed note.

"It's from Hallowed Currade," he said. "I'm to wait on a reply."

"Wait a moment," Ginnevra said. She turned away from him to open the note. The paper bore only a few lines in a cramped, wavering script Ginnevra nevertheless had no trouble reading. Turning back to the boy, she said, "Tell Hallowed Currade I'll be there in one hour."

The boy nodded and disappeared down the hall.

"I guess I have something to do, after all," Ginnevra said, folding the note. "Hallowed Currade wants me to attend upon her at the sanctuary."

"She needed to send a note for that? Couldn't she have given the young man a spoken message?" Eodan sat up and ran his fingers through his black hair, combing it down.

"The note means it's an official summons, for an official assignment." Excitement bubbled up inside Ginnevra. "My first official assignment. I wonder why they didn't wait for me to finish my justicer's training?"

"Because something awful has come up, and they can't afford to wait?" Eodan said with a smile.

"Pessimist." Ginnevra sat beside him again. "I guess I'll find out. I hope I'll be back before the sun can roast me in my armor."

An hour later, Ginnevra, bearing her sword over her mailed shoulder, crossed the plaza at the heart of Devoyenne. She walked wide around the famous white marble fountains. They depicted the creatures worshipped by people before the coming of the Faith, the so-called holy children. Ginnevra didn't know the names of the godlings, so the statue of a bear standing on its hind paws, water pouring out of an urn it held over its shoulder, meant nothing to her.

The presence of the eight fountains made her uncomfortable. She wasn't sure why the Faith endured their presence, especially when the sanctuary was built right next to that constant reminder of the religion the Faith had displaced. She reminded herself that the godlings were made up by humans and had no power to challenge her beliefs. She still felt uncomfortable.

The Devoyenne sanctuary, on the other hand, cheered her. Its five black spires pointing heavenward gleamed darkly in the morning sunlight, their tips bright gold—real gold, probably. The men and women passing it slowed to admire the black marble facings and the inlaid silver traceries of abstract patterns that circled the building at head height. More silver outlined the arched doorway where no doors had ever stood.

Ginnevra's steps slowed as she approached the sanctuary. It looked so vulnerable to attack, and yet she knew from personal experience that it was guarded against evil. She hated that the protections laid upon it didn't know to distinguish between "monster" and "evil." When they'd first arrived in Devoyenne and reported in to the sanctuary, Eodan had tried to enter and had bounced off the doorway in a crack of thunder and a flash of white light. It had taken some talking, and the written word of the Blessed, to convince the anointed that Eodan was no threat.

For a moment, the memory angered Ginnevra. It wasn't fair that Eodan could turn his back on his creator, repudiate the Bright One entirely, and still be treated like a monster. The anointed of Devoyenne behaved with politeness when they encountered Eodan—*outside* the sanctuary, of course—but most of them still looked frightened of him, and they cast wary looks her way when they thought she couldn't see. Ginnevra had to remind herself frequently that centuries of fear and distrust of werewolves couldn't be erased overnight. She still hated the situation.

Today, though, Eodan's race didn't matter. She was receiving her first assignment as a prime of the Blessed. The anointed could give her all the wary looks they wanted.

The interior of the sanctuary was cooler than it should be, though Ginnevra didn't know if it was architecture or a grace that did it. Small lanterns lit the space dimly, revealing a round room paved in polished granite with three doors leading off it. One of the doors was wider and taller than the others, and Ginnevra headed that way.

The door opened before she reached it, and a short, round woman with an unusually thin face bowed to Ginnevra. "Prime Cassaline," she said. "Please, come this way."

"Hallowed Currade," Ginnevra said politely.

The door opened on a chapel filled with wooden pews stained black and lacquered to a bright gloss. Currade led Ginnevra past the altar table to a smaller door and ushered her inside. Ginnevra had seen Currade's office once before and been impressed at the décor. As a Revered, Currade had traveled the Lordagne and beyond, all the way across the sea to Illiou and even Olagunah, and had brought back mementos of her travels. Ginnevra turned her back on a figure of a shepherd carved in rosewood she wished she could examine closely and took a seat when Currade gestured.

Currade sat behind her desk and moved aside a glass paperweight flecked with gold. Behind her, water sheeted from an arm-long slit in the wall into a long, deep basin. An eternity fountain, and one larger than any Ginnevra had seen before, not that there had been many of those. The water caught the lamplight and reflected it back like moonlight on a sheet of ice. "You already know this is about an assignment," Currade said. "The Blessed requested your presence here so she could give it to you directly."

Ginnevra's earlier excitement turned to dread. "Um... thank you?"

Currade smiled. "It's not unusual," she assured Ginnevra. She stood and withdrew her grace, a torus of jet wrapped with silver wire, from beneath her black robe and gripped it in one hand. "*By Your grace we speak as one,*" she said in a low voice.

The water stilled and hung motionless, just as if it were actually frozen. A pale blue glow radiated from it, and Ginnevra smelled lightning, sharp and biting and clean. The blue glow shifted like heat haze, and then it sank into the sheet of water, turning it milky. Then a woman's face appeared, as clear as if the water were a window she looked through. She was pale, with black hair pulled back from her face, and her eyes were pure black, with no white or iris.

Ginnevra rose and drew her sword, saluting. "Holy One," she said.

The Blessed smiled. "Ginnevra Cassaline," she said. "I'll be brief. I need a negotiator to handle certain sensitive matters with the head of a city-state. You're nearby, and I judge you to have the qualifications necessary."

Ginnevra crushed feelings of uncertainty about her qualifications. "I'm ready, Holy One. Where am I to go?"

The Blessed hesitated. "I'm sending you to Quinizelle."

CHAPTER

THREE

Dizziness struck Ginnevra, and for a moment she was back in the inn's private parlor, with Filippa saying *We ended up in Quinizelle.* "Are you sure?" she blurted out, then blushed hotly.

The Blessed didn't smile. "I understand why you might feel doubtful. Are you concerned for political reasons, or personal?"

"Both," Ginnevra said. "Though—I'm sorry, I don't mean to criticize. You know more about Quinizelle than I do. I just believed the Faith wasn't welcome there, after Dianetta Napolle's death."

"Relations between Quinizelle—more accurately, Quinizelle's king—and the Faith were strained well before that tragedy." The Blessed's thin eyebrows drew down over the bridge of her nose, curving up at the ends. "But there are still worshippers there, and King Paolo Napolle, while hostile, has not demanded they or our anointed leave."

"King Paolo was so angry," Ginnevra recalled. "That seems unexpectedly generous from his perspective."

"From ours as well," the Blessed said. "We understand grief, and King Paolo does not worship as we do. But I have had reports in recent months of increased violence by the citizens of Quinizelle against our people, and King Paolo hasn't done anything about it. *That* is something no one should put up with, regardless of the past. I want you to present our case to the king and request him to intervene."

Ginnevra nodded, though inside her heart quailed at the thought of a diplomatic mission. She was terrible at diplomacy— saying one thing and meaning another, listening for unspoken meaning, delivering the polite lie.

"But that is not your only concern," the Blessed said.

Ginnevra glanced at Currade, who stood silently beside the frozen waterfall. "I'm not afraid. I do wonder if I'm the right choice. I mean, it's not as if the king will know who I am, that I was in the company that failed to save his sister, but he might see any paladin as a reminder of his loss."

"He might," the Blessed said. "But he is the ruler of a city-state, and a man grown, and he should not allow his personal tragedy to turn him into a child. If he is someone who lets past resentments cloud his judgment, that is also something we should know. And we can't know that unless we challenge him. My primes are the ones I send on missions like this one. If I send a different negotiator, he will believe I fear giving offense, and that will give him power over us."

"I understand." Understanding didn't make Ginnevra feel better.

The Blessed's image shifted slightly. "And what about your personal tragedy? How will it affect you?"

"I won't let it," Ginnevra said promptly. "It's in the past. I did what I had to do and I have nothing to reproach myself for. I'm not saying I'm entirely comfortable returning to Quinizelle, but I won't let you down."

"I believe you." The Blessed smiled. "Hallowed Currade has detailed instructions for you. In general, however—you will request King Paolo to stop the violence against believers in the Faith, and you will tell him that if he fails to intervene, we will withdraw our economic support from Quinizelle."

"What economic support?" Ginnevra immediately felt stupid. Maybe this was common knowledge and she had just demonstrated her ignorance.

But the Blessed's expression didn't change. "Quinizelle's existence depends on the silver mines it sits on top of. The Faith is a major purchaser of their silver; you know how much silver paladins alone use, in treating weapons and mail for protection against the Bright One's creatures. If we chose to go elsewhere to meet our needs, Quinizelle's economy would suffer." Her lips curved up on one side in a wry smile. "It would disadvantage us, too, but I care more about the welfare of my people than about temporarily increased expenses. And the winner in a negotiation is the one who is willing to walk away."

"So we have a weapon King Paolo is weak against," Ginnevra said.

"Precisely. Though, having said that, I would prefer you not use that weapon immediately. If you can present our request amicably, the king will have the opportunity to show what a kind and generous ruler he is without being forced to it. These are his subjects, after all." The Blessed's face grew slightly larger, as if she had leaned closer to the magical window. "Have you other questions?"

"I—actually, yes. How should I contact you to tell you the king's decision?"

"There is a sanctuary in Quinizelle. You may ask Hallowed

Nevante to communicate via this grace." The Blessed raised a hand and gestured at the space around her head. "If you have any other questions about the information I've given Hallowed Currade, ask, but I trust in your intelligence and faith to work out most of the answers for yourself."

Ginnevra couldn't decide if that was a compliment or a warning. She saluted the Blessed, somewhat awkwardly given the close quarters. "It's my honor to serve."

"Please give my regards to Eodan. I hope you are both well," the Blessed said.

Ginnevra's gaze flicked again to Currade, who looked so bland she was obviously concealing some other emotion. "We are. We've had no problems." Not totally true, but the minor conflicts she and Eodan had had with the anointed in Devoyenne weren't something Ginnevra wanted to whine to the Blessed about, especially in Currade's presence.

"Good." The Blessed nodded. "May the Dark Lady's blessing of strength and wisdom be upon you, Ginnevra Cassaline." The milky blue glow intensified, and the image vanished. A moment later, the water resumed its endless falling cycle.

Ginnevra let out a deep breath. She turned to Currade and said, "I don't know how usual that was."

"The Blessed takes a personal interest in any mission she sends a prime on," Currade said. "I have your detailed instructions here."

She crossed the room to a wall of cubbies like a black honeycomb and removed a fat, short scroll case, which she handed to Ginnevra. Ginnevra uncapped it and shook a thin sheaf of heavy papers into her hand. "Why send this instead of telling me everything directly?"

Currade shrugged. "I assume there are details enough that the Blessed doesn't expect a prime to be able to remember all the verbal instructions—unless memory is one of a paladin's enhancements?"

"No, not really." Ginnevra flipped through the pages without reading them. Time enough for that when she wouldn't bore Currade by making her wait while she studied them. She thought about saying something about how the Blessed approved of Eodan, and how that ought to be a lesson to the anointed, but she decided that would be childish. Currade almost certainly had gotten the message.

"If there's anything we can do to speed your journey, just ask," Currade said. "You'll want to take ship to Paese, and—but you know how long the overland journey from Paese to Quinizelle is, if you've been there before."

"Yes, it's a two-day ride and then another day traveling through the mountain passes." Ginnevra managed not to blush this time. Currade hadn't sounded judgmental, but it still felt as if she'd intended to remind Ginnevra of the last time Ginnevra had made that journey and how disastrous that trip had been.

"We'll supply you for the journey, then." Currade took a seat behind her desk. "If you'll let the Revereds know what you need?"

"Thank you, I will." Impulsively, Ginnevra added, "I'd send Eodan, but we both know that wouldn't work."

Currade regarded her placidly. "I believe the Blessed's assurances that your companion means us no harm."

"But that's not the same as accepting who he is."

Currade shrugged again. "He's a werewolf. We've fought his kind long enough not to rest easy around him. You need to accept people's limitations, prime."

Ginnevra opened her mouth for a hasty reply, then thought better of it. "I suppose," she said instead. "Thank you for your assistance, Hallowed. I'll return this afternoon."

All the way back to the inn, Ginnevra wrestled with herself.

She hadn't accepted Eodan at first, either—had threatened him with death, even. So she didn't know why she expected others to be more well-adjusted. Probably her love for him made her want others to, not love him, obviously, but see in him the many good qualities she appreciated.

She stopped on one of the bridges crossing the river Devoyenne straddled and watched the water rush seaward for a few moments. The Varaigne River was wide enough to make bridging it a challenge, but humans thrived on challenge, and the Varaigne was spanned by not one, but four bridges, each wider than the last. Ginnevra, facing upstream, watched the water lash the pilings in a lather of foam and wondered at what point the river water became seawater, and whether high tide reached this far upriver. It wasn't full noon yet, but the heat of the day made her consider a swim.

She wasn't sure whether or not she, personally, thrived on challenge. She never backed down from one, of course, but it wasn't as if she sought out fights. And despite what she'd told the Blessed, she was a little uncertain about returning to Quinizelle, going back to the scene of her greatest failure. But she wasn't going to let that uncertainty run her life.

A handful of people loitered in the street outside the inn's door when she arrived. Some sat on the paving stones despite their not-very-clean condition, and one or two held their stomachs as if in pain. The ones standing moved aside for Ginnevra, their eyes round with astonishment; she nodded politely as she passed.

The door to the private parlor stood ajar, and Ginnevra heard Eodan's voice coming from within. "...hold his hand, but I assure you he won't feel anything," he was saying.

Ginnevra stood outside the door and peered through the crack. An elderly woman knelt beside one of the chairs in which sat a young man whose head lolled back as if he was unconscious. Eodan held a large, blunt needle in his gloved hand and forced the young man's jaw open with his bare left hand. Deftly, he maneuvered the needle into the man's mouth. Something hissed wetly, and the young man jerked, making the woman cry out and clutch his hand to her bosom. Eodan removed the needle and set it on a nearby table, which was already covered with pots and metal tools and rolled bandages.

"That should help the abscess," he said. He picked up a bundle of dry, sticklike herbs and walked wide around the chair to touch the bundle's end to the small fire burning in the hearth. He let it burn for a moment, then blew out the fire, releasing a pungent odor. Returning to the young man's side, he held the smoldering herbs beneath the patient's nose and waved the odorous smoke toward him. The man jerked again, and his eyes fluttered open. His hand flew up to touch the side of his face.

"It still hurts," he said in a whining, nasal voice.

"The pain will ease over the next week," Eodan said. He bent over the table and scribbled something on a piece of paper. "Follow these instructions to make a poultice for the abscess, and apply it six times a day with a linen cloth until the sore heals." He handed the paper to the old woman, who clasped it in both hands and pressed it to her chest the way she had the young man's hand.

Eodan helped the young man stand and kept a hand under his elbow when he wobbled. The old woman inserted herself beneath the man's other shoulder. "Thank you so much, sieur, so very much," she said.

"It's my pleasure," Eodan said.

He accepted the coin the woman gave him and turned toward the door. His smile widened when he saw Ginnevra. Ginnevra held the door open for the pair; the young man seemed still not fully aware of his surroundings and didn't acknowledge her, but the woman gaped and tried to bow. Ginnevra steadied her and said, "Good day to you, madama."

When the outer door closed behind them, Ginnevra said, "Should I call the next person? There's a queue outside. Isn't queueing interesting?"

"I'd rather know what you found out at the sanctuary," Eodan said. "There's no hurry—unless someone is bleeding heavily."

Ginnevra shook her head. "We're leaving sooner than I expected," she said, and summed up what the Blessed had told her. Eodan listened in silence with his brow furrowed the way it got when he was intent on a problem. Finally, she said, "The sanctuary has offered to outfit us, so I'll go back there this afternoon. We'll probably leave day after tomorrow."

"You sound so calm about this," Eodan said. "Aren't you at all worried?"

"There are so many things I could potentially worry about I've decided not to dwell on any of them," Ginnevra said. She leaned against the table and fiddled with a length of bandage. "Worrying won't make my job easier."

"No, but it would be a natural response." Eodan prodded the fire into life again, then set down the poker. "I won't tell you what to feel, but if there's anything you want to talk about—"

Ginnevra set aside the bandage and wished she weren't wearing her armor. Holding him close would ease her heart, but her mail was coated in silver that was inimical to werewolves. "I love you, and I love your generosity of spirit. But I'm fine. It's just one of life's weird coincidences that Filippa showed up just before I'm sent to Quinizelle. I promise I'm not secretly afraid of going back there, or of failing again, or anything like that."

"I know you're not." Eodan carefully kissed her, long and sweet, making her head spin. "I'll finish up here today and pass the word that I'm leaving. And pay the innkeeper something extra for her generosity in renting me this room during the day."

Ginnevra touched his cheek lightly with her gloved hand. "If I'm worried about anything," she said, "it's that cold weather comes earlier in the mountains. I really hope it doesn't snow while we're there."

"We'll buy you a cloak," Eodan said.

FOUR

A week later, Ginnevra thought back to that conversation and huddled deeper into her fur-lined cloak. The shopkeeper had looked at her like she was crazy for wanting anything that heavy when summer's heat was still fierce, but he'd sold it to her at a good price. It was of heavy twilled cotton dyed deep green, thick enough to keep off all but the heaviest rain. The bear's fur lining the inside still smelled faintly of the lavender the shopkeeper had stored it in as a preventative against moths, a nice, comforting smell. Eodan had laughed when she put it on for the first time, saying she looked like a bear herself, but Ginnevra hadn't cared so long as she stayed warm.

This evening, a heavy mist hung in the mountain passes, promising rain before midnight. They would be well inside Quinizelle by then, Ginnevra judged. Far to her left, a sliver of moon hung above the horizon, barely visible against the setting sun. Tomorrow was the dark of the moon, the first day of the new month, and Ginnevra looked forward to celebrating it with other worshippers at the Quinizelle sanctuary. Even if it rained.

Dauntless picked his way carefully up the road, which was wide and well-trafficked, though not by wagons. The steepness of the grade would make that impossible. Ginnevra wondered how the citizens of Quinizelle managed their trade. They would need supplies, and then there was all that silver to transport down the mountain. Ginnevra hadn't cared about any of that the last time she was here. She wasn't sure she really cared about it now except as a curiosity. But if she was going to threaten the king's economic stability, maybe it needed to matter to her.

The steep road would have been practically vertical if it hadn't zigzagged across the mountainside, making travel possible. Weeds and tough grasses grew on every even remotely horizontal surface, clinging to the bases of trees whose roots emerged from the very stone and bent parallel to the cliff faces. Their foliage glimmered in the last light of the setting sun with the condensation from the fog, making the place feel like a land from a dream.

Ginnevra glanced over her shoulder at Eodan, who wore a light, waterproof cape over his usual shirt and breeches and seemed unaffected by the chill and damp. "I see lights ahead," she said.

"So do I," Eodan said. He patted Ginger's neck and then shook water off his palm. "I'm looking forward to a hot meal."

"They make a delicious roast pork glazed with honey here. It's like nothing I've ever tasted before." Ginnevra eyed the distant lanterns, gleaming like fallen stars. "Though that could just be the mountain air. I know I said I hate the cold, but the air is invigorating."

"This isn't cold. It's not even close to cold."

Ginnevra shivered. "I don't want to know what you've experienced that you can say that. You northerners are always quick to brag about how you walked ten miles in waist-deep snow barefoot and got nothing worse than a sniffle from it."

"We are a hardier folk, true," Eodan said.

"And yet you were the one who complained about the heat wave last month and insisted on a cold bath every day. I'm not sure how hardy that is."

Eodan laughed. "So we both have our preferences. It's too bad there isn't anywhere that meets both our requirements for comfort."

Ginnevra looked uphill again. At that distance, the regular shapes of human construction were visible despite their being the same color as the mountainside. "If we travel far enough, maybe we'll find it."

The sun was halfway below the horizon when they arrived at Quinizelle's gate. The road, bounded now by a short curb barely waist-high to stop the unwary from accidentally walking off the cliff, widened into a small paved area too tiny to be called a court-yard. An arch of tawny stone surrounded thick, iron-banded oak doors that were blackened in places from a long-ago fire. The walls extending to either side of the gate were of rough stone anyone might have climbed—if not for the sheer drop fifty feet to the next curve of the road.

Two men wearing hardened leather jerkins and round, narrow-brimmed helmets looked down at Ginnevra and Eodan from atop the arch. "State your business," the man on the left said. His thick black mustache bobbed as he spoke.

"Ginnevra Cassaline, prime of the Blessed, and my companion Eodan, here on Abraciabene business," Ginnevra called out. With her armor, she was obviously a paladin, something that had been part of her decision to wear it that day. Now she hoped she hadn't made a mistake. Nobody was likely to turn her away, but they might decide to give her a hard time, and she was tired and hungry and did not want trouble.

The man on the right turned and shouted at someone out of sight behind the door, "Open up!"

One half of the enormous door began creaking open. The guard on the left said, "You're almost too late, paladin. These gates open for no one after sunset."

"Then I'm glad we made good time," Ginnevra replied. It surprised her how relieved she was that her first interaction with Quinizelle was not hostile. It wasn't that she was afraid of getting in a fight so much as she was conscious of being there as more than just herself.

The door shuddered to a halt, and Ginnevra saw three more guards in the same armor hovering just beyond it. She nudged Dauntless forward. "Thank you for your welcome," she said, though they all looked more nervous than welcoming. But none of them had drawn their weapons, heavy spiked maces that would do serious damage to an opponent, and none of them sneered or said anything antagonistic like—

"Paladin," said the first guard, and Ginnevra brought Dauntless to a halt and watched the man with the mustache descend a narrow, steep flight of stairs from his position on the wall-walk. He trod the steps heavily, making them shake. He stopped about ten steps from the ground, putting him well above the level of her head, and said, "You need to watch yourself in Quinizelle. We aren't interested in a paladin's interference in our business."

Ginnevra examined him. He wore a purple knot of rank on his right shoulder that Ginnevra thought indicated a sergeant, or some similar rank. Despite his strong words, he didn't sound hostile, but he stood like someone ready for a fight.

"Sergeant—is that correct, sieur?" she asked.

The sergeant nodded once, curtly.

"Sergeant, I am here as a negotiator with King Paolo on behalf of Abraciabene. While it's true I am authorized to prosecute justice throughout the Lordagne, I understand Quinizelle does not recognize my remit. So I won't interfere unless someone requests my help." She cast an eye over him again and added, "I am not here to challenge your religion."

The sergeant's gaze moved to Eodan. "And you are...?"

"The paladin's companion," Eodan said. He had maneuvered Ginger to stand next to Ginnevra so his full height was clear by comparison to hers. Now the sergeant looked nervous. Caught between amusement and annoyance that he clearly didn't think of her as a threat, at least not compared to Eodan, she put a hand on her greatsword where it was strapped to Dauntless' saddle. The sergeant's attention immediately fixed on it.

"Are we free to go?" Ginnevra said.

The sergeant's mustache twitched. "Certainly," he said, though he sounded like the word was pulled out of him, it was so grudging. "Welcome to Quinizelle."

Ginnevra nodded and rode on.

The street was narrow and surprisingly empty, with only a few pedestrians and no other horses occupying it. Lights burned at all the windows at ground level, which boasted grilles bolted to the window frames, and at many of the windows above, some of them three or four stories high. Every building was built of the same warm, tawny stone as the wall, though the stones were smaller and irregular in shape. Ginnevra glanced up as they passed beneath one of the many arches built out over the street, taking advantage of the empty space for more housing. There was a light in the window that dimmed as someone walked between it and the lantern, and then Ginnevra and Eodan passed beneath the arch, their horses' hooves clopping loudly over the cobbles.

Eodan came up beside her. "I'm not sure what just happened," he said. "Why would anyone believe a paladin is less of a threat than anyone just because he's bigger than she is?"

"People who don't see paladins in action always assume we're too small to be a credible threat," Ginnevra said. "It's why the Goddess's warriors are all women, so Her grace and power are made evident. If She blessed a man with a paladin's enhancements, people might believe he was strong on his own because men tend to be stronger than women. In granting women Her blessings, She makes it clear that their abilities come from Her and aren't inherent."

"I remember you saying something like that before," Eodan said. "He's lucky you *weren't* interested in starting a fight. Not that you'd ever attack anyone just to prove a point, right?"

"Don't think I've never been tempted." Ginnevra sighed. "Let's go to the sanctuary and see if they have a place for us to stay. Not in the sanctuary, obviously, but Hallowed Nevante was supposed to arrange something."

They passed a couple of taverns, doing good business by the sound of revelry, and then some shops closed for the night. The smells of cooking food drifted from somewhere nearby, rousing Ginnevra's hunger. For a moment, she considered stopping for a meal. Then she recalled that the sanctuary was expecting them that evening, and it would be uncivil to make them wait while she had some of that famous roast pork in honey.

More sounds of conversation, and a fiddle's high skirling melody, came to Ginnevra's ears. This time, the noise didn't fade as they passed, though the fiddle stopped mid-phrase. Ginnevra brought Dauntless to a halt. "Do you hear that?"

Eodan tilted his head, listening. "A fight. It's down the next street. That sergeant said—"

Someone in the distance cried out, a terrible, frightened sound. Ginnevra cursed and urged Dauntless into a trot. "He didn't say let someone be assaulted. Let's go."

They rounded the corner onto a street even narrower than the first, one where more arches darkened the already dim sky. Ginnevra, whose vision sharpened after sunset and was at its keenest at the dark of the moon, saw everything as if it were day. Six or seven figures scuffled about twenty feet away, while a few others hovered nearby, making the tentative movements that said they wanted to intervene but were afraid to. One of them, female by the pitch of her voice, screamed, "Help! Someone stop them!"

Ginnevra slid down with Eodan half a breath behind her and ran toward the fight. One of the watchers, the one who'd screamed, hurtled toward them and met them halfway. "Please —" the woman began, then looked Ginnevra up and down and said, "No, don't!"

Ginnevra heard more cries, these of pain, and put the woman to one side, ignoring her odd reaction. Eodan hadn't stopped running when she had and reached the fight a few steps ahead of her. He plunged into the melee and dragged two men off a third. Somebody else was kicking a man who lay curled in on himself on the ground. Ginnevra grabbed the kicker and twisted his arm high behind his back, dragging him away. She shoved him to the ground. "Back off," she said.

The man scuttled backwards, his eyes wide. "Let's go!" he cried out. "Now!"

Three of the others immediately disengaged from the fight, one of them wrenching out of Eodan's grip. All four took off down the street, not looking back.

Ginnevra knelt beside the fallen man. "It's all right, they're gone," she said. "Are you badly hurt?"

Something struck her in the side, impacting harmlessly on her cuirass. Ginnevra turned. "What—"

"Leave us alone!" the shrieking woman shouted. "Haven't you people done enough harm?"

"Excuse me?" Ginnevra said. "We haven't hurt anyone." She

stood and put a hand on the woman's shoulder, stopping her from attacking again.

"Berria, stop," one of the other watching women said. "They ran off those thugs. There has to be a reason."

"A reason for these people to turn on their own?" Berria shouted. She slapped at Ginnevra's restraining hand. "Don't touch me, Goddess-worshipper."

Ginnevra withdrew her hand. "Are you Torunes?"

"Ginnevra, this man needs help," Eodan said. He was kneeling beside the fallen man. "His ribs are cracked and I think he has internal injuries. We need to get him someplace I can get a better look."

"We don't want your help," the one remaining man said. His eyes were both swelling shut and a long cut, now clotted, had bled heavily down his right cheek. "Get out of here. Follow your friends."

Thoroughly confused now, Ginnevra said, "What friends? We arrived in Quinizelle less than an hour ago."

"You're all the same, you Goddess-worshippers," Berria spat. "Think you're entitled to knock us around—well, we don't have to put up with that."

Ginnevra closed her eyes and let out a deep breath. Opening her eyes again, she said, "Hold on. Do you mean to say those were Faithful who attacked you? Because you're Torunes?"

The man laughed. "Don't sound so surprised. We all know the truth, so there's no point you pretending to innocence."

"But—we were told it was Torunes who were assaulting the Faith."

"Not tonight, it wasn't," Berria said. "Leave Carriolus alone. We care for our own people."

"And I suppose you're all physicians?" Eodan straightened,

though he remained kneeling. "Because I am, and I'm sure he needs my help."

Berria snorted. "We take care of our own," she repeated, though she didn't sound quite so sure.

The man bent and lifted Carriolus into his arms. It disturbed Ginnevra that the wounded man didn't move, even though with broken ribs that maneuver would have hurt like hell. "Please," she said, "let us help. I don't know what started the fight, but I assure you—"

"It's none of your business, paladin," Berria said, making "paladin" sound more like "filth." "Back off."

Ginnevra watched the little group walk away, her mouth open. Eodan got slowly to his feet. "What just happened?" he said.

"I don't know. That's not at all what I expected." Ginnevra shook her head. "We need to get to the sanctuary. Someone there must be able to explain all this."

Conflicting thoughts spun through her head as they rode through increasingly quiet streets. The Blessed had been very clear that it was believers in the Faith who were in danger. But those men and women who'd been attacked had not only claimed otherwise, they'd made it sound as if attacks like that one were common. Either someone was lying, or the problem in Quinizelle wasn't prejudice, it was religious war.

The Quinizelle sanctuary nestled into the side of the mountain and looked as if it were still in the process of emerging from it. It was the only sanctuary Ginnevra had ever seen that was painted black instead of being clad in marble or basalt facings. It was built like all the other buildings in Quinizelle, narrow and four stories tall, but with its windows bricked over and painted the same ebon black as the walls, it looked more like a carving of a building rather than anything anyone lived in. But lanterns burned on either side of the black door, and Ginnevra smelled the warm, rich odor of a stable nearby.

She followed her nose around the corner and discovered a cave hollowed out behind the sanctuary, well-lit and so warm Ginnevra felt comfortable for the first time all day. The space was divided into stalls by wooden partitions, over which two horses peeked, interested in the newcomers.

An elderly man with wispy white hair was engaged in sweeping the space in front of the stalls. He startled at their entrance, then smiled. "My lady," he said, "welcome. We were expecting you. I'm Harrus. Let me care for your mounts."

Ginnevra dismounted. "Ginnevra Cassaline," she said, extending a gloved hand. "And my companion, Eodan."

Harrus eyed Eodan as if impressed by his size, but not as if he knew Eodan's race. "Welcome to you both. Please, go right in. You can trust me with horses. I was practically raised by them."

Ginnevra handed over Dauntless' reins with a smile. She hadn't realized how much that encounter with the Torunes had unsettled her. "Where should we go?"

"Take the back door, my lady, the front door is locked." Harrus led Dauntless to the nearest stall. "I'll get some of the acolytes out here to help."

"The front door is locked?"

Ginnevra hadn't meant to sound so startled, even horrified, but to her knowledge, sanctuary doors were never locked. Harrus' smile fell away. "Because of the troubles, my lady," he said, ducking his head as if he was embarrassed.

Ginnevra almost asked *What troubles?* But Harrus definitely looked upset enough she thought better of pushing him. Besides, that was a question better put to Hallowed Nevante. "I see," she said. "Thank you, Harrus, if you're sure it's all right that we go in the back way?"

"Of course, my lady." Harrus led the way to a door cleverly hidden by a fold in the mountain and opened it, revealing a warm, golden light illuminating a short hallway. "Take the door at the far end and then follow the stairs to the ritual chamber. Someone there will summon Hallowed Nevante." He pushed ahead of her and opened the first door on the left, saying, "Come, you layabouts, there's work to be done!"

Ginnevra and Eodan stepped back to let Harrus and his two assistants exit. Ginnevra walked through the doorway and stopped when Eodan hesitated. "Eodan—"

Eodan pointed at the hall beyond. "I can't enter."

Ginnevra had forgotten this was the sanctuary, thanks to the homely nature of the entrance; between the smallness of the door and the rough, cavernous stable, it looked like the back door to someone's house. "I'm sorry," she said, her heart aching with the unfairness of it all. "Wait here? I'll be back as soon as I can."

Eodan nodded. "I'll help with the horses."

Ginnevra squeezed his hand lightly and released him. *Someday*, she silently vowed, though fulfilling that vow seemed unlikely.

The hall was very short and very narrow and smelled sharply of vinegar, a clean, biting scent. Unlike the sanctuary's exterior, the hall was painted bright cream, even the stone ceiling, and the golden light emanated from four iron lanterns also painted cream. The door at the far end, though was only cream-colored on this side; on the other side, it was stained dark to blend with the dark hallway beyond.

Ginnevra shut the door behind her, blinking as her eyes quickly adjusted to the dim light cast by flickering lanterns burning low. This hall was much longer, with no doors to interrupt its sheer blackness, and it smelled of incense. Ginnevra's disquiet faded. It was hard for her to stay agitated within the darkness and peace of the Goddess's sanctuary.

She removed her helmet and coif, tucking them under her arm, and walked down the hall, listening for signs that anyone else was there. It was unlikely the sanctuary was empty, though it certainly felt that way. But someone tended the lanterns, someone burned the incense, and Ginnevra's fancies were in her imagination.

She reached the end of the hall—the front end, since the hall terminated in a large black double door with iron handles and two small window slits no wider than her palm. Iron panels that could be slid back currently covered each window slit. Ginnevra tried the door latch; locked, as Harrus had said.

Stairs painted the same black as the walls ascended from the door into more darkness. Ginnevra still didn't hear any movement or distant speech. She put one foot on the bottommost step and winced at the loud creak that echoed up the stairwell. Somebody knew she was coming now.

She continued up the stairs, which creaked and squealed with every step no matter how she walked. Finally, she gave up trying to be unobtrusive and strode decisively upward, past the first landing and then the second. Each landing opened on more hallways, these lined with doors. The ceilings were low, the corridors narrow, and despite herself Ginnevra felt hemmed in, as if she'd stepped into what she thought was familiar territory and instead found herself in a maze.

Over the sound of the creaks, she heard light footsteps descending toward her. She paused on the next landing and waited. Soon, a woman rounded the stairs and stopped a few feet away, enough that Ginnevra had to look up to meet her eyes. The woman was dressed in the full-sleeved black robe of a Revered, and her dark brown hair was bound up messily at the nape of her neck.

"Paladin—I mean, prime," she said, stammering slightly. "Welcome to the Quinizelle sanctuary. I am Revered Aperrede."

"Ginnevra Cassaline," Ginnevra said, saluting her. "May I speak to Hallowed Nevante?"

"Of course. Follow me." Aperrede led Ginnevra to the top of the stairs. There, instead of narrow, low, claustrophobic corridors, the space opened up into a single large room with a high ceiling, empty of furnishings. Lanterns that burned brighter than the ones downstairs illuminated the painted floor, which showed a series of abstract curves and lines defining a large circle. The phases of the moon made another circle on the ceiling.

Two people, a man and a woman, stood near the center of the circle, conversing quietly. The woman held up a hand, silencing the man, and walked forward to meet Ginnevra before she could step into the circle. "Prime Cassaline," she said. "I'm Hallowed Raina Nevante. Welcome."

"Thank you, Hallowed," Ginnevra said. "I'm sorry if I interrupted something."

"No, not at all. Revered Bariatte and I were discussing plans for the morning's new moon ceremony." Nevante gestured in the man's direction. "I understood you have a companion. The werewolf."

Her casual reference to Eodan, as if werewolf were an occupation no more terrifying than carpenter or merchant, startled Ginnevra into saying, "He can't enter the sanctuary. That doesn't mean he's evil."

"I see. I hadn't realized." Nevante still sounded casually uninterested in the subject. "Fortunately, we arranged for you to be housed in a hostel closer to the royal palace. It seemed more convenient. Revered Bariatte will escort you."

"Thank you," Ginnevra replied automatically. "I'm sorry, Hallowed, but I'm not used to any of the anointed accepting Eodan so easily."

"The divine inscrutability works wonders beyond our comprehension," the Hallowed said. "A werewolf who has turned his back on his creator is not the strangest thing I've ever heard of. Now, if you'll excuse me, I'm sure you want to settle in."

"Yes—wait." Ginnevra held up a hand. "Eodan and I interrupted a fight on our way here. Some of the Faithful assaulted a group of Torunes."

"That's unlikely," Nevante said. "We have been dealing with daily assaults by Torunes who believe we are easy targets because their king opposes the Faith. Naturally, I've told the Faithful not to retaliate, but you can understand how some of them might not be able to abide by that guidance, especially if their families are involved. I can't tell them not to defend themselves."

"The Faithful involved fled when Eodan and I intervened. That doesn't sound like they believed they were in the right. Is that what the stable master meant when he said you'd had some trouble here?"

Nevante shook her head. "You're new to Quinizelle, prime, and it won't take long before you see the truth of what's going on. I assure you the Faithful are innocent victims. Women and children have been attacked. Shops have been looted and burned. And King Paolo does nothing. You are here to put an end to that." She turned her back on Ginnevra. "Pandolfus, please guide the paladin and her companion to the hostel."

The man bowed his head. "As you wish, Hallowed."

Ginnevra cast one glance over her shoulder before following Revered Pandolfus Bariatte out of the ritual chamber. Nevante had resumed her place in the ritual circle and had tipped her head back to look at the ceiling. She hadn't once sounded disturbed, not afraid nor concerned nor angry, and Ginnevra didn't know what to make of that. All Ginnevra was sure of was that that confrontation between Torunes and Faithful had not been a misunderstanding, and it had not been a matter of the Faithful defending against a Torune attack. She had the sinking feeling that nothing about this was as straightforward as she'd hoped.

Ginnevra left the sanctuary the next morning feeling more cheerful than she had the previous night. The morning's ceremony welcoming the new month had invigorated her, reminding her of her vows and the Goddess's promise to support Her people in their trials. Only a few people had been present, Hallowed Nevante, both the Revereds, and seven Dedicates, and the ceremony had felt as intimate as Ginnevra remembered from her time with a paladin company. She and Nevante hadn't talked about Ginnevra's mission, and Ginnevra had been able to focus for a time on the purity of her service to the Goddess and not on the difficulties sure to come.

Now she walked through the rainy streets back to the hostel, silently thanking the Devoyenne shopkeeper for the cloak he'd sold her. It had begun raining sometime after midnight, and the rain hadn't let up since. Stupid mountains and their stupid rainy, cold climate. She liked rain fine so long as she didn't have to be out in it. Maybe the king wouldn't have time for her today, and she could stay indoors with Eodan, maybe read, maybe nap. Maybe more vigorous activities...

Nobody paid her any attention, just an anonymous woman in a nice cloak. She'd left off her armor in part because it was uncomfortable when rain seeped through the joints and in part to observe the city without being an explicit representative of the Faith. Nothing unusual caught her eye, but then almost everyone was as huddled in on themselves as she was, trying to accomplish their business as quickly as possible. Nothing about the city suggested religious war.

She rounded a corner and ascended another slope to the hostel. She'd forgotten how *vertical* Quinizelle was, how much of it was built on the mountain peak that had never been leveled. It was no wonder she never saw any wheeled vehicles bigger than a handcart; these streets would be impossibly slick after a winter storm, and Ginnevra guessed Quinizelle saw a lot of those. Her calves ached from the constant up and down motion.

The hostel Nevante had chosen was small and, while not luxurious, definitely catered to an elite clientele. It looked like a typical house, four stories tall and narrow, but little bushes grew in pots on either side of the front door, and all the windows were large and paned with thin, perfect glass. Ginnevra had learned when she and Eodan had arrived the previous night that there was someone on watch at the door at all times, not to prevent theft but in case a visitor might need something at midnight. That struck Ginnevra as more extravagant than anything else.

She nodded politely at the woman sitting beside the front door and ran up the stairs to the third floor, where she and Eodan had their room. Rooms. All right, so *that* was the most extravagant thing Ginnevra had ever seen. She and Eodan had a suite of rooms, not only an oversized bedroom but also one of those newfangled cubbies called a water closet for relieving oneself.

Ginnevra had used it hesitantly, remembering the comfortable family outhouse she was used to from her childhood. This didn't stink like that had, but it was so unfamiliar she had an irrational feeling she was doing something wrong.

Eodan was sitting in one of the room's two armchairs, turning the pages of a book. He didn't look at all as if he'd only begun learning to read a few weeks ago. He set the book aside when Ginnevra entered. "There's been no word."

"I know it's too early to expect a response, but I hoped... I want to get this over with." Ginnevra sat in the chair next to him. Its back and wooden armrests were broad and wide, and two cushions embroidered in the Fayonne manner padded its seat.

"Even I know this won't be resolved with one meeting," Eodan said.

"I meant this initial meeting. I want to know who I'm dealing with and what to expect." Ginnevra tilted her head back and sighed. "I hope he doesn't know this is my first negotiation. That would weaken my position considerably."

Eodan took her hand. "It will be fine. And now we should eat."

"You waited for me?" Part of Ginnevra's personal new moon observance was fasting until the ceremony was over, not a hardship since it happened at dawn, but she felt bad that Eodan had gone without food on her behalf.

"I only woke about half an hour ago. It's no problem."

Someone knocked on the door, and Eodan stood. When he opened the door, a young woman with damp hair and a round-cheeked face waited there. She wore a rain cape over a fine white linen shirt and a forest green doublet belted with a maroon leather belt. A sash, also maroon, crossed her chest diagonally from her right shoulder and was tied in a knot above her left hip. Boots stained dark with rainwater left puddles on the floorboards.

"I've a message for the paladin Ginnevra Cassaline," she said.

"I'm here," Ginnevra said, joining Eodan at the door.

The girl reached beneath her cape and removed an oilcloth packet sealed with a blob of dark green wax. She extended it to Ginnevra, bowed, and hurried away down the hall.

"I guess she wasn't counting on a response," Ginnevra said. She turned away, examining the seal. The wax bore the impression of a stylized animal of some kind. "I can't tell if this is a dog or a wolf."

"It's a cat," Eodan said, looking over her shoulder. "Pointed ears and whiskers."

"Oh, right." She broke the seal and withdrew a sheet of paper. "Well, that was fast. King Paolo Napolle requests my attendance upon him at three o'clock this afternoon. I'm to present myself at the receiving hall for admittance." She folded the paper in half. "I don't know if that's normal. I know nothing about royalty."

"Neither do I, but if he responded that quickly, he's concerned." Eodan resumed his seat. "He'd have put you off for days if he wanted to prove his power over you. Over the Faith, by extension."

"That makes sense. How do you know that?"

Eodan glanced out the window. "It's a guess," he said, so flatly Ginnevra was taken aback.

Impulsively, she said, "You mean, that's how werewolves do it? Eodan, you don't need to hide from me. I would never pry, but I don't think you—"

"I'd rather not think about it," Eodan said. "Forget I said anything. And I don't even know if humans are like werewolves that way."

He sounded so harsh, so unlike himself, Ginnevra turned her back on him and walked to the window. "I think you're right," she said. "But let's talk about something else, all right? I don't think you can come with me. The message didn't say 'bring a friend.'"

"No, that would look bad," Eodan said, sounding a little more normal. "I thought I would explore the city, maybe see if I can find any more evidence that Torunes are attacking the Faithful. I didn't like that fight last night."

"Neither did I. And the Hallowed dismissed it as impossible, despite the fact that the attackers fled the way guilty people would." Ginnevra sighed. "I don't like not knowing things. If it's not true that the Faithful are the victims, that will change how I approach the king."

She heard Eodan's footsteps, and then he put his arms around her. "Food," he said. "Then we'll wait the rain out."

"What will we do?" Ginnevra turned around in his arms to face him.

Eodan smiled. "We'll think of something."

THE RAIN SUBSIDED to a seeping drizzle around noon, a heavy mist that beaded on the canopies over the merchants' carts when Ginnevra finally ventured out. This time, she wore her armor, cursing inwardly at how much work it would take to ensure the wet didn't affect the silvered steel. It was too bad the silvering process didn't waterproof the metal, though Ginnevra couldn't imagine why anyone should even expect that. She reminded herself that paladins didn't complain about things they couldn't help and trudged onward, her sword banging against her hip.

With her gloved hand, she swept water off her helmet before it could condense into droplets and fall into her face. The few pedestrians walked wide of her, though none looked more than reasonably wary. No one accosted her or threw things, both of which she'd steeled herself against. Of course, this was an upper-class part of Quinizelle, and maybe that extended to the inhabitants being better mannered than most.

The palace squatted at the top of the city, nearly at the top of the peak, and the streets leading to it were even steeper than elsewhere in Quinizelle. Ginnevra saw some past general's influence in their construction; getting an invading army up to the palace would be difficult, the more so if that army was being shot at as they came.

The palace also looked like it was meant solely for defense, with its sheer thirty-foot walls, its crenellated towers that would provide excellent cover for the archers Ginnevra had imagined, and the heavy iron portcullis that at the moment was winched out of the way, leaving the entrance open but not welcoming. On seeing it, Ginnevra wished she'd ridden Dauntless to this meeting. The palace's entire appearance seemed calculated to make visitors feel small. She straightened her shoulders and tugged gently on the sword belt slung over her shoulder to adjust the lie of the greatsword. She would not let imagination get the better of her.

The road leading to the gate was raised above street level. Ginnevra would have called it a causeway if a river had flowed beneath it, but it was just a big arched street with waist-high curbs on either side to prevent anyone walking off accidentally. Four soldiers wearing hardened leather armor reinforced with steel plates stood guard at the gate, halberds held erect rather than at the ready. One of them, a woman with a long scar along the right side of her jaw, stepped into Ginnevra's path. "State your business," she said, but in a tone of voice that suggested she already knew.

"Ginnevra Cassaline, paladin and prime of the Blessed," Ginnevra replied, "summoned to present myself to his majesty,

King Paolo Napolle." She kept her gaze fixed on the guard, whose own gaze never flinched.

"Prime Cassaline," the guard said. "You will proceed into the courtyard and wait for an attendant. Do not stray beyond that mark. Unescorted armed strangers are not tolerated within the palace."

"I understand."

For some reason, that made the guard blink with surprise. Ginnevra wondered what response she'd expected. Then the guard said, "Proceed," and stepped out of the way. Ginnevra saluted her, gloved fist to below her throat the way she would another paladin. She hoped to startle another unguarded reaction out of the woman with that salute, but the guard showed no sign she knew it was an unusual gesture. Ginnevra walked past the guards and through the short tunnel through the outer wall into the courtyard.

In full sun, the courtyard would be cheerful, with its yellow-tan stone construction that would take the sun's rays and reflect them back to warm the whole area. With the rain still drizzling, it wasn't anything but dreary. Gates that were a smaller version of the enormous main gate, but without portcullises, lay at opposite ends of the courtyard, both of them closed. Stairs ran up both sides of the wall immediately opposite Ginnevra, meeting at a landing at the top of the wall that spread out to become another courtyard in front of what Ginnevra judged to be the inner keep.

She turned in a circle, conscious of her promise not to go anywhere—probably she didn't need to interpret that directive so literally, but she meant to be cooperative until that didn't get her anywhere. More stairs flanked the gate, leading to the wall-walk, and there were guards with crossbows posted there. They paced the length of the wall-walk in both directions, their attention turned outward, though Ginnevra was sure they knew she was there and were only pretending to ignore her.

"Prime Cassaline?"

She turned on her heel to see a middle-aged man running toward her, splashing through the puddles with no care for his shoes. They were going to be ruined, Ginnevra reflected, but she said nothing. He almost certainly knew his feet were soaked.

The man slowed to a halt before her. "I am Lord Pattero Alamanne," he said, "and it is my honor to escort you to his majesty's presence." He bowed low and then made a grab for his flat velvet cap as it slid over his thick, graying hair. The cap was dark with rainwater in places where it pressed closest to his head. Another item of clothing Pattero would need to replace, unless the velvet they had in Quinizelle wasn't the kind that water instantly ruined. Ginnevra had never had contact with nobility—the Blessed didn't count, even though she was of the noble house that ruled the city-state Fayonne—and she wished she dared ask if deliberate waste was a noble quality. Or maybe it was just that Pattero was so wealthy he could afford to ruin his shoes and his hat and replace them as easily.

But she was there to negotiate, not to discuss comparative social classes, so she only said, "Thank you, Lord Pattero. Let's get out of this rain, shall we?"

Pattero led the way up the stairs and into the keep. The door opened on a vast receiving chamber, tiled in black and white and lined on both sides with pillars that held up the curved roof. Intricate murals covered the ceiling, but Pattero set too fast a pace for Ginnevra to be able to examine them. Instead, she paid attention as the lord exited the chamber and led Ginnevra through a series of winding passages, some of them windowed, all of them carpeted in something thick and plush she left wet footprints on.

Just as she'd started to suspect Pattero was trying to unsettle her, maybe even get her lost on purpose, he pulled open half of a double door and bowed. "There's a mark on the carpet," he whispered, so low only Ginnevra's enhanced hearing made it out clearly. "You'll see it. Stand there and go no closer." He held out both hands. "You can leave your sword with me."

"The hell I will," Ginnevra said, startled into a frank response. "This is my badge of office. You're not entitled to carry it."

Pattero's eyes widened. "But, Prime Cassaline, surely you understand no one can enter the king's presence armed unless it is his own trusted guards. We make no exceptions."

Ginnevra regarded him and concluded, irritably, that he was telling the truth. She unslung the sword belt from her shoulder and coiled it around the blade. "I'll leave it here," she said, walking to one side and propping the greatsword against the wall. "Nobody touches it. That means nobody. I'll know if you interfere with it, and we will have a problem. Do you understand?"

Pattero swallowed, making the lump of his throat move convulsively. "I understand," he said, still whispering. "I assure you nothing will happen to it, my lady."

No one else here had addressed her as "my lady." Instinctively, Ginnevra checked the lie of Pattero's doublet and saw a barely perceptible lump beneath it, just below the neckline where a grace would hang. Suddenly his haste to greet her, and his politeness, came into focus. "You're—" she began, then thought better of it. If King Paolo was hostile to the Faith, Pattero might be keeping his religious affiliation private. "Thank you," she said instead, and walked through the door.

This room was smaller than the reception chamber, but was otherwise identical: murals on the ceiling, plush carpet on the floor, rows of pillars holding up the roof. Guards armed with pikes too keenly edged to be purely ceremonial flanked the door; they didn't move at Ginnevra's entrance, but she felt their attention on her. More guards stood at regular intervals along the wall and on either side of two other doors just as grand as the one she'd come in by. Ginnevra assessed their height and build and judged she could neutralize six of them before being overwhelmed. She had no intention of fighting the king's guards, but she believed in having a plan to defeat any potential enemy. This habit had saved her life three times already.

A carved wooden throne stood at the far end of the room, surrounded by almost two dozen men and women dressed in silks and velvets who never got too close to the man on the throne. By the way they stood, they had been conversing in groups of three or four when she entered, and her entrance had stopped them in place as if they had been frozen like Hallowed Currade's eternity fountain. All of them stared at Ginnevra, but she was used to being stared at and didn't feel there was anything more intimidating about being stared at by nobility.

She walked forward until she reached a dingy mark on the carpet. It looked like the kind of mark that came from hundreds of people stepping in that spot over centuries. That put her within twenty feet of the throne and the people gathered around it.

The man on the throne regarded her silently, his eyebrows and lips drawn down in a frown. He was too thin to be truly handsome, but the unusual light gold shade of his eyes gave him a striking appearance nonetheless. He wore a richly embroidered doublet over knee breeches and fine woolen hose, all in shades of gold and brown that looked so comfortably warm Ginnevra had to suppress jealousy. The velvet and wool would be impossible to fight in. Despite the richness of his clothing, he wore little jewelry, just a thin silver circlet confining his longish black hair and a gold chain with links as fat as the first joint of her thumb. He sat with one ankle crossed over his other knee, a relaxed pose Ginnevra thought indicated fake composure.

"Your majesty?" she said.

King Paolo inclined his head. "And you are the paladin representative of Abraciabene. We had word of your arrival." He spoke precisely, enunciating each word as if he could taste it and didn't like the flavor. Between that and his scowl, Ginnevra's resolve to remain calm wavered. She'd never met anyone as hostile as this who wasn't actively trying to kill her.

Hoping she concealed her disquiet, she saluted him, again with the paladin's salute because she didn't know what else was appropriate. She wouldn't have given him the salute to the Blessed even if she'd had her sword. "Thank you for your welcome, your majesty." Pretending this was an ordinary interaction seemed the only option, at least for now.

"We are pleased to confer with our counterpart in Abraciabene on matters of mutual interest." King Paolo sat up, putting both feet on the floor and leaning forward slightly. "We are sure we can arrive at a satisfactory conclusion." His unusual eyes narrowed as he watched her, his gaze never leaving her face.

Ginnevra swiftly glanced over the assembled crowd of... courtiers, that was the right word, yes? The courtiers stood still as statues, with only their eyes moving to indicate whom they were looking at. At the moment, every gaze was fixed on the king. Why he kept referring to himself in the plural, Ginnevra didn't know, unless he meant that there was someone else who would be involved in the discussions?

"I hope so, your majesty," she replied. Surely they weren't supposed to start negotiations with all these people around? There was so much she didn't know. "I know the Blessed is very interested in resolving matters, um, amicably. And unrest can't be good for your city, regardless of who starts it."

Murmurs rose up from the watching courtiers, and Ginnevra was instantly sure she'd said the wrong thing. She pressed her lips tightly together—she knew enough not to make matters worse by trying to retract her statement when she didn't know what about it had upset them—and took a parade rest stance she hoped conveyed confidence.

King Paolo raised a hand to his mouth and pressed two fingers to his lips as if he, too, intended to lock his words away. Then he said, "We believed Abraciabene to have already made up its mind as to guilt in this matter."

"I'm here to determine what's fair for both of us, your majesty," Ginnevra said. "But I think that's best saved for a private discussion."

King Paolo didn't reply. He stayed quiet for so long that the other mutters hushed. Ginnevra, feeling nervous, turned her attention on the walls of the throne room. Banners of forest green and maroon draped the two long walls, and round decorative shields hung between them, four on each side. Each shield was quartered, with colors decorating them, one silver and brown, another red and white, a third—

Ginnevra drew in a startled breath as surprise shot through her, freezing her in place. High on the left-hand wall, hanging where anyone could see, was a shield quartered in gold and gray, with a chevron pattern on its bottom left and a wolf's head on its upper right.

"Abraciabene claims our people have assaulted yours," a new voice said, breaking through Ginnevra's stunned surprise.

The speaker was a man standing near the king, close enough to touch the throne—closer, Ginnevra realized, than anyone else. He was not dressed like the others. The men wore doublets and hose similar to King Paolo's, the women wore straight-skirted gowns with stiff, form-shaping bodices, but this man wore a long gray robe that fastened from hem to chin with a row of bone toggles. Black-banded sleeves that dragged the ground and a black cowled hood thrown back from his unusually pale face gave him the look of someone deep in mourning. While he was clean-shaven, his gray-streaked hair grew more than long enough to compensate. Sharp black eyes stared Ginnevra down, daring her to defy him.

"Are you saying that's not true, sieur?" she said, raising her chin slightly, though not enough to be a gesture of defiance.

"Goddess-worshippers do not care whom they hurt in the

cause of bringing others to their Faith," the man said. "Torunes have been assaulted by your Faithful—what do you say to that?"

"I know," Ginnevra said.

The man had opened his mouth to say something else, but those two words caught him off guard. Before he could recover, Ginnevra said, "I believe the matter isn't as simple as one set of innocents being preyed on by religious zealots of a different faith. As I said, I'm here to work out a solution. And you and I, sieur, have not been introduced."

The man shut his mouth abruptly. King Paolo said, "This is High Priest Rainaldus Mastarcce. He is the spiritual leader of our —that is, the Torune religion."

"Mastarcce?" Ginnevra almost asked if he was related to one of her former teachers, Dedicate Emella Mastarcce, but she looked again at Rainaldus' sharp eye, at his glowering countenance, and decided that even if there was some distant relation, he would never admit to being kin to an anointed of an opposing faith. "I'm pleased to meet you, High Priest. I assume you are an advocate for your religion in this matter?"

"I am." Ice could have crystallized on Rainaldus' words. "And I have no intention of allowing you to intimidate his majesty into making a decision that will hurt these people."

"The Faithful are citizens of Quinizelle too, High Priest," Ginnevra said.

"That's enough," King Paolo said, rising from his throne. "We will begin discussions tomorrow morning at ten o'clock. You will attend upon us then."

"Of course, your majesty." Ginnevra saluted again, thinking that he had yet to call her by her name—by any title, for that matter. She shot another glance at the shield on the wall. "Should I return here?"

"You will be given a guide." The king straightened his doublet and took a few steps that coincidentally—or maybe not coincidentally; Ginnevra's ignorance frustrated her—took him toward a door in the wall beneath the wolf shield. Rainaldus followed close behind.

"Thank you, your majesty—and may I ask—" Ginnevra took a step after him, but the men and women surrounded him, and he was through the door before she could gracefully ask him about the shield. Six of the guards followed the crowd, and then the door shut, and Ginnevra was alone with the six remaining guards, who continued to ignore her.

She let out a deep breath and unclenched her right hand, which had closed without her noticing. Normally, she would have had a sword pommel to hang onto. She'd never realized how much she depended on her sword to calm her.

She turned to leave and let out a gasp when it turned out Pattero was right behind her. "Were you here the whole time, standing there like a vulture?" she demanded.

Pattero smiled, the first natural expression she'd ever seen from him. "I was at the door. I promise I am not meant to watch your every move. But I *am* supposed to escort you to the gate."

"King Paolo must be afraid of something," Ginnevra said without thinking. At Pattero's shocked expression, she quickly added, "That is, I don't mean to criticize, but where I come from, the lords who behave that way are the ones who have enemies."

"It's not my place to comment," Pattero said. "This way, please."

"I'm sorry," Ginnevra said. "I'm afraid I don't know much about Quinizelle's nobility. Do those shields mean something?" She pointed at the nearest shield, which was red and white with a bird sketched on one quadrant.

"Those represent the six noble houses," Pattero said without stopping.

"But there are eight shields."

"Six extant noble houses, I should have said." Pattero paused at the door and looked back at Ginnevra, who hadn't moved. "Please follow me, prime."

"They're so interesting," Ginnevra said. She pointed at the gold and gray shield. "What animal is that? A dog?"

"That is a wolf, my lady." Pattero took a few steps toward Ginnevra.

"Oh, of course. I see it now. So each of these represents a noble house, or something like that? What house is that one?"

Pattero sighed deeply. "The Zuccare family, my lady. The wolf's head indicates that they consider themselves under the aegis of Lopone, child of Torun. Torun is the chief of the old gods. Now, will you please come with me?"

Ginnevra gave the Zuccare shield one last look. Pattero's impatience to be gone concealed a hint of fear whose source Ginnevra couldn't identify. She changed her mind about asking for more details about the Zuccare family for the moment. "Of course, Lord Pattero," she said. "I'm afraid my curiosity got the better of me. But you should be more careful. No Torune would refer to Torun as one of 'the old gods.'"

Pattero stopped with his hand on the door. "I don't know what you mean."

"I'm guessing it's not common for someone of the Faithful to hold noble rank here," Ginnevra continued, taking a few more steps toward him. She lowered her voice so no one farther away than Pattero could hear. "I won't give you away, but I do wonder how you manage it."

Pattero wouldn't look at her. "It's not your business to delve into mine, my lady," he said. "My religion is my own." He spoke quietly, glancing at the guards, who remained still and decorative as statues.

"Lord Pattero, I'm here because the Faithful are being attacked." Ginnevra took a final step to stand beside him. "But I've learned the attacks aren't going just one way. What is going on in Quinizelle?"

With one hand still on the door, Pattero gripped the handle with his other hand, then pushed the door open and walked through. Ginnevra followed him and waited while he shut the door. "The Torunes didn't start the conflict," he said in a low voice. "It was the Faithful. Some of them harassed Torunes, and the Torunes fought back. I think the religious aspect was coincidental, but those Torunes claimed they were persecuted for what they believed. Then they began harassing the Faithful. That is likely when you were sent for."

"So it is religious war, or the beginnings of one," Ginnevra said.

Pattero nodded. "You surprised the king. We all knew the substance of the message that went before you. The Blessed was very clear that she put all the blame on Torunes for the violence—"

"Because that's what she was told," Ginnevra protested.

"What matters is that King Paolo expected you to make demands, not propose a real negotiation." Pattero's eyes met hers finally. "He hates you. Hates all paladins. But now he's confused, and I believe that gives you an advantage."

"You know him that well?"

Pattero nodded. "His wife is my half-sister, Benitta. I've learned to watch him closely against the day when I might need to defend her. Paolo is not a bad man, and he's not a bad king, but his station is a great burden, and that affects his judgment."

The longer Pattero talked, the more questions Ginnevra had. "You probably shouldn't be telling me this," she said. "Your loyalty is to your king."

"My loyalty is to my Goddess," Pattero said, touching the lump of his grace that lay beneath his doublet. "And to my king. I want peace in this city, my lady, and I believe you can deliver that. Peace will strengthen King Paolo, and that is something else I want." He rested his hand on the door again. "That is all I can say."

Ginnevra looked around. No one had disturbed her sword or the sword belt she had carefully looped around it to fall if anyone touched it. That was a relief. She wasn't sure what she would have done if anyone had interfered with it.

The rain had stopped, though clouds still covered the sky and no sunlight warmed the stones of the keep. Pattero said nothing more as they crossed the courtyard, but when they reached the gate, he bowed and said, "Prime Cassaline, I will be here tomorrow morning to escort you to your audience with the king."

"Thank you, Lord Pattero," Ginnevra said, returning his bow.

The guards at the gate gave her suspicious looks she ignored. With her sword over her shoulder, she retraced her path to the hostel, scanning her surroundings as she walked. No one looked happy to see her, which disturbed her. Obviously the Torunes would be wary, but she expected the Faithful to at least not walk wide of her. And she didn't believe *everyone* she met was a Torune.

Eodan was gone when she arrived at the hostel, but he had left a note scrawled on the endpaper torn from his book: *gone to explore, back soon.* His handwriting had improved dramatically in the weeks since he'd started learning to read and write. Ginnevra removed her armor and inspected it before drying it thoroughly with a spare cloth and arranging it in one corner of the room. Then she changed out of her damp shirt and settled into one of the well-cushioned chairs. From that position, she could see a wedge of gray sky and the walls of the building next door. The sight comforted her. She always felt more confident in a city.

She stretched her legs out and propped her stocking feet on the bed. It hadn't occurred to her at the time, but in not simply demanding the king protect the Faithful from being attacked, she could be said to have failed at her mandate. She hadn't been sent to Quinizelle to do anything but defend her people. But the situation wasn't as it had been reported, and Ginnevra was sure if the Blessed knew the truth, she would want Ginnevra to do exactly as she'd told the king: work out a solution to the conflict. If that was possible.

Ginnevra thought back to her first meeting with Hallowed Nevante. The Hallowed had been very clear about her position with regard to who was being attacked, which either meant she was ignorant of the truth or she refused to accept the truth. Scowling, Ginnevra added a third possibility, that Hallowed Nevante encouraged the Faithful to either actively defend themselves or take the initiative and attack Torunes first. She hated to even consider it, not because she had any illusions about Hallowed, who were after all still human, but because her job would be a thousand times more complicated if she were fighting her religious superior as well as a hostile king.

And then there was the shield.

Ginnevra pressed the heels of her palms against her closed eyes and groaned. So Filippa had been right about something: the crest those mercenaries had given her really did exist. That didn't mean they were telling the truth about the man they claimed to have seen. They might have picked a crest at random to get rid of Filippa. Or they were telling the truth, and some other person had stolen the crest and pretended to be a—Zuccare, that was the name. Zuccare.

The door opened. "You're back," Eodan said. "I found a place that cooks that honey pork roast you were talking about. And it's almost time for a meal."

Ginnevra sighed. "Yes. We should eat."

"Don't sound so enthusiastic." Eodan sat next to her and took her hand. "How did it go, meeting the king?"

"Not as I expected." Ginnevra stood and tugged on Eodan's hand, making him rise. "Let's eat, and I'll tell you everything."

The tavern Eodan had found was in a part of Quinizelle that wasn't exactly rundown, but had a slightly seedy atmosphere Ginnevra found unexpectedly comforting. Nobody there stared at her as if they expected her to attack. Instead, the tavern's patrons huddled in on themselves, either sitting alone or in pairs, and drank in morose silence. The place was quiet and dimly lit, and it smelled deliciously of honey-glazed pork roast.

The wooden tankard the tavern's server put in front of Ginnevra also smelled good, and Ginnevra sipped and then took a longer drink. "I didn't realize I was so on edge," she said. She kept her voice low though no one was close enough to hear. The tavern gave her a feeling of privacy, between the dimness and the way all the other patrons kept their distance from Ginnevra and Eodan and from each other.

"Then it didn't go well," Eodan said.

"It was unexpected rather than a failure." Ginnevra recounted the details, straining to remember the king's words as exactly as possible. The longer she talked, the more details she recalled, some of them she hadn't fully been aware of at the time. The still silence of the courtiers that was more frightened than respectful. Rainaldus' dark, fathomless eyes, and how his gaze never left her face even when his king spoke. The tension in King Paolo's body that had increased when she said she was there for the sake of justice.

"There's more going on here than a dispute between religions," she concluded. "But I'm not sure whether any of it is my business. If King Paolo is worried about a challenge to his rule—"

"Is that what you think it is?"

"I don't know what it is. But everyone was frightened in a way that suggested they feared what King Paolo might do. Everyone except Rainaldus." Ginnevra sighed and took another bite of pork. "Maybe the king is too erratic to deal rationally with me."

"You can't start from that assumption," Eodan said. "There'd be no point in negotiating from there."

"I know. I can only go to that meeting and hope for the Goddess's guidance." She pushed her plate away. The food was delicious, but it sat like lead in her stomach. "And then there's the shield."

"So Filippa was telling the truth. She was onto something."

Ginnevra discovered her earlier objections, the possibilities that said Filippa was still wrong, had vanished. "I wanted her to be wrong, but whatever else has passed between us, I can't believe Filippa would lie to me. And the simplest explanation is that this Quinizellan noble house was behind the massacre."

Eodan raised an eyebrow. "But?"

Ginnevra sighed again. "No 'but.' It's just that I don't know what to do with that information. Reviving a four-year-old disaster won't change the past."

Eodan stared past her, his lips compressed as if he was holding back words. Ginnevra recognized that look. "You think I'm wrong," she said.

"I think you're not looking at this properly," Eodan said. "And maybe that's not wrong, given what happened. But to me it seems these Zuccares committed murder and got away with it. They assassinated a member of the Quinizellan royal family. If this were any other murder, wouldn't you want to bring the killers to justice? And don't you think the king will care about punishing the people who were actually responsible for his sister's death?"

Ginnevra's face felt tight and hot. She stared down at her hands, loosely clasped on the tabletop. "It's not that simple."

"I said I'm not sure you're wrong, beloved. You suffered a terrible tragedy, and that has to influence your reactions. But you're the one who told me paladins face the hard things so others don't have to. I think maybe you should consider putting aside the personal aspect of this crime so you can pursue justice." Eodan put a hand over her joined ones.

Ginnevra closed her eyes. For a moment, she again saw flashing swords and heard the screams of women and horses. "You're right," she said, looking at him again. "This doesn't have to be about Filippa's quest to change what happened. We don't let murderers escape punishment just because it's been years since they committed their crime."

Eodan nodded. "So—what happens next?"

"I find out anything I can about the Zuccare family." Ginnevra moved her hand so she could clasp Eodan's. "I'll need more than just a charcoal sketch if I want to accuse them of murder. I should learn what benefit they got out of Dianetta Napolle's death. She was leaving Quinizelle for an arranged marriage, so it wasn't as if she was still part of Quinizellan politics, at least not directly."

"An arranged marriage? What's that?" Eodan asked.

"Nobles in the Lordagne—probably all over the continent— often make political marriages between their families to strengthen ties and promote their interests. Sometimes to head off potential fights. Rulers supposedly are less likely to go to war against their own family members, though I'm not sure how well that works in practice." Ginnevra observed Eodan's look of appalled disgust and said, "I take it werewolves don't think that way."

"We mate for life, with someone we've made a personal and intimate connection with," Eodan said. "And politics is only tangentially a part of that. A dominus or a domina can't exercise power through his or her children." His look of disgust briefly became one of anger. "And those roles aren't supposed to be inherited."

"I don't know those words."

Eodan hesitated only a moment before saying, in a lower voice than before, "A pack has a male leader and a female leader. Dominus and domina. They're each responsible for guiding different aspects of pack life. But they're chosen by mutual accord, by the whole pack agreeing."

Ginnevra wanted to press him for more details, but she didn't like the look in his eye, like he was gearing up to snap at her. She suppressed an irrational fear and said, "And you and I are mates." It felt like a reminder more than a question.

The look vanished, and he smiled at her. "We are. Which is better than some political arrangement, right? How did Dianetta Napolle feel about the marriage?"

"She was cheerful about it. I think she saw it as an adventure. She spoke often of how much she'd liked Paese when she'd visited in the past, and once or twice she said something about how at least Paolo had picked an intelligent man for her husband. She was very quick-witted." Ginnevra's heart ached with memory and with a closer pain.

"You know," she added, "the more I think about it, the angrier I get. I don't think it's blasphemy to say Dianetta could have lived a long, contented life if not for those murderers, and to mourn the loss of that life. I grieved over my sister paladins, but at least they died doing what they'd sworn to do. I don't want Dianetta's killers, not the mercenaries, but the ones ultimately responsible for her death, to get away with that."

Eodan's smile widened. "Now you sound more like the woman I love."

"Meaning I wasn't thinking clearly?"

"Meaning you are powerful in the cause of justice, and that's something I love about you." Eodan squeezed her hand. "Let's go, and you can make a plan for investigating the Zuccares. And one for talking to the king in the morning."

Ginnevra stood, still holding Eodan's hand. "I do feel better when I have direction and a clear goal. In this case, I need to find someone who will tell me all about the Zuccare family. And I think I have a place to start."

SEVEN

T he next morning, Pattero escorted Ginnevra into the receiving hall and down a hallway in the opposite direction from the throne room. Unlike the one she'd seen the previous day, this hallway was long and straight, with a row of stained glass windows running its entire length. That side of the palace faced west, so at the moment the hall was dim, but Ginnevra judged the walls would blaze with color in the afternoon.

The facing wall was hung with portraits in a long line, all of them somber in shades of brown and deep red. Their true colors were distorted by the indirect light coming through the stained glass. At sunset, the faces would look garish, like children's drawings where skin was green or blue or whatever other color struck the artist's fancy.

Though the portraits didn't interest Ginnevra, the stained glass windows did. She wished she had time to stop and examine them more closely. "This is beautiful art. The windows."

Pattero slowed for a few steps. "Do you know, I've never

thought of them as art," he said. "I suppose I'm so used to seeing these windows I never think about them."

"Do you live in the palace?"

"I am a courtier," Pattero said, "and that means I must be available to wait upon his majesty at his majesty's pleasure. But I have not always lived in the palace. Until two years ago, I lived in my family's home."

Ginnevra nodded. "Your family must be important, if your sister—half-sister—married King Paolo. Does Alamanne have one of those shields?"

"We are one of the six noble families, yes."

Pattero didn't sound worried or frightened, which told Ginnevra she wasn't on shaky ground yet. "What are the other families?"

Pattero shot her a wary glance, which Ginnevra found odd. Surely there was nothing secret about the nobles of Quinizelle? "Napolle, of course. Alamanne, Nazarente, Gualterre, Zuccare, and Monalde."

"I remember you said Zuccare was the one with the wolf's head on their shield. What made them choose that?"

Pattero's eyes narrowed. "You seem very interested in the Zuccare family, my lady. Why is that?"

Ginnevra didn't hesitate. "It's wolves I'm interested in, Lord Pattero. Most places in the Lordagne don't use wolves as symbols because of the Bright One's werewolves. But I suppose, if Quinizelle still holds to the old religion, a wolf's head wouldn't mean that here." She watched Pattero out of the corner of one eye while still overtly observing the windows. He looked suspicious, which roused her curiosity. Maybe there was more to investigate here than she'd thought.

"To Torunes, the wolf is a sacred symbol, representative of Lopone, who is the oldest child of Torun," Pattero said. "A Torune is dedicated to one of the holy children on his first birthday, and that totem guides him throughout his life. But in Quinizelle, the oldest families are under the aegis of one of the holy children, and each takes that symbol to represent their family. The Alamanne family crest, for example, bears the image of Accone, the Eagle."

"And what role do those six families play within your government?"

Pattero came to a halt. "Did I somehow give you the impression that I am disloyal to my king?"

Ginnevra fixed her full attention on him. Pattero's color was high, and he had clenched one hand into a fist. "It's a simple question, Lord Pattero, and I meant no disrespect. I have been to Quinizelle exactly once before, four years ago, and I know very little about your government. To me, that seems like something I ought to remedy if I'm to negotiate fairly with King Paolo. If you don't want to answer that question, maybe you'll do me the honor of telling me why it's a treasonous one?"

Pattero's ruddy complexion paled. "I—" He stopped and swallowed, visibly calming himself. "I overreacted. Please pardon my abruptness."

"So things are not well with the king and his nobles," Ginnevra continued. "I don't think it's disloyal to explain to me what's going on, unless you think it will give me some unfair advantage. Lord Pattero, I promise I'm not interested in anything but seeing that the Faithful in Quinizelle aren't persecuted under official authority. You said you want peace in Quinizelle. Help me achieve that."

Pattero glanced away. "We will be late. There's no time."

"Then tell me as we walk." Ginnevra took a few inviting steps in the direction they'd been going. After a moment's hesitation, Pattero strode ahead, making Ginnevra stretch to keep up with him.

"King Paolo has no heir," he said, speaking quietly though they were the only ones in the hall. "He and my sister Benitta have been married for just over two years, and Benitta has had no children. Some of the noble families would like Paolo to name one of them as his heir—as a temporary measure, naturally."

"I see. Which families?"

"House Alamanne has made the case that they are already connected to King Paolo through Benitta. House Nazarente ruled Quinizelle generations ago and claims they are hereditarily predisposed to protect the kingdom. And House Zuccare is the most powerful of the houses, financially and socially. They insist they would be Quinizelle's most staunch defenders, having greater resources to do so."

The hall came to an end at an interior courtyard, tiled in pale gray and black in a pattern that reminded Ginnevra of the chevrons on the Zuccare family crest. Pattero walked rapidly across it without deviating from his straight path. "But you should not believe the king is weak," he continued. "He commands the loyalty and respect of every Quinizellan, and he will not permit insubordination."

Ginnevra examined her surroundings. Three more wide halls opened off the courtyard, all of them brightly lit by lanterns. She and Pattero were headed for the one directly opposite, where two armed guards waited. "He didn't strike me as weak," she said. This was farther afield than she'd wanted to go in her inquiry, since the only house she cared about was Zuccare. Casting about for a way to turn the conversation around, she said, "So do you consider those houses to be loyal? Nazarente, and Zuccare?"

"Their loyalty has never been questioned before," Pattero said. "House Zuccare in particular has always had close ties to House Napolle. But when it is a throne in question, everyone's loyalties are strained."

Ginnevra leaped on that opening. "What kind of close ties? Marriages?"

Pattero gave her another narrow-eyed look. "We are here," he said, gesturing. The two guards stared straight ahead, not at Ginnevra, but their grip on their weapons was firm, and Ginnevra didn't doubt they were very aware of her. Beyond the guards, a short hall extended to an arched doorway with the door standing open.

Ginnevra cursed herself for not being quicker of thought. "Thank you, Lord Pattero," she said. She would have to find a way to interrogate him later.

She took a step down the hall, but Pattero's discreet cough brought her to a halt. "Your sword, Prime Cassaline," he said.

Scowling, Ginnevra unshouldered her blade and wrapped the sword belt around it before propping it against the wall, behind the guards. She fixed Pattero with a warning glare. Pattero smiled and bowed. "No one will touch it, prime."

Two more guards flanked the door inside the room. Ginnevra ignored them. All her attention was on the bookcases lining the walls. She had come to reading later than her brothers, having been more interested in rough play and exploring her home city than academics, and only her decision to become a paladin had changed that, as paladins were required to be literate. She'd been fourteen when she'd made the belated discovery that her favorite stories were all written down, and that a paladin was not only free to read whatever she wanted, she was actively encouraged to.

But this room surpassed all her deepest literary desires. She'd seen libraries that looked interesting at first glance, but were filled only with boring legal tomes or dry histories commissioned by an elector or prince to justify his rule. The books here were beautifully varied, and most of them appeared to be new, which meant they were more likely to be printed than engraved or handwritten.

And the smell... the perfume of leather and thick paper and ink filled the air, preventing the room from feeling close and stifling as its lack of windows would otherwise do.

Ginnevra realized she'd been staring and collected herself. An ebony table stood near the center of the room, its legs intricately carved in abstract patterns, its feet shaped like lion's paws. Two matching chairs, equally intricate in design, faced each other across the table. King Paolo sat in the one facing the door. He watched her intently, his brows furrowed and his mouth curved in a slight frown.

Ginnevra approached the table and put a hand on the high back of the unoccupied chair. "Good morning, your majesty," she said. "May I be seated?"

King Paolo nodded minutely. Ginnevra pulled the chair out and sank into it. She hated having her back to the door, and hated even more having her back to two armed men, but she could hardly refuse without insulting the king, and that would mean failing before she'd even started.

She settled herself as comfortably into the seat as she could, which wasn't very; the chair was hard, and her cuisses dug into her thighs. After a moment's thought, she removed her helmet and coif and put both on the table to her left. The king watched her movements in silence. That made Ginnevra more nervous and inclined to fidget. She instead interlaced her gloved fingers and rested them in her lap.

Still, the king said nothing. Ginnevra took a calming breath and let it out. "Your majesty," she said, "thank you for agreeing to meet with me as representative of the Blessed."

King Paolo arched one heavy black eyebrow. "We did not believe," he said in that same precise way Ginnevra remembered from the throne room, "we had much choice."

Not an auspicious beginning. "I hope you mean that we are

86

both interested in coming to terms. Your city can't be satisfied with so much religious unrest."

"You don't care about our city's welfare." The king leaned forward slightly. "Don't pretend to altruism. This is about the Faith's demands of us. We would like to remind you that the Faith has no dominion here. Quinizelle is open to believers of both religions, Torunes and Faithful. And we reject utterly Abraciabene's insistence that Quinizelle bow to its rule."

Ginnevra's mouth fell open in astonishment. "That's not what I was sent here for."

"Is it not? Then you deny that Abraciabene claims its people have been innocent victims of assault by Torunes, and that we are to make amends to the Faithful regardless of the circumstances?" King Paolo hadn't raised his voice, but the intensity of his speech unnerved Ginnevra.

"That's what we were told, your majesty," she said, "but when I arrived in Quinizelle, I witnessed an attack—"

"The witness of a paladin is worthless," King Paolo said. "You would say anything so long as it got you what you want."

"Excuse me?" Ginnevra's heart pounded, demanding she leap into action. "Do you question my word?"

"Quinizelle learned four years ago what the word of a paladin is worth," the king said. "And we do not forget."

"Which 'we' is that?" Ginnevra snapped. "You mean *you* haven't forgotten. I'm sorry for your loss, your majesty. Lady Dianetta Napolle was a wonderful young woman, and her death was a tragedy. But dozens of others died trying to keep her safe, including fourteen paladins, and most of us had nothing to do with treachery. And none of that has anything to do with why you and I are here today."

King Paolo shoved his chair back. "'Most of us.' Us. You were one of that company."

"I was." Ginnevra realized her hands were clenched tightly and relaxed her grip, but her heart continued to hammer in her chest and her skin felt stretched to breaking across her cheeks.

"You *dare*," King Paolo whispered. "Your damned self-righteous leader *dared* to send someone complicit in my sister's death—"

Ginnevra shot to her feet. "I nearly died trying to keep her safe!"

"It is that 'nearly' that condemns you," the king roared. "Paid off to let her die—you think I give a damn about your survival if it meant losing her?"

Ginnevra slammed a fist on the tabletop. "You think hanging onto your grief will change the past? You—"

She heard the guards approaching and spun, shoving the chair to slam into the nearest bookcase and bracing herself for an attack. The guards stopped several feet away and brandished their halberds. The sight of the weapons brought Ginnevra to her senses. She was faster than any polearm, and disarming and incapacitating these guards would be simple. But it would also be the end of any hope of negotiations.

With a superhuman effort, she turned her back on the guards, raising her hands to show she was unarmed. "Your majesty," she said, "I wish to apologize. I should not have threatened you, even implicitly."

King Paolo's eyes narrowed. He rested both hands on the tabletop. "We are not afraid of you," he said, and to her surprise Ginnevra saw it was true; the king's hands didn't tremble, and his voice was steady.

"I'm glad of that, because I don't want to be feared," she said. "Your majesty, I can see your grief is powerful. I can't tell you I understand how you feel, because Lady Dianetta wasn't my sister. She was, however, someone I was sworn to protect, and *you* will never understand what it meant to me that I failed."

The king's jaw relaxed, and he pushed away from the table, standing straight to look Ginnevra in the eye. He was a little shorter than she, but he held himself as regally as if he didn't feel the lack. "Your apology can't bring her back."

"No, it can't." Ginnevra gazed back at him. "I won't ask for your forgiveness, because the one I failed was Dianetta. But I can ask you to let go your anger, if only for the time it takes to resolve this other matter."

King Paolo sank into his chair. "Abraciabene claims no fault in these attacks, just as they claimed no fault in my sister's death."

"Captain Ercole was judged guilty, and it was determined she acted alone," Ginnevra said. The words made her feel unexpectedly uncomfortable, as if she'd condemned Ercole all over again. Almost she brought up the Zuccares, but the knowledge that she still didn't understand what had happened stilled her tongue. "I don't know what reparations the holy city made to you, if any. I was still injured when the trial concluded. But—please, your majesty, can't we let the past stay in the past? It really has nothing to do with the current attacks. And I don't believe Torunes are entirely at fault."

"You don't." It was a statement, not a question, and yet for the first time Ginnevra felt the king wasn't as certain as he seemed.

"I saw an attack on my arrival in Quinizelle that I believe was initiated by the Faithful," she said. "I don't know if it was retaliation, or if the Faithful were unjustified in fighting, but it's something we should consider, don't you agree?"

King Paolo's expression hardened. "You try to lull us into complacency with your pretended altruism?"

Ginnevra felt like screaming. "I'm trying to discover what's really going on, and so should you!" she exclaimed. "What do *you* want, your majesty? A reason to run the Faithful out of Quinizelle entirely?"

The king slapped his hand palm-down on the tabletop. "This meeting is over," he said. "We have nothing more to say."

"Well, I do," Ginnevra said. "Abraciabene will not endure its Faithful being harassed in their own homes. I've already said I believe the truth is somewhere between these extremes, but if we can't come to an agreement, I am authorized to withdraw Abraciabene's economic support from Quinizelle."

"A threat? How typical," King Paolo said.

"A consequence," Ginnevra replied. "Your majesty, I request you investigate these allegations further. I will do the same. I believe we can discover the truth together—*if* you are willing to be openminded about the matter."

She held the king's gaze, praying silently that he would see sense. King Paolo stared back at her, his eyes still narrowed. Finally, he said, "We will summon you again when we are prepared to discuss further. You have our leave to depart."

Ginnevra saluted him with the paladin's salute, but perfunctorily, not caring whether he thought it was rude. She snatched up her helmet and coif and tucked them under one arm—she'd be damned if she'd delay even one minute longer in the king's presence to put them on—then turned on her heel and made for the door. Her quick movement startled the guards, who stepped back involuntarily, lowering their weapons. Ginnevra ignored them. Even one-handed, she didn't consider them a threat.

EIGHT

Once through the door, she squeezed her eyes shut and thought about screaming again. Then she donned her coif and helmet and strode down the short hallway to where she could retrieve her sword. Holding it calmed her, though she had no intention of using it on anyone in the palace. She slung the belt over her shoulder and shrugged it into a comfortable position.

Pattero, standing a few feet away, watched her in silence. The guards maintained their statue-like stillness, but Ginnevra caught the one on the left looking at her and glared until his eyes flicked forward. It was impossible to tell what he thought of her, given how motionless his face was, and Ginnevra still didn't care about the opinions of guards. Not in the mood she was in, at any rate.

"I'll escort you to the gate, Prime Cassaline," Pattero said, bowing. He was back to looking placid and showed no sign that he'd noticed her foul mood, though she hadn't concealed it. His placidity irritated her further. Pattero, the king, that arrogant priest Rainaldus, all those frightened courtiers, even Hallowed

Nevante—all Ginnevra's encounters in Quinizelle came to a bubbling boil inside her. She had a simple job to do, and everyone seemed bent on complicating it. Diplomacy could go hang.

"Lord Pattero," she said as she and Pattero crossed the gray and black courtyard. "Tell me about your noble houses. Who rules, and what does that rule entail?"

Pattero gave her a startled look. "I'm not sure why you want to know."

"That's my business, Lord Pattero. Just answer the question." Ginnevra managed, just barely, not to snarl at the man.

"Well..." Pattero cleared his throat. "I'm sure it's like any noble family anywhere. There's a head of the household, usually the oldest male of the oldest generation, and he's responsible for making alliances and apportioning household or business duties among the other family members. He also owes service to the king, though that service is almost always delegated to some other family member because the head of the house is too busy to spend all his time waiting on the king. It's why I'm here in the place of my father."

"And who is the head of House Zuccare?"

"My lady—"

"Lord Pattero," Ginnevra said, stepping in front of him and bringing them both to a halt, "do you know what this is?" She swung her greatsword to hang between them, grounding the tip so the pommel was level with Pattero's chest.

Pattero gazed at it uncomprehendingly. "It's your sword, my lady."

"No, Lord Pattero. This is the symbol of my oaths as a paladin. It is the symbol of my role and my responsibility. I'm here in an official capacity, and that capacity is as an investigator of truth. If you won't answer my very simple questions, I'll have to start wondering *why not*." Distantly, she heard her inner voice reminding her that this man had been helpful, was probably an ally, and she might be ruining the possibility of making him a friend, but anger and a sense that she had on some level already failed shouted that voice down.

Pattero's eyes were wide, and his mouth hung slack. "I meant no disrespect," he said.

His obvious fear and dismay struck her a blow to the chest, dispelling some of her anger and rousing her guilt. She was meant to protect humanity, not terrorize it.

"Forgive me, Lord Pattero," she said, feeling more genuinely contrite than she had when she'd apologized to the king. "I'm not used to diplomacy, and I still have a lot to learn. I know you're interested in protecting your king, and you don't want to be disloyal to him, but I promise nothing I'm trying to discover is intended to hurt King Paolo or discredit him or even put him at a disadvantage."

"Then—why do you care about the Zuccares?" Pattero asked. "If it's not to support them in their bid to become Paolo's heir?"

Ginnevra shouldered her blade again. "I don't have any interest in the succession of Quinizelle. And I can't tell you the details of my investigation. I just need information about House Zuccare." She knew she sounded more suspicious the longer she talked, and she wished now she'd found some other way of getting the information she wanted. Pattero had seemed the perfect source that morning, before it turned out Ginnevra's possible prey was involved in the complexities of an inheritance squabble.

"I won't betray my king," Pattero said. "I want you to swear on your sword that you won't use anything I tell you against him."

"Because you want House Alamanne to inherit the throne?" Ginnevra asked.

Pattero's gaze hardened. "Because my sister loves him," he said, "and her child will rule Quinizelle someday."

Something Pattero had said the day before clicked into place. "And all this inheritance mess is a threat to her," Ginnevra said. "I swear on my sword I will not act against Paolo Napolle."

"House Zuccare's head is Jiuseppe Zuccare," Pattero said. "He's a staunch Torune and makes no secret of his desire to see the Faithful banished from Quinizelle entirely. He's also loyal to the throne, claiming that House Zuccare's long support of the Napolles makes him the best choice for the king's heir. But—"

"But, what?" Ginnevra prodded when Pattero didn't continue immediately.

Pattero shook his head. "I'm not sure I trust any of the families who are mixed up in this, and that includes my own father. They all claim to have Quinizelle's best interests at heart, but to make that claim, they also can't be completely disinterested or altruistic. Each of them wants power, and my feeling is Jiuseppe Zuccare is more interested in power than he is in the welfare of Quinizelle."

"Just Jiuseppe?"

"All of them. But you asked about the Zuccares." Pattero shook his head again. "I don't know what else I can tell you. I don't believe Jiuseppe Zuccare would ever act against Paolo, for what it's worth. The people love Paolo and Benitta, and they'd turn against anyone who tried to harm them."

Ginnevra thought about that for a moment. None of it seemed to have anything to do with assassinating Dianetta Napolle, at least on the surface. "Thank you," she said. "We should go. And I'm sorry I lost my temper."

"You were right, it's none of my business what you investigate," Pattero said. "Was there anything else?"

Ginnevra walked beside Pattero out of the courtyard and

down the long hallway of stained glass marvels. "Is there a reason the palace always seems so empty?"

Pattero blushed faintly. "The king ordered the halls cleared for your arrival," he said. "He didn't want you to encounter anyone you might, um, corrupt."

Ginnevra was too emotionally weary to be more than mildly annoyed at this. "He hates paladins. Hates me specifically, now that he knows I failed to protect Lady Dianetta."

Pattero came to a stop. "You were there," he said. "Your captain took bribes to let those men slaughter her like an animal." His voice was low, and he wouldn't meet her eyes.

"That's what the trial said," Ginnevra heard herself say. She closed her eyes and cursed herself inwardly. Any moment now she'd turn into Filippa and start ranting about conspiracies and injustice. "We did our best, Lord Pattero. I nearly died protecting her. I don't know if that means anything to you, but...we did our best."

Silence. Ginnevra's weariness redoubled. Coming here had been such a mistake. Then Pattero said, "Dianetta was dear to me. Not romantically, but we were close, and... afterward... I hated paladins for a long time. I used to go to your sanctuary and fight with the anointed—arguments, I mean, screaming fights. They never fought back. Revered Bariatte, he put up with me shouting the worst abuse you can imagine, and he always left me with the Goddess's blessing. And then the day came when I went to the sanctuary and asked the Revered to explain why any loving God or Goddess would let such injustice happen."

Ginnevra held her breath, fearing interrupting Pattero's reminiscence with even something so small as an exhalation.

Pattero bowed his head and smiled. "I don't know why his answer comforted me. I mean, it makes no sense that anyone would worship a Goddess who doesn't make your life easier. But I came to believe that what happened to Dianetta wasn't a punishment from Torun or the indifference of the Goddess. It didn't have anything to do with Dianetta not being good or pure enough. And then I was ready to accept the Goddess's blessing of comfort as I grieved. I was sanctified a few months later." He patted the lump of his grace where it lay on his chest.

"I'm sorry I couldn't save her," Ginnevra said.

"I know. For a long time, I wished I'd convinced her to stay in Quinizelle." Pattero shrugged. "But you know where that thinking leads. There's no guarantee she'd have lived if she'd stayed here. She might have married someone else and died in childbirth, or been taken ill with influenza, or been run over by a maddened horse. I just wish they'd found out who bribed that captain. I can't help feeling the true villains got away with their crime."

Again, Ginnevra had to close her lips tight on what she suspected. For the first time, the idea of discovering the truth about Dianetta Napolle's death excited her. "I understand," she said. "It's not blasphemy to wish for justice."

Pattero escorted Ginnevra all the way to the gate. "Good luck," he said, and then reddened slightly. "I mean—sorry, I still have old habits to break."

"That's all right." The Faithful didn't believe in luck, good or bad, but Ginnevra understood Pattero's meaning: there was nothing wrong with wishing the Goddess's blessings of strength and wisdom upon a coming endeavor. And her talk with Pattero had lifted the feelings of anger and despair that the argument with King Paolo had filled her with.

She left the palace and strolled down the long, straight slope, reflecting again how slick these stones would be come winter. That alone resolved her to be done with her investigation before that time.

The street below the palace teemed pleasantly with men and

women going about their business, far more than there had been the day before. Ginnevra didn't let herself be bothered by how many of them got quickly out of her way. So long as nobody spat or threw things, she could ignore the hostility and fear.

Her stomach rumbled unexpectedly. A glance at the sky told her it was nearly noon, which surprised her; she hadn't thought the meeting had taken so long. She looked around for a street vendor and found one a few dozen yards away, selling skewers of meat and grilled tomato. Hesitating, she considered her options. If the seller was Torune, she might not like Ginnevra interfering with her custom, and the simple act of buying food might start a fight Ginnevra couldn't win regardless of what weapons she did or did not use. On the other hand, Ginnevra's peaceful interactions with the people of Quinizelle might set a good example. And Ginnevra had never liked pretending to be something she wasn't just to keep the peace.

She strolled toward the vendor, nodding and smiling pleasantly and getting almost no response in return. That was better, again, than spittle and stones. Silently, she joined the queue. How queueing had reached this tiny city-state, she didn't know, but she again marveled at how civilized an innovation it was. How orderly. Lining up to enter a city, that made sense, but that someone had thought to extend that idea elsewhere... it really was remarkable.

Three people waited ahead of her. The woman immediately in front of her held the hand of a small child who stared wide-eyed at Ginnevra. Ginnevra didn't know anything about children younger than about twelve, but this one was waist-high to his mother and had long brown hair that fell into his eyes. She smiled at him, and the child, rather than ducking behind his mother, gaped until his mouth was as wide as his eyes.

Ginnevra waved at the child, the merest wiggle of her fingers.

That made the child step sideways, bumping into his mother's legs. "Fino," the woman said, "don't—" She turned to see what Fino was looking at and gasped.

"Sorry," Ginnevra said. "I'm afraid I startled your little boy."

The woman closed her mouth and drew the child closer to her. Her eyes never left Ginnevra's. Ginnevra held onto politeness with both hands and smiled, then looked away to where the vendor served the woman at the head of the queue. The woman turned around and, biting into a chunk of meat, strolled toward Ginnevra.

It was Filippa.

NINE

S urprise rooted Ginnevra to the spot. She felt as stunned as little Fino, eyes wide, mouth hanging open. Filippa took another step before seeing Ginnevra and coming to a halt. She swallowed her mouthful and didn't take another bite, watching Ginnevra with what anyone else would have thought was calmness. But Ginnevra had once been closer to Filippa than anyone else, and she recognized the tiny lines of tension at the corners of Filippa's eyes, the way her lips paled slightly from being pressed together hard. She wondered what Filippa saw when she looked at her.

They watched each other for a moment, neither moving. Then Filippa closed the distance between them. "It's good food," she said, gesturing with the skewer. "They grow the tomatoes in special houses that stay warm year-round, over some of the hot springs in the mountains."

"I wondered," Ginnevra said.

Filippa lowered the skewer. "It's none of my business," she said, "but I'm wondering why you're here in Quinizelle."

"I didn't follow you, if that's what you mean," Ginnevra retorted. "It's paladin business."

"I assumed as much." Filippa's lips thinned again briefly. "I'm sure I don't have to tell you why I'm here. I didn't seek you out."

"I know." Guilt unexpectedly surged through Ginnevra. She didn't owe Filippa anything, but the knowledge that she'd decided to pursue the investigation after telling Filippa she wouldn't made her feel like a liar. And yet the truth was far more complicated than simply admitting she'd changed her mind. For a moment, her memories battered her, making her heart ache over old betrayals. She pushed them away and made herself focus on the present.

She realized the queue had stopped moving, with even the vendor watching this exchange with interest, and realized further her appetite was gone. "Excuse me," she said to the short man behind her, and stepped out of line.

"Didn't you want food? Don't let me stop you," Filippa said.

"It's fine," Ginnevra said. "I'm not that hungry. And I don't think I could eat if we just passed each other on the street like strangers."

"It's not like we have anything left to say to each other, Ginnevra." Filippa backed away from the vendor's cart, giving Ginnevra space to follow. She wasn't wearing the short sword she'd had in Devoyenne, and her heavy knee-length coat showed signs of heavy wear. More memories struck. Filippa had always hated the cold as much as Ginnevra did.

"Maybe," Ginnevra said. She wrestled with herself again. Filippa wasn't a paladin anymore; she was after the solution to the mystery for all the wrong reasons. Ginnevra shouldn't involve her.

"You're looking for information on House Zuccare," she said.

Filippa's eyes widened. "You found it, too. The insignia."

"I wasn't looking for it. It was a coincidence. Don't think I agree with you." The words spilled out of Ginnevra, harsh and urgent.

"It doesn't matter. This is proof."

"It *does* matter." Ginnevra stepped closer to Filippa. "Eodan convinced me this is a matter of bringing a murderer to justice. That's not at all the same as trying to change the past."

Filippa nodded, a short, curt gesture. "You're right. It's not the same. I know you don't want to help me, and that's your prerogative. But isn't there some way we can work together?"

Her eyes were as dark and intent as Ginnevra remembered. They'd looked that way any time Filippa found a new puzzle to solve. Another ache struck her in the middle of her chest, this one of longing. "I... don't know," she said. "I'm here to negotiate peace between Quinizelle and the Faith, not investigate an old murder. But I don't think there's any harm in asking questions."

"I can show you what I've found," Filippa said. "Then you can decide what you want to do with it." She looked at the skewer in her hand as if she'd forgotten she held it, then lowered it again.

Ginnevra glanced back at the palace. If House Zuccare was involved somehow in Dianetta's murder, proving their complicity might disrupt whatever fragile understanding existed in Quinizelle's government, and it might make her assignment harder. But even thinking that made Ginnevra impatient with herself. Paladins were a force for justice, and justice shouldn't be robbed by political expediency.

"Show me, then," she said. "And we'll see where that takes us."

FILIPPA HAD TAKEN a room at an inn close to the gate, where many businesses catered to the few travelers who braved the mountain heights. The inn was closer to being a tavern with a few rooms to let, which gave it a cozy feeling Ginnevra appreciated. It reminded her of so many other places she'd stayed when she was with a paladin company: small, dingy, and smelling of onion. Ginnevra hadn't understood why paladins, who were respected as representatives of the Goddess, would ever stay anywhere but the best places. Then Captain Ercole had pointed out that those small, out-of-the-way inns benefited from increased custom after paladins slept there. It had changed Ginnevra's perspective on a number of things.

She hadn't thought of Captain Ercole in a long time, not as she'd been before the disaster. Her first company, her first captain. Ercole had reminded Ginnevra of her Aunt Caterrina, also a paladin. Both women were quick to laugh and quick to start a fight in the name of justice; both treated Ginnevra like a true paladin and not a girl barely a woman. Ercole's reputation as a hard taskmaster was earned; she had insisted her company practice with sword and mace until they were exhausted, then drill some more. Ginnevra had groused about it until the night her training saved her life.

It hurt to think of Ercole taking her own life. She had been so vital, so dedicated to the Goddess, and Ginnevra hadn't believed the news at first, though it was Filippa who'd told her. Ercole's suicide felt like a final betrayal. Ginnevra blinked away angry tears and cursed herself for a fool. It had been four years. More than long enough for the past to stay buried.

She followed Filippa up the stairs to the second floor and down a narrow, dark hall to the third door on the right. The room beyond was small and dimly lit by sunlight passing through the single grimy window. Ginnevra walked over to it and peered through the thick glass that distorted the street below into a greenish, wavy dreamscape, like a world seen through water. None of the pedestrians thronging the street looked up. No one ever looked up, in Ginnevra's experience.

Filippa reached beneath the mattress of the room's one narrow bed and pulled out a flat leather portfolio tied with worn black ribbons. She extended it to Ginnevra. "I doubt anyone suspects me to care about searching for this, but there's no sense not taking precautions."

Ginnevra untied the ribbons and opened the portfolio. Several sheets of paper in varying shades of cream or white and in different sizes lay within. The top sheet was Filippa's drawing of the Zuccare shield, unfolded but still creased. Ginnevra set the portfolio on the bed and flipped through the pages. "This is a lot for—how long ago did you connect that insignia with House Zuccare?"

"I found someone in Devoyenne who identified the shield as a Quinizelle crest, but she didn't know which house. That was a week ago." Filippa leaned against the door and crossed her arms over her chest. "I took ship the day after we spoke."

"So did we. You couldn't have beaten us here."

Filippa shrugged. "I got off at the Belladine River and took the high route instead of sailing all the way to Paese. It cuts two days off the travel time."

"That's an incredibly dangerous route!" Ginnevra paused in sorting through the papers to stare at Filippa. "You might never have made it here."

"Somewhere in the last four years, I stopped caring so much about what could happen to me." Filippa's mouth curved up on one side in a cynical smile. "How's that for not believing in destiny?"

Ginnevra scowled. "So you came to Quinizelle three days ago, then. That's still very fast work."

"Some of that is what I wrote on the ship. It's everything I've learned since the massacre. The first two pages after the drawing are more recent."

Ginnevra drew those pages out from the rest and set them above the portfolio. Filippa's handwriting had always been neater than hers, neat as a fabulist's, and she had organized her notes in labeled columns. "There's more here than just House Zuccare."

"Quinizelle is in the beginnings of a succession crisis. I investigated all three of the houses who would like to rule. I thought it was possible one of them might have arranged for Dianetta's death as the first step in getting rid of King Paolo's heirs."

That had not occurred to Ginnevra. "Four years ago? Isn't that a little long to wait to make another move?"

"Possibly," Filippa said. "Right now I'm still gathering information. I don't want to draw conclusions."

Ginnevra read the rest of the pages. "You have the names of the House rulers and their heirs, and some details about their lives—how did you learn all this?"

"With the succession in question, it's all anyone is talking about." Filippa began unbuttoning her coat. "Most Quinizellans are more interested in speculating on the king's bride and when she'll conceive, but there are those who've already taken a side— for the good of the city-state, of course. They say they want the stability of knowing who will inherit if something happens to the king, but my sense is they'd like to be on good terms with the future ruler. And all of them are quick to try to convince others of why their candidate is the best choice."

"Makes sense." Ginnevra turned over the last paper and considered her options. Filippa really didn't have any right to Ginnevra's information; she wasn't a prime, wasn't even a paladin, and Ginnevra ought to take these papers and use them herself. But the idea made her uncomfortable, and she didn't think it was her lingering attachment to Filippa that did it. Filippa had done good work—better work than Ginnevra, though maybe that was just because she'd had a head start—and Ginnevra didn't want to throw away a resource. Even if she wished Filippa had never come back into her life.

"According to my source, House Zuccare wouldn't move against the king," she said. "My source claims the people love King Paolo and his wife and wouldn't support anyone overthrowing House Napolle. But I don't think he's considered the possibility that someone might act in secret."

Filippa stood up straight. "Is that what you think? That House Zuccare plans a coup?"

"I'm not interested in drawing conclusions prematurely, either. I'm just saying, so long as King Paolo doesn't choose an heir, those three Houses have incentive to take more drastic action." Ginnevra gathered the pages in her hands and squared them up. "What concerns me more is that the head of House Zuccare, Jiuseppe, is strongly opposed to the Faith to the point that he'd like to see all of us out of Quinizelle. That gives him motive to want to see the Faith discredited."

"I hadn't heard that," Filippa said. "Motive enough to arrange for the king's sister to be assassinated?"

"I think so. But I'd need actual proof to be able to denounce him to the king." The king who hated paladins and didn't believe their sworn word. "A *lot* of actual proof."

"You'd need evidence that Jiuseppe gave the order," Filippa said. "That's a good place to start."

"It's a terrible place to start," Ginnevra said. "It's far too broad in scope and will take a lot of time. I'm not sure I should ignore my actual duties for this."

"You're here on assignment. Can you tell me what?" Filippa asked.

"It's not a secret. I'm supposed to negotiate with King Paolo to stop the persecution of the Faithful in Quinizelle." The memory of her encounter with the king angered her again, enough that she added, "And I'm also not sure if that's even possible. King Paolo hates me for failing to defend his sister, and he's about as rational as anyone filled with hate can be."

"Wouldn't it help your negotiations if you could prove the Faith wasn't to blame for Dianetta's death?"

Ginnevra blinked. "It—well, possibly. I hadn't considered that."

"You'd need either someone's sworn statement—someone believable—or some kind of physical evidence," Filippa added. "That means getting close to House Zuccare. It will be difficult if they're opposed to the Faith, unless that means Jiuseppe Zuccare is eager to challenge the Faith's representatives—"

"Slow down," Ginnevra said. "I can't walk into their estate and demand to speak to Jiuseppe. This requires subtlety."

"Which is why I ought to do it." Filippa took the loose pages from Ginnevra and rolled them together, slapping the tube against her palm. "I'm nobody. I can get inside and learn the family's weaknesses, then pass that on to you for your frontal assault."

"This isn't a battle, Filippa."

"A figure of speech." Filippa fixed Ginnevra with her gaze again. "You can't go nosing around these noble houses without making somebody wary and maybe ruining any chance of proving the Zuccares are guilty. I can."

Again, Ginnevra felt uneasy. "I'm not sure that's a good idea. Maybe this isn't an official investigation, but it should be, and that makes it my responsibility."

"And your responsibility is to proceed with your investigation in the best and most efficient way. Which means delegating," Filippa said.

Ginnevra eyed Filippa narrowly. Filippa sounded calm and reasonable, but there was a familiar light in her eye. It was the light that said Filippa was in the grip of a new obsession—though it was probably more accurate to say it was a new approach to an old obsession. "You can't act on your own," she said. "You bring what you learn to me, and I'll decide how we act on it."

"You're the one who can make use of any proof I find," Filippa said.

"Right."

Ginnevra walked back to the window and looked down at the street. The plan made sense, and it was just her lingering feeling that she was doing something illicit that made her uncomfortable.

"What if you don't find anything?" she asked. "What if it turns out there's nothing to find?"

"Then I'll start over," Filippa said. "And I won't involve you. I know how you feel, Ginnevra. And I understand. We don't share the same beliefs anymore. But right now, we have a chance to achieve both our goals. Don't feel guilty about that."

"I don't feel guilty," Ginnevra said. She pushed away from the window. "I'm staying in a hostel by the palace. I'm afraid I don't know Quinizelle well enough to give you directions, but anyone in the area can probably tell you where the paladin is staying."

"I'll be in touch." Filippa tapped the rolled papers against her palm again. "That man, Eodan—is he your lover?"

"Yes." Ginnevra didn't know why the question made her want to blush. She hesitated, considering whether she wanted to reveal Eodan's race. Usually, she looked for ways to teach humans about the nature of the werewolves who turned their backs on the Bright One, but the idea of explaining it to Filippa felt uncomfortable, and she wasn't sure why. At the very least, it would mean extending this also-uncomfortable conversation, and her hunger had returned.

"I didn't think you'd ever want a long-term relationship," Filippa said. "Not with how shy you always were around men you were attracted to."

"Eodan's different," Ginnevra said. "And I've changed."

Filippa's smile fell away. "I guess we both have."

They faced each other in silence for a long, awkward moment. Ginnevra felt the unexpected urge to continue the conversation. To ask what Filippa had done and seen in the last four years. To press her to explain how she'd changed. She hated herself for caring. Filippa had abandoned her. Ginnevra didn't know why that still mattered.

"I have to go," she said, and turned away. "Contact me when you learn something."

"Ginna," Filippa said. "I'm sorry."

Ginnevra knew exactly what she meant. "I'm not," she lied, and closed the door behind her.

She trudged through the streets, feeling as if a black cloud enveloped her even though the day was clear and sunny and even warm. She barely noticed the pedestrians who got quickly out of her way. Between fighting with the king, intimidating Pattero, and talking to Filippa, this had been the worst morning she'd had in a long time.

She found herself thinking of Eodan with greater fondness than usual. If the Goddess loved her, he was at the hostel, and she could throw herself on him and let him hold her while she poured out her misery. She didn't even need to make love with him; she just needed comfort. And food. Her stomach had decided it had had enough of her indecision, and it growled like an angry dog in its hunger.

She slowed her steps and finally looked at her surroundings. She hadn't been paying attention to her path, and to her dismay, she didn't recognize the street. It was narrower than the one outside Filippa's inn and looked older, the buildings soot-stained from what might be centuries of torches and leaning slightly toward the street so the clear sky was barely a sliver high above.

Ginnevra sighed. The delay was her own fault, but she almost wished she had an excuse to take her frustrations out on someone. But none of the other pedestrians so much as looked at her, and she wouldn't bully someone no matter how they treated her. She remembered coming down hard on Pattero and inwardly winced. All right, *going forward* she wouldn't bully anyone. She had the feeling she was going to have trouble keeping that promise.

Since no one wanted to meet her eyes, she decided to take a more direct approach. She stepped in front of the next person who tried to pass her and moved with him when he shifted to the side. "Excuse me, sieur, I'm afraid I'm lost. Can you direct me to the palace?"

The elderly man glared at her from beneath his flat, brimless cap. "Leave me alone," he grumbled. "Not interested in speaking to any of you Faithful. You ought to leave and never come back."

"Why is that, sieur?" Ginnevra suppressed her first reaction, which was an angry retort, and managed to sound politely curious. "Have the Faithful injured you somehow?"

"Told you to leave me alone," the man said, and pushed past Ginnevra.

She watched him walk away and saw, beyond him, furtive movement that stood out against the normal background of citizens walking through the streets. A couple of figures hurried from one stoop to the next, pressing themselves into the scant shelter of the doorways and glancing around before moving to the next.

109

Confused, Ginnevra started walking in that direction. If they intended not to draw attention to themselves, they were going about it all wrong. On the other hand, no one else seemed aware of them as anything but two young men, or possibly women with short hair, so maybe their technique was effective on someone not a paladin.

She was twenty feet away when the two stopped at the same door, pressing themselves to either side of the frame. Ginnevra couldn't tell what made that building special; it had the same single window barred against thieves that every other building on the street had, the same door with faded and peeling dark blue paint. Again, no one paid the two any heed, and yet Ginnevra had the feeling they intended something malicious.

She quickened her pace just as the one on the right grabbed the latch and flung the door open. Both hurried inside, and the door swung nearly shut. A muffled scream that cut off sharply reached Ginnevra's ears, followed by the sound of breaking glass.

Ginnevra broke into a run.

TEN

S he slammed through the door and came to a halt just inside. The room was dimly lit by a couple of lanterns as well as what little sunlight came through the dirty window, and at first glance looked full of looming hulks. She registered the presence of shelves crammed with boxes before focusing on the people who'd all frozen in place when she entered.

One of the young men Ginnevra had pursued held a balding middle-aged man up against the wall by his shirt collar with his other hand raised for a powerful blow that hadn't yet landed. The other thug stood over a girl sprawled on the ground, brandishing a knife at her. All four stared at Ginnevra. Ginnevra kept her eyes on the knife and spread her hands wide. Possibly this wouldn't end in bloodshed, but likely the best she could do was make sure it wasn't innocent blood that was shed.

"Back away," she said. "Now."

Nobody moved. The thug threatening the girl said, "You can't hurt us. The law will come down harder on you than us if you do."

The voice was a woman's, but Ginnevra didn't think that made her less dangerous.

"I don't want to hurt you," Ginnevra lied. "I want you to leave these people alone. Step away now."

The thug holding the man against the wall swung his victim around so the man ended up in front of him like a human shield. "I think you should leave," he said. "This is none of your business. Paladins have no authority in Quinizelle."

Ginnevra shrugged. "You have a point," she said. Then she removed her helmet and put it on the nearest shelf, shoving boxes and a few odds and ends aside to make room. She propped her sword against the same shelf, looping the belt over its hilt. She unbuckled her greaves and dropped them on the ground, then began working the fastenings of her cuisses.

Everyone watched her in stunned silence. Ginnevra continued to watch the woman with the knife. Her grip had relaxed, but not enough. The girl on the floor darted glances at the thug, then at Ginnevra, but she didn't move. Ginnevra prayed silently she'd continue to hold still. The last thing they needed was for the woman to remember the girl was there and take another hostage.

She dropped her cuisses atop the greaves with a dull clang and then tackled her pauldrons. The middle-aged man worked his mouth like he wanted to say something, and Ginnevra glared him into silence before returning her gaze to the knife and its wielder. Finally, she unbuckled her cuirass and stood there in her chain mail sleeves over her dark red gambeson and coif. "That's better," she said.

"What in the hell are you doing?" the male thug said.

"Getting comfortable," Ginnevra said, and lunged for the knife.

The woman barely had time to move before Ginnevra grabbed her wrist and spun her around. She slammed the woman's hand into the nearest shelf, making her cry out and lose her grip on the knife. It hit the ground and skittered away, bouncing and rattling into a corner. Ginnevra switched her hold on the woman and wrenched her arm high behind her back, making her gasp in pain. Swiftly Ginnevra kicked the back of her knee so she dropped to the floor.

"Now," she said, "let's try this again."

To her surprise, the middle-aged man had freed himself from the thug's hold and was now brandishing a heavy length of polished oak. The thug had backed against the wall with his hands held out in a nonthreatening gesture. "Don't," he said.

The man brought the cudgel down on the thug's head, making him collapse. Ginnevra shouted, "Wait! Stop!"

"He threatened my Orenna," the man said in a low voice. "I ought to beat him to death." He swung the cudgel again, this time slamming it into the thug's chest.

"I said *stop*," Ginnevra shouted. She shoved the woman to the ground and said, "Stay there." With a few strides, she reached the man's side and wrenched the cudgel out of his hands.

"I've a right to defend myself," the man said. He was breathing heavily and what was left of his hair was disordered. "The Hallowed herself said so."

"You're Faithful?" Ginnevra lowered the cudgel.

"They've persecuted us for weeks," the man said. His eyes widened, and he said, "She's getting away!"

Ginnevra spun and ran after the female thug, bringing her down just inches shy of the door. "I said *stay there*. You're going to face charges for this."

The woman laughed. "No justicer in Quinizelle will punish us for wanting to rid the city of the Faithful. We didn't do anything to them."

"She said she'd kill me if Papa didn't give up the cashbox!" the girl, Orenna, said. "She said it was what we deserved!"

Ginnevra began to wonder what kind of nightmare she'd walked into. She pulled the female thug to her feet and marched her to her compatriot's side. "Sit." The woman sat. She didn't spare so much as a glance for her partner. Ginnevra knelt by the man's side and checked his pulse and then his breathing.

"He's alive," she told the middle-aged man. "But he's not in good shape."

"Good," the man said smugly. "Serves him right."

"And if you'd killed him? What would happen to Orenna then?"

The man's smug expression vanished, and he looked nervously at Orenna, who had retrieved the knife and looked like she wanted to use it on her assailant. Silently, Ginnevra held out her hand for the weapon and tucked it into the belt securing her gambeson.

"One of you needs to go for the guards, or whoever takes charge of criminals in Quinizelle," she said. "I'll watch these two until you return."

"It won't matter," the man said. "We're Faithful. Nobody in power gives a damn about what happens to us. It's why we have to fight back ourselves."

"You're still Quinizellan citizens. I can't believe that doesn't matter." Ginnevra stood and regarded her prisoners. "And I can't exactly drag these two through the streets, even if this one regains consciousness. You have to do *something*."

The man nodded. "Wait here," he told Orenna, and left the shop, slamming the door behind him.

Ginnevra looked at Orenna. "Are you all right? She didn't hurt you?"

Orenna shook her head. "Papa's right. It won't matter that they attacked us."

"That's so very wrong." Ginnevra crouched again beside the woman and said, "You attacked them because they're Faithful? Or was it theft, and you picked this place because you figured they were defenseless?"

The woman sneered at Ginnevra, but said nothing. Ginnevra shrugged and got to her feet. Now that the immediate danger was past, she could examine her surroundings more closely. Shelves crowded together in an irregular pattern made the shop feel even closer than the dim lighting. It wasn't just boxes packed onto the shelves, it was curios and knickknacks and wooden bowls and all manner of odd things. Ginnevra recognized a second-hand store when she saw it. Probably the man and his daughter didn't have much in that cashbox, which meant the attack had been intended to harm someone of the Faith.

"I don't understand any of this," she said, partly to the woman on the floor and partly to herself. "Torunes and Faithful coexist peacefully all over the Lordagne, so why not here? Granted, Torunes are a very small minority most places, and maybe that's it. Maybe with the Faith being such a powerful presence, there's no need to persecute Torunes, and Torunes aren't numerous enough to persecute the Faithful." She didn't say anything about the city-state of Savorola, which was antagonistic to the Faith; the Savorolans were hostile to Torunes as well.

The woman glared up at Ginnevra. Ginnevra glanced at her once and then ignored her. She paced slowly back and forth in front of her captives. "And Lord Pattero Alamanne claims the Faithful started the conflict. I don't think he has reason to lie about that. But it doesn't matter who starts a feud—what matters is who finishes it. And right now it looks like the Torunes have the upper hand."

She turned her attention on the woman. "I don't like bullies," she said. "I don't care what reason they have, bullies don't deserve any respect. You attacked this place because you figured you were stronger than the owners, and I'll wager you took pleasure in that. I don't know if it's true that a justicer will take your side regardless of what you do, but I promise I will see real justice done regardless."

"You've got no power here," the woman said, her lips curling back in a snarl.

"Not as a paladin," Ginnevra said. "But I am a prime of the Blessed with authority to negotiate with your king, and I guarantee I'll find a way to turn that power toward seeing you punished."

The door opened. The middle-aged owner walked in, followed by three guards. Ginnevra strode forward to meet them. "Thank you for coming so promptly," she said.

The guard in front looked Ginnevra up and down. "You don't look like a paladin," he said. His voice was deep and gruff, and his eyes were small and deeply set.

Ginnevra pointed at the pile of armor on the floor and the sword propped nearby. "I'm acting as a concerned citizen, since I don't have authority to execute justice in Quinizelle."

"I see." The guard brushed past her to kneel beside the two thugs. "What happened here?"

"We were browsing this man's wares when that woman burst in and attacked us," the female thug said. "I demand you take her into custody."

Ginnevra silently cursed herself for not expecting this. She overrode the shop owner's sputtering protest with, "I'm sure that sounds plausible. Maybe she can explain why, having attacked her, I then sent this man to bring you gentlemen here instead of leaving? And why I haven't stolen any of their things?"

The guard eyed Ginnevra narrowly, making his eyes almost disappear into folds of skin. "This is Reena Naccione and her partner Gittanus Revellini," he said. "Known thieves. That still gives you no right to attack."

"She defended us!" Orenna shrieked, and burst into tears.

"Sounds like you got a little of what's coming to you," the guard said to the shop owner. "Maybe you'll be less quick to make mock of your neighbors. Get them up, fellows."

The other two guards hauled Reena and Gittanus to their feet. Gittanus was barely conscious, but with the guard's help he was able to stagger behind Reena toward the door. The first guard turned back to Ginnevra. "You got lucky," he said. "Don't go attacking Quinizellans again."

Ginnevra stared him down, clenching her teeth together to hold back angry words. The instant the door shut behind the guards, she said, "What did he mean that you made mock of your neighbors?"

The shop owner looked away. "It's just words. They insult us, we insult them—it's not like that makes us deserving of being robbed and maybe beaten."

"And you think that's what the Goddess teaches?" Ginnevra said, all her anger erupting at once. "That it's right to ridicule others for their beliefs? You should both know better than that."

"It's not like we're supposed to lie down and take that abuse," the man spat back at her. "The Hallowed said we can fight back if we have to. We're not going to be victims."

"The Hallowed—" Ginnevra ground her teeth again. "Look, this isn't going to be the only attack. You need to find common ground with your neighbors, or the fights are going to escalate until someone gets hurt or even killed."

"It won't be us," the shop owner said.

His belligerent stance made Ginnevra feel suddenly weary.

Without speaking, she donned her armor. The creaks and clanking as she did so sounded louder than usual in the silence of the shop. Orenna and her father watched Ginnevra until she shouldered her sword, then Orenna opened the door and held it for her. Ginnevra walked away without looking back.

She was still lost, and now she was ravenous, but her black mood made both those things feel distant and unimportant. At the next corner, she whispered, *"By Your grace I come home,"* and a gentle tug behind her breastbone pointed her the way north. It said something about Quinizelle that she hadn't thought to invoke that grace before. She hoped she wasn't falling into the habit of concealing the outward expression of her religion. That was something she'd sworn she would never do.

With the grace's guidance, she worked her way back around to the palace, and from there it took almost no time to reach the hostel. No one accosted her; no one did more than move quickly out of her way.

When she reached her room, Eodan wasn't there. The black mood swelled into true misery. She hadn't realized how much she'd counted on seeing Eodan and being able to pour out her troubles to him. Sighing, she removed her armor and piled it in a corner, removed her coif and gambeson, and headed out the door. Food first, and then it was time to accost Hallowed Nevante. Ginnevra couldn't ignore any longer the possibility that she was behind some of the animosity Ginnevra had come to Quinizelle to address.

THE SANCTUARY in full daylight looked unexpectedly tawdry, like it was trying too hard to stand out from the other buildings that backed against the mountain. Close to, Ginnevra could see the black paint was peeling at the bricked-over windows and around the lintel, revealing the paler stone beneath. The peeling paint made a strange contrast to the sharp line where the sanctuary shared a wall with its neighbor, as if someone had laid a plumb line down the building's side and painted so far and no farther.

Ginnevra stood across the street from the sanctuary and watched people pass. No one veered wide around the sanctuary the way they had around Ginnevra earlier, but no one approached it closely or slowed to look up at it. As she observed more closely, she noticed that almost everyone averted their eyes from it, though they didn't make their aversion obvious. Ginnevra guessed that many of them didn't realize they were doing it. Maybe if she stood there long enough, she could identify which of those passing by were Faithful. But that sounded boring and pointless. After a few minutes' watching, she crossed the street and entered the stable.

The smell of horses and manure calmed Ginnevra's nerves somewhat. She'd eaten a lackluster meal off a barrow, she didn't know where Eodan was, and almost everyone in the city hated her for what she represented, but there was Dauntless, peering over his stall, and she could never stay truly upset in his presence. She hurried to his side and took his face in her hands. "I bet you don't like this city, either," she whispered. "Though I'm sure Harrus is treating you like a king."

"That I am, my lady," Harrus said, startling Ginnevra with his silent approach. "He's a good lad, if a bit too clever for his own good."

"I should have warned you he has a habit of playing tricks on new people. It's his way of testing your character." Ginnevra patted Dauntless' nose. "I hope he hasn't been too much trouble."

"No, though I think Sertus has learned a valuable lesson about approaching unfamiliar animals." Harrus laughed. "You've no need to worry, my lady."

"Thank you, Harrus." Ginnevra gave Dauntless one last pat and headed for the sanctuary's back door.

This time, the short hallway smelled of an unfamiliar roast meat that made Ginnevra's stomach protest its earlier, unsatisfying meal. The smell wafted through the door connecting the back rooms with the black sanctuary halls as if it meant to follow Ginnevra, taunting her. She sternly told her stomach it could wait and hurried up the stairs. She met a pair of acolytes on the stairs, but neither of them stopped to question her, and when she reached the ritual chamber at the top of the sanctuary, she found she was alone.

She slowly circled the chamber, observing it closely as she hadn't had time to during yesterday's ceremony. A real artist had been at work here; the unknown person had painted the ceiling in abstract curves of gold and silver that gleamed like real metal. The curves cradled images of the moon in its varying phases.

Ginnevra stopped beneath the full moon. She'd only rarely seen it depicted—it was the Bright One's emblem, after all, symbol of corruption and evil—but she couldn't remember seeing it painted so realistically before, shaded with the faint patches that in the real moon made irregular patterns across its surface. The curves surrounding it were entirely of silver, which Ginnevra thought was a nice touch. Silver to bind the Bright One.

"Prime Cassaline," Hallowed Nevante said from behind her. "Is there something I can do for you?"

Ginnevra had only spoken to the Hallowed twice before, but that had been enough for her to realize Nevante had no use for small talk. Since it had also been enough for Ginnevra to decide she didn't like the woman very much, she was just as happy not to have to pretend to amiable conversation. "I have some questions," she said. "What exactly have you told the Faithful with regard to this religious conflict?"

Nevante's eyebrows raised nearly to her hairline. "That sounds like you take issue with my handling of the situation."

"I don't know what your handling has been like, Hallowed. But I've encountered a handful of people whose responses all implied that you've encouraged the Faithful to retaliate. Is that true?"

Nevante pursed her lips briefly. She walked toward Ginnevra, one slow step at a time. "There is nothing in the Goddess's Faith that says Her worshippers must endure calumny and violence. I have told our people they are allowed to defend themselves. Are you suggesting otherwise?"

"I'm not. I do have to wonder whether your words aren't being misconstrued by some. It's not a long step from 'defend yourself' to 'strike first so they can't strike you.'" Ginnevra took a parade rest stance she knew was slightly aggressive, but Nevante's attitude was aggressive as well. It was better Nevante not believe she could intimidate a paladin.

"I have been clear on the subject," Nevante said, coming to a stop two feet from Ginnevra. She clasped her hands together so her long, full sleeves covered them entirely. "But I see no problem with Torunes being shown the error of their ways. Unless you mean to suggest that their religion has any validity to it."

"I was taught to be respectful of those who haven't yet come to the Goddess's Faith," Ginnevra said. "She loves all of us, even those who worship differently."

Nevante smiled, an indulgent expression like that of a parent watching their child take a first step. "If that were so, there would be no point in sanctification, would there? Or receiving a grace? I bear no ill will toward Torunes, but I have a responsibility to the

Faithful, and I refuse to apologize for acting on that responsibility."

Ginnevra's heart beat faster as if she were going into combat. Maybe verbal combat counted as far as her reflexes were concerned. "I'm told it was the Faithful who first aggressed on Torunes."

"I'm sure that's not true," Nevante said. "We've lived in peace here for centuries. Why would the Faithful feel compelled to start a fight? We know we have the true faith, and that makes fighting over it unnecessary."

"The Blessed can't put up with our people being victimized," Ginnevra said. "That's why I'm here. But I'm sure she also doesn't believe the Faithful are at all justified in harassing others not of the Faith. I'm not going to make demands of the king that will protect the Faithful only to have the Faithful use that protection as a shield behind which they can continue to persecute Torunes."

"Are you saying you won't do your sworn duty?" Nevante's smile vanished. "You're here for a reason, prime, and if you won't carry out those orders, I'll send to Abraciabene for someone who will."

Ginnevra closed her hand on a sword pommel that wasn't there. "Oh, I will most definitely do my duty," she breathed. "But I'm not your puppet, and I'm not here to blindly follow your orders. I will resolve this situation justly, even if that means disappointing you." She strode past Nevante toward the stairwell. "And, Hallowed Nevante?" she said over her shoulder. "If you think you can send to Abraciabene over and over until you get a paladin willing to bow to you, think again."

She hurried down the stairs, though she didn't think Nevante would follow her. It was more that she wanted desperately to get away from the Hallowed before her inclination to slap the woman overrode her good sense. She had never thought a Hallowed could be so bigoted as to ignore the dictates of her own Faith.

Immediately, Ginnevra felt embarrassed at behind so critical. She'd grown up assuming the Faith was all there was, and it had taken time for her to shed that early, uncritical belief. Not that long ago, Ginnevra had thought of Torunes as less worthy because they didn't share her religion. Even now, she felt mildly uncomfortable in their presence, acutely aware that they were different in a fundamental way, and she had to work at being evenhanded and polite. But a Hallowed ought to be different, particularly one who'd had decades to overcome the prejudices Ginnevra struggled with.

She left the stable with only a nod for Harrus and a last pat for Dauntless, intent on getting back to the hostel. Hopefully, Eodan would have returned. If not, maybe the hostel had a bath house; a good long soak might help her sour mood. She scowled at a woman who passed her too closely and felt pleased to see her recoil before guilt over that pleasure set in. Some prime she'd turned out to be.

ELEVEN

G innevra had braced herself when she approached the hostel owner, preparing for more hostility. But the woman was of the Faithful, and she had led Ginnevra to the bath house herself, saying, "We haven't many guests at the moment, and the baths are fed by a hot spring, so take as long as you need." Her kindness made Ginnevra's throat tighten against self-pitying tears.

Now she stretched out in the tub, which was large enough to accommodate her long legs, and breathed in the warm, moist air. She'd scrubbed and rinsed well and washed her hair before climbing in, and she felt not only clean but perfectly relaxed. All the trials of the day floated at a distance, for the moment only dimly remembered. All that was missing was Eodan.

She couldn't imagine where he'd gone in this unfamiliar city. Human civilization fascinated him; maybe he was out exploring for exploration's sake. Or he might be looking into setting up as a traveling physician. Whatever it was, she hoped he would return soon. Even with her troubles temporarily distant, she wanted to talk to him about what she'd learned. She'd become used to working out solutions with his help. Maybe that made her a terrible prime, if she couldn't solve problems on her own, but she chose to see it as making the best use of her resources. And if other primes didn't have the sense to find companions as intelligent and sensible and handsome as Eodan, that was their own lookout.

Someone rapped lightly on the bath house door. "Ginnevra?"

Ginnevra sat up, making the water in the tub slosh. "Eodan. Come in."

Eodan opened the door the narrowest crack that would admit him and slipped inside. He shut the door behind him and leaned against it, looking her over with a familiar light in his eyes. "You're almost finished. I wish I'd returned sooner. I'd have scrubbed your back. Among other things."

Ginnevra stood and swiped warm water off her body. "Where have you been? I missed you."

She immediately regretted how whiny she'd sounded. Eodan's eyebrows rose. "That was unexpected. I didn't realize you wanted me here waiting on your return."

"No, I—that's not it. Sorry." She dried herself off and hung the cloth on a peg near the door. "It's been an awful day, and I need someone to talk to. That's all."

"I see." Eodan stepped to one side for Ginnevra to open the cupboard where she'd put her clothes to protect them from most of the muggy air. "I went for a long walk, mostly to see what Quinizelle looks like. I asked about local physicians, and I talked with some people about the king and the families who want to be his heir. Did you know there's a succession crisis brewing?"

Ginnevra paused in putting on her breeches. "I do. Filippa told me."

"Filippa?" Eodan sounded more shocked than Ginnevra felt was justified, and it made her feel guilty all over again.

"Yes," she said. "She's here in Quinizelle. She found out about the origin of that crest and followed the evidence here. We—I agreed we should share whatever we find, even though we have different goals."

"I see," Eodan said, sounding so neutral it set off warning bells in Ginnevra's head.

"Is something wrong with that?" she asked.

Eodan shrugged and handed her her shirt. "I was under the impression that you wanted nothing to do with her. I don't want you making decisions you'll regret later."

Ginnevra pulled the shirt on over her head and tucked the hem into her waistband. "Eodan, I have no idea what I feel anymore. She was my closest friend and she betrayed me and everything we both stood for. Now I'm in a position where I need her help, but I don't know if I'm doing the right thing in accepting it. All I know is that I don't want our past to stop me from bringing a murderer to justice."

"I understand," Eodan said. He put his arms around her waist and pulled her close. Ginnevra snuggled into his embrace, enjoying the heat of his body, a few degrees warmer than human normal.

"That's some of why I needed you," she murmured. "You are so good at seeing to the heart of things."

"I'm not always that even-tempered," Eodan said. "What were the other things?"

"Let's go upstairs, and I'll tell you," Ginnevra said.

The chairs weren't big enough for them to share one, so they ended up in bed, fully clothed but cuddling close together. Ginnevra recounted the whole day's adventures, meeting with the king, Pattero's revelations, encountering Filippa, stopping the robbery, and the unsatisfactory meeting with Hallowed Nevante. Eodan listened in silence, and when Ginnevra wound down, he said, "You've had a very full day."

"I feel like it was forever ago I left this morning. And despite all that, I have no idea what to do next. I feel like I'm standing at a crossroads where half a dozen roads intersect with no guide as to which one to take." Ginnevra scooted in closer. "I told the king I intended to find out the truth behind these religious attacks, but I'm starting to worry that means arresting a Hallowed. I told Filippa I'd let her investigate the Zuccares, so I'm waiting on her return with new information. Everything looks like a dead end."

"I learned something you might be interested in," Eodan said. "I don't know if it's something to investigate, but it's relevant. Some of the wealthy citizens of Quinizelle have put together a protection fund to help Torunes who've been injured in attacks by the Faithful. Wounded, or had their property stolen or destroyed —any kind of suffering, the fund is meant to ease."

Ginnevra whistled, low and long. "And some of those who've been attacked retaliate. Doesn't that mean those wealthy citizens are more or less paying people to attack the Faithful? By removing the costs of doing so?"

"Indirectly, yes." Eodan's breath sighed across her forehead. "I was thinking, suppose the people behind the fund have set it up like that on purpose to support attacks on the Faithful? Attacks that can't be linked to them?"

Possibilities bloomed in Ginnevra's mind. "That is definitely something I should look into," she said, and kissed Eodan. "But not in my official guise. Nobody in Quinizelle is going to talk to a paladin."

"It's unlikely," Eodan agreed. "Does that mean you're going to conceal your identity? Because you've said you'll never do that."

"I won't. However, I don't have to proclaim what I am."

Ginnevra kissed him again, longer this time. "And if they find out the truth about me, I'll trust in the Goddess that I can make use of that, too."

Eodan captured her hand and pressed it close to his chest. "Food," he said. "And then I want—"

"So do I," Ginnevra said.

THE FOLLOWING morning dawned gray and cloudy, with the smell of rain in the air. Ginnevra dressed warmly in ordinary clothes, leaving off her gambeson even though its padding made it the warmest thing she owned that wasn't the fur-lined cloak. That, she donned readily, ignoring Eodan's chuckle. "I know, it makes me look like a bear," she said. "Bears are warm during the winter."

"Bears hibernate during the winter," Eodan pointed out. "I doubt you want to sleep away four months of your life."

"Don't bet on it." She kissed him swiftly. "What will you do today?"

"I put word out about a visiting physician. In Quinizelle, people don't go to a physician, the physician comes to them. So we'll see how many requests I get." Eodan's arm snaked around Ginnevra's waist. "Come back around noon, and we'll eat together."

"I will. Have I mentioned I love you?"

Eodan's blue eyes gleamed. "Not recently."

"That's what I thought." She hugged him close, pressing her cheek against the side of his neck and breathing in his werewolf musk. "I love you. I'll be back soon."

Despite the oncoming storm, the streets were as full as they'd been the previous day. Ginnevra observed how quickly everyone walked and concluded they wanted to finish their business before it rained. Few people paid her any attention, and most of those who did stared at her cloak enviously. Ginnevra didn't mind those kind of looks.

She'd given her next steps much consideration. Torunes didn't have places of worship the way the Faithful did, so she couldn't go to a Torune chapel or sanctuary to ask about a Torune protection fund. She didn't think it was a good idea to ask around where Eodan had gone the previous day, in case someone thought it was suspicious that two foreigners in as many days were interested in a fund that didn't benefit them. And it seemed unlikely that the Faithful at the sanctuary knew about it, if only because Ginnevra was certain Nevante would have mentioned it.

But there was someone—two someones—who probably knew about the fund and might even be its beneficiaries already. She just needed to track them down.

She had to ask a couple of people where the justiciary was before finding someone willing to give her directions. It turned out to be on the far side of the palace from her hostel. As she walked through the streets beneath a thin drizzle of rain, she considered whether she was wrong, and her paladin's armor and sword were more likely to get her what she wanted. Certainly justicers all over the Lordagne respected what it represented, and even here in Quinizelle it stood for power. But she remembered the guards from yesterday, and concluded she was as likely to be kicked out of the justiciary as given respect if she was wearing it.

She had seen any number of justiciary buildings throughout the Lordagne, all of them stony and dark and low to the ground regardless of their surroundings. None of them would ever be mistaken for anything but what they were: places to confine criminals. Except this one. It looked like a mansion, one built of the same tawny stone as everything else in Quinizelle, with turreted towers and an oak double door twice Ginnevra's height. She nearly walked past it before noticing that all the lower windows were bricked over and guards stood at the door, armed and alert as she hadn't seen anywhere else in Quinizelle but the palace.

Ginnevra backtracked and hurried up the flagstone path, noting in passing the fine garden surrounding the mansion. She couldn't guess why anyone would care so much about making the justiciary beautiful. The rain was coming down harder now, fat drops tapping her head and shoulders hard enough she felt them even through the heavy cloak. Getting inside was now a priority.

At the door, the guards moved to intercept her, stopping her about five feet from the entrance with their cudgels raised in warning. "State your business," the female guard said.

"I'm here to see two of the prisoners," Ginnevra said. "Reena Naccione and Gittanus Revellini."

"You family?" the male guard said.

"No." Ginnevra smiled pleasantly. "I stopped them assaulting a shopkeeper and his daughter. I have some questions for them."

The guards exchanged glances. Both of them wore identical expressions of puzzlement, their foreheads wrinkled in thought, and their cudgels dipped slightly. "Questions?" the male guard said. "If you're telling the truth, and I'm not saying you are, they got captured in the act. I don't see that there's many more questions to be answered."

"I think they're part of a larger organization," Ginnevra said, which was true enough. "And why would I lie about that? Even if many people try to see prisoners they've no relation to, what would be the point?"

"Might try to help them escape," the male guard said. "Strangers aren't allowed in. Move along."

"But—suppose I had a complaint to register with a justicer?" Ginnevra protested. "Or had some other business? You'd let me in then, right?"

"Don't try to fool us," the female guard said. "We already know what you want. It's no good lying."

Ginnevra ground her back teeth together. "Fine," she said, glaring at the two. The guards, who'd moved closer to the door to take advantage of the little roof's scant shelter, eyed her warily. She wasn't going to accomplish anything by standing there, and they certainly wouldn't let her wait out the storm in the justiciary doorway. So she tugged her cloak's hood securely over her face and strode back the way she'd come.

TWELVE

With the heavy raindrops beating down on her head and shoulders, she ran through the streets toward the hostel. It didn't take long for her to realize she was going to be soaked through, fur-lined cloak or not, if she didn't take shelter before reaching it. The empty, dimly-lit streets made Ginnevra think mad thoughts about plagues and invasions. It was the endless drumming on her skull that sent her imagination running wild.

She caught a glimpse of a sign outside one business as she passed. No name, but the picture of a foaming tankard told her what she needed to know. She veered around and dashed for the entrance, skidding to a halt outside before opening the door decorously. She immediately thanked the Goddess for encouraging politeness in Her paladins, because another patron stood just inside the door, someone Ginnevra would have crashed into had she not been careful. Ginnevra stood aside and held the door for the man, who nodded his thanks before putting up the hood of his oiled leather cape and heading out into the storm.

When the door closed behind him, Ginnevra surveyed the tap room. There weren't many patrons at that hour, and they all had the appearance of heavy or habitual drinkers, their shoulders rounded as they leaned forward over their drinks, their eyes fixed on mug or glass, their hands trembling whenever they weren't holding something. None of them looked up, though a few glanced her way without moving. Ginnevra did them the courtesy of not staring.

She removed her cloak and folded it loosely over one arm, where it immediately soaked her sleeve. So long as it was just the outside and not the lining that was wet, she could put up with a little dampness. The cloak had only been soaked through once before, but Ginnevra had never forgotten the stink of bear fur that filled the air as it dried.

The barkeep looked up when she approached. "You want something?" he asked, in a doubtful tone of voice. It said Ginnevra wasn't the sort of person he was used to serving before noon.

"A dry place to wait out the storm, honestly," Ginnevra said with a smile. "But I'll take a pint of ale. Anything to warm me up. I am not used to your weather."

"Not from around here?" The man pulled a wooden tankard from beneath the bar and filled it with a dark, rich-smelling stream from a tapped barrel.

"Just visiting." That didn't count as concealing her identity, since she wasn't afraid of being known as a paladin here; she simply didn't want to give anything away to a stranger.

"From the lowlands." The barkeep nodded. "Much warmer there than here, I imagine. I've never been out of Quinizelle."

"It's a lovely place to call home," Ginnevra said. Then, remembering what Eodan had told her, she asked, "Is it true the king is going to choose an heir from among the noble families of Quinizelle?"

The barkeep's expression hardened. "He's not a fool, so I doubt it," he said. "Fastest way to get himself killed I can think of."

"I don't—" Ginnevra paused, enlightenment dawning. "Oh. Because if he names an heir, they'd have no reason to want him alive anymore. He'd be in the way of them becoming king."

The barkeep tapped his nose knowingly. "So I think he'll string them along until the Lady Benitta has a child. Should be any time now she'll conceive, I'm sure of it."

"I hope so." Ginnevra sipped her ale, which was surprisingly good and did warm her up. "But what will those families do if they're not chosen? Would they go to war anyway?"

"Who knows?" the barkeep said with a shrug. He turned away to put a bottle of whiskey on the rack behind the counter, then turned back to Ginnevra and leaned in close. "It would be treason for them to take a stand against the king, but I've heard how at least one of them might do it," he said, his voice low and confidential. "House Zuccare has talked a good line about them being natural heirs, but I think they just want someone more religious on the throne."

"Is King Paolo not very devout, then?" Ginnevra almost asked about what it meant that Rainaldus was part of the king's court, but realized in time that might be knowledge a stranger to Quinizelle wouldn't have.

The barkeep let out a short bark of a laugh. "He's a strong believer, and don't let anyone tell you otherwise. But he hasn't taken a hard line against the Faithful, and there are some who think that makes him unsuited to rule Torunes."

"But...those Faithful are citizens, aren't they? Why should they be punished for their religion?"

The barkeep's eyes narrowed. "You one of them?"

"I am. Is that a problem?" Ginnevra retorted. She took another long drink, deciding if she was going to be evicted, she'd enjoy herself first.

"Guess that's not so unlikely, you being a foreigner." The barkeep's hostile look disappeared. "But you Faithful, you did your best to wipe out the worship of Torun and his children throughout the Lordagne. So I'm not sure where you get off being upset when we fight back."

Ginnevra took another drink to give herself a moment to consider her response. "It's true, the coming of the Faith meant a lot of Torunes converted to the new religion," she said, watching the barkeep carefully. "We could argue over how much of that was demanded by the Blesseds of the past. I imagine you and I were taught different things about that era. But what matters is what we do here and now. Where I come from, the Faithful are taught to be respectful of everyone regardless of their beliefs. I don't think anyone should suffer because of their religion."

She felt so stupid saying this. The Faith hadn't tried to wipe out the Torune religion; it had been a welcome alternative to the violent, misogynistic religion that then dominated the Lordagne. Its anointed had demonstrated miracles, true miracles in which the hand of the Goddess was clear, unlike the superstitions of the Torunes that had no divine power behind them. As far as Ginnevra was concerned, her Faith was the true religion. But she knew better than to challenge someone's beliefs in his own home, or business in this case.

"And I also don't think it's ever right to persecute someone because they're not like you," she added. That, at least, was a solid truth she could stand on.

"Bold words," the barkeep said, but he still didn't look or sound hostile.

"Do you agree, then?" Ginnevra asked.

The man smiled. "I'm still serving you, aren't I?"

Ginnevra saluted him with her tankard. "You are indeed."

She tipped back the last drops of ale and set the tankard down. "So, House Zuccare is more devout than the Napolles?"

"Very much more," the barkeep said. "I don't think anyone gets more devout than them. They started that Benevolent Fund, they pay for religious instruction for the young, High Priest Rainaldus is at their beck and call. I've heard they've set aside part of their estate as a place of worship even."

Ginnevra wasn't listening. Her mind had caught hold of something interesting. "High Priest Rainaldus?"

"He's like your Blessed—he's the chief religious authority over Torunes, except only in Quinizelle," the barkeep said. "He's performed great miracles."

Ginnevra doubted that, but again, there was no point arguing. "I'd heard he attends on the king, too."

"The king calls on him for advice all the time, or so it's said. He's the wisest and most respected man in Quinizelle. You want another?"

Ginnevra listened. She couldn't hear the rain drumming on the street outside anymore. "If it's stopped raining, I should probably go." She pushed a couple of larins across the counter, hoping the barkeep wouldn't object to them being of Abraciabene minting.

The barkeep swept up the coins without a blink. "Good luck to you."

Ginnevra gathered up her still-wet cloak and nodded a farewell.

The rain had gone back to being a light drizzle, and Ginnevra decided to take her chances rather than stay and feel obliged to drink more than she really wanted. There was still some time before noon, and after her conversation with the barkeep, there was something she wanted to do.

Getting directions to the Zuccare estate was simple. No one even looked at her funny for asking. Oddly enough, it was near the hostel, and she had passed it twice in her travels to and from the palace. Or maybe that wasn't odd, since many of Quinizelle's nicest and most expensive houses clustered near the palace, as if wealth attracted wealth.

She strolled past the estate, examining it. Even that didn't set her apart; the people who'd dared the rain for this neighborhood all slowed to look at the mansion behind its stone wall topped with iron spikes. Ginnevra stopped at the gate, an iron-barred monstrosity decorated with grinning baby-faced cherubs. Cherubs were one of two things she knew about the Torune religion, those and that there were eight holy children of Torun; cherubs were supposed to be spirits of the natural world, brought into being by Marena, Torun's wife and goddess of the sea. Ginnevra found them deeply unsettling.

She peered through the bars. The mansion was of a darker yellow stone than most buildings in Quinizelle, and none of its windows, not even the lowest ones, were barred. She guessed the Zuccares believed their spiked wall was enough protection. The house itself was plain, with sheer walls rising to crenellated tops where—oh. So they believed their spiked wall and a dozen guards armed with crossbows was enough protection. Ginnevra couldn't argue with that.

Grateful that she wasn't expected to break into the Zuccare estate, Ginnevra strolled back the way she'd come. The rain made Quinizelle unexpectedly beautiful, deepening the golden-tan of its stones and filling the air with the rush of water running off the eaves. Flowers grew in pots or in the upper casements, and raindrops collected on their petals and magnified their brightness. If it hadn't been so cold, Ginnevra might have considered settling here for a while.

She turned a corner and nearly ran into a mass of gray-robed men coming the other way. Their first rank stopped, causing those behind to pile into them. Irritated murmurs rose up from the crowd as the ones in back demanded to know what had happened. Ginnevra backed up a few steps. "Sorry about that," she said.

"You should watch where you're going," one of the gray-robes said. He was the one whose toes she'd nearly stepped on. "We have the right of way."

"I don't see why," Ginnevra said. "It's a blind corner, so neither of us could see the other. That calls for caution on both sides, don't you think?"

"I should have expected no less than disrespect from you," a new voice said. The crowd parted to reveal Rainaldus Mastarcce, tall and dour in his gray and black clothing. His hood was thrown back from his face, and his long, graying hair was damp but not soaked through. He came to a halt less than a foot from Ginnevra. "The followers of the Goddess care nothing for the beliefs of others."

"As I said, I didn't see you all," Ginnevra replied, "so I could hardly have intended disrespect. I didn't realize this was a religious processional."

"Ignorance of our customs does not excuse rudeness," Rainaldus said. "Stand aside."

Ginnevra closed one hand into a fist, reining in her anger. "I know there is bad blood between the Faithful and Torunes. I'm here to put an end to it. I hoped you and Hallowed Nevante would feel the same. There's no reason our religions have to live in enmity."

"You would do better to control Nevante. She is the one goading her people into attacking the innocent." Rainaldus' expression was as stony and hard as the mountain.

"It's not a one-sided conflict, High Priest. I've seen both sides attack the innocent." Ginnevra wasn't sure the Torunes she and Eodan had rescued that first night were innocents, and she didn't think Orenna and her father were completely blameless, but Rainaldus didn't look like someone interested in the details.

Rainaldus' brows drew down until they nearly met above his nose. "You challenge me, woman?"

No one had ever called her "woman" in that tone of voice, as if there were something inherently weak or stupid about being female. Ginnevra's temper flared. "You're ignorant, bigoted, and full of your own self-worth," she snapped, "so yes, I'm challenging you. Torunes look to you for guidance, and if you aren't willing to rein them in, I have to wonder whether you don't have some personal stake in this conflict!"

The murmuring grew louder and angrier. Rainaldus was red as a ripening tomato. "How *dare* you," he snarled. "Leave my presence now, or I won't answer for the consequences."

Ginnevra swiftly assessed Rainaldus' followers. There were fifteen of them, none of them younger than middle-aged, but they were angry and they had the look of men who were eager to defend their beliefs and the man who personified them. She could probably fight them off, and she wasn't likely to be badly hurt, but if word got around that a paladin of the Goddess had beaten up a pack of holy men, or whatever they were, she might as well lie down in the street and let them trample her to death.

"I'm leaving," she said, "but I'm not giving up on my mission. Consider that carefully, High Priest." She turned on her heel and strode away, cursing herself. She was terrible at diplomacy, but that had been a new low even for her.

She worked her way around to the hostel, not wanting to even come within sight of the gray robes, and stomped up the stairs to her room. Eodan wasn't there. She flung her cloak at one of the chairs with such force it rocked on its back legs. Now that the immediate challenge was over, she felt cold and miserable inside. It didn't help that she might be right about Rainaldus being involved. If Nevante had encouraged the Faithful to take matters into their own hands, why should Rainaldus not do the same with the Torunes? Which meant she had *two* holy people to fight.

She sank down onto the bed and buried her face in her hands. Convincing King Paolo looked like her only option now, and it seemed increasingly likely she would have to carry out the Blessed's threat. Nothing about that possibility comforted her. "Goddess," she prayed aloud, "I lack wisdom. Please, guide my hand in Your service. And forgive my short temper. I'm afraid it may have ruined my chances. Help me forge a path that will protect Your servants."

She paused, closing her eyes and letting her shoulders droop so her tension would fall away. "I want these people to live in peace, even the ones who don't believe in You," she said, surprising herself. "I know You won't impress a given future on anyone, and it's their choice how they live, but if You don't mind, show me how to reveal that possibility to them. Ever in Your name."

No voice responded, to Ginnevra's relief. The Goddess had spoken to her once before, and while it was a memory she cherished, it had also unsettled her. She didn't like the idea of being singled out; that was the sort of thing that led to pride, and she was already special by virtue of being a prime of the Blessed.

She remembered what she'd said to Rainaldus and her face burned with embarrassment. It didn't matter how rude he'd been, that didn't entitle her to lash out, certainly not at someone she might otherwise have wanted on her side. Though that desire was irrelevant, because she was sure Rainaldus was not interested in seeing both sides of the conflict any more than Nevante was. It no longer mattered who'd started it; it was going to go on until someone stepped in and made it stop. And that someone was probably Ginnevra.

The door opened. "Oh, you're back," Eodan said. "You're not going to believe who I attended on this morning."

Ginnevra sighed. "King Paolo."

"Close. It was the Lady Benitta." Eodan's expression was grim, his eyes bright with suppressed emotion. He entered the room fully and closed the door behind him. "But I *know* you can't guess what I discovered."

"Is it something good? Lady Benitta is expecting a child?"

Eodan shook his head. "I think King Paolo may be infertile," he said.

THIRTEEN

Ginnevra gasped. "That's impossible. How can you know? Did you examine him?"

"It's just a guess," Eodan said. "I knew the citizens of Quinizelle were concerned about Lady Benitta's ability to conceive. It turns out that concern is downright panic among the courtiers who wait on her. They call on every physician who comes to Quinizelle to treat her, in the hope that one of them will come up with a solution. And given that we've only been here two days, they are very alert to those arrivals."

"So they expected you to enhance her fertility?"

Eodan sat in the chair that didn't have Ginnevra's cloak slowly soaking its cushions. "They said they wanted me to confirm her health, but everything they didn't say told me they were hoping for a miracle. Lady Benitta herself was very polite and accommodating. Amazing, that, when you consider how many physicians have treated her in the last two years. And some of them were probably charlatans, so you can add to that the likelihood that she's endured some quackery during that time."

Ginnevra felt a pang of sympathy for Pattero's sister. "Is there medicine for barrenness? But—you said you thought it was King Paolo with the problem."

"I'm getting to that." Eodan leaned forward. "It's hard to examine a woman's reproductive organs for flaws or damage, unless there are tumors or excessive bleeding. Usually all any physician can do is see that her humors are in balance and that she's eating a diet rich in foods that encourage fertility. I asked a lot of questions and performed several tests, and as far as I can tell, there's no reason she shouldn't conceive. None."

"Which means..." Ginnevra felt cold. "But without an heir, King Paolo falls prey to whichever of the noble houses convinces him to make them his heir. We could be looking at actual war in addition to religious war."

Eodan nodded. He looked tired now, as if delivering this news had sapped his energy. "I doubt the king will be willing to let me confirm that guess, even though that would be best for everyone."

"But if he names an heir, he might as well hand over the throne immediately. He becomes an obstacle that house would want removed as soon as possible." Ginnevra rubbed her eyes with the heels of her palms. For a moment, she envisioned leaving Quinizelle that night, abandoning her mission and letting the city fall into chaos. There certainly wasn't anything she could do to stop it.

"You're not here to fix the succession, Ginnevra. You're meant to stop the religious persecution. Hang on to that." Eodan removed her hands from her eyes and clasped them. Ginnevra looked at him and was stunned at the intensity of his expression. He had faith in her when she didn't have faith in herself. Her vision of leaving dissolved.

"I'm not sure I can even do that," she said, and told him what had happened with Rainaldus. This time, she felt guilty as well as embarrassed. "I shouldn't have lost my temper," she said. "But he was so dismissive of me, I wanted to strike back."

"Understandable," Eodan said. "But you're right, that didn't help. On the other hand, it probably didn't turn him from an ally into an enemy. If he believes the Faithful are at fault, he's not likely to change his mind just because you're nice to him."

"I know." Ginnevra squeezed Eodan's hands and smiled. "It's done, and I can't take it back."

"Let's get something to eat—"

Eodan's words were interrupted by a knock at the door. When he opened it, the hostel owner stood there, holding a folded and sealed piece of paper. "This came for you," she said, handing it to Ginnevra.

Ginnevra turned it over to look at the seal. The yellow wax was clearly imprinted with chevrons and a wolf's head. "Who brought this?"

"A girl in the gray and gold of House Zuccare," the hostel owner said. "She wouldn't stay for a reply. I'll just leave you to it, shall I?" She smiled and closed the door.

"This really is a remarkable place," Eodan said. "Most hostels or inns, the owner would have stayed in the hope of learning something gossip-worthy."

"It's the one good thing about Quinizelle," Ginnevra said. She broke the seal with her thumbnail. "All right, there are other good things, but that's the one that most directly affects us."

She scanned the contents of the paper, her eyebrows rising gradually higher until they nearly reached her hairline. "Well, this is unexpected," she said. "We're invited to a gathering at the Zuccare mansion tomorrow night. It's to celebrate Giuseppe Zuccare's son receiving his yearling totem, whatever that is—actually, I remember Lord Pattero saying something about

Torunes being dedicated to one of their religion's holy children on their first birthday, and I suppose that could be what this is."

"They're inviting a paladin to witness a Torune religious ceremony?" Eodan's eyebrows rose to match hers. "That seems unlikely."

Ginnevra handed him the paper. "Read it yourself."

"You know my reading skills aren't up to diplomatic language," Eodan said, but he read the paper anyway, his lips moving occasionally as he sounded out an unfamiliar word. "This doesn't sound very welcoming. It sounds like they'd rather you not come. Why would they invite you if they didn't want you?"

"I don't know. I wasn't raised in a wealthy or noble household to know their rules. Maybe it's a formality? In Talagne, where I was born, everyone in our neighborhood was invited to wedding celebrations, even people the family didn't like. It could be that." Ginnevra accepted the paper back from Eodan. "But I'm not going to pass up the chance to get inside the Zuccare estate. Suppose Filippa couldn't manage whatever she had in mind? I need to know if Jiuseppe is behind both the religious strife now and the massacre four years ago."

"What can you do with that information? If both Rainaldus and Hallowed Nevante believe they're justified in setting their people against each other, knowing Jiuseppe is ultimately responsible probably won't change their minds." Eodan shook out Ginnevra's cloak and handed it to her. It was still damp, but only on the outside.

"It's something I can take to the king and use to make him put pressure on the two religious leaders." Ginnevra hoped this was true. It was more of a plan than she'd had an hour ago, so she clung to it.

They walked through the rain-slicked streets hand in hand, breathing in the fresh, cold, wet air. Others had ventured out now that the rain had stopped, and Ginnevra saw street vendors setting up from where they'd huddled to wait out the storm. Most of them looked soggy, but their wares were untouched by rain.

"What do you know about Torunes?" Eodan said abruptly.

"Why do you ask?"

"I was thinking about that dedication ceremony, and whether there's any validity to it. Are the Torune gods real?" Eodan steered her around a puddle, warming Ginnevra's heart.

"We're taught not," she said. "When the Faith came to the Lordagne, it was brought by anointed from Illiou, across the sea. They weren't antagonistic or violent, just taught the Goddess's religion wherever they could. Which meant coming into conflict with Torune priests. The records all say that the anointeds' faith defeated every challenge the priests brought against them. It was a time of miracles like nothing we have today." She'd loved stories of that time when she was a child, even though as she'd gotten older she'd learned that not all of them were one hundred percent true. They were still wonderful stories.

"Our lore says the Torunes who challenged the anointed used trickery and misdirection rather than divine power, and that and the Goddess's doctrine of compassion and love for others appealed to the Lordagni. That's why the Faith spread widely and rapidly. But—" Ginnevra paused to let a man on a horse cross the street in front of them. "I don't believe in the Torune religion, and I wonder why other people do, if there's no truth to it. Why would anyone commit to a religion they couldn't prove was true?"

"What did you do before you were a paladin?" Eodan asked.

Ginnevra blinked. "What do you mean?"

"I assume taking oath as a paladin convinced you your religion was true, because you were altered by the Goddess's gift. Increased strength, keener senses, all of that." Eodan stopped her and made her look at him. "But you worshipped the Goddess before that, so how did you know it was the right thing to do when you hadn't seen evidence to prove it?"

"Oh," Ginnevra said. "Well, everyone who has a grace draws on the Goddess's power to work small magics. So we know She exists and cares enough about us to give us Her power in that way."

"But that doesn't have to be the Goddess," Eodan said. "It could be magic inherent to the grace. Maybe obsidian and jet and pearl are all magical, and you're tapping into that magic when you invoke a grace."

A chill touched Ginnevra's heart. "You're not serious, are you? There's no such thing as magic inherent to objects."

"There could be. Maybe that's where the Torune religion came from—they worship the mountain and sea and river, right? Natural forces—"

"All right, I get it," Ginnevra snapped. "I just know, Eodan."

"I'm sorry." Eodan did look remorseful. "I don't believe any of that. I have enough evidence of the Bright One to know her counterpart the Goddess is real. But I think your question is valid. If the Torune religion is all made up, why would anyone follow it?"

Ginnevra sighed. "I'm grateful I don't actually have to answer that question. I suppose people can fool themselves into believing things if they really want to. And I've seen conjurers perform sleight of hand and other tricks. Some of them pretend they're doing real magic, as part of the show. Those can be very convincing. Maybe the Torune priests are like that."

"The conjurer we saw in Uparde certainly seemed capable of magic. I still don't understand how he made that woman disappear." Eodan turned a blind corner, and Ginnevra tensed, remembering her unexpected encounter with the gray-robes. But no one was there, and Eodan continued down the new street without any sign of apprehension. "But they don't actually claim to work divine magic," he added.

"No. Everyone knows it's part of the fun, pretending it's real magic." The new street was wide enough to allow for a small market to spring up, with a dozen wagons selling fruits and vegetables. Ginnevra wondered where all the food came from. Transporting all their food up the mountain would make living in Quinizelle expensive.

She dodged someone who hurried in front of her intent on a wagon full of bright red apples. It was nice to be anonymous after receiving so much wary attention in her armor, and she reminded herself not to get used to it. Avoiding being snubbed wasn't a good reason to pretend to be something other than she was.

"But if this yearling totem ceremony involves a Torune priest performing their rites," she said, "we might get a close look at what passes for their divine magic. That might tell us something."

Eodan paused beneath a sign depicting a steaming cauldron and pushed the tavern door open. "Maybe that's why you were invited. So they can show the paladin the might and power of Torun."

"If it's as simple as an intent to intimidate," Ginnevra said, "I'll attend gladly."

THE FOLLOWING EVENING, Ginnevra reflected on her careless words and wished she could take them back. She plucked at the satiny fall of her overskirt, lifting it so she could see her feet. Those, at least, were clad in her own boots, polished until they shone. She'd flatly refused to wear the thin-soled slippers that matched the gown.

"I haven't worn a dress since I was thirteen," she complained.

"And that was for my sanctification, so I wore it for all of half an hour. Skirts are unnatural."

Eodan raised both hands, displaying all his fingers with both thumbs folded down, and gave her a meaningful look. Ginnevra glared at him. "What?"

"That's the eighth time you've said that," he replied. "Almost as many times as I've pointed out that according to the hostel owner, this is what noblewomen wear for public formal events. And almost as many times as I've said you could probably wear anything you like that isn't the armor and no one will blink."

Ginnevra scowled harder. "You don't have to be so reasonable. Besides, *you* look good. I look like I've been stuffed into this thing like a pig in a poke." She smoothed the fabric of her bodice and then knocked gently on its stiffened front. The thing pushed her breasts abnormally high and made her ribs feel strapped into a cage.

Eodan surveyed her from head to toe. Then he walked with slow, deliberate steps to stand in front of her and put his hands on her hips. "You know I think you're beautiful whatever you wear," he said in a low voice, "but this gown makes you look like an exotic stranger I'd love to get to know better. And I like what it does for your figure." He pulled her toward him until she was pressed against his body. Gently, he ran his fingers down the side of her neck and along her shoulder, which the gown left mostly bare. Ginnevra shivered with pleasure.

Eodan kissed her collarbone. "Of course," he whispered, "if you've changed your mind about the ceremony, I'd be happy to help you out of that gown." His lips brushed hers, feather-light, sending a rush of desire through her.

"All right," she said breathlessly, "so the gown isn't awful."

Eodan kissed her again, more firmly, and said, "Please say you've changed your mind."

The twinkle in his eye told her he was only half serious, and Ginnevra laughed. "Later," she said. "All right, I'll stop bitching about the gown. Though I am concerned about my ability to fight in all these skirts."

"You don't think it will come to a fight, do you?" Eodan straightened his formal doublet and brushed lint off his breeches. His clothing was as suitable to the event as Ginnevra's, but nothing could make him look like anything but a warrior given his size and the breadth of his shoulders. He'd tied his hair back in the short tail Ginnevra had observed on the courtiers surrounding King Paolo, and the hairstyle gave his face unexpected and attractive definition.

"I always assume a fight is a possibility," Ginnevra said. "Then I'm pleasantly surprised when I'm wrong."

"That attitude is so typical of you I can't believe I had to ask," Eodan said. He extended a hand to her. "Shall we see what adventure awaits us, my lady?"

Despite her resolve to stop dwelling on how much she disliked wearing a gown, Ginnevra couldn't help feeling grateful for her boots. The streets had dried since yesterday's storm, but they were still dirty, and Ginnevra imagined feeling every cobble through the thin soles of the abandoned shoes. The toes of the boots were visible with every step, but Ginnevra doubted anyone would look at her feet, not when her short hair, so dramatically different from the noblewomen she'd seen at King Paolo's court, would draw more immediate attention.

The sun had nearly set, and almost no one was still on the streets, but the pedestrians all stared at Ginnevra and Eodan as if they were a couple of exotic, possibly dangerous animals loose in Quinizelle. Ginnevra chose to ignore the stares, though she hated that it made her look aloof and arrogant not to acknowledge those they passed. She hoped walking wasn't a mistake. There were no horse-drawn carriages in the city, and she hadn't liked the look of the palanquins popular among the wealthy; they were too confining and potentially an obstruction if things did come to a fight. So walking was the most practical option.

As they neared the Zuccare estate, Ginnevra's doubts multiplied. Palanquins thronged the street ahead, pausing at the cherub gate to deposit their passengers, who alighted gracefully and with the kind of offhanded carelessness that meant utter confidence. Even as a prime of the Blessed, Ginnevra hadn't had much to do with nobility. She'd never felt so out of place in her life.

"Don't be nervous," Eodan said. "I'm sure they can sense fear."

"I'm not nervous. Sense fear? How is that possible? Some kind of Torune magic?"

Eodan chuckled. "I was joking. Sort of. I meant that nervousness is generally easy to detect, even if you don't have extraordinary senses. You have no reason to be nervous. If anything, *they* ought to be nervous around *you*. You do represent a threat to their faith, after all."

"I won't hurt them." Ginnevra realized her hand was clutching Eodan's arm too tightly and made herself relax. "And it's not nervousness, precisely. I just dislike going into a situation I know nothing about."

"That's reasonable, but don't let it affect your behavior. Remind yourself you can take the head off anyone who threatens you, assuming I don't beat you to it."

The image of herself and Eodan tussling over an aggressor made Ginnevra laugh. "All right. I'll try to look at this as a challenge. And there's so much to learn here, not least who Jiuseppe Zuccare is. Taking off *his* head might be in the offing, depending on what he does."

They strolled up to the cherub gate, which stood wide open,

brushing past a man in a fur-trimmed doublet who made a noise of protest. "Excuse us," Ginnevra said politely, but didn't stop walking.

"Do you know who I am?" the man demanded, walking swiftly to close the distance between them.

Ginnevra looked at Eodan, who shrugged in a "it's up to you" gesture. Well, it wasn't as if she intended to keep her identity secret. She turned around, bringing Eodan with her, and said, "No. Do you know who *I* am, sieur?"

The man's pudgy face flushed. Despite the chill in the air, beads of sweat clung to his hairline. "I am Lord Ugolino Sighere, and I do not endure rudeness from no-name pretenders to nobility."

"That does sound awful," Ginnevra said. "My name is Ginnevra Cassaline, and I am a prime of the Blessed. This is my companion, Eodan. I wouldn't dream of pretending to nobility, but I was polite just now, and I have to ask myself what Quinizellan manners demand that you felt entitled to be rude to me."

Sighere's complexion paled the longer Ginnevra talked. When she finished, he swallowed visibly, glanced from Ginnevra to Eodan and back again, and said, "You have the nerve to come to this sacred ritual?"

"I was invited, my lord, and I believed that invitation to be genuine." Ginnevra smiled. "I'm sure Lord Zuccare's confidence in his religion extends to not fearing contamination by mine."

"But—"

"We look forward to seeing the ceremony," Eodan said. "Excuse us, my lord." He turned, tugging on Ginnevra's arm, and set off at a brisk pace up the flagstones of the walk extending from the street to the mansion's front door.

"Sorry about that," he murmured when Ginnevra started to

complain. "I could tell you were gearing up for an argument, and while I'm sure it would have been a spectacular one, I don't think you should expend energy on a minor noble when Jiuseppe Zuccare and that High Priest are around here somewhere."

"True. Thanks for saving me from myself."

Stairs guarded on both sides by stone railings ascended from the walk to the front door. Like the gate, the two halves of the front door stood wide open, and yellow light illuminated the wide courtyard surrounded by low, neatly-trimmed hedges. Guards stood at either side of the massive front door, but they paid no attention to the guests streaming past. Ginnevra eyed them as she and Eodan approached and concluded Jiuseppe must be confident in his name and reputation to protect him from uninvited visitors. Even so, the sharp edges on the guards' polearms and the cross-bowmen visible atop the walls warned Ginnevra that Jiuseppe wasn't entirely unconscious of danger.

Their pace slowed as they neared the door thanks to the number of guests thronging it. When Ginnevra was close enough, she realized why; a short distance past the doors, the hall opened up into a chamber a good thirty feet tall that extended to left and right at least forty feet in both directions. Its arched ceiling was a riotous mass of color. Ginnevra blinked, and the color came into focus. The ceiling was a mural painted with such incredible detail Ginnevra had to remind herself to keep walking so no one would pile into her. She didn't know what the mural represented, but from the arrangement of the figures, some human, some anthro-pomorphized animals, she guessed it told a story, or maybe a group of stories.

"Extraordinary, isn't it?"

Ginnevra turned to face the speaker, who was a man about her own age with dark hair and a pleasant face. He had his head tipped back to survey the mural. "History and fable combining to make something greater than either," he continued. "What do you think?"

"I don't know those stories," Ginnevra said.

The man's gaze swiftly fixed on Ginnevra. His eyes narrowed. "You're the paladin."

"Ginnevra Cassaline, prime of the Blessed," Ginnevra said, "and my companion, Eodan."

The man ignored Eodan. "I'm surprised you didn't show up in full armor. It's no less than I'd expect."

The dismissive tone of his voice angered Ginnevra, but she locked away a hasty response and said, "I would never be so rude as to antagonize my host that way. And I don't believe I've had the pleasure of your name, my lord."

"No, you have not," the man said. "I am Jiuseppe Zuccare. Your host."

CHAPTER

FOURTEEN

S hock and surprise rendered Ginnevra temporarily mute. She'd expected someone older, someone with a cruel face and hard eyes, someone with the capacity to order a massacre written on his skin, not this youthful man who under any other circumstances Ginnevra might have dismissed as innocuous. She ignored the instinct that demanded she launch herself at him, screaming accusations, and said, "Then I thank you for the invitation, my lord. I admit I didn't expect it."

Jiuseppe regarded her with a cold, unfriendly stare. "And yet you accepted."

A creeping sensation of unease made Ginnevra say, "Did you think I wouldn't?"

"I did not believe," Jiuseppe said, "that a paladin of the Goddess would want to attend on an event sacred to Torun."

Now Ginnevra was certain she'd done wrong in coming. Her earlier supposition that the invitation had been a formality she was expected to ignore seemed increasingly likely. But leaving now, acknowledging that she'd made a social misstep, would not only be embarrassing but would ruin her chance to learn something that might condemn Jiuseppe. With a polite smile, she said, "I believe the fighting between religions here in Quinizelle is rooted in mutual misunderstanding and ignorance of one another's beliefs. I saw your invitation as an opportunity to learn more about Torun and his teachings. It's generous of you to offer to share what must be a sacred experience. Thank you."

Jiuseppe's eyes widened slightly, and a look of confusion replaced the cold expression. "You are here to impose the Faith on Quinizelle," he said, but with a hint of uncertainty.

"No, I came because we believed the religious persecution was one-sided," Ginnevra said. "Now that I know the truth, I want to see that Torunes and Faithful can live peacefully as they did four years ago."

Eodan tensed. Ginnevra kept her eyes on Jiuseppe. At the words "four years" his lips whitened, but otherwise he did not react. "The Faith made promises it didn't keep," he said. "Is it any wonder Quinizelle turned its back on that religion?"

Ginnevra closed her hand tightly on Eodan's sleeve. "There are still Faithful in Quinizelle," she said, "and they are still citizens. They don't deserve to be persecuted any more than Torunes do."

"The Faithful are a rot within our city." Jiuseppe's voice hardened, and he spat words at Ginnevra like stones. "Their presence offends Torun. Better they leave entirely than continue to corrupt Quinizelle."

The urge to attack Jiuseppe grew stronger. "Are you saying you encourage violence against the Faithful, Lord Jiuseppe?"

"I do not condone any kind of violence. But the Faithful should recognize where they are not wanted." Jiuseppe's lips curled in what could have been a smile had his eyes not been completely without humor.

Even Ginnevra's lack of diplomatic experience recognized the double meaning in that. She chose to ignore his veiled demand that she leave. "How fortunate for the city that your opinion is only one of many," she said, smiling sweetly. "Lord Jiuseppe, I don't believe I've introduced my companion, Eodan. He's a physician."

"Thank you again for the invitation," Eodan said, his deep voice lower than Jiuseppe's and as placid as a lowland stream. "What do the murals depict? They're quite lovely."

Jiuseppe's gaze flicked toward the ceiling, then back to Eodan. "I—they are representations of the creation of the world by Torun and Marena. The birth of the eight holy children. But I doubt any Faithful really cares about our mythology."

"I'm not of the Faithful," Eodan said. "And I'm interested in the different ways people believe."

Now Jiuseppe looked thoroughly confused. "Not of the Faithful? And you're her lover? You're no Torune, either."

"The world is a complex and beautiful place," Eodan said. "I don't think it's so strange that Ginnevra might care about understanding religions other than her own, no stranger than my own interest, at least."

Jiuseppe stared at Eodan in silence. "Enjoy the evening," he finally said, but in a distracted way that said he was thinking of something else. He nodded curtly and walked away.

Eodan gently pried Ginnevra's fingers off his arm. "So we weren't meant to come," he murmured. "Do we make a polite and inconspicuous exit?"

"I won't be chased away just because I didn't understand their subtle codes," Ginnevra said in the same low voice. "Jiuseppe all but confirmed he was behind the massacre."

"He expressed a desire to see all Faithful removed from Quinizelle. That's not the same thing."

"All right, he confirmed that he could have done it. He certainly hates the Faithful enough." Ginnevra rested her hand on Eodan's arm again, this time gripping loosely. "I want to learn more about Jiuseppe before this ceremony begins. Maybe we should separate. That will give us more opportunities to question people."

"All right," Eodan said. He sounded skeptical.

"What's wrong with that plan?"

Eodan shrugged. "Nothing, except...how sure are you of controlling your temper?"

Ginnevra tamped down on the surge of irritation his question roused. "I have self-control, Eodan. I'm not going to start a war in the middle of the Zuccare estate."

"I didn't mean to give offense," Eodan said.

"I'm not offended," Ginnevra lied. "I'll see you shortly." She walked away without waiting for his response.

Almost immediately, she wished they'd stayed together. The room was hot and overcrowded, filled with people dressed more nicely than Ginnevra who ignored her as she passed between them. Her awareness that this was not the social situation she was accustomed to made her want to shrink in on herself. She drew in a breath of warm air scented with flowery perfume and hot lamp oil and straightened her spine. It didn't matter that she wasn't socially adept or used to conversing with the wealthy and noble; she was a paladin, prime of the Blessed, and that gave her a rank at least as high as anyone else's.

She circled the room once, not trying to make conversation with anyone, just assessing her surroundings. She didn't intend to start a fight, but she liked to be prepared in case someone else did. The chamber wasn't furnished, and Ginnevra couldn't tell if that was always the case or if someone had removed all the furnishings for this gathering. Dozens of silver lamps hung on the walls well above head height, illuminating the wonderful ceiling without obscuring it. Above the lamps, rows of glass-paned windows reflected the lamp light, which turned them into sheets of gold.

She reached the far end of the room from the front door and paused, intrigued by what she found there. It looked like a wooden crate big enough to hold a couple of full-grown men bent over, but it was built with such elaborate care it might contain the treasures of a kingdom rather than anything ordinary. Ginnevra circled it without touching it and discovered it was a little more than waist high to her. A white marble basin bigger around than Ginnevra could encircle with both arms was set in the crate's top. Oddly, it had a drain with a metal plug in its base. The marble was pretty, with pinkish streaks matching the darker gray ones.

A whiff of a familiar scent reached her nose. Ginnevra leaned closer, still unwilling to touch the basin.

"You should stay away from the ceremonial bath," someone said. Ginnevra jerked upright and turned to find Pattero Alamanne at her left elbow. "Nobody here is crass enough to approach you in warning, but if you touch it, you might start a fight."

"Nobody crass enough but you?" Ginnevra's response was sharper than she'd wanted, but he'd startled her, and she was already on edge.

Pattero smiled. "I choose to trade on the relationship the king has impressed upon us. I would rather not see this ceremony disrupted."

"But you're not—" Ginnevra lowered her voice and nodded at the barely-visible lump of Pattero's grace.

"Taking new oaths doesn't mean I'm contemptuous of the old ones," Pattero said. "I no longer believe as I once did, but I grew up in the Torune religion and I respect how it shaped me. Which includes respecting its rituals." He took Ginnevra's arm and steered her away from the basin. "Though this one…you may find it disturbing."

"Does it have something to do with blood?" Ginnevra asked.

Pattero stopped and released her arm. "Then you know."

"I don't know anything. I smelled blood on that basin." Ginnevra looked over her shoulder to where Rainaldus now stood by the basin. The black look he gave her made Ginnevra shudder involuntarily. He clearly wished violence was an option. "I didn't touch it, so I don't know why the High Priest is so angry."

"This is one of our—the Torunes, I mean—one of their most sacred rituals," Pattero said. "Even your presence here could be considered a taint. Why did you come? You couldn't have believed yourself welcome."

Ginnevra blushed. "I was fool enough to take the invitation at face value."

"It doesn't matter. Just don't interfere, whatever you see." Pattero had his attention on Rainaldus as well. The High Priest sat cross-legged beside the basin and gripped something small in both hands. His eyes were closed, and his lips moved in silent speech or prayer. Ginnevra was struck by how closely Rainaldus resembled an anointed in that pose, though no male anointed would wear his hair that long.

"That's ominous," Ginnevra said. "How awful is this ritual?"

Pattero looked her way. "It's—"

"Thank you all for coming," Jiuseppe said, his voice ringing out above the noise of the crowd. "Today is my son Piettro's first birthday, and I ask you all to witness his dedication, as he takes his first step on the path that leads to Torun."

The crowd shifted forward, carrying Ginnevra and Pattero with it. Ginnevra ended up several ranks back from the basin, which relieved her mind. She didn't want to be close for whatever this was, not only because she'd usurp a spot some believer might want, but because she hadn't liked the sound of Pattero's warning. Her imagination flitted through a dozen possible scenarios involving blood, each more disturbing than the last. Animal sacrifice, perhaps? It wouldn't mean injuring the child, or Pattero would have said so immediately... unless he was so used to the dedication ceremony shedding a child's blood meant nothing to him.

A lovely woman with dark eyes emerged from the door behind Jiuseppe, dressed in a loose-fitting blue silk robe the color of the night sky that made her look to Ginnevra as if she was in mourning, though likely Torunes didn't associate that color with grief. She carried a naked child in her arms, and a little girl wearing a small version of the robe toddled close behind, her chubby hand twisted into the woman's skirt. The younger child had stuffed his fingers into his mouth and was drooling around them. Ginnevra didn't know anything about children; she was the youngest of her parents' brood and had grown up surrounded by older siblings and cousins, and paladins didn't have much contact with children as a rule. She hadn't thought a year-old child would be so large.

The woman handed the boy to Jiuseppe, who bounced him twice before putting his hands beneath the child's arms and lifting him high above his head. "My son, Piettro!" he shouted.

Everyone around Ginnevra, including Pattero, cried out some word Ginnevra didn't know. By the liquid sound of the polysyllables, she guessed it was in Sezarni. She held very still, not wanting to be a distraction even though no one was looking at her.

Jiuseppe lowered Piettro, who blinked at the gathered crowd and continued to chew on his fist. "High Priest, will you bless my son with Torun's gift?"

Rainaldus, who'd been standing behind the basin, walked with slow, measured steps around the wooden crate to stand in front of it. "As you have asked, so you will receive," he said. With the same slow deliberation, he unfastened the bone toggles of his robe until it lay open from neck to hem. Two gray-robed attendants, one of whom Ginnevra recognized as the man she'd confronted in the street, stepped behind Rainaldus and slid the robe off his shoulders and arms, then carried it to one side.

Beneath the robe, Rainaldus wore plain black trousers, roughly woven and tied with a hemp cord at the waist. His chest was lean and hairless and paler even than his face, though not by much. He tilted his head back and closed his eyes, breathing deeply enough that the rise and fall of his chest looked strained. Then he returned to his place behind the basin.

Ginnevra watched, fascinated, as Rainaldus raised both arms high and tilted his head back again. Thin white scars striped the undersides of his arms like hair-fine bracelets. Ginnevra suddenly had a strong suspicion of what Pattero had meant by "disturbing." She tried to step backward, but the crowd held her in place, and she felt equally strongly that she shouldn't disrupt the proceedings, however she might feel about them.

Rainaldus spoke a long string of words in Sezarni, then clasped his hands over his head and said, "By the holy children, show us, Torun, upon whose guidance Piettro Zuccare may rely, now and until the end of his life. *O volte minianame!*"

All the others clasped their hands together as Rainaldus did, but over their hearts, and repeated the words *O volte minianame*, not quite in unison so the effect was like hearing stones rolling downhill. Ginnevra's discomfort increased. She didn't belong here, and she couldn't help feeling guilty at intruding, even though she didn't believe their religion was anything but false tradition.

Rainaldus, without looking down, extended a hand to Jiuseppe. Jiuseppe withdrew a knife from his belt and handed it

164

over hilt first. Rainaldus tested the edge with his thumb. He held his other hand outstretched over the basin and once more spoke in Sezarni. Ginnevra was prepared for the moment he drew the knife's edge across the underside of his arm. Dark red blood sprang up immediately from what Ginnevra judged was a deep cut, but Rainaldus didn't flinch. He flexed his forearm, and the blood spilled faster, dripping into the basin.

More words in Sezarni, and Rainaldus made a second cut, just as deep and inches from the first. From Ginnevra's position, she couldn't see how much blood had accumulated in the marble basin, but it had to be more than a little. For the first time in her life, she felt queasy at the sight of blood.

Rainaldus switched the knife to his other hand and repeated both cuts on his right arm. Blood dripped into the basin. The smell of it made Ginnevra sick. No wonder the Lordagni of centuries past had taken up the Faith, if this was what Torun expected of them. Ginnevra was grateful that it wasn't the child they felt compelled to bleed. She wasn't sure she could stand by and watch that.

After what felt like forever, the blood flowed sluggishly, and Rainaldus moved his arms so they were no longer poised above the basin, though he didn't bind up the wounds. "Our blood runs through Torun's veins," he declared, "and his blood speaks to us. Show me the child."

Jiuseppe held Piettro under his arms again, this time at arm's length directly in front of him. One of the gray-robes gave Rainaldus a whisk brush and then stepped back. The brush wasn't much more than a handful of bristles bound at one end and stained dark at the other end. Rainaldus dipped the brush into the basin and stirred its still-unseen contents three times counter-clockwise, then three times clockwise. He tapped the bristles lightly against the edge of the basin. "By his blood we see the future," he said, and flicked the brush at Piettro.

The blood spattered the boy's face and chest with dozens of red dots, some much larger than the others. A few missed and struck Jiuseppe, who didn't flinch. Behind them, the woman closed her eyes and smiled as if she'd had a vision of eternity. Rainaldus stepped forward and with his right forefinger drew lines connecting several of the blood specks. Ginnevra became aware that everyone around her now leaned forward, watching Rainaldus intently, and that people here and there were whispering to their neighbors.

Rainaldus stepped back. Whatever he'd drawn in blood on the child's chest didn't look like anything real; if anything, it looked like a lot of straight lines connected at random. But the crowd's whispering grew louder and more excited, as if the spectacle were a race they all had a stake in.

"Lopone has accepted Piettro Zuccare," Rainaldus exclaimed.

Excited shouting filled the air, and all around her men and women clasped hands or pounded one another on the back. Ginnevra didn't dare move. Her earlier defiance of Quinizelle's customs had vanished. This was definitely something she shouldn't have been present for.

She scanned the room as best she could without moving, searching for Eodan. He wasn't within sight. Discouraged, she watched Rainaldus as he once more lifted his arms above his head, chanting more words she couldn't understand. Four gray-robes surrounded him, one of them backed nearly against the wooden crate. They, too, held their arms high, but their eyes were closed and they were swaying to a melody Ginnevra couldn't hear. Their fingers moved in complex patterns Ginnevra watched closely. She felt as if she were on the verge of understanding something important.

A rush of wind filled the room, bringing with it the smell of autumn in the mountains. Golden light ringed Rainaldus' arms in four places, glowing so brightly Ginnevra had to look away. She blinked to clear her vision and turned back in time to see Rainaldus wipe the remaining blood from his arms with a wet cloth.

The wounds were completely healed.

Ginnevra stepped forward once, came up against a couple of guests, and then with a muttered oath she pushed them aside and made her way through the crowd to Rainaldus. "What was that?" she demanded.

The gray-robes were helping Rainaldus back into his robe. The High Priest glared at Ginnevra. "It's not enough that you insinuate yourself into our sacred ceremonies, now you must challenge me on my faith?" He sounded angry, but his expression was triumphant, the look of a man who knows he has won.

"You healed yourself. I want to know how," Ginnevra said.

"Because my faith is false tradition, is that it?" Rainaldus buttoned his robe, not looking at Ginnevra. "Torun grants me his healing, paladin. Just as your Goddess grants hers. You would do well to abandon your assumptions."

"But—" Ginnevra managed to stop short of saying his religion was all lies and deceit. Based on what she'd seen, she wasn't sure anymore that was true.

"Quinizelle is blessed by Torun," Jiuseppe said. He'd given his son back to the woman, who now stood nearby, listening in. "We don't want the Faith here. We don't need the Faith here. You should take that information back to your Blessed instead of wasting your time trying to build unity where no one wants it."

Ginnevra closed her mouth. She bowed briefly to Jiuseppe, then to Rainaldus. "I appreciate your perspective," she said. "I don't agree with you, because I don't think anyone should be forced to leave their home because of their religion. And I will continue to do what I can to bring Torunes and Faithful together in harmony. Congratulations on your son's dedication." She turned on her heel and walked away.

The crowd had spread out, and men and women in Zuccare gray and gold moved through the room carrying trays. The tall, narrow glasses on the trays were filled with red wine that was uncomfortably close in color to Rainaldus' blood. Ginnevra smiled and shook her head at a man who offered her his tray. She hadn't learned any more about Jiuseppe, but she didn't care. She needed to get out of this place.

She stood and turned in a slow circle, searching for Eodan. He was a head taller than most men; he ought to be immediately visible. How unfortunate that she didn't dare climb on that wooden crate to survey the room.

A serving woman came up beside Ginnevra. "Drink, madama?"

Ginnevra turned, startled. It was Filippa.

FIFTEEN

Ginnevra automatically took a glass from Filippa's tray. "What—" she began, then thought better of asking stupid questions when she knew why Filippa was here. "How did you get in?" she asked instead.

"House Zuccare is always short of servants," Filippa said in a low voice. Her lips barely moved, but Ginnevra had a paladin's hearing and Filippa might as well have shouted. "Vinita Zuccare, Jiuseppe's wife, is a real harridan. She's convinced Jiuseppe is just a breath away from sleeping with the maids. I figure I only have a few more days inside before she sends me packing." Filippa smiled wickedly. "More than enough time."

Ginnevra lifted the glass to her lips to conceal their movement. "You've been here two days?"

"Three. Like I said, getting hired was pathetically easy. And the Zuccares see servants as furniture. I'm not sure why Vinita is so paranoid about her husband's fidelity, because he never so much as looks at the female servants." Filippa made a slow turn, pretending to scan the room for someone in need of a drink. "I need to move. Scout's circle?"

Ginnevra nodded and turned away.

She'd taken several steps toward the front door before Filippa's comment registered. Scout's circle. A company maneuver in which riding partners swept an area by circling in opposite directions counter to each other, describing a figure eight that covered all the ground between. The ache of memory throbbed through her, and she briefly squeezed her eyes shut against it. She tried to summon up outrage that Filippa had dared remind her of their shared past, but all she found was weary resignation. She couldn't afford to reject useful tactics out of anger or spite.

She circled the room, not meeting anyone's eyes in case someone else knew who she was and felt compelled to challenge her, and met Filippa near the center of the chamber. Filippa's tray was emptier than before. "Nobody ever looks at the servers," Filippa said. "I'll be glad to get out of here."

"Have you learned anything yet?" Ginnevra tilted her head back as if examining the mural.

"Servants always gossip more when their masters are cruel or demanding," Filippa said. "The Zuccare servants aren't at all secretive. But it's not good news. Jiuseppe didn't order the massacre."

Ginnevra closed her mouth on a surprised exclamation, keeping her attention on the ceiling painting to prevent a visible reaction. "Are you sure?"

"Four years ago, his brother Jiovanni was head of House Zuccare. Jiuseppe wasn't even in Quinizelle." Filippa again made her slow turn, pretending not to pay any attention to Ginnevra.

"He might still have been behind it. He's rabidly opposed to the Faith, and I'm sure he's capable of ordering an assassination to discredit it." The picture directly above was of a mouse hiding from a lion. It probably had great significance to a Torune. To Ginnevra, it just looked silly.

"Everything I learned before proved that it took great resources to arrange for the ambush. According to the servants, only the head of the house has access to its wealth. Everyone else is dependent on the generosity of that person. Jiuseppe couldn't have managed it." Filippa completed her turn and once more faced Ginnevra, though her gaze was fixed on someone beyond her.

Ginnevra pressed her lips together in frustration. "So it was Jiovanni. Move again."

She once more passed through the room, this time distracted enough by her thoughts that she didn't see any of the people who made way for her. If Jiovanni Zuccare was responsible instead of Jiuseppe, that was it for exposing a murderer. She couldn't demand justice from a corpse. Anger filled her, an unexpectedly fierce anger. She hadn't realized how much she wished she could prove someone guilty of using her company to conceal a murder.

She angled her path so she and Filippa met near the front door. "So that's it," she said. "Jiovanni is dead, which makes his guilt or innocence irrelevant."

She risked a glance at Filippa and was surprised at how fiercely pleased she looked. "There's something else," Ginnevra said.

"There are several servants—older men, naturally—who remember Jiovanni. All of them agree that he was thicker than mud and never did anything without consulting his brother." Filippa's smile broadened. "*And* one of those servants hinted that there'd been suspicious circumstances surrounding Jiovanni's death. I don't like to take him completely at his word, because he's the sort of man who sees conspiracies in everything, but all of that taken together paints a detailed and gruesome picture, don't you think?"

Ginnevra's breath caught. "Jiuseppe manipulates his brother into hiring mercenaries to attack and kill Dianetta and her retinue, and then Jiuseppe has Jiovanni murdered to cover his tracks. It's not proof, but it's worth following up on." She swiftly glanced around, but no one was looking their way and no one was close enough to overhear. "I'll see what I can find."

"I'll keep asking questions," Filippa said. "And yes, I'll be careful. I always am."

"I know," Ginnevra said. She didn't watch Filippa walk away.

She raised the wine glass to her lips again, but the scent of the red wine was resinous enough she knew she would hate the taste. Maybe Jiuseppe Zuccare didn't want his hospitality to encourage his guests to stay long. Well, Ginnevra was past ready to leave. It was time to make a serious effort to locate Eodan.

She inhaled deeply, searching for the werewolf musk, but there were too many bodies obscuring that scent. As good as her senses were, she couldn't track by scent the way Eodan could. Grinding her teeth in annoyance, she set out to search the crowd.

She reached the basin without seeing or hearing or even smelling Eodan's presence. The gray-robes were dismantling the structure, which came apart cleverly in sections that fitted together without nails. The man she'd confronted in the street knelt nearby and unscrewed a silver flask from beneath the basin, which was now empty of blood save for a thin pink film slicking its white surface.

On a whim, Ginnevra approached him. "Excuse me, sieur—"

The man's lips peeled back from his teeth in a snarl. "I'm not interested in talking to the likes of you."

Ginnevra had experienced too many shocks that night to be

daunted by one underling's hostility. "I was just wondering if the ceremony makes the High Priest's blood sacred. It was very impressive."

The man screwed the cap onto the flask and tucked it away inside his robe. "We don't discuss holy matters with heathens."

Ginnevra raised an eyebrow. "I thought you weren't afraid of me."

He jerked upright. "Of course I'm not!"

"You must be afraid I'll use your knowledge against you, or you'd be quick to challenge me with your beliefs." She probably shouldn't push him, but she was still on edge from not finding Eodan and needed a tiny victory.

"I wouldn't expect you to understand the ways in which life blood is holy to Torun," the man said. "We use it in many rituals—"

"That's enough, Ciorrus," Rainaldus said from behind Ginnevra. She'd heard someone approaching, so she didn't react except to turn to face the High Priest.

"I appreciate the lesson," she said. "Will you tell me now how you managed that healing?"

"I don't share holy secrets with those hostile to my religion," Rainaldus said. "It's enough to say I am servant to my God, and he rewards my service."

"All right," Ginnevra said. "I still think—" She realized she didn't want to complete that sentence. Her belief that the Torune religion was false, and its divine magic mere trickery and deceit, had trouble standing in the face of what she'd seen. Weariness swept over her, and she said, "Good night, High Priest. I apologize if I interfered."

She made her way through the thinning crowd toward the front door. She still saw no sign of Eodan. Maybe she should leave anyway. It wasn't as if he didn't know the way back to the hostel, and she didn't need an escort.

She stopped near the door to look at the mural again. The image just inside the door, the one every guest would see first upon entering, was a glowing male figure who stood surrounded by eight animals all bowing to him. The next picture showed the same male figure, but the animals now stood on hind legs like people, and they were all the same size, which made the mouse as big as the bear. Ginnevra knew the so-called holy children had been brought into being by Torun himself, not conceived with his wife Marena, but that was all she knew. What Marena thought of that—Ginnevra shook her head. Marena wasn't real, so she couldn't think anything.

Rapid footsteps drew her attention. "There you are," Eodan said, taking her by the upper arm. "Where have you been?"

He sounded exasperated, as if he hadn't been the one who'd disappeared when she needed him. Ginnevra snapped, "I should ask you that. I've been searching for you for an hour."

"We haven't been here that long," Eodan pointed out.

That made her angrier. "I suppose that makes everything all right, then? We haven't been here that long? What was so important you couldn't at least find me to tell me you'd be busy?"

Eodan released her. "Nothing," he said. "Obviously I should have followed you around like a lap dog instead of trying to learn more about Jiuseppe. Are you ready to leave, or did you want to go on fighting in public?"

"I'm not the one who started it," Ginnevra said, and stormed out the door and down the stairs.

She could hear Eodan following her and thought about speeding up to get away from him, but his legs were longer and that was a fool's errand. Even so, he stayed a few paces behind her, which was as good as leaving her alone. The night was cold, but she felt even colder than the brisk wind could account for, cold and empty and aching inside. She didn't know how that interaction had turned so hostile so quickly. She hadn't wanted to lash out at Eodan, but he'd made it sound like she was the one at fault when he'd been the one to disappear, and before she knew it, she'd said things, and he'd said things, and now...

The air was cold and clammy, and she wished she had her cloak. She didn't care if it made her look stupid. This city was awful, Torunes were awful, and she ought to leave it behind and tell the Blessed Quinizelle could go to hell on its own terms.

Ginnevra sighed. Awful or not, the city didn't deserve to fall into outright religious war, if only because of the many innocent people who only wanted to live their lives in peace. Which meant she couldn't go anywhere until she'd either succeeded or proved the goal was impossible.

To keep from remembering fighting with Eodan, she reviewed what she knew. Almost everyone in power in Quinizelle was Torune, and most of those either didn't care about the religious conflict or believed Torunes were in the right. Jiuseppe was at the head of that latter group and might have had Dianetta Napolle assassinated to put himself that much closer to ruling Quinizelle the way he believed it should be.

Or... A new idea struck. Maybe Jiuseppe hadn't wanted to rule, not four years ago at least. Maybe he'd wanted King Paolo more inclined to hate the Faithful and rid the city of them. But for all Paolo was prejudiced and hateful, he hadn't taken any drastic measures to eliminate the Faithful. That would explain why Jiuseppe had waited so long after Dianetta's death to make another move; if he had only wanted Quinizelle to be a Torune city-state, he might have been satisfied with Paolo making it happen. And when he didn't, Jiuseppe would have taken more steps. Like, for example, demanding to be made Paolo's heir.

Ginnevra recognized the hostel door a scant moment before she would have passed it in her distraction. She shoved it open, making it bang against the wall, and strode up the stairs without closing it behind her. She was angry and heartsick, but she didn't want to slam the door in Eodan's face.

In their room, she threw herself into one of the chairs and yanked off her boots, tossing them into a corner behind her. She didn't look up when Eodan entered. He silently took the chair beside her and removed his own boots with less force than she had. Now that they were in the quiet of their room, Ginnevra found her anger had cooled from a white-hot fury to a smoldering despondency. They'd never fought like this before, not in all five months they'd been together. She wasn't sure what that meant. Eodan had said more than once that werewolves mated for life, but suppose that didn't take into account being so angry with each other they couldn't come back from it?

She stood and walked to the window, which was a dull gray square Ginnevra's enhanced vision saw clearly. Curtains shrouded it from outside view, and she ran her fingers along their smooth surface before reaching behind herself to unlace the stiff bodice. It took her a moment to fumble along the tangle of ribbons to find their ends. She tugged, but the ribbons didn't come loose. Closing her eyes in frustration, she felt her way up to the knots and picked at them, wishing her nails were longer.

Hands gripped hers, moving them away. Eodan said nothing, but she felt the gentle tugs that said he was working the knots loose. Sharp anger coursed through her again, fury that he could presume she wanted his help or his closeness. He thought, after what he'd said, how dismissive he'd been, that he could make it all right with this small kindness?

In that moment, she saw herself jerking away from him. Saw him leaving the room in silence. Saw herself waiting the next day, and the next, for him to return. Saw herself finally leaving Quinizelle alone. Ginnevra didn't believe in inevitability, but she did believe the future was what you made of it, one choice at a time. And that small choice could lead to only one place.

So she stood still as his fingers untangled the knots and loosed the ribbon binding the bodice. With every passing moment, her anger ebbed until it was an echo of itself. Finally, he removed his hands, and Ginnevra lifted the bodice away and held it so the ribbons brushed the floorboards. She drew in a deep, unconstrained breath. "Thank you."

Eodan said nothing. Ginnevra took a few steps away from him and set the bodice on the clothespress at the foot of the bed. She felt emptied out, too devoid of emotion to even want to speak. She unfastened the tapes tying the overskirt around her waist and stepped out of it, letting it puddle on the floor. Then she sat on the edge of the clothespress and gathered up the hem of the kirtle, but didn't immediately pull it off over her head. Wealthy women were mad to wear so many different articles of clothing, but at least they stayed warm in winter.

Behind her, Eodan resumed his seat. The lack of rustling movement told her he hadn't yet undressed. Wealthy men wore as many layers as the women, something else Ginnevra thought was insane. Or maybe the point was to show off how much expensive fabric they could afford. Her overskirts and bodice were brocaded satin, her kirtle was silk, her chemise beneath the kirtle was the finest linen Ginnevra had ever felt, and yet she'd looked like a dowdy country girl beside some of those noblewomen at the dedication tonight.

She wriggled out of the kirtle and spread it on the bed, smoothing out wrinkles before folding it neatly. Buying it had been a mistake, because when would she ever have the opportunity or need for courtly clothing again? But the seamstress had been so enthusiastic, and an unsuspected, deeply hidden desire for femininity had taken Ginnevra by surprise. And then Eodan had looked at her—

A cold fist gripped Ginnevra's heart. She removed her chemise and put on the linen shirt, coarser than the chemise, and cotton drawers she usually slept in. A wintry chill had seeped into the room after nightfall, but she didn't climb into bed. Instead, she sat in the chair next to Eodan, folding her legs beneath her and hugging her knees.

Eodan shifted his weight. "You're cold," he said. "You should get under the blankets."

Ginnevra shrugged. "I'm not sleepy yet."

He ran a hand over his face, pushing back hair that had come free of its cord. In the dimness, his blue eyes appeared colorless, like the eyes of a specter, but no specter would have such well-defined features. "Ginnevra," he said. "Ginnevra, I apologize."

Ginnevra's heart lurched. "You're angry with me."

"I worried when I couldn't find you. I was afraid something had happened, that you'd started a fight—"

"How dare you!" Ginnevra shouted. "I'm not some out of control lunatic, Eodan. You keep acting like I'm going to fly into a rage and kill someone. What makes you think—"

Eodan closed his hand over Ginnevra's wrist, startling her into silence. "That's why I'm apologizing. You're right. I know how difficult this assignment is, and I know you face challenges you're not accustomed to in fulfilling it, and you've had some hostile encounters. But my fears about you losing control aren't rational. You are strong, and competent, and you care about making Quinizelle better for everyone, Torune and Faithful. And I shouldn't have doubted your character."

Ginnevra wanted to pull away from him, but she couldn't

without turning it into a dramatic rebuff. "I didn't know you felt that way."

"I want the world to see the woman I know." Eodan's hand tightened on her wrist briefly. "I suppose my second-worst fear is seeing you dismissed and belittled by people who only see you in a moment of weakness. But I shouldn't have let that fear dictate how I treated you."

Ginnevra closed her hand into a loose fist. "Second-worst fear?"

Eodan let go of her. "My worst fear," he said in a low voice, "is that you'll tell me to leave and mean it."

"I—" Ginnevra's heart pounded painfully again. "That's your worst fear?"

Eodan tilted his head back and let out a long, harsh stream of breath. "We're not married," he said. "By human standards, there's nothing keeping us together, no oaths, no words spoken by an anointed. And unless the Goddess changes her mind about accepting the worship of my kind, that's never going to change."

"You told me you consider me your mate."

"I do. But you're not a werewolf. My feelings aren't binding on you." Eodan shifted his weight again, this time looking at his knees. "If you decide to walk away, I can't stop you. If you tell me you want me gone, I will have to leave."

Ginnevra regarded him, how he sat slumped in his chair, his hands resting loosely on the armrests, his head bowed. Then she rose from her seat and knelt before him, taking his right hand in her left. "Marriage is important," she said. "My parents always said they felt their union was stronger because the Goddess blessed it, in the person of Revered Canzonelle. But that ceremony doesn't stop people cheating on their spouses or leaving each other. It doesn't stop love turning to hate. I was so afraid, tonight, that this fight was too much for us to get past, and I think maybe it almost was."

She pressed his hand to her cheek. His skin was dry, callused, and warmer than her own, and it sent a shock of heat through her body she welcomed. "I'm sorry," she said. "I was already on edge, and I overreacted to your words because I was frustrated and I wished you'd been with me all night. Please forgive me."

Eodan leaned forward, his fingers curving around her cheek. "I think, if we can forgive each other, we're not as badly off as we fear."

Ginnevra covered his hand with hers. "I know we can't be married yet," she said, "but you should know I consider myself bound to you by oath, just as surely as if an anointed said the words. However angry I get, I will never use the absence of marriage vows as a weapon against you. You are the one I love, now and forever."

Eodan smiled. "I'll hold you to that," he said, and leaned forward to kiss her.

They kissed in the quiet darkness, not holding each other or touching except where their lips met, fervent kisses that to Ginnevra felt like the seal on a promise rather than the prelude to more physical activities. She almost wasn't aware of the chill in the air. But after a long, blissful moment, a convulsive full-body shiver ran through her, and then she couldn't stop shivering. Eodan put his arms around her and held her close, warming her. "You paladins, thinking you're immune to the environment," he said. "Get into bed, beloved, and I'll join you shortly."

Ginnevra promptly dove beneath the heavy quilted comforter and wrapped her arms around her chest. Eodan removed his courtly attire and piled it on the clothespress rather than putting it away neatly. "It can wait until morning," he said when she commented, "and this is faster." He snuggled up beside her and took her in his arms. "Better?"

"Much." Lying with Eodan always felt like cuddling with her own personal fire, but one that warmed rather than burned. Ginnevra's shivering soon subsided. "I don't want to fight with you again," she said. "Can we promise never to argue like that from now on?"

Eodan chuckled. "I think the nature of life means we'll have other arguments. The best we can do is promise not to let those arguments destroy what we have."

"I can promise that." Ginnevra closed her eyes and breathed in the werewolf musk. "So much happened tonight. I wanted you with me—I don't mean that as complaint, understand, just that I'm used to having your perspective on things."

"I can tell you right now that ceremony was deeply disturbing. I don't know what it's like for humans, but werewolves don't do blood magic unless it's in the service of the Bright One."

"I was more disturbed by how High Priest Rainaldus' wounds healed. That wasn't sleight of hand or trickery, but it can't possibly be Torun's power." Ginnevra shivered again.

"Still cold?"

"No, unsettled. I know Rainaldus couldn't have drawn on the Goddess's power, but what else is there?" Ginnevra nestled in closer. "If Torun is a real god, don't you think the Goddess would have said something?"

"I don't know that much about how your religion works. Maybe She doesn't think humans need to know that kind of thing. Or maybe Torun is in opposition to Her, and She wants to keep that opposition a secret."

"I suppose that's possible, but it feels unlikely, given that She makes no secret of Her animosity toward Her Bright Sister." Ginnevra yawned. "I'm too tired to think about it anymore.

Tomorrow will be soon enough for pondering theological questions."

"I almost wish they were questions you could answer with your sword," Eodan said. "We might see more progress."

"I haven't ruled that out yet," Ginnevra said.

CHAPTER

SIXTEEN

T he summons from King Paolo came the following morning as Ginnevra and Eodan were dressing. Ginnevra read it aloud once the messenger was gone. "'The paladin Ginnevra Cassaline is commanded to wait upon his majesty King Paolo Napolle at ten o'clock of the morning this day.' I don't know what to be more annoyed at, the short notice or the fact that he thinks he can command me."

"To me, that sounds like he wants to put you at a disadvantage so he doesn't have to admit that Abraciabene has him cornered," Eodan said.

"That's reasonable, I suppose." Ginnevra tossed the note on the unmade bed. "I wish I were more certain of what I intend to tell him. Or, actually, certain of his response. I couldn't tell the first time where his loyalties lie. If he's more committed to his religion than to his city, there might not be a solution to this mess."

"You mean a solution you can be happy about," Eodan said. "The Blessed's instructions are the ultimate solution."

"I know." Ginnevra sighed. "I thought about communicating with her, asking for advice, but I feel that would be like going crying to my mother for help. Nothing that's happened has invalidated my instructions. It's not the Blessed's fault I don't like them."

Eodan took her hand and squeezed it lightly. "You're compassionate, and you care about the well-being of strangers. That makes you better suited to this task than someone who would blindly follow instructions that will make the situation worse. If you have to tell the king Abraciabene will no longer buy silver from Quinizelle, it will be because you've exhausted all the other possibilities. That's all anyone can ask."

"It's hard not to wonder if someone else might have been better for this job." Ginnevra sat to put her boots on. "But that verges on blasphemy. Besides, nobody else would have the interest or inclination to seek out Dianetta Napolle's murderer, and after talking to Filippa last night, I feel more certain that we can bring Jiuseppe to justice."

"Assuming he was his brother's puppet master."

"Right." Ginnevra donned her cloak and slung her sword over her shoulder. "We'll get food, and then I'll see what the king wants." She sighed again. "Let's hope he's in a reasonable mood."

When she arrived at the palace an hour later, Pattero was there, not in the courtyard but on the street outside the gate and portcullis. Ginnevra's impulse to joke about his eagerness died when she saw the look on his face, set and hard, his jaw rigid enough to use as a nutcracker. He didn't say anything, merely nodded in greeting and indicated she should follow him.

They crossed the courtyard in silence, with Pattero setting a ground-eating pace Ginnevra had to stretch to keep up with despite having longer legs than he. When they entered the inner keep and were past the first set of guards, she said, "Is something wrong, Lord Pattero?"

"Nothing that concerns you," Pattero said sharply.

This rudeness coming from someone Ginnevra had judged to be almost terminally polite surprised her. She opened her mouth to push for a more enlightening answer, then shut it again. Her curiosity didn't entitle her to pry into Pattero's affairs, and since she had no reason to believe his bad mood had anything to do with her assignment, she should mind her own business.

They crossed the gray and black courtyard and halted at the same short corridor Ginnevra had seen before. She unslung her sword without being prompted and set it against the wall, behind the guards. Pattero watched in silence without meeting her eyes, his expression still angry. Ginnevra didn't acknowledge him. She strode down the hall and pushed open the door, which this time stood ajar.

The guards inside the room stood further to alert when she entered, though neither of them looked at Ginnevra. The guard on the left shifted his weight enough to make his halberd quiver, as if both man and weapon were afraid and didn't want to show it. Ginnevra ignored him. A frightened guard was a guard who might overreact and get other people killed, so it was better she not do anything to increase his fear.

King Paolo once again sat behind the table, facing Ginnevra. Ginnevra approached and sat without waiting for an invitation. He already knew she opposed him to some extent; time for him to remember she wasn't a supplicant or a subject.

The king interlaced his fingers and rested them on the table. Ginnevra observed the table was otherwise completely clear of papers or books or pens. She couldn't remember if it had been that way on her first visit. If it was a sign that the king intended to be recalcitrant—but there was no point borrowing trouble.

"Prime Cassaline," King Paolo said. "You challenged us the last time you attended upon us. We do not appreciate being told what to do, particularly by a representative of a religion opposed to ours."

"I'm sorry if you took my request as an order, your majesty," Ginnevra said. "I recognized that you have resources to investigate the situation in Quinizelle that I lack. And I did you the courtesy of assuming you care about the well-being of *all* your subjects." Politeness was fine in its place, but Ginnevra had no intention of letting the king control the conversation.

King Paolo's lips pressed together briefly, and his knuckles whitened. "And what has your investigation revealed?" he said. "Or did you mean us to do all your work for you?"

"Not at all, your majesty. I have evidence that the religious strife in Quinizelle is being incited by both Torunes and Faithful." Ginnevra hesitated, then decided she could hardly make the king like her less, and his opinion of her was irrelevant anyway. "I believe both Hallowed Nevante and High Priest Rainaldus are to blame for encouraging their followers to fight the opposition, so to speak."

The king's scowl deepened. "And it was Hallowed Nevante who struck the first blow."

"I don't know, your majesty. I couldn't find out where it started. But I'm not sure it matters, not if both sides are committed to making an end." Ginnevra felt a twinge of guilt at saying this. If Pattero was right, it was Faithful who had struck the first blows, but since Ginnevra couldn't prove Hallowed Nevante had been behind those blows, she didn't want to lay blame at her feet.

"You would have High Priest Rainaldus humble himself when he was not the first to attack?" King Paolo's voice rose in pitch enough to make him sound outraged.

"I *said* I don't know that's how it went, your majesty," Ginnevra replied, keeping a level tone. "And I think both the High Priest and the Hallowed should set the example for their followers by acknowledging their own culpability in this situation. It doesn't have to come to one humbling him or herself before the other."

"But one must go first," King Paolo said. "And we do not believe it is the High Priest's duty to be that one."

Ginnevra's heart sank. "You want Hallowed Nevante to make amends before High Priest Rainaldus."

"We believe that is fair. The Faith should show its willingness to respect the Torune faith." The king's voice had returned to normal, but his knuckles still showed the white of tension.

"That doesn't suggest two religions living side by side as equals," Ginnevra said. "You want the Faith subordinate to the Torune religion."

"The Torunes are in the majority in Quinizelle. It is only reasonable that they hold a higher status." King Paolo smiled, a thin-lipped little smile Ginnevra wished she could slap off his face. "As the Faith is predominant elsewhere in the Lordagne."

Ginnevra stared him down. King Paolo hadn't been rude, but his smug pleasure at making demands Ginnevra couldn't challenge grated on her nerves. Well, she wasn't there to promote religious equality, just to stop persecution. "Then I suppose you should ask Hallowed Nevante to make a statement."

The king shook his head. "We believe it is you who should instruct Hallowed Nevante to respond," he said, still smiling. "We cannot make it a royal command without inflaming anti-Torune sentiment further, given that we are Torune ourselves. Doing so would mean imposing our will on another faith. So much the better if Hallowed Nevante came to this conclusion on her own."

Ginnevra suppressed a desire to scream out her frustration. "I can ask her," she said, "but even the command of a Hallowed is not perfectly binding on the Faithful. What will you do if the strife continues?"

"We believe it will not come to that."

"That's not good enough." Ginnevra leaned forward. "I am here to stop the religious persecution, your majesty, not to see the leaders of two faiths exhort their people. It is *you* who bear the ultimate responsibility for peace in your city-state, and it is *you* who Abraciabene will hold responsible for the treatment of its Faithful. I need your assurance that if the words of the Hallowed and the High Priest aren't enough to stop the violence, you will step in."

King Paolo pushed his chair back and stood. "You will not make demands of us," he said.

Ginnevra rose as well. "I shouldn't have to, your majesty."

The king's lips compressed again. He gave a dismissive wave. "Convince Hallowed Nevante to stop her people aggressing on Torunes. Then we will talk further."

"And you will instruct High Priest Rainaldus to do the same," Ginnevra said.

"When the Faithful stop attacking, we are certain the High Priest will not need to be commanded." King Paolo stared Ginnevra down. "You are dismissed."

Ginnevra clenched her teeth together to stop herself shouting accusations at the king. With a curt nod, she turned and stormed out of the room.

For the few steps it took her to reach the end of the hall, she imagined what she might have done differently. The Blessed hadn't said she was to abase herself, and Ginnevra wished she'd threatened the king with the economic sanctions she had authority to impose. He wouldn't have been so smug or so quick to demand concessions then.

She picked up her sword and examined it rather than slinging it over her shoulder, not for flaws or possible damage, but for the sake of what it represented. True, it ate at her to be a supplicant in even a small way, particularly to someone who so gleefully wanted her religion in a subordinate position, but the goal was freedom from persecution for everyone in Quinizelle, and what harm did it do to be the first to apologize? Unless it gave the other person power over you. Ginnevra silently snarled. She would talk to Hallowed Nevante, and worry about the future once that was done.

Pattero still looked thunderously angry when she reached his side. He turned without a word and led her back across the courtyard.

When they were halfway across, Pattero came to a halt. Ginnevra looked at him again; his angry expression had disappeared, and he looked uncertain. "Is something wrong, Lord Pattero?" Ginnevra asked.

"I don't know," Pattero said. His attention was on one of the other halls opening off the courtyard. With a slower stride, he set off again, changing direction. Ginnevra now saw a woman standing in that hall, dressed in court finery with her hands clasped in front of her. She watched their approach, her face composed and neutral, but the jewels dangling from her earlobes trembled.

When they were near enough for quiet speech, the woman said, "My lady wishes to speak with the paladin."

"Prime Cassaline is to go nowhere except where she is directed by the king," Pattero said. "Your mistress knows that."

"My lady chooses to pay the price if the king is angry," the woman said. "And you know he is never angry with her."

"That is not a given," Pattero said, but he sounded resigned. "Very well. Where is she?"

"Follow me," the woman said.

This new hall was dimly lit by lanterns trimmed to burn low. They cast their flickering light over long rows of portraits depicting dour men and haughty women, all of them garbed in fine clothes in styles ranging over a century. Ginnevra's boots sent up echoes off the polished wooden floor and the walls covered with yellow brocaded satin that gleamed gold where the light struck them. Pattero's softer soled shoes made as little noise as whatever the woman wore; her feet were invisible beneath her full skirts.

At the end of the hall, an ornately carved door matching the ornately carved frames of the portraits stood. Its brass latch was shaped like a strand of ivy leaves. The woman set her hand to the latch. "My lady trusts your discretion," she said, and pushed the door open. Birdsong twittered within, and bright sunlight painted a wedge across the floor at Ginnevra's feet.

Ginnevra wanted to protest. Discretion was all very well—the Dark Lady cherished secrets, and honored those who kept them— but suppose this woman's mistress was someone Ginnevra shouldn't speak to, someone who might ruin her chances of getting King Paolo to cooperate? Reasoning that it was too late to protest, she followed the woman inside, with Pattero close behind.

From the sound of birds and the brightness of the light, she had expected the door to lead outside, possibly to a walled garden. Instead, Ginnevra found herself in a warm, slightly muggy room that smelled strongly of oranges and green growing things. Wide-bladed grasses and flowering shrubs grew in planters lining the walls and making a path through the room; miniature trees in pots, lindens and aspens and orange trees, marked where the path turned corners.

Colorful, tiny birds like spun sugar confections perched in the trees, their pastel blues and yellows and pinks bright against the green and gold. A larger bird, this one richly colored in bands of green and yellow, took flight from a tree near Ginnevra's head and soared across the ceiling, which was marvelously constructed of clear glass set in an iron framework. Ginnevra gaped in wonder.

"They are astonishing, aren't they?"

Ginnevra dragged her attention from the beautiful ceiling to face the woman who approached her now. She was small, with delicate features that were beautiful mostly in their daintiness, and she wore the same kind of courtly clothing her attendant did, but on her it looked natural instead of affected the way it did on every other woman Ginnevra had seen at court or at Jiuseppe's ceremony. Ginnevra couldn't imagine this woman in breeches and shirt.

The woman stopped in front of Ginnevra. "Thank you for coming," she said. "I'm Benitta Napolle. And I hope you are the answer to my prayers."

SEVENTEEN

"Lady Benitta," Ginnevra said automatically. Her mind had already raced ahead, coming up with reasons why the king's wife would want to speak to her, and speak to her secretly. Ginnevra had no doubt no one but the four of them knew Ginnevra was here.

Benitta smiled. "You're confused. That's understandable. Let's start at the beginning, shall we? It's essential Paolo not know I spoke to you. He is afraid of what you represent, and it would hurt him dreadfully to know of this meeting."

"I don't understand," Ginnevra said. "Why hurt? I can see why he is afraid of me, but I don't have the power to do anything to him personally, even if I wanted to."

"Because he trusts me to be as one with him in all his dealings, and he would see my speaking to you behind his back as a betrayal." Benitta gestured. "Come this way."

Ginnevra didn't move. "Then he will be angry with you if he finds out. I can't allow that, my lady."

Benitta chuckled, a low, rich sound deeper than her speaking voice. "Paolo is never angry with me. He turns his emotions inward—anger, fear, sorrow. It's not the best reaction for a king, but better that than a ruler who flies into rages at every slight, real or imagined. Please. Let's sit. I have only half an hour free before my absence will be noticed." Again she gestured, and Ginnevra followed her along the path.

They passed between waving grasses that brushed Ginnevra's legs, turned a corner, and stopped where the path opened up into a small paved circle clear of plants. In its center stood a round table and two chairs, all three of wrought iron painted white. A tiled mosaic covered the tabletop, its deep blue and red and purple tesserae glimmering in the sunlight like pools of liquid pigment.

Benitta sat and indicated Ginnevra should take the other seat. Benitta's attendant took up a position behind Benitta; to her surprise, Pattero stood behind Ginnevra's left shoulder. She was too curious about what that meant to be concerned about having him at her back, especially since he was unarmed.

"I apologize for the lack of refreshments, but bringing food for two people to this place would raise suspicions," Benitta said. "And, as I said, it's essential this meeting not be discovered."

"Then, if we're being frank," Ginnevra said, "what exactly do you want from me, my lady?"

Benitta slipped her hand between the folds of her voluminous overskirt and withdrew something small on a silver chain. "A pocket, sewn into the side seam," she said when Ginnevra raised an eyebrow. "They're very practical. I'm sure soon every skirt will have them."

She opened her hand and displayed an irregularly shaped piece of obsidian about an inch across on its longest side, wrapped in silver wire and dangling from the chain. An obsidian grace.

Ginnevra sucked in a startled breath. "You're Faithful." Reflexively, she shot a glance at the attendant, who looked not at all surprised or horrified.

Benitta nodded. "I was sanctified over three years ago, after Pattero's conversion. I wanted to know why he stopped being angry all the time. Then I was curious about the differences between my religion—the Torune religion—and the Faith. The simplicity of what it teaches appealed to me, and..." She shrugged, and put the grace back in her pocket.

"But King Paolo hates the Faith," Ginnevra blurted out.

Pink tinged Benitta's small cheeks. "Will you indulge me in a story?" she said. "Once there was a young woman who met a man very different from herself. He was charming, and attractive, but the young woman didn't care for him. She thought she wanted a different life for herself. Then she came to know him, how his charming, confident demeanor concealed pain and fear. She saw that he needed her. That he loved her. And gradually, her feelings changed."

Pattero shifted, the fabric of his doublet rustling against itself. Benitta's gaze flicked to him, then settled back on Ginnevra. "This young woman had a secret," she continued. "Something the man would be angry about and hurt by if she told him. It was a secret that mattered deeply to her, so she decided she would tell her love, to give him the opportunity to accept her as she was. But when she met him intending to reveal all, he surprised her by asking her to marry him. And the young woman's resolve failed her. She agreed to become his wife. And she kept her secret hidden in her heart."

Ginnevra brushed her fingers across the black pearl she wore at her throat. "You've been married for two years," she said. "That's a long time to keep a secret."

"Two years, six months, three days," Benitta said. "At first, I thought it would be easy. I was new to the Faith and I had no idea how much its ceremonies and traditions mattered to my everyday worship. But...I couldn't wear my grace without Paolo noticing. I couldn't celebrate the dark of the moon. I sneak out occasionally to meet with Revered Bariatte, for religious instruction and guidance, but it's dangerous. Anyone who knows me and saw me there would tell Paolo, and that would be far worse than if he learned the truth of my religion from me."

"Then... I'm sorry, I still don't understand. What do you need that I might be the answer to your prayers? Do you want me to stand with you when you tell King Paolo the truth? Because I can tell you right now that would be a mistake."

Benitta shook her head. "I want you to bless me to have a child," she said.

Ginnevra blinked. "You want *what?*"

"Revered Bariatte taught me that faith in the Goddess works miracles." Silver tears streaked Benitta's cheeks. "My faith isn't enough. I hoped the faith of a paladin might be."

"I—" Ginnevra's thoughts raced again. "I wouldn't know where to begin. For one thing, petitioning the Goddess for a child is like asking for a destiny. So I can't do that."

"But you can bless me that my womb will be fertile. You can bless me with strength and health." Benitta clasped Ginnevra's hand in both of hers. "I know the Goddess will listen to one of Her own."

A memory rose up, Eodan telling her what had come of his examination of Benitta, and the memory was so strong Ginnevra recognized it as the Goddess giving her a nudge. "Lady Benitta, I need to tell you something privately," she said. "Just the two of us."

"Sephronia keeps all my secrets," Benitta said, "and I know all of Pattero's. You can say whatever you like in front of them."

"Trust me, this is something for your ears alone," Ginnevra said. "If you want to tell them, that's fine, but this is about more than just you."

Benitta glanced up at Sephronia. "Wait by the door," she said. Sephronia immediately walked away. Pattero hesitated, then followed her.

Ginnevra waited until the two were obscured by the trees and grasses, then leaned in close. "You were visited by my companion Eodan," she said. "The physician."

"He's why I thought to speak to you. He told me about traveling with you, and the stories were so interesting I didn't mind the discomfort of the examination." Benitta wiped her eyes. "Is there something wrong with me? I thought he was the sort of man who wouldn't keep a secret from me for my own good, but maybe I was wrong."

"You weren't wrong." Ginnevra took a deep breath. "Eodan thinks the problem, the reason you haven't conceived, isn't a flaw in you. He thinks it may be King Paolo who is infertile."

Benitta's eyes widened. "No," she said. "No, that can't be right. It has to be me."

"Why do you say that?" Ginnevra asked.

Benitta rose and paced restlessly in a tight circle beside the table. "Because he will take it personally," she said. "He'll blame himself for being less of a man, and I don't know if I can convince him—oh, this is a nightmare." She grabbed the back of the chair, gripping it like it was her worst enemy's neck.

"I'm sorry," Ginnevra said, feeling more awkward than ever before in her life. "Eodan wasn't sure—that is, he thought there was a good chance it wasn't you—but I'm sure that's why he didn't tell you. He doesn't like to diagnose anything when he's not confident."

Benitta shoved the chair away with such force its iron feet

made a *skree* against the stones of the path. "This is my fault," she said, anger distorting her lovely features. It was like seeing a kitten in a rage, except that would have been funny and there was nothing amusing about Benitta just then. "I should have told him the truth—this is the Goddess punishing me—"

"Stop," Ginnevra said, rising to tower above her. "That's not how it works. We make our choices, step by step, and those steps build our future. Nothing about what you chose made you or King Paolo incapable of having children. That's the challenge the Goddess gave you. And you won't disappoint Her in anything you do unless you choose to blame that challenge on someone or something else."

Benitta sagged. "I can't tell him. It will break his heart."

"You shouldn't tell him unless you have proof. Otherwise it's just being cruel." Ginnevra's heart ached. She'd never imagined feeling sympathy for the king in any way, but seeing him through his wife's eyes roused her compassion.

"Sit," she told Benitta, and resumed her seat. "I don't really understand how the human body works. That's Eodan's realm. But I believe in miracles. I can pray with you, and that might help, but..." Another thought came to mind, and before she could tell herself it was stupid, she said, "I think you need to tell King Paolo about your religion. He needs to know you're Faithful."

Benitta paled. "I can't. Not after so much time has passed. He'll think I deceived him—because I deceived him, of course. I can't do it. If he hates me—"

"I know it's hard, but you can't be fully united with your husband if there are secrets between you." Words poured out of Ginnevra from some source deep within her. She'd felt this way before, this sense of rightness, and she let herself swim in it, ignoring the part of her that was afraid of being lost. "You were right before when you intended to tell him before he proposed. He needs to be able to choose for himself, not have you choose for him."

"I can't," Benitta repeated. "Between this, and the fact that I haven't had children... he'll see an opportunity to divorce me. It won't matter that I'm not the infertile one."

"You don't know what the future holds. That's your fear talking. Have faith that the choices both of you make will lead somewhere wonderful." Ginnevra clasped Benitta's unresisting hand. "I think you can do that."

Benitta closed her eyes and let out a long, deep breath. She pulled away from Ginnevra's loose grip. "I have to go."

"But you'll tell him, won't you?"

"I don't know. Maybe." Benitta rose and straightened her skirts. "I'll consider it."

Ginnevra figured that was the best she would get from Benitta. She bowed politely and made her way through the plants to the door, where Pattero and Sephronia still waited.

Outside, Pattero said, "You didn't say anything to hurt her, did you?" His earlier hostility had vanished.

"Not on purpose," Ginnevra said. "I told her the truth, or at least my best guess as to the truth. It's up to her how she reacts to it."

Pattero nodded. "I've been telling her she needs to tell Paolo her true religion for months," he said, as if that was the right response to Ginnevra's words. "She shouldn't go on pretending to follow a different religion. It's not good for either of them."

"Do you think King Paolo would cast her off for being Faithful?" Ginnevra lowered her voice, though they had reached the courtyard and the guards were gone.

"I don't know. I hope not. It's been four years since Dianetta died, enough time to blunt the pain. At least, it has for me—Paolo doesn't have the Goddess's guidance to heal his spirit. Even so, he ought to see that the present is more important than the past. But I don't know him well enough to be sure he loves Benitta as much as she loves him." Pattero put a hand on Ginnevra's arm, bringing her to a halt just inside the stained glass hall. "You're a paladin. Is Benitta under condemnation for living a lie?"

The question made Ginnevra uncomfortable. "I'm not qualified to make that judgment. But if she meets often with Revered Bariatte, I'm guessing not. He wouldn't agree to keep seeing her if he thought she was an unrepentant sinner."

"I hope you're right," Pattero said.

PATTERO ESCORTED Ginnevra through the gate and to the end of the raised causeway. "May I ask how things are progressing, or is that paladin business?" he asked. His earlier bad mood had evaporated completely.

"It's confidential, at least for now." Even if she hadn't been sure she shouldn't reveal the substance of her argument with the king, Ginnevra didn't see how it would help matters to have it be known that the highest authorities of the city's two religions were behaving like spoiled toddlers fighting over the same scrap of blanket. "I can tell you I think we're closer to a solution that will stop the fighting." That was nearer to a lie than Ginnevra liked. She chose to think of it as anticipatory optimism.

Pattero looked skeptical. "If that solution requires High Priest Rainaldus to back down, I don't know that you'll ever be close enough. He is utterly convinced of the rightness of his position and sees himself as a lone beacon against the forces of darkness— darkness, in his worldview, being a bad thing."

"I hope he can be convinced to be reasonable," Ginnevra said.

"Please, don't tell me how forlorn a hope that is. I still have a job to do."

Pattero smiled and saluted her, a courtier's salute of right hand pressed flat against chest and a shallow bow. "I wish you strength and wisdom, my lady."

He hadn't said "good luck" that time, Ginnevra realized as she walked away from the palace. She wondered what it must be like for him, concealing his religion so thoroughly. That couldn't be right, even by the standards of a Goddess who delighted in a well-kept secret. Religion was supposed to guide and support you, not be a burden you couldn't reveal to anyone.

The sky was clear for once, with only a few white clouds drifting high above, not the sort of clouds that promised rain. The sun's bright radiance transformed Quinizelle, making it seem cheerful rather than dour. Still, Ginnevra was grateful for her cloak; the sunlight had little warmth to it, and the cool, crisp mountain air made her cheeks tingle.

But she seemed to be the only one who thought the day less than perfect. More people thronged the streets than before, and it seemed every other plaza hosted an impromptu market filled with shouting, cheerful people. Even Ginnevra's appearance, in plate mail and cloak with the sword's hilt bobbing above her shoulder, didn't do more than part the crowds. She got the usual stunned stares, but no one accosted her or shouted rude remarks. Her despondent mood lifted slightly. If only she didn't have to talk to Hallowed Nevante...

The crowds thinned before she reached the sanctuary, but she'd already noticed that few people used this street who didn't have actual business there. Ginnevra walked around the corner to the stable and greeted Dauntless. The blue roan hurried forward to meet her, warming her heart with his eagerness. "I've missed you, you great ninny," she whispered as she stroked the side of his face. "I promise we won't be here much longer." She hoped that was a promise she could keep.

Inside, the back rooms of the sanctuary smelled deliciously of spicy sausage and pasta, reminding Ginnevra that it was nearly noon. She hurried through the corridors and up the stairs, passing a couple of acolytes who gaped at her, until she reached the ritual chamber. Again, no one was there. Well-concealed doors painted a flat black to match the walls surrounded the chamber, their lines nearly invisible in the low light. Ginnevra eyed the decorations above each one and chose the door topped by a painting of the dark moon.

When she knocked on it, someone's muffled voice bade her enter. She pushed the door open on a room that reminded her of Hallowed Currade's office back in Devoyenne, complete with eternity fountain and desk. Hallowed Nevante sat behind the desk, reading from a leatherbound gospel. The black leather gleamed as if new, but the edges of the pages were worn, their gilding missing, and Ginnevra judged this was actually a much-used book that had been re-bound.

Hallowed Nevante set the gospel aside on its open face. "Is there something I can do for you, prime?"

"I hope so," Ginnevra said. "May I sit?" She didn't want to sit, because sitting in armor was uncomfortable, but standing for this discussion, looming over the Hallowed like a harbinger of doom, was a bad idea.

Nevante gestured at the room's other chair. Ginnevra sat, perching on its edge. "I've just spoken with King Paolo. We agree that both Faithful and Torune have been responsible for the religious persecution currently plaguing Quinizelle."

"That is an oversimplification," Nevante said. "The Torunes outnumber the Faithful. They have greater power over us."

"That may be, Hallowed, but the point is that matters have escalated past whatever beginnings might have started this."

"Then the king believes the Faithful should submit meekly to being beaten, their homes and businesses vandalized?" Nevante's voice rose to a pitch not quite a shout. "He cannot consider himself a just ruler if he allows some of his subjects to persecute others."

"King Paolo recognizes that it is not right for either religion to attack the other," Ginnevra said. Her heart was beating fast the way it did when she was about to go into battle, and she made her voice remain calm despite her impulse to shout back at Nevante. "But he does not want to step in and make demands on religious matters. He believes the king should remain neutral."

"Does he." Nevante's voice lowered. She sounded skeptical. Since Ginnevra had more or less made that up, Ginnevra couldn't blame her for doubting it. But based on the conversation Ginnevra had had with the king, she felt safe making those claims, particularly since she *was* certain the king didn't want any part of this mess.

"I assure you King Paolo wants a peaceful resolution," she said. "But he depends on you and High Priest Rainaldus to take the first steps. He requests that you make a proclamation to the Faithful, instructing them to stop attacking Torunes and to stop retaliating for attacks on them by Torunes."

Nevante shot to her feet. "Meaning we are to lower ourselves first? To concede that we were at fault? Impossible!"

"Someone has to go first, when it's a reconciliation, Hallowed Nevante," Ginnevra said, remaining seated. "King Paolo believes—"

"This is *not* the king's idea," Nevante said. Her chest heaved with rapid, angry breathing. "This is the work of Rainaldus, that thrice-cursed bastard. He wants the Faith subservient to him. Well, we will not stand for it."

"It isn't like that," Ginnevra said, uncomfortably aware that that was probably a lie. "King Paolo simply wants a show of good faith on both sides, and he's asked that the Faithful be the first—"

"No." Nevante's face was red with anger. "No. Unacceptable. If he's so committed to a show of good faith, let the Torunes be the ones to back down first."

Ginnevra's heart sank. "But the Faithful were the first to strike, according to my sources. Don't you think—"

"To hell with your sources," Nevante snarled. "We are a persecuted minority in Quinizelle. If we abase ourselves, if we admit to any culpability in this war, the Torunes will use that as an excuse to go on persecuting us. Rainaldus will claim that we deserve what we get, and the king will support him. There is no way I will order my people to give in unless the Torunes back down first."

"Hallowed Nevante," Ginnevra began.

"It will not happen," Nevante said. "I would rather see the Faithful endure holy suffering for the rest of time than require them to abase themselves before their persecutors. You can take that to the king, Prime Cassaline."

Ginnevra recognized the set to the Hallowed's jaw as sign that further argument was pointless. She stood. "Hallowed Nevante, this means actual religious war," she said. "Please reconsider. Without your cooperation, I will have to invoke economic sanctions, and everyone in Quinizelle will suffer. Please."

"If you have the authority to force King Paolo to do the right thing, I wonder that you haven't used it yet." Nevante glared at Ginnevra. "You should consider where your loyalties lie, prime." She put an emphasis on the final word that made Ginnevra's cheeks warm with anger.

"My loyalties are to seeing the persecution stop," she said. "I don't want the Faithful hurt for what they believe. I also don't think they're entitled to hurt others in the name of defending the Faith. That's not what the Goddess expects from us."

"You don't get to tell me what the Goddess wants," Nevante said.

Ginnevra bowed swiftly and left the room.

She stormed down the stairs, glad not to encounter anyone she might snarl at. She knew half her anger was because she agreed with Nevante in one respect: Rainaldus would never admit to guilt, would not instruct his followers to stop the persecution, and would use any concessions from Nevante or the Faithful as a weapon against them. And it infuriated her that she had let King Paolo maneuver her into a position where she would be the instrument of that plan.

She sped through the stable without a nod to Dauntless—she didn't like inflicting her ire on her horse, even indirectly—and stomped through the streets, holding her sword so it didn't swing into her legs. Usually that was a minor irritation, easily ignored, but today it would inflame her mood further.

People got out of her way rapidly now, casting wary or even scared glances over their shoulders as they hurried to the side. Ginnevra didn't care anymore if she scared random pedestrians. If Torunes felt entitled to persecute the Faithful, they should try persecuting her and see what they got. Bullies were all the same, wherever you went—quick to attack someone weaker than they, quick to fold when someone bigger showed up. The way she felt, she would welcome a chance to attack someone who deserved a beating.

She realized someone was pacing her just as she felt a tug on her belt pouch. Quick as a snake, she grabbed the thief's wrist and dragged him in front of her, twisting his arm high behind his back and making him yelp. "What the *hell* are you doing?" she shouted.

The noise and the thief's struggles to escape drew plenty of attention, but Ginnevra didn't care. She looked the man—no, boy—over. He was barely an adolescent, with longish dark hair and a snub nose, and he fought vainly against her grip. Ginnevra changed her hold on the boy so she could look him in the eye. "If you thought me an easy target, you're mad. What did you think would happen, snatching my purse in broad daylight surrounded by witnesses? That was the sloppiest grab I've ever seen."

The boy stopped struggling and glared at her, but Ginnevra knew sullen fear when she saw it. "Stupid bitch lied to me," he muttered. "Said you wouldn't see me."

"*You* were stupid to believe that. Or did you not realize a paladin's senses are superior to an ordinary person's?" Ginnevra gave him a little shake. "You're going to the justiciary. Maybe some time in a cell will straighten out your thinking."

The boy's eyes widened. "No, don't! It wasn't for real!"

That was a lie, but Ginnevra didn't care. "Wasn't it? We'll let the justicers straighten this out."

"She said I'd be invisible! She said you wouldn't see me 'long as I had the token!"

The boy struggled again, and Ginnevra shook him harder to make him hold still. "What token? Someone lied to you."

"See, it's right here." The boy stopped trying to pry Ginnevra's fingers loose and reached for the neck of his loose-fitting shirt. He wore a leather thong around his neck attached to something beneath the fabric. With a shaking hand, he pulled the thing out.

Ginnevra froze. The leather strip was threaded around a black pearl set in a hematite bezel. It had been four years since she'd seen it last, but she recognized it immediately. Filippa's paladin's grace.

Part of her mind protested that Filippa shouldn't have it, that she was no longer entitled to wear it or even carry it. It was over-ridden by her mouth saying, "Who gave you this?"

The boy's restless, frightened movements stilled. "Can't say," he whispered. "Not supposed to talk about it."

"Did she give it to you freely? And she said it would be a fine joke to play on the paladin if you stole her purse?"

His face clearing, the boy said, "Right. But she lied. She said that thing would make me invisible to you. So joke's on me, isn't it?"

Ginnevra felt as if all the air had been sucked out of her lungs. "Yes," she managed, "I suppose she should have played the trick on me herself, if she wanted. Why didn't she?"

The boy gave a one-shouldered shrug. "Can't tell," he said, and once more the lie was written on his face. "Not supposed to send messages for my lord's prisoners. It's more than my life is worth."

"We wouldn't want that," Ginnevra said. Then, making a guess, she added, "Your Lord Jiuseppe is strict, isn't he?"

"Stricter than my pa, and he used to whup me good," the boy said.

It confirmed the last of Ginnevra's suspicions. "Well, you told me nothing, and if it was all a harmless joke, I don't see the need to involve the justiciary."

The boy's face brightened. "No?"

"In fact," Ginnevra continued, "I think it was cruel of that woman to play a trick on you, prisoner or not, and you shouldn't tell anyone what happened. You don't want anyone making fun of you when it was you who were the victim, right? And you certainly wouldn't want Lord Jiuseppe knowing about it." She released the boy and gave him a little shove.

The boy nodded vigorously and sped away. Ginnevra watched long enough to see him disappear into the crowd. Then she ran.

It was fortunate people got out of her way, because a paladin's strength and endurance meant Ginnevra was an unstoppable armored juggernaut while running, and heart-pounding fear gave her feet wings. She hurtled through the streets until she reached the hostel, praying the whole way that Eodan was there and not out exploring or treating patients.

She pounded up the stairs and threw open the door. Her heart lurched with relief when she saw Eodan there, seated in one of the chairs rolling strips of fabric for bandages. He blinked at her abrupt arrival. "Something wrong?"

"Jiuseppe Zuccare captured Filippa," Ginnevra panted. "We're going to rescue her."

CHAPTER

EIGHTEEN

E odan absently set the bandage he held aside, his full attention on Ginnevra. "What happened?"

"I don't know." Swiftly, Ginnevra told him about the would-be thief and displayed Filippa's grace. "Jiuseppe must have found out Filippa was snooping around. Goddess knows what conclusion he drew, but he must assume something dire if he ordered her confined and commanded it be kept a secret. She was clever to find a way to reach me." Unexpectedly, a laugh escaped her. "I guess some things don't change."

"Ginnevra, are you sure this is a good idea?" Eodan's frown brought Ginnevra back to earth.

"You mean, because of our past?" Ginnevra shook her head. "It's not about friendship. She and I are working together on this. I can't let her be captured and possibly killed just because she— look, it doesn't matter, all right? She reached out to me for help, and I need to give it to her."

"I meant because you're talking about breaking into a powerful Quinizellan noble's estate. You're a representative of a political entity, more or less. That could start a war. At the very least, it will ruin your chances of an amicable resolution to Abraciabene's problem." Eodan's frown deepened. "You need to consider this carefully."

"I—" Ginnevra closed her mouth. "You're right," she continued after a moment. "If I'm caught, they won't go easy on me because I'm a paladin. But I have more than one mission here. I want to prove who was really behind the massacre. Filippa, what she learned in the Zuccare estate, is key to that. And if she knows something I can take to the king, that will give me a powerful weapon for accomplishing my other mission. I think it's worth the risk."

Eodan stood. "That's reasonable. So, it sounds like we need a plan. If she's being held in the estate, that will make rescue difficult."

"I know." Ginnevra removed her helmet and set it in the corner, then took off her coif and ran her fingers through her hair. "But the moon will be rising soon, and it hasn't reached its half, which means the Dark Lady's influence is still strong. That will give us an advantage while sneaking in."

"You want to sneak in now? Before sunset?"

"Maybe. It's a possibility. Since I don't know how long ago she was captured, I don't want to delay. Jiuseppe struck me as the sort of person who'd resort to torture quickly and wouldn't believe any answers he got regardless." Ginnevra unbuckled her armor and began setting the pieces next to the helmet. "Let's start by taking another look at the walls."

The Zuccare estate looked bigger in the bright sunlight than it had at night. Ginnevra and Eodan held hands so they looked like nothing more than sweethearts out for a stroll—Ginnevra hoped they did, anyway—and casually circled the estate, now and then taking side streets to conceal their interest. The wall was no more than seven feet high, topped with the iron spikes she'd noted before, but those were really only a deterrent to casual thieves. Ginnevra could climb the wall easily.

No, the real danger was the crossbowmen positioned high atop the mansion. The crenellated walls gave them enough cover that it was hard to see them at all times, which meant timing the gaps in their patrol was almost impossible. Ginnevra carefully didn't look directly at them, which might have drawn their attention to her. She stopped Eodan at the back of the estate and turned him so they faced each other, with Ginnevra looking over his shoulder at the mansion. "Kiss me," she said, putting her arms around his shoulders.

Eodan raised an eyebrow. "You don't have to ask twice," he said, drawing her into his arms.

Ginnevra kept her eyes open while they kissed, most of her attention on the crossbowmen. Two of them were watching her kiss Eodan, elbowing each other and pointing. Ginnevra could practically hear the lewd comments. She took a moment to enjoy the kissing, then drew back. "Thanks."

Now both Eodan's eyebrows raised. "Thanking me for kissing you, that's new," he said with a smile. "What did you see?"

Ginnevra took his hand and continued down the street. "They're more distractable than professionals would be. That helps us, but it worries me that Jiuseppe didn't hire the very best. It's out of character, at least as far as I understand his character, and it means he might not be as predictable as I'd like."

"Let's go with being cautiously relieved that the entrance will be easier." Eodan cast a glance at the wall and tugged on Ginnevra's hand to draw her into its shadow, out of sight of the crossbowmen as they walked. "Do you still think we should try to get in now? I can think of two ways to get me inside, but I'm not sure either of them are good ones."

Ginnevra raised an eyebrow. "What did you have in mind?"

Eodan grinned. "Aside from leaping the wall in wolf shape? Physicians are welcome anywhere. And I learned last night that Vinita is overanxious about her children's health. It's common knowledge that she makes frequent use of Quinizelle's physicians for ailments that either turn out to be minor or imaginary."

"But she didn't summon you. And we can't wait for that to happen." Ginnevra turned a corner, taking them away from the estate. She didn't look back to see if the crossbowmen were still watching.

"No, but there's a good chance one of those children is 'ill' after the strain of the ceremony. If I show up on her doorstep offering my services, they'll probably let me in." Eodan stopped and looked back the way they'd come. "But I'd be watched wherever I went, so I'm not sure how helpful that would be."

Ginnevra followed the line of his gaze, but most of the mansion was now out of sight. "You're right, that would limit your movement. And although I can be nearly invisible with the right grace, there are probably too many people moving around in the daytime for entering now to be practical. We'll have to wait for nightfall." She cast an eye on the eastern horizon. "Let's finish preparations, and let the dark moon watch over our endeavors."

She didn't dare pray that Filippa was all right. Instead, she prayed that she would have the strength and wisdom that would carry her through the next several hours.

SEVERAL HOURS LATER, well after nightfall, Ginnevra looked out her window at the wedge of black sky visible from that angle. The buildings blocking the rest of her view looked as clear-edged as if it were daylight, though dimmer. She couldn't see the moon, nearly at its half, but she knew it was about an hour from setting. Time to go.

She picked up her empty rucksack and settled it on her shoulders. Eodan rose from where he'd been putting on his boots. "It's possible the Zuccares are still entertaining guests," he said. "I learned last night, from talking to people at the dedication, that nobles in Quinizelle often throw parties that last until dawn."

"I'm counting on them not wanting to host two big events two nights in a row," Ginnevra said. "If I'm wrong, well, that just makes this more complicated. But we can't delay any longer."

"We're as prepared as we can be. No point worrying, right?"

Ginnevra kissed him. "Thank you for coming with me. I don't want to do this alone."

"As if you could stop me," Eodan said with a smile.

Ginnevra thought about that as they descended the stairs and nodded at the night host, who sat patiently by the front door. It wasn't quite true, because if something came up that only a paladin could handle, Eodan wouldn't push to join her. He wouldn't be happy about it, but he was sensible. What *was* true was that she was now part of a team, two people supporting each other with everything they had.

That brought her back to thinking about Filippa. They'd been the best of friends, closer than sisters, and since Ginnevra had never had a sister, the relationship had been unexpected and powerful. Filippa's betrayal, coming so closely on the heels of the massacre, had devastated Ginnevra more than if Filippa had died at the hands of those bandits. Mercenaries. The distinction didn't matter much, not to the ones they'd killed.

Of course, it mattered if it meant Ginnevra could prove Jiuseppe Zuccare had arranged for mercenaries to murder Dianetta Napolle. And that meant rescuing Filippa. Ginnevra composed a silent prayer as she and Eodan walked through the dark streets: *Goddess, You have guided me this far. Help me deliver justice for Dianetta and my lost paladin sisters and all those caught up in Zuccare's plot. Strengthen my body and mind that I might be Your instrument in helping to bring peace to Quinizelle. Ever in Your name.*

There weren't many people on the street at that hour, though Ginnevra suspected that was because they were in an expensive residential area rather than on the main street with all its well-lighted taverns and inns. No one met Ginnevra's eyes when they passed. With that kind of furtive behavior, how many others out that night intended crime? So long as no clever thief decided this was the night she would rob the Zuccare mansion, Ginnevra didn't worry about it. That was probably dereliction of duty, but she doubted Quinizellan law enforcement wanted her help, so there was no point taking on extra burdens.

Eodan took her arm and drew her close. "We're here. Around back?"

Ginnevra nodded. She slowed her pace so she and Eodan, arm in arm, once more looked like a courting couple. She didn't bother looking for the crossbowmen. They passed the great front gate, closed now, and Ginnevra snuck a peek through the bars. Lanterns lit the doors, but most of the windows were dark. No party tonight. The cherubs' blank eyes caught the light, seeming to wink at her. Ginnevra suppressed a shudder.

They strolled around the corner, then turned down the first street they came to and walked its length before returning via a different street that brought them out behind the mansion. This time, Ginnevra kept a close eye on the crenellated walls, counting. Three crossbowmen guarded the rear approach of the mansion, but only two of them were even a little alert. The third walked a short loop near the southeastern corner, but his attention was to the south and west, toward the front of the mansion. Ginnevra couldn't figure out what he was so interested in, but it didn't matter.

She wished she knew what the estate looked like on the far side, beyond the wall, whether there was a door, or a garden, or one of those hedge mazes becoming popular throughout the Lordagne—there were a lot of things she wished for she wasn't going to get. At some point, she had to act on faith.

She checked the watchmen again. With her night-enhanced vision, they were as visible as they'd been that afternoon. The two guarding the rear walked from opposite corners to meet in the middle. From their pace, Ginnevra guessed they didn't have a clear view of the back wall, but they'd certainly notice if someone came over it. At least, someone who came over it the conventional way.

She let Eodan guide them down the street behind the mansion as she watched the guards' paths. When they reached the opposite ends of the walls, she said, "Now," and hurried with Eodan into the shelter of the wall, making them invisible to the guards.

"Smart guards would notice that we disappeared," she whispered. "But if these guards were smart, they wouldn't walk a path that puts both of them where they don't see the back wall at the same time. I think we're all right." She removed the rucksack from her shoulders and opened it.

Eodan was already removing his clothes and handing them to Ginnevra, who stuffed them into the rucksack. "You're sure this grace will conceal us both?"

"Mostly sure. That is, unless the Goddess decides not to grant it. I've seen it invoked on someone other than the invoker, if that's what you mean."

Eodan wrestled his boots off, and Ginnevra crammed them atop his clothes and put the rucksack back on. "I suppose we'll find out." He shimmered silver, and then the enormous black-furred wolf stood beside her. Ginnevra ran her hand over his head and patted his shoulder, which was nearly chest high to her.

"Stand close," she said. Eodan shifted until he was pressed against her legs. Ginnevra drew in a deep breath and let it out slowly. Touching her grace with the tip of her forefinger, she whispered, *"By Your grace the shadows fall."*

Her whole body tingled so hard it sent a convulsive shiver through her. Eodan's body trembled violently, enough that she felt the vibration through her legs. Immediately she crossed the street to give herself a running start, turned, and raced toward the estate wall. In half a dozen quick strides, she reached its base and leaped to grab the top. One hand slapped the smooth stone; the other curled around the base of an iron spike. She swiftly hauled herself up, avoiding the other spikes, and lowered herself to where she could drop to the ground. Moments later, she felt the air move as something flew past overhead. Eodan landed ten feet away and took a few running steps to slow his momentum, barely audible in the stillness. First hurdle passed.

This part of the estate grounds was a garden, but a sprawling, wide-open one. Dozens of flowerbeds and the occasional tree spread out from mansion to outer wall, but no hedges provided cover for intruders, no leafy bushes cast irregular shadows that might conceal human ones. Without stopping to see if she'd been spotted, Ginnevra ran for the mansion behind Eodan, who swiftly outpaced her.

She was aware of carrying, not a shroud of darkness, but a distortion in the air surrounding her. Though her vision was clear ahead, out of the corners of her eyes the garden looked fractured as if she were seeing it through a sheet of cracked, milky glass. Ahead, Eodan was all but invisible as the effect made him seem part of his surroundings, a heat haze at most. Ginnevra tamped down on the surge of satisfaction running unseen past the guards gave her. It was too soon to be confident of their chances.

She reached the mansion without hearing any shouts of alarm or the whistle of crossbow bolts and pressed herself against the wall, breathing heavily more from excitement than exertion. Even without the concealment grace, she and Eodan were now actually invisible to observers above unless they leaned over the parapets and looked straight down. Even someone standing at one of the windows, with their small panes of clear glass set in lattices of black leading, would have trouble perceiving them.

Ginnevra tipped her head back and surveyed the mansion. It was four stories tall, judging by the windows, with the top story being shorter than the others. Servants' quarters, possibly? There were no windows at ground level, which Ginnevra assumed was a security precaution. Somebody was paranoid, but not paranoid enough.

To her left, the flat stone wall of the mansion extended all the way to the corner without interruption, at least eighty feet. It looked almost exactly the same on her right, except for a single small door set into a stone arch about twenty feet from where she stood. Its elaborate latch and handle echoed the leaves of the trees, and the weathered bronze revealed the mansion's age as the stone did not.

Ginnevra sidled along the wall until she reached the door. The wood was stained black and lacquered to protect against the elements. She pictured this garden blanketed with snow, the winds beating more snow against the door, and shivered involuntarily. Then she shivered again as another strong tingle ran through her. Her peripheral vision cleared, and the wolf appeared, standing on the far side of the door. Ginnevra had used the concealment grace often back when she'd been a paladin with a company, and she was used to how it lasted only as long as the

Goddess believed the paladin needed it. She hoped this meant there was no one beyond the door they would need to be invisible to, but likely it was just that nothing could conceal a door opening, and Ginnevra needed to have faith in her abilities.

The wolf's body shimmered silver, and Eodan rose from a crouch and extended his hand for the rucksack. "Now what?"

"Give me a minute." Ginnevra brushed her fingers over the lock plate, which was burnished smooth and well cared for, then pushed down on the latch. It didn't move. There was no keyhole, which meant the locking mechanism was accessible only on the other side. That was another hint that someone did care about security; they just didn't know what threat to ward against.

In Quinizelle, with so few Faithful and anointed to invoke the Goddess's graces, it was unlikely anyone considered how those might be used illegally. Though it was also true Ginnevra wasn't aware of anyone ever using the firelighting grace to spark arson, or of paladins using their darksight to break into a house. Whether the Goddess would even grant an invocation for those uses, Ginnevra didn't know. But it was time for her to find out.

She laid her left hand, slightly cupped, against the lock plate and pressed her fingertips firmly against it. With her right hand, she grasped the latch. "If this is wrong, I'll find another way in," she whispered, "but—*By Your grace I clear the way.*"

A click sounded, the faintest distant sound barely perceptible even by her enhanced hearing. Something shifted, and she depressed the latch. The door opened a hair-fine crack, surrounding the black wood with a thin line of pale gray, indicating a distant light source. Ginnevra let out a breath. That grace was intended for making a path through heavy undergrowth or snow, and that the Goddess had allowed it here reassured Ginnevra that she was doing the right thing.

Eodan finished putting on his boots and nodded. Ginnevra

pushed the door open barely enough for them to slide through, and Eodan shut it behind them. She had guessed, based on the stairs that led to the front door, that the windowless foundation housed things like kitchens and pantries. With luck, that meant it also had a room where an intruder could be confined. Ginnevra had hoped this door opened on a hallway that led deeper into the house.

Instead, they'd entered a small but not cramped chamber, lined on one side with solid oak cabinets stained a deep brown and polished until they shone. The smell of the wax overwhelmed any other scents, but Ginnevra wasn't a werewolf to track or identify humans by any but the strongest odors. Wooden benches with backs carved with trees and flowers sat against the other wall. Across from the door, a narrow stairwell rose into light, not very bright and dimmer here at the bottom of the stairs. Ginnevra didn't like the look of the stairwell. It almost certainly went to the public places of the house, not where they wanted to go.

Eodan opened one of the cabinets. "Cloaks," he said. "A lot of different sizes. I imagine this is where people dress for warmth if they want to walk in the garden during stormy or wintry weather."

"That's even worse news than that we're not in the servants' quarters," Ginnevra said. "The garden is for decoration, not for food, so it's the private space of the Zuccare family rather than a kitchen garden. And that means the stairs definitely don't go where I'd hoped."

"We could try looking for another entrance."

Ginnevra shook her head. "Going in and out risks drawing attention. We'll just have to make do. Besides, maybe I'm wrong, and they're holding Filippa in an unused bedroom upstairs."

Eodan settled a chain around his neck. A flat oval of obsidian in a steel frame dangled from it. "Let's try to stay together, though. Splitting up offers them two chances to discover us instead of just one."

"And whisper if you have to use this. The sound carries a lot farther than you'd imagine." Ginnevra patted the matching obsidian pendant that hung around her neck. It was no bigger than the first joint of her thumb and was highly polished to a mirror shine. Revered Bariatte hadn't asked any questions about why she needed them, and Ginnevra thought he might suspect she intended something underhanded he would need to deny knowledge of. He was much easier to deal with than Hallowed Nevante. Too bad men couldn't be Hallowed, because Bariatte would make an excellent leader of the Quinizelle sanctuary.

She rubbed her fingerprints from the shining obsidian surface and made her way slowly and silently up the stairs, followed by Eodan. If this let out in that enormous hall where the dedication had been held, they might be discovered before they'd gotten anywhere. But that was a defeatist thought, and dwelling on the possibility wouldn't help them succeed.

She heard no one moving on the floor above, but she hung back anyway, staying close to the left-hand wall and stepping with caution. Eodan moved more silently than a man his size ought to be able to manage, but she was used to that by now. The stairs didn't creak, for which she was grateful, though that was a mixed blessing; creaky stairs could warn them of unwanted company as well as giving their position away.

A faint floral scent came to her nose, nothing strong enough to tickle, and then the smell of wax polish again. Still no sounds of movement. At the top of the stairs, the narrow stairwell turned into a narrow hall about ten feet long that opened into a larger space, dimly lit. Ginnevra took a deep, calming breath, let it out slowly, and walked silently to the end of the hall.

NINETEEN

S he peered out through the opening into the next room. It wasn't the vast great hall, thank the Goddess, but a smaller yet still empty chamber with doorways on either side and a big opening straight ahead. That one did lead to the great hall, the source of what little light there was—enough light that Ginnevra's enhanced vision saw her surroundings clearly. The front doors were visible from where Ginnevra stood.

Long-stemmed lilies in tall vases, the source of the floral scent, stood in each corner of the small chamber, beneath portraits of elegant, sneering men and women who bore a striking resemblance to Jiuseppe around the eyes and mouth. A thick gold and gray flowered carpet filled the center of the floor, leaving polished floorboards circling it so it looked like a flowered island in a wooden sea.

Ginnevra walked forward, staying well to the left so she wasn't as visible from the great hall. Eodan went right, mirroring her path. The doorway on Ginnevra's side led to a room filled with long couches and chairs, their tapestry cushions fat enough nobody could sit comfortably on them. A wide fireplace, currently empty, occupied the far wall. Again, no one was there.

Ginnevra hurried past the doorway anyway, casting a quick glance across the chamber at Eodan; the other room was a dining hall, with a table big enough to seat forty. More tall vases stood in both dining room and sitting room, and the floral smell had grown stronger. Ginnevra pinched her nose against a sneeze and crept to the edge of the wide opening, peering around the corner.

The great hall was as empty as everything else they'd seen. With no crowds thronging the space, it looked even more enormous than it had the previous night. Lamps of frosted, milky glass, turned low for the night, shed a faint light across the floor and cast strange shadows over the ceiling murals. Ginnevra scanned the room quickly for other exits and saw a few doors off to the right, all closed, as well as another opening leading to the sitting room on that side.

Across the hall, to the right of the outer doors, a staircase wide enough for five people to ascend at once, arms linked, rose to a landing lit by another of the lamps. Two more closed doors on that side offered no hint as to what lay beyond them.

Ginnevra hurried to join Eodan, though she still perceived no one nearby who might notice them. "There have to be stairs going down somewhere, but they're behind one of those doors."

"Or she's upstairs," Eodan whispered back. "If the top floor is servants' quarters, that's a lot of small rooms someone could be locked into."

"Time to see if the Goddess is willing to help us further," Ginnevra said. She felt for the leather thong she wore around her neck and withdrew Filippa's grace, closing her hand around its smooth surface. She'd only ever seen this done, and the times she'd tried it herself, it had failed, but her captain at the time, Biasca Attanante, had said the grace was finicky because you had to be within a certain distance of the individual you sought, and that distance was never the same from person to person. Ginnevra hoped she was close enough.

She closed her eyes and drew in a deep breath, then released it slowly, relaxing the tense muscles of her shoulders and letting her head droop. She let herself become aware of the smooth black pearl in her hand, of its warmth as if it were a living thing, of its rounded contours interrupted by the hematite bezel, of the roughness of the leather woven around it. In a whisper so low she didn't think even Eodan heard it, she said, *"By Your grace the two unite."*

She felt a pulse of force like someone squeezing her fist, and then her hand began to throb, but pleasantly, like a heartbeat. The pearl warmed until it felt like a nearly extinguished ember, one that didn't burn her skin. Ginnevra held up her fist to shoulder level and examined it. Her hand didn't look any different than before, but when she blinked, she saw a dim red glow superimposed on the blackness behind her eyelids. She closed her eyes; her fist still glowed red. She wasn't sure how that helped, unless she was willing to walk blindly through the mansion, guided by Eodan. That wasn't the worst idea she'd had that day.

"Did it work?" Eodan whispered.

Ginnevra nodded, her attention still on her hand. "It did something, anyway." She waved her hand back and forth between them. When her hand was closer to the great hall, the throbbing intensified, not by much, but enough that she could tell the difference. She closed her eyes again and saw the red glow was deeper in color, but brighter, two things that ought to have contradicted each other. "We'd better move quickly. I don't know how long this will last."

They crossed the hall, their footsteps quiet on the wooden

floor. Halfway to the stairs, Ginnevra said, "It's definitely this way. The pull is very clear."

"Most of the house is in that direction," Eodan said.

"Pessimist." Ginnevra mock-scowled at him. "Stay close, but not too close."

Eodan nodded.

The stairs were finished with a glossy shine that wasn't slick underfoot. Once again, Ginnevra's feet made practically no noise on the treads, and the stairs didn't creak. How old was this mansion, anyway? It was her experience that old houses creaked no matter how well maintained they were. Maybe if you were as wealthy as the Zuccares appeared to be, you could replace your staircases every hundred years or so. Though, in that case, was the house really old if parts of it were constantly renewed? It was an odd thought, and Ginnevra pushed it aside. Time for foolish wonderings after she'd achieved her goal.

The stairs rose to a wide landing and continued upward. Ginnevra slowed as she neared the second floor, listening, watching. Still nothing. More dim lights burned in the hall where the stairs ended, illuminating several doors to the right. To the left, at the end where Ginnevra and Eodan stood, two more short staircases rose to an elevated area that lay in darkness.

Ginnevra waved her fist slowly from right to left and felt the increase in pressure that marked her path. "That way," she whispered, pointing left at the dark area at the top of the stairs. They didn't rise very high, since there were only four of them, but even her enhanced vision couldn't help in total darkness.

A click echoed in the stillness, the sound of a latch opening, and a door opposite where they stood began to open. Ginnevra grabbed Eodan's arm and tugged him up the short stairs. They ended at a landing at the base of more stairs, these steep and narrow, going up. Eodan and Ginnevra ducked around the far side of these and crouched. Footsteps sounded on the floorboards, and a woman came into view. She wore a dark gown with a white wraparound apron and had her hair pinned severely around her head. From Ginnevra's position, the woman resembled Filippa, or at any rate was dressed the way Filippa had been at the dedication. Servant, probably.

Ginnevra watched the woman walk away from them down the hall and knock on a door, then open it at a muffled command. She released a breath. "That was close."

"We should have encountered more people than we have," Eodan said. "We should be grateful the Zuccares go to bed early."

"The pearl is leading us up again," Ginnevra said. "Let's go."

The small stairs felt utilitarian, not like the broad stairs below that were meant to be seen and admired by guests. Though there was enough room for Ginnevra and Eodan to walk side by side, they continued as they'd done before, with Eodan following Ginnevra, who held her fist in front of her and occasionally closed her eyes to assess the red glow. It continued to deepen. Ginnevra didn't dwell on what it meant that they hadn't reached Filippa yet. She was in the house somewhere, and the pearl would find her, and that was all that mattered.

The stairs brought them to another landing and a broad, long hallway lined with doors. It looked just the same as on the floor below, with a carpet running down its center and more vases, these short and squat, sitting on small tables between the doors. Paintings of landscapes far from Quinizelle and its mountains hung above the vases. Ginnevra waved her fist at the hall and felt no increased pressure.

She glanced at the stairs, which continued upward, and then at Eodan. Eodan nodded. Ginnevra put her foot on the first step and jerked back, startled, when it let out a tiny moan, barely louder than the sound of a man turning over in his sleep. She hesitated, then held out her fist. The burning sensation and pressure increased. Carefully, she rested her foot on the step again, far to the right, and then put her weight on it. No noise.

Slowly, she raised her other foot and took another step. This time, the creak was so quiet she could barely hear it, which meant nobody else in the mansion would. Even so, she proceeded up the stairs with caution, testing each step before committing to it. Behind her, Eodan walked where she did, but even that didn't stop his weight making more noise than Ginnevra. She listened hard for signs that anyone heard them. Between the strain of listening and the need to step softly and the burning, pulsing sensation in her hand, she felt tuned to a breaking point, all her nerves taut and twanging.

They climbed the stairs, which were narrow enough and made enough sharp turns Ginnevra wondered how anyone had gotten furniture up them. Maybe the mansion had been built around its contents. The darkness of the stairwell gradually lightened until Ginnevra could see clearly again, and then they were at the top and the light was bright enough for normal vision. Ginnevra took a few more steps, putting herself out of Eodan's way, and made her shoulders relax again.

This hall wasn't as wide as the ones below and was very plain, with plastered walls painted a dull cream rather than wood paneling and no carpet. The only thing the halls had in common was many doors lining both sides of the corridor. Lanterns hung on the walls, cheap brass ones without the frosted glass that made the lamps below glow so steadily. Two of them burned low, their flames flickering faster than the others. There were no windows, and nothing to indicate what lay beyond the doors.

Ginnevra extended her fist and began a slow, measured walk down the corridor. The floor creaked with every step, not loudly, but enough to make her wince inwardly. If someone emerged from one of these rooms, they'd have to act fast to subdue that person, because just one scream would be enough to turn their rescue into a rout.

Her fist suddenly blazed with heat, and she gasped and dropped the pearl, swiftly catching the thong with her other hand so it swung free without hitting the floor. It didn't look any different than usual, and Ginnevra no longer felt heat radiating off it.

She had been so focused on the pearl she hadn't been paying attention to her surroundings. Now she saw she had stopped between two doors on either side of her. Both were identical. Neither bore any indication of what lay beyond them.

Ginnevra grasped the pearl again. It was cool to the touch, and when she closed her fist around it, it didn't send any pulses of force through her. She cursed silently and turned to Eodan. "It's one of these, but I don't know which."

"No guesses?" Eodan whispered back.

She shook her head. "And there's no grace that will tell me which to choose. We'll just have to take our chances." She looped the pearl around her neck and shook out her hands. The left one, the one that had gripped the pearl so tightly, tingled as if the blood was returning to it. Ginnevra breathed in deeply, let the breath out, and relaxed. She considered praying for guidance, decided that was too close to praying for a desired future, and examined the doors once more. Neither was locked—none of the doors were made to lock, she noticed—and the latches were identical brass handles with a thumb plate that depressed to engage the latch.

Ginnevra grasped the left-hand one and slowly pushed down on the thumb plate, which moved with the faintest sound of metal grinding against metal and then clicked when it was fully depressed. To Ginnevra, the click echoed down the hall. She reminded herself that no ordinary person could hear it and pushed the door open.

The room beyond was lit only by the faint light of the moon coming through the one small window, but that was more than enough light for Ginnevra to make out a bed, a clothespress, a small table by the head of the bed, and a chair pushed to the side of the room opposite the bed. Dark blotches on the wall indicated where the occupant had hung clothing, shapeless in the dimness, on pegs. The room was empty.

Ginnevra backed out and let the door swing shut. She caught it before it closed entirely and said, "Did you hear that?"

Eodan didn't respond. He was looking back at the stairwell, which had begun to creak with the weight of someone ascending the stairs.

Ginnevra looked at the door opposite. Filippa was probably in there, but otherwise it was a total unknown and therefore a danger. She grabbed Eodan's arm and tugged, pushing the nearly-closed door open again with her other hand. They hurried inside, and Ginnevra shut the door, leaving it open a crack. Both of them leaned close and listened.

The stairs stopped creaking, and heavy footsteps sounded against the bare planks of the floor. Whoever it was didn't bother to conceal their presence and didn't seem to be in a hurry. Ginnevra's imagination presented her with a dozen possibilities. She didn't dwell on the chances that the person was the occupant of this room.

The footsteps came closer. Ginnevra breathed slowly, calming her racing heart. Probably this person was a servant heading to bed—though didn't servants have to stay up late in case their masters needed something? It didn't matter. If this became a problem, they would handle it when it happened.

Gradually, the footsteps slowed until they came to a halt—

right outside the door where Ginnevra and Eodan crouched. For a moment that felt stretched to breaking, nothing happened. Ginnevra pictured the person looking at their door, wondering why it wasn't closed. Then she heard the grind and click of a latch being engaged, and the creak of hinges. Their door wasn't moving.

She let out a breath and closed her eyes in a silent prayer of thanks. Then someone spoke, his voice muffled by the door. "Let's see if you're more cooperative now that you've had time to consider your position."

Jiuseppe Zuccare.

Ginnevra's heartbeat, which had almost returned to normal, sped up until her chest hurt from the pounding. Across the hall, the hinges squealed again, and the door thumped shut. Ginnevra and Eodan stared at each other. Eodan looked as horrified as Ginnevra felt. "Now what?" he said.

"If we go bursting in there while he's present, he'll denounce me to the king as a spy or a traitor or—I don't know what else, but it can't be good." Ginnevra looked at the door as if she could see through it and its neighbor through willpower alone. "But if he plans to torture her—"

"We don't know that's what he has in mind." Eodan shook his head. "But we can't count on him being willing to restrict himself to questions. Not if he's behind the massacre."

Ginnevra straightened. "I won't leave her to him. We'll have to take our chances, and hope the Goddess is willing to inspire a solution."

She pulled the door open, not bothering to keep it silent. She and Eodan arranged themselves to either side of the other door. Ginnevra put her hand on the latch and nodded at Eodan, who nodded back. Then she thrust the door open swiftly and rushed inside with Eodan at her back.

TWENTY

They were inside with the door safely shut before anyone else reacted. Jiuseppe Zuccare stopped half turned toward them, his brows furrowed in a scowl and his mouth opening to say something that by the look of him would be scathing. Filippa sat tied to a chair, glaring at Jiuseppe over a gag. Her eyes widened when she realized who had entered. Then she shook her head violently in a clear signal to Ginnevra to get out.

Jiuseppe's mouth slackened in astonishment. "Who—" He looked puzzled now, as if he didn't recognize Ginnevra. That didn't last long. "Paladin," he said. "What are you doing—" He glanced at Filippa, then back at Ginnevra, and finally turned on Filippa again. "Who *are* you?" he demanded of her. "You're no paladin. And yet it's too much to believe this is coincidence that *this* one—" He jabbed a finger at Ginnevra— "invaded my house for some other reason and happened to stumble on you. You're working together."

"Get out of my way," Ginnevra said. "She's coming with me."

Jiuseppe's astonishment faded, replaced by a cunning, half-lidded look of contemplation. "And you're the physician," he said to Eodan. "I suppose paladins really are easily bought, but what made you decide to throw away your principles to work for House Alamanne?"

"Work for—is that what you believe?" Eodan said.

Ginnevra held up a hand, hoping Eodan would understand she needed to do the talking. "You think we're spies for the Alamannes?"

"That one claimed to be searching out weaknesses in my security so she could steal from me." This time, Jiuseppe pointed at Filippa. "A transparent falsehood. It's obvious she's working for my enemies."

Filippa's eyes were so wide Ginnevra hoped they didn't burst from their sockets. Her obvious distress made Ginnevra feel uncertain. Filippa had managed to get word to her, and why do that if she hadn't wanted to be rescued? And yet she looked as if she was desperate to communicate something vital, something that would make a difference, and had practically willed Ginnevra to turn around and leave without her.

"So you believe *I* am working for your enemies, too?" she asked. "A paladin and a prime of the Blessed?"

Jiuseppe sneered. "Paladins have no honor. All Quinizelle knows it. No wonder you defiled my son's dedication with your presence—it was part of Mazzeus Alamanne's plot to weaken and discredit me."

"You really are a fool," Ginnevra said. "You know damn well paladins can't be bought. It was you who arranged for Dianetta Napolle's murder. Captain Ercole was your victim as surely as the rest of us. And I'll make sure the king knows the truth."

Jiuseppe's eyes narrowed. "You're spouting nonsense. Your desperation to avoid public condemnation is pathetic, if you think you can get away with making up lies to discredit me."

Ginnevra looked past Jiuseppe at Filippa. She'd stopped straining against her bonds and her head sagged, but she was still breathing heavily from exertion. She looked so perfectly despondent Ginnevra knew instantly she'd missed something important in Filippa's unspoken warning. Nothing for it but to forge ahead.

"We have evidence that House Zuccare was behind the ambush," she said. "The man who hired the mercenaries wore the Zuccare insignia. You manipulated your brother Jiovanni into arranging for Lady Dianetta's murder. You wanted King Paolo to evict the Faith from Quinizelle entirely. When that didn't happen, you worked to increase strife between the Faithful and Torunes, hoping to get rid of us some other way. But you've failed, Jiuseppe. When we tell the king what happened... well, I'm sure he'll be interested in pursuing justice for his beloved sister."

Jiuseppe's face had gradually reddened as Ginnevra spoke. "You *dare*," he shouted. "As if I gave a damn about you pathetic Faithful. Your time is over, and I don't need to do anything to hasten that ending. I'm going to have you arrested for breaking into my house and threatening me and my family. We'll see if the king is willing to treat with you at all then!"

He stepped forward, pushing past Ginnevra, only to run into Eodan. "Get out of my way, or it will go the worse for you," Jiuseppe snarled.

Eodan put a hand on Jiuseppe's shoulder and stepped sideways, blocking the door. "I don't think so," he said. "Ginnevra?"

Ginnevra only hesitated for a moment before drawing her belt knife and cutting Filippa free of the gag. Filippa spat and worked her jaw for a moment. "Damn it, Ginna," she said hoarsely. "We used to be able to practically read each other's minds."

Ginnevra swallowed a sharp retort about why they weren't that close anymore. She didn't want to mention her past in front of Jiuseppe. "What the hell has you so worked up?"

"Let go of me," Jiuseppe demanded. "Help! Someone—"

Ginnevra crammed the gag into his mouth, making him choke briefly. She set about cutting Filippa's bonds. "You sent word. Didn't you *want* to be rescued?"

"At least that much went right," Filippa said. She massaged her wrists, but didn't stand up. "I was trying to communicate that Jiuseppe isn't our man."

"What?" Ginnevra swiveled to look at Jiuseppe, who was struggling impotently against Eodan's implacable grip. "How can you be sure?"

"Because four years ago he was Dianetta's lover," Filippa said.

Ginnevra's mouth fell open. "But...Filippa, that's not proof! Suppose he was jealous of her leaving him for another man, and decided if he couldn't have her, no one would? Or maybe they parted on bad terms, and he figured he could use her as a weapon against the Faith? Love gets corrupted and warped all the time."

"I investigated all those possibilities," Filippa said. "I read his correspondence—"

Jiuseppe's muffled, angry cry and lunge forward startled both Ginnevra and Filippa. Eodan restrained him more securely. "Sorry," he said. "You read his letters—but he'd only have half of the correspondence, right? Dianetta would have the other half."

"He had all the letters, tied up with ribbons in a box I'm sure he thought was well hidden," Filippa said with a grin. "I'm guessing Dianetta gave his back to him before leaving Quinizelle. She was a smart lady—too smart to go to her wedding carrying love letters from another man. Anyway, he kept them packed away like they were precious, a reminder of something he cared about. Not the act of someone intent on assassinating his lady love."

"He might still have done it," Ginnevra protested, but in the face of Filippa's certainty it was hard to continue to argue against her conclusions. "Suppose he's the type who can lie to himself about his motives?"

"People who do that show it in other ways," Filippa said. "Jiuseppe isn't like that. You may hate me, Ginnevra, but you can't deny I'm skilled at seeing to the heart of people."

"I don't hate you," Ginnevra said automatically. "All right. Suppose this is all true. What now?"

"I still believe Jiuseppe has something to do with the religious strife." Filippa stood and stretched. "I'd hoped you would find me without Jiuseppe being here as well, and we could escape and have no one be the wiser."

"I wasn't going to let him torture you," Ginnevra said.

"He's no danger to me," Filippa said.

Ginnevra stalked to Jiuseppe's side and patted up and down his legs. She pulled a nasty-looking dagger from a boot sheath and brandished it. "This isn't a belt knife, Filippa."

Filippa paled slightly. "I'd have been fine," she said weakly.

Ginnevra thrust the dagger through her belt. "Eodan?"

Eodan shook Jiuseppe hard enough that he temporarily stopped struggling. "We can tie him to the chair and leave him, but that won't stop him telling the king what we did. And that will be the end of any hope of a peaceful resolution to this mess."

"Let's start with the chair, and I'll think of something." She stood back and watched Eodan and Filippa salvage the longest pieces of rope and tie Jiuseppe hand and foot to the chair. Given that the king was already hostile to her, and that he'd set her the impossible task of getting Hallowed Nevante to abase herself, Ginnevra didn't actually care if Jiuseppe revealed what had happened here tonight. It likely wouldn't make a difference. But *someone* had ordered the murder of Dianetta Napolle, and Ginnevra wanted more than anything to know who that was.

She squeezed her eyes tight shut for a moment. It wasn't

Jiuseppe. It hadn't been his brother Jiovanni, unless someone other than Jiuseppe had manipulated him. Someone who couldn't arrange it on his or her own, someone who hated the Faith—

Ginnevra's breath caught. There was a possibility, someone she should have suspected immediately, except that Jiuseppe was such a perfect candidate. But she needed more facts. And since she couldn't interrogate everyone in Quinizelle, she would have to start here.

She turned her back on Jiuseppe and the others and laid two fingers against her grace, whispering, *"By Your grace I hear true."* A high, clear tone came out of nowhere, echoing in her ears, and then died away, leaving her ears itching. She resisted the urge to scratch and turned around. No one else reacted as if they'd heard the sound. Eodan stood behind Jiuseppe. His eyes met hers, and he raised an inquiring eyebrow. Ginnevra shook her head minutely, though she wasn't sure what she intended to convey. She'd explain everything to him later.

Filippa looked confused when Ginnevra handed her Jiuseppe's dagger, but she gripped it at the ready. Ginnevra stood in front of Jiuseppe, who glared at her. Then she tore the gag from his mouth and let it dangle loose in her hand. It was damp and warm and unpleasant, but she might need it again.

"Don't shout," she said as Jiuseppe drew a deep breath. Without being prompted, Filippa laid the edge of the dagger against his throat. Jiuseppe subsided, but he continued to glare at Ginnevra. "We're going to have a little talk. You're going to answer my questions truthfully, and this lady won't resort to the knife."

"I will tell you *nothing*," Jiuseppe snarled.

"I don't think that's true." Ginnevra smiled pleasantly. "You see, I think you want to know the answers as much as I do. And I have a feeling you'll be surprised at what you learn."

Jiuseppe's glare faded slightly. "You're babbling."

Ginnevra shrugged. "How long has High Priest Rainaldus Mastarcce been manipulating you?"

"High Priest—" Jiuseppe's jaw slackened in confusion. Eodan and Filippa stared at her, their identical looks of astonishment making them look like a couple of startled statues.

"It was obvious once I stopped making assumptions," Ginnevra said. "That's the problem with evidence—it doesn't always tell the whole story. We believed because the man who hired the assassins that killed Dianetta wore your insignia, the Zuccares were responsible."

"You *liar*," Jiuseppe spat. "No Zuccare would have done it. And even if we'd wanted to, Jiovanni was too stupid—" His voice cut off, and his eyes widened as if he'd had a realization.

"Jiovanni was too stupid to think of it on his own," Ginnevra finished for him. "So we assumed you were behind your brother's actions, and that you'd killed him to keep the secret."

Jiuseppe wrenched at his bonds and succeeded in nearly tipping the chair over. Eodan grabbed the chair back and steadied it. Jiuseppe's eyes never left Ginnevra's. "How dare you make such foul accusations! I swear I'll see you dead for that!"

Ginnevra reflected that he was talking a lot for someone who'd said he wouldn't answer her questions. So far, he hadn't said anything true or false for the grace to register it. "Then you deny setting mercenaries to kill Dianetta and her escort?"

"You're damn right I deny it!"

The same clear tone rang out like a bell in Ginnevra's ears. Truth. She was convinced her new theory was correct, but she wasn't going to be a fool twice. "And you didn't murder your brother?"

Jiuseppe struggled to free himself again, but not as violently.

"I've never killed anyone," he said, "not like you, you demonic bitch."

Eodan slapped him across the back of his head, making his head snap forward. "Watch your language."

"It's fine," Ginnevra told Eodan as the bell-like tone faded. It was still possible, based on how she'd worded that question, that Jiuseppe had arranged for Jiovanni's death and was telling the literal truth that he hadn't done the deed himself, but Ginnevra was satisfied he wasn't deceiving her. "So it was Rainaldus' idea to arrange for Dianetta's death."

"That was the act of a faithless coward," Jiuseppe said. "You're so desperate to prove your captain wasn't at fault you're willing to accuse a holy man of depravity. High Priest Rainaldus would never hurt another person."

Ginnevra regarded him closely. "I think he just didn't involve you in the plot. You wouldn't have agreed to it. Sacrifice Dianetta for the sake of the Torune religion, as a ploy to get the Faith out of Quinizelle—it was effective, it was almost perfectly successful, but you would have considered the cost too high." Time for a different strategy. "Whose idea was it to start the Benevolent Fund?"

"I'm done answering your questions," Jiuseppe said. "You'd better start running, because when I'm free I'm going to denounce you to King Paolo."

"Well, that won't get us anywhere." Ginnevra smiled again. "I'll tell you what. You answer all of my questions, and I'll escort you to the king myself and admit to any charges you want to lay against me."

"Ginnevra!" Eodan exclaimed. Jiuseppe hissed as Filippa's incautious jerk of surprise cut a thin line across the side of his throat.

Ginnevra made a curt, silencing gesture. "Well, Jiuseppe?"

Jiuseppe's glare changed to something calculating. "It was my idea," he said.

Nothing sounded in Ginnevra's ears confirming the truth of this statement. "I don't believe you. You arranged it, true, but someone else gave you the idea."

Jiuseppe started to shake his head, but thought better of the gesture when he came up against the knife. "All right, it was in a discussion with a group of like-minded Torunes who are influential in Quinizelle. What do you care?"

Still Ginnevra didn't hear the ring of truth in his words. "That's where you proposed it. But someone else said something that influenced you. Who was it? Think, Jiuseppe."

Jiuseppe opened his mouth and shut it again. Then he said, "High Priest Rainaldus...he told me of the suffering of our people at the hands of the Faithful and said it was a shame there wasn't anything to support them." His voice sounded oddly distant, as if coming from deep within memory.

The sound of the bell hadn't faded when Ginnevra asked, "And who suggested you present yourself as King Paolo's potential heir?"

Jiuseppe blinked. "That was—High Priest Rainaldus. He said..." He moistened his lips with his tongue. "He said Quinizelle should be ruled by someone committed to our religion."

"And he implied that that day should come sooner than the natural course of King Paolo's life?"

"That's a lie," Jiuseppe said, but without force. "You're suggesting the High Priest manipulated me. All my decisions are my own, paladin."

"Except you're not sure now." Ginnevra took a step forward and leaned in. "You're looking back over everything Rainaldus has said to you, and you're questioning his motives. You know the High Priest is dedicated to his religion, and you're most of the way to being convinced you've been his pawn for a long time now. How sure are you that Rainaldus wouldn't do whatever it takes to hound the Faith out of Quinizelle? Including murder?"

Jiuseppe's jaw tightened. "I trust him with my life," he said.

No bell sounded in Ginnevra's ears.

Ginnevra stepped back and crossed her arms over her chest. "Zealots are dangerous," she said. "We have a story of a paladin captain named Mennagrande...this was about fifty years ago, long before my time, but her example is one nobody wants to forget. Captain Mennagrande became convinced that it was her duty to force others to obey the Goddess's will more perfectly, so they could be assured of a place in heaven. That's not how it works, but she believed her paladin's oaths entitled her to make those demands."

She caught Filippa's eye. Filippa's expression was grim, as if she too were remembering that story. "Eventually, that captain's obsession grew to the point that she started executing people she believed had achieved purity. In the name of sending them to the Goddess unstained, you see. She killed fourteen people before the Blessed struck her down."

"That's foul," Jiuseppe said. "And your Goddess never took Her blessing from that captain."

"She did," Ginnevra said. "But when Mennagrande continued on her quest anyway, the Goddess didn't stop her—not directly, anyway. And a lot of people wondered if that meant the Goddess approved of her deeds. But I—we—were always taught the Goddess allows us the freedom to choose, to see what we will do to others in Her name. Jiuseppe, I saw Rainaldus work magic in his god's name. Torun blessed him despite his crimes. Maybe that means Torun approves, or maybe it means Torun is waiting to see what other worshippers will do about it. Worshippers like you."

She held out her hand for the dagger. Filippa put the hilt in her hand. "Rainaldus is a zealot, and he's corrupting your religion," Ginnevra said, "but I don't think you'll be willing to stand for that." She slid the dagger beneath Jiuseppe's bonds and sliced the ropes apart. "Now," she added, cutting his other wrist free and handing him the dagger, "shall we meet at the palace tomorrow? I doubt the king will be happy about us invading his privacy at this hour."

Jiuseppe bent and cut the ropes binding his ankles. He thrust the dagger into his boot sheath and stood. "Get out," he said. "Before I change my mind."

"But I promised—"

"I said *get out*. This isn't your business." Jiuseppe pointed at the door. Ginnevra inclined her head, hoping he wouldn't think she was mocking him, and left the room.

She didn't turn to make sure Eodan and Filippa had followed her. She just made for the stairs, walking rapidly. When she rounded the first turn of the stairwell, she broke into a run.

The three of them pounded down the stairs, no longer trying to stay silent. They met no one on the stairs or in the halls, and made it to the back door with no trouble. Ginnevra pulled them all close together and invoked the concealment grace, not waiting for Eodan to change shape, then sped across the garden after Filippa. The moon had set, and a storm was rolling in, thick gray clouds turning the night blacker than before.

She had to give Filippa, then Eodan, a boost to the top of the wall before taking a running leap that nearly had her clearing it entirely. Outside, they ran again, Eodan in the lead this time. When the grace wore off, they were most of the way back to the hostel. Eodan came to a halt on a corner three streets away and bent over, breathing heavily. "Now what?"

"Do you think he'll denounce you to the king?" Filippa asked.

Ginnevra shook her head. "I suppose it's possible, but I gave him too much to think about. Right now I'd wager he's revisiting all his interactions with Rainaldus and coming to some unpleasant conclusions."

"That was a tremendous risk, beloved," Eodan said.

"I know, but it felt right. If Rainaldus is behind all our mysteries, that makes Jiuseppe as much his victim as anyone, and he deserved to know the truth." Ginnevra stretched. "I'm exhausted now. And if I'm wrong, and a squadron of guards shows up at our hostel in the morning to haul me in front of the king, I want to get a good night's sleep first."

Filippa continued to look skeptically at Ginnevra. "We need to discuss this further," she said. "Not tonight. But if it's High Priest Rainaldus we intend to take down, that requires a different plan."

Ginnevra nodded. "Are you all right? Jiuseppe didn't hurt you?"

"No. I told you, I don't think he intended torture." But Filippa didn't look certain. She added, "I'll meet you tomorrow at the Empty Flask—you know where that is?"

"We can find it." Ginnevra hesitated. "I'm glad you're well."

"I'm glad you understood my message," Filippa said. She nodded and ran off into the darkness.

Ginnevra and Eodan trudged back to the hostel in silence. The man on duty at the front door watched them enter and head for the stairs, but said nothing, not even a greeting. Ginnevra felt too tired for conversation, so that was just as well.

In their room, while undressing, Eodan said, "You didn't give her back her grace."

Ginnevra's hand automatically gripped her belt pouch. "I didn't."

"Did you have a reason for that?"

"I don't know." Ginnevra shook the grace on its thong into her palm. "Maybe I don't believe she ought to carry it, even if she doesn't wear it properly. Or maybe I just forgot. It was a busy night."

Eodan put his arms around her and pulled her close. "Old loves are the hardest to let go, even if you feel you should."

Ginnevra rested her head on Eodan's broad shoulder and sighed. "I can't stop remembering our friendship. How close we were. How she made me walk away from her."

"She made you? Ginnevra, how was that not your choice?"

"Because—" Ginnevra stopped, struck by memory. "Because I wouldn't have done it if she'd kept her oaths. I couldn't do anything else."

Eodan slid a hand across her back, a comforting feeling. "Beloved," he said, "I think on some level you know you're the one who abandoned her."

Ginnevra sucked in a startled breath. She pulled back enough to look Eodan in the face. "I didn't. Did I? She... Eodan, she left the Faith."

"And you left her."

Ginnevra nodded slowly. "I did. I'm the one who walked away. But I don't know what else I could have done."

Eodan kissed her forehead lightly. "Maybe that's something you should consider."

"I will. But not tonight. I'm exhausted."

"Then let's sleep, and we'll see what the morning brings," Eodan said.

Sleep came quickly to Ginnevra, and she woke hours later to the sound of rain striking the window. She knew at once she'd slept longer than usual without the sun's rays to wake her. Rather than rising immediately, she rolled over and nestled against Eodan's side, relishing the warmth of his body.

Someone knocked lightly on the door. "My lady paladin, there's a messenger for you downstairs."

Ginnevra groaned and sat up. Beside her, Eodan stirred and blinked at the ceiling. "What messenger?" Ginnevra asked.

"She gave her name as Filippa Genovarde and says it's urgent."

Ginnevra groaned again. "Would you send her up? I'll see her here." She stood and pulled her shirt over her head.

"You don't suppose Jiuseppe sent guards after Filippa instead?" Eodan said.

"I doubt it. I have no idea what could possibly be so urgent." Ginnevra finished dressing and pulled her boots on. She eyed Eodan, who was putting his own clothes on, and added, "I hope it's not so urgent we can't have breakfast."

Another knock sounded. Ginnevra waited for Eodan to tie the laces of his trousers, then opened the door. Filippa was out of breath, her eyes wide. She gripped the sides of the doorway as if she needed their help not to fall over. "Ginna," she said, "Jiuseppe Zuccare is dead."

TWENTY-ONE

"Dead?" Ginnevra said. Filippa's appearance had startled her so much the word at first had no meaning. Her last sight of Jiuseppe emerged from memory, of how angry and resolute he'd looked. It was not the face of someone who was dead. She gripped the edge of the door as an anchor to the present and blinked the memory away. "But we spoke to him only hours ago."

"It happened sometime in the early morning, after we left. The news is spreading all over the city." Filippa's breathing quieted, and she stepped inside the room and shut the door. "I went to the estate to collect my things—"

"That was dangerous. Suppose Jiuseppe had told people you were a spy?" Ginnevra said.

Filippa shrugged. "It was worth the risk. Anyway, I talked to some of the servants, and they all said Jiuseppe's manservant found him around six-thirty when he took him his breakfast. Nobody agreed on how he died, so I think everything else they said was rumor. But nobody was talking murder, so it wasn't an assassin who somehow made it past the guards."

"Like we did," Eodan said.

"Yes, but we didn't kill him," Ginnevra said. "And I doubt anyone else could have bypassed the Zuccare estate protections."

"True, but it's also a huge coincidence if he died of natural causes hours after speaking to us," Filippa said, "and I don't believe in coincidence."

Ginnevra sat in a chair and began pulling on her boots. "Neither do I. The most likely explanation is that one of his enemies succeeded in assassinating him. Which means it has nothing to do with us, except that we're back to the beginning with regard to the massacre. Even if Rainaldus was behind that, we have no way of proving it."

"Unless that's why he was killed," Filippa said.

"You mean, killed to prevent him speaking against Rainaldus?" Ginnevra stood and stamped her feet, settling the boots firmly. "How would Rainaldus know?"

"I don't know." Filippa's lips were taut and her jaw set tightly. "Maybe that's impossible. It's just the worst possible explanation I can think of."

"Because it means Rainaldus knows more than we are aware of," Eodan said, his eyes distant with thought. "Suppose Torun gives him insights that will protect him? Lets him eavesdrop on potential threats?"

"Torun's not real," Ginnevra said, but she didn't feel as certain as she sounded. She remembered the golden light healing Rainaldus' wounds. That hadn't been trickery. "And if he is, I'm not willing to ascribe more power to him than is reasonable."

"We're a potential threat, Ginnevra," Eodan said. "I think we should consider whether we need to protect ourselves against Rainaldus' retaliation."

"If we don't know what Rainaldus is capable of, protecting ourselves is impossible. We can't anticipate every possible threat." Ginnevra slung her sword over her shoulder. "Let's get something to eat and see about learning more of these rumors. If Jiuseppe's death is public knowledge, some of them might turn out to be true."

The rain had subsided to a drizzle Ginnevra put up her hood against. She looked at Eodan and Filippa, whose heads were also covered, and reflected that they looked like a little group of mourners headed to a funeral. It felt unexpectedly appropriate, given that they'd possibly been the last people to see Jiuseppe alive. Ginnevra didn't like him any better now that he was dead, but she was starting to reconsider her first impressions of Jiuseppe as an arrogant, self-centered noble who cared more for his status than for the truth. He hadn't insisted Ginnevra turn herself in as she'd promised, and he'd sounded like he intended to investigate her allegations. It was unlikely he would have turned out to be an ally, but he might not have been an enemy, either.

The three of them ate meat pies bought from a street vendor who huddled in on himself, daring the rain even though they were the only ones gathered around his cart. The man brought up Jiuseppe's death voluntarily. "I heard he had a bad heart," he said. He seemed not at all put off by Ginnevra's sword. "Shame about that. All the Zuccares are prone to heart problems."

"Is that what killed Lord Jiovanni Zuccare?" Eodan asked.

"Oh, no. He was waylaid by thugs looking for a rich mark." The vendor leaned on his cart with one hand and gestured with the other in a way that suggested wielding a knife. "But probably he'd have gone the same way if that hadn't happened. Still, you have to laugh."

"Really? Why is that?" Ginnevra asked, startled by the man's sudden amusement.

"Oh, because they're all wealthy as kings, and yet they die as easily as anyone. No good having a pile of gold in your basement if your body gives out on you." The vendor laughed again. "Want another pie? You made short work of that one."

"Thanks, no," Ginnevra said, wiping her mouth. The pie had been hot and savory with a flaky crust, far better than she expected from street cuisine, but it had also been filling enough she didn't need a second.

She turned away from the cart and pulled her hood lower over her forehead. The chill in the air made her wish briefly for her nice, warm bed. "Well, you were right about Jiuseppe's death being news, if that man is anything to go by," she said when they were out of earshot of the vendor.

"I hadn't heard the thing about the Zuccares having weak hearts," Filippa said. "I wonder how true it is."

"It sounds like we need more information," Eodan said. "It's not too early to visit a few taverns, see what the gossip is." He tapped the hilt of Ginnevra's sword. "But we might want to leave this behind. That man was talkative, but I think most people will be silenced by it."

"I was going to suggest we split up, anyway," Filippa said.

It had been four years, but Ginnevra hadn't forgotten that particular tone of Filippa's voice, careless indifference masking a deeper hurt. "You think we don't want you with us."

Filippa met Ginnevra's eyes without flinching. "Do you?"

Ginnevra's face warmed with anger and embarrassment. "I'm not so rigid I can't accept help, whatever the source. I said I don't hate you."

"But I'm a reminder of the past you'd rather not have." Filippa continued to stare her down. "It doesn't matter, Ginnevra. I don't want to impose on you. Look, let's meet back at your hostel in two hours, all right? We really will be more efficient if we separate." She turned and walked away without waiting for a response.

Ginnevra stared after her, her mind numb and her heart aching. She remembered what Eodan had said the previous night about Ginnevra being the one who'd abandoned Filippa four years ago. She'd told herself at the time she didn't have a choice, and she felt that was still true. She was a paladin, Filippa wasn't, and their lives had to diverge. But now Ginnevra wondered if she'd done the right thing in so completely cutting her best friend out of her life. Had it hurt Filippa this badly watching Ginnevra walk away, hurt as much as Ginnevra now ached watching Filippa's retreating form?

Ginnevra blinked tears away. Heartache wasn't a good enough reason not to do what was right. But maybe it was a sign that she *hadn't* done what was right.

She took Eodan's hand for reassurance, but said, "Let's go. You're right, the sword is a liability."

Eodan held onto her hand when she would have pulled away. "Ginnevra."

"I've never felt this uncertain before, Eodan," Ginnevra said. "I thought it mattered more that I stick to my principles, and I still believe that. Paladins make hard choices, and we don't let personal pain get in the way of doing the right thing. But what if I'm wrong about what the right thing was?"

"I can't answer that, beloved." Eodan drew her along with him as he proceeded down the street. Their boots sent splashes of water up from the puddles that formed between the uneven cobblestones. "Am I right that you're worried about what forgiving Filippa will mean to your paladin's oath?"

"Yes. Sort of. I don't think she was right to abandon her vows and the Faith, and I'm afraid if I forgive her, that's like saying she didn't do anything wrong." Ginnevra stepped wide of a larger puddle. Raindrops hitting its surface showed that the storm had gotten worse. "I'm supposed to be the Goddess's representative, and if I don't stand for what She teaches, I might as well abandon my oaths too."

"Do you want my opinion?"

"Always."

Eodan bowed his head and said nothing for a moment. Just as Ginnevra was about to ask him what he was thinking, he said, "Among my people, forgiveness is a mark of one's own ability to change. It means rejecting the power someone who's wronged us has over us. It's not about pretending not to have been hurt, or telling the other person it was all right that they did whatever it was they did."

"So, does that mean I should stop feeling pain when I think about what happened?"

"It's not about that, either. Just—" Eodan lifted his head and gazed at the overcast sky. "I suppose in your case, by werewolf tradition, you would accept that both you and Filippa made choices that put you at odds, and you would decide to stop seeing Filippa's choice as deliberately intended to hurt you."

Ginnevra considered that for a moment. "I think I understand. You mean, see Filippa's side of the disagreement."

"That too, but mostly I meant letting go of constantly telling yourself how you were hurt by her actions." Eodan's steps slowed. "What is going on there?"

Ginnevra was already looking ahead to their hostel. A loose grouping of armed men stood near the door. They wore the gold and gray of House Zuccare on their surcoats. "That can't be good."

"Should we walk away? Whatever they have in mind is going to delay us," Eodan said.

"True, but I'd spend the whole day wondering about it if we left now," Ginnevra said.

They were within fifteen feet of the guards before any of the men—all men, Ginnevra noted, and wondered if that mattered—noticed their approach. That man's gaze fixed on the hilt of the sword that bobbed next to Ginnevra's ear. He turned around fully and drew himself up to attention, but awkwardly, reinforcing Ginnevra's earlier observation that the Zuccares didn't hire the best.

"Paladin Cassaline," he said in a booming voice that sounded like it was trying too hard to intimidate. "You will come with us."

"Will I?" Ginnevra said with a smile.

The other guards turned and stood at attention, raggedly as some of the men were slower on the uptake than others. The first guard said, "At the request of Lady Vinita Zuccare, paladin."

Ginnevra blinked, but gave no other sign she was startled by his words. "Lady Vinita? May I ask why the lady wishes to see me?"

The guard shifted his weight awkwardly and wouldn't meet Ginnevra's eyes. "Our instructions are to summon you to meet with Lady Vinita. On a personal matter. Her business is her own."

A personal matter. Ginnevra didn't think Vinita knew about her nocturnal visit to Jiuseppe, though that could be totally wrong. Jiuseppe might be the kind of man who discussed everything with his wife. On the other hand, what Ginnevra had told him might not be the sort of thing Jiuseppe wanted to share with anyone, even his wife. She couldn't draw any conclusions based solely on the fact that the man's widow had sent a squad of household guards to summon her.

She cast her gaze over the assembled guards. Most of them stared at her, though a few eyed Eodan as if assessing him as a threat and not liking their conclusions. They all moved restlessly, tiny shifts of arms and legs that said they were very nervous. Ginnevra noted that they bore truncheons rather than swords or maces. She sensed the king's hand in that decision; King Paolo, fearful of being overthrown by one of the noble houses, would certainly not want his enemies armed with more deadly weapons. How that squared with the crossbowmen atop the Zuccare estate, she didn't know, but it didn't matter.

"I see," she said. "Then I'm free to refuse."

The first guard licked his lips, a swift motion of his tongue, and swallowed as if to moisten his throat. "Lady Vinita would prefer that you do not."

"I'm sure she would." Ginnevra glanced at Eodan, who nodded minutely. An invitation to exactly where they wanted to go—teasing the guard was fun, but Ginnevra had no intention of missing this opportunity. "Very well. I take it you'd like us to go now?"

"You will come with us," the guard said, drawing himself up to his full height, which was a few inches short of Ginnevra's. Despite her annoyance at his attempt to intimidate her, she couldn't help being impressed at his bravery in the face of what he clearly believed was a dangerous enemy. Then she was annoyed again at his assumption that she might feel entitled to attack him unprovoked in the middle of the street, as if paladins were vicious and ungoverned. She tamped down on her annoyance and smiled pleasantly, gesturing to him to lead the way.

"March out," the guard said, and Ginnevra found herself and Eodan surrounded by guards. That, she would not stand for.

"I don't think so," she said, taking a few sideways steps that moved her out of the crowd. "You'll go first, and we will follow."

"It's meant to be an honor guard," the guard said, once more licking his lips nervously.

"Thank you, but no," Ginnevra said. "You'll have to show honor some other way." She shifted the muscles of her back and shoulder to make the sword bob up and down. The guard's attention immediately fixed on it. His eyes widened, and his jaw briefly slackened in fear. Ginnevra instantly felt guilty. His fears were unfounded, but that was no reason to play on them for her own satisfaction.

"It really is all right, sieur," she said. "It's not as if I'm going to run away, is it?"

The guard nodded and returned to his position at the head of the squad. Ginnevra and Eodan took their places at the rear of the group. Ginnevra found the pace the guard set was unexpectedly rapid. "I hadn't thought about how they would feel to have us at their backs," she whispered to Eodan.

"It's not as if you could lead the way," Eodan whispered back. "If they're afraid, there's nothing we can do about it."

"I'm certainly not going to give anyone ideas by showing up at the Zuccare estate looking like a prisoner." Ginnevra adjusted her grip on her sword belt. She wanted to talk about why Vinita Zuccare wanted to speak with her, but not where the guards could potentially overhear. So instead she covertly surveyed the people they passed. There weren't many, because the rain beat down harder now, but the few on the street gawked at their procession, as much at the guards as at Ginnevra and Eodan. Ginnevra didn't acknowledge the stares. Anywhere else, she might have made sure people knew where she was going, in case her "host" tried to make her disappear, but no one in Quinizelle cared about the fate of a paladin, and she didn't think the Zuccares had the resources to make that happen.

Two of the guards wrestled the cherub gate open when they reached the estate, and the rest of them trooped inside to the short entry hall leading to the great hall with its astonishing murals. The guards looked uncertain, but they didn't proceed further, so Ginnevra put back the hood of her cloak and stood dripping on the fine wooden floor.

A door that had been invisible opened, and a woman dressed in a gray and gold tunic over a linen shirt and a floor-length black skirt approached Ginnevra. "You are welcome here," she said, bowing. "You and your companion will please accompany me."

Another couple of servants, these male and wearing trousers under their tunics instead of skirts, followed the woman out of the small door. Ginnevra looked past them into the room, which was plain and bare by comparison to the rest of the mansion. One of the men bowed to her; the other bowed to Eodan. "They will take your cloaks and see that they are dried," the woman said.

This was a level of courtesy Ginnevra had not expected—or maybe it was just that Vinita didn't want strangers dripping rainwater all over her house. She removed her heavy cloak and draped it wet side out over the servant's arms. His expression didn't change, which impressed her.

The woman bowed again and gestured for Ginnevra and Eodan to follow her. The great hall was more brightly lit than it had been the previous night, but Ginnevra didn't gawk at the murals this time. She pretended she didn't know where she was going as the woman led them up the broad stairs to the hallway above. The scent of lilies drifted delicately to Ginnevra's nose before they rounded the landing and proceeded to where the second short flight of stairs went up. The woman didn't pause there, but took them across the hallway to one of the closed doors. She rapped lightly on it and then pushed it open without waiting for a response.

The room beyond was warmer than the rest of the house, and some of Ginnevra's tension eased with the simple pleasure of not being cold. A fire burned brightly in the fireplace to the left, drawing so cleanly not a hint of smoke escaped into the room. That, to Ginnevra, said "wealth" more even than the many chairs upholstered in tapestry shot with real gold threads or the fine steel mirror hanging on the wall opposite the fire. She took a few steps into the room and stopped before her dirty boots could touch the carpet woven in what she recognized as the Fayonne manner.

A woman sat near the fireplace, leaning forward slightly as if to soak up the heat. Ginnevra recognized her as the woman who'd held Jiuseppe's son the night of the dedication. She was as lovely as Ginnevra remembered, with large dark eyes and black hair arranged informally in a low roll at the base of her neck. Her kirtle was as informal as her hair, a somber and unadorned dark gray with a high neck, and over the kirtle she wore a loose over-robe rather than the form-fitting bodice Ginnevra expected. She didn't rise when they entered. The door clicked shut behind them, but Ginnevra didn't take her eyes off the woman to see if they were alone.

"Paladin," Vinita Zuccare said. "I didn't think you would come. Let alone with your companion."

Ginnevra raised an eyebrow. "You asked so politely, and I was curious. I didn't think you and I had anything to say to one another."

Vinita stood. "I suppose in a sense, that's true." She walked forward, her gaze fixed on Ginnevra. "Though you must know why I summoned you."

"I don't, sorry. Would you care to enlighten me?"

Vinita's neutral expression gave way to a snarl. "I want to know why you seduced my husband," she said.

TWENTY-TWO

S tunned shock flashed through Ginnevra, numbing her cheeks briefly and making her hands tighten into fists. "I beg your pardon?"

Vinita continued to walk forward until she faced Ginnevra directly. She tilted her head like an inquisitive bird, likely a raptor. "I don't see it," she said. "I'm far more beautiful than you. Maybe it was the thrill of sleeping with the enemy. Or maybe you're willing to do things I'm not—"

"Stop," Ginnevra said. "I didn't have sex with Jiu—Lord Jiuseppe. Why in the Goddess's name would you believe that? He hates—hated me."

Vinita's lips tightened briefly. "Don't bother denying it. I have proof in Jiuseppe's own hand. With his last breath, he tried to communicate with you. Not with me, his own wife, mother of his heirs, but with some upstart worshipper of a degenerate Goddess—"

"Watch your tongue," Eodan said just as Ginnevra said,

"Insult me if you like, but it won't change the fact that I never spoke to Jiuseppe but a handful of times at your son's dedication."

"I don't believe you."

"Of course you don't. You're so worried about the hold you had on Jiuseppe's loyalties you see infidelity everywhere." Ginnevra remembered Filippa's assessment of Vinita and added, "I doubt Jiuseppe was ever unfaithful to you, but I'm sure the servant girls you fired so he wouldn't be tempted don't care about that."

Vinita snarled again. "I have a right to protect what's mine."

Ginnevra shook her head. "If that's all you wanted, Lady Vinita, we'll show ourselves out. I'm sorry for your loss."

"You wanted his wealth, didn't you?" Vinita said. "Well, prepare for disappointment, because a man's wishes aren't honored unless they're enshrined in law. Even a dying man's last request isn't legally binding on his estate."

Ginnevra had half turned away, but this brought her back around to face Vinita. "What are you talking about? Money? Why would Jiuseppe want to give me money?"

"It's not yours," Vinita said. "I imagine you meant to take everything from me, didn't you? My husband, my money... none of that belongs to a foreign harlot."

"I told you to watch your tongue," Eodan growled, taking a step forward.

Vinita ignored him. "I wanted you here so I could tell you face to face that you failed. I'm his wife. You're just the slut he kept on the side."

Ginnevra's arm shot out, stopping Eodan from advancing further. "Lady Vinita, you're delusional," she said, keeping an even tone though she dearly wanted to slap the woman. "I didn't have an affair with Lord Jiuseppe. If he said otherwise, he was lying. I have no interest in sleeping with a man who's married to someone else. I swear that on my sword. Now, we'll leave you to your grief."

Vinita's eyebrows drew down over the bridge of her nose, and for the first time, Ginnevra saw uncertainty in her eyes. "You're the one who's lying," she said, but not as forcefully as she'd spoken before. "Why else would he want to speak to you?"

"I don't understand."

Vinita reached into her sleeve and withdrew a folded piece of paper. "This was under his hand when Carlitto found him this morning," she said. She handed it to Ginnevra.

Ginnevra opened the paper. She'd never seen Jiuseppe's handwriting, but she guessed it wasn't usually this sloppy or shaky. In wobbling letters that grew increasingly faint and illegible, he had written, *paladin knows where to* and then a couple of scrawls that didn't make any words Ginnevra understood.

She showed the paper to Eodan. "Cryptic," Eodan said. "What did Jiuseppe want, and why would you know about it?"

"Clearly he was referring to how you pleasured him," Vinita said.

"That's disgusting," Ginnevra said, but absently, all her attention focused on the note. *paladin knows where to*... Where did Jiuseppe mean that Ginnevra would understand? "This has to do with—the thing we talked about last night," she said to Eodan. "But I don't get it."

Eodan took the paper and squinted at it. "I think the word after this is 'find,'" he said. "Find something. Something Jiuseppe hid, maybe?"

"Hmm." Ginnevra returned her gaze to Vinita. "Where did Jiuseppe die?"

"I'm not telling you anything," Vinita said. "Get out."

"You invited me here. I think that deserves a little consideration. It wasn't in here, and I'm guessing it wasn't his bedroom, if he died in the act of writing a message. Does he have a study?"

"I said *get out*." Vinita pointed with a shaking hand at the door.

Ginnevra regarded the woman, how her lips were white with anger despite the tears in her eyes, and made a decision. "I don't think Lord Jiuseppe died of natural causes, my lady. And I think he wrote that note because he knew I was the only one who would guess the truth."

Vinita lowered her hand. "Are you trying to distract me with baseless accusations? Jiuseppe died of natural causes. A weak heart."

"Jiuseppe was investigating something that would have devastated Quinizelle if it came out," Ginnevra said. "It's not impossible someone would have wanted him silenced. You know he had enemies, my lady. Why couldn't one of them have gotten to him?"

"You mean poison," Vinita said. She dashed away tears from her eyes. "How do you know all this? And why do you care? This isn't your city, paladin."

"It doesn't matter how I know," Ginnevra said. "Jiuseppe knew what I suspected, and I think he must have left something —some piece of evidence pointing to his killer, maybe."

Vinita shook her head. "It's preposterous. You have no proof."

"I can examine the body," Eodan said. "Some poisons leave evidence of their presence. And there are often signs that indicate how someone died. If it wasn't heart failure, I might be able to prove that."

For the first time, Vinita looked fully at Eodan as if she hadn't really been aware of his presence. "You're a physician."

"I am. And I want to know the truth, Lady Vinita." Eodan rested a hand gently on her shoulder. "I think you must have loved your husband very much to be so angry at the thought of his being unfaithful. Let us help you discover what really happened."

Ginnevra thought it was more likely Vinita was afraid of being cast off by a philandering husband who found someone he liked more than he liked her, but she didn't voice that opinion. Instead, she said, "If Jiuseppe had evidence that will bring someone to justice, I want to know what it is. Can you help us?"

Vinita hesitated. She looked again at Eodan, who smiled slightly in encouragement. "You can examine his body, and the study where he was found," she said, "but I have no idea what evidence Jiuseppe might have hidden."

"Leave that to me," Ginnevra said.

She waited patiently while Eodan examined Jiuseppe's body. The servants had taken the body to his bedroom and arranged it neatly on the bed. To Ginnevra, dead bodies were nothing more than empty vessels to be returned to the earth or air, and unless she'd had a hand in making them so, she didn't see anything worth noting in their condition. But Eodan took his time, removing Jiuseppe's clothing and turning the body on its side, looking for Goddess knew what. Vinita had stayed for only a minute before turning pale and hurrying out, instructing Ginnevra to return to the sitting room when they were done.

She leaned against the wall and ran her fingers up and down the smooth scabbard of her sword. "So, was it a heart attack?"

"I don't think so, though it's hard to tell afterwards," Eodan said with an air of distraction that said he wasn't fully listening. "There's no obvious sign of poison, and most of the poisons I know of that leave no visible trace are the kind that act instantly. I doubt someone entered Jiuseppe's study and forced him to ingest a poison that would kill him that way. Not to mention that he wouldn't have had time to write even a partial message."

"Not a poison, then." Ginnevra sighed. "The fact that he wrote me a message as he was dying suggests some urgency. Like he knew he was under attack."

"I wonder," Eodan said, still in that distracted way. "His face is blue-tinged like he suffocated. There are no marks to show he was choked to death, and no sign of a struggle. If he had died in this room, I'd suspect his killer of having murdered him while he slept. But he was fully awake, as far as we know, and in his study." He rolled the body onto its back again, and after a moment's pause started dressing the body.

"I think this is as far as we're going to get with Jiuseppe's murder," Ginnevra said. "Someone suffocated him, but we don't know how. I'm more concerned about finding whatever he hid."

"Whatever it was, he put it somewhere you'd know to look." Eodan stepped away from the bed and regarded Jiuseppe. "I can't believe there would ever be a point where I'd wish nothing bad had happened to him."

"Me too." Ginnevra straightened. "It's something to do with the massacre and High Priest Rainaldus' involvement. If he learned something that would prove Rainaldus was behind Dianetta's murder—"

"How could he have, in that short a time? It couldn't have been more than eight hours after we spoke that he was killed," Eodan said.

"I don't know, but it's the only thing that makes sense, because if he'd known something before that, he wouldn't have been surprised at the possibility of Rainaldus being our villain, and he would probably have told us about it." Ginnevra began pacing, back and forth in front of the door. "He learned something, and it was something important, because he hid it where no one but I would find it. And I bet it wasn't meant to be a permanent hiding place, because I won't be in Quinizelle forever."

"It's a hiding place only you would think to check, too," Eodan said.

Ginnevra nodded. "Let's start with his study."

Vinita somewhat sullenly led them to Jiuseppe's study, which was adjacent to his bedroom. "Did you find anything about his death?" she asked Eodan.

Eodan waited until they were inside the study with the door safely closed before replying. "It wasn't heart failure or poison. Someone suffocated him. I don't know how."

Vinita's eyes widened. "That's impossible."

"It almost is," Eodan agreed, "but I'm certain of it."

Ginnevra ignored this conversation and prowled the room. It felt smaller than it was due to the heavy oak paneling covering the walls, dark and dour. Two wide windows with tiny glass panes didn't make the room feel any larger, though they would let in plenty of light on a day less overcast than this. The fireplace, with its hearth made of river stones and the gray marble mantel, was empty and cold. Ginnevra knelt beside it and ran her fingers through the ash, then felt around inside the chimney. She didn't expect to find anything, which was exactly what she found.

"What are you doing?" Vinita demanded. "Leave that alone!"

Ginnevra ignored her, too. She dusted her fingers off on her trouser leg and continued her examination. The desk had its back to the windows so anyone sitting at it would have plenty of natural light to work from. A couple of loose, blank sheets of thick, pale gray paper lay atop it, next to a crystal and gold inkwell that was half full of black ink and a quill pen with a blunted nib. Bookcases filled not with books but with expensive-looking knickknacks flanked the door, over which hung a small version of the Zuccare shield Ginnevra had seen in the palace great hall.

Ginnevra ran her fingers over the top of the bookcases and

displayed gray dust clinging to them. "I thought you had servants for that," she said.

"Jiuseppe doesn't let anyone in here. Didn't. Only himself and me, on occasion." Vinita glared at Ginnevra. "I think you're wasting my time."

Ginnevra cocked her head and looked at the shield more closely. "Eodan, would you bring me that chair?"

Eodan carried the chair from behind the desk and positioned it beneath the shield. He steadied the chair as Ginnevra stood on its seat. She touched the top of the round shield, examining it more closely. Her fingers came away clean. "Someone's handled this recently," she said, "and..." Her voice trailed off as she remembered herself telling Jiuseppe that someone wearing House Zuccare insignia had hired the mercenaries who killed Dianetta, her entourage, and fourteen paladins. That insignia, this shield, were the only things Ginnevra and Jiuseppe had in common. The only thing Jiuseppe knew Ginnevra would remember.

She gripped the shield with both hands and worked it free of the wall. Behind it lay a crevice about a handspan wide and tall. "Here, take this," she said, lowering the shield so Eodan could take it from her. Vinita made a noise of protest, but Ginnevra ignored her. She peered into the crevice, which was narrow and dark enough that even her vision had trouble making anything out. She gave her eyes a moment to adjust, confirming there wasn't anything alive in there, before reaching inside. Her fingers brushed rough-textured paper, rolled up like a scroll, and then touched the smoother surface of a ribbon tied around the paper.

Gingerly, she slid the thing out of the crevice in case she was wrong and this was something old that needed delicate handling. But the paper was new, gray-tinged and matching the pages on the desk. The dark blue ribbon tied around it was wider than her first two fingers together and had been knotted tightly. Dangling from one of the ribbon ends was a yellow wax seal impressed with the Zuccare insignia.

"What is that? Give it to me!" Vinita said.

Ginnevra stepped off the chair and turned away from Vinita, keeping the scroll out of the woman's reach. Once more ignoring the woman, who made another grab for it, she slid the ribbon off the scroll rather than trying to untie the knots and unrolled it. There were actually three papers, covered in neat handwriting that slightly resembled Jiuseppe's dying message. Ginnevra read *I, Jiuseppe Zuccare, head of House Zuccare, put my name and seal to this affidavit* and the previous day's date.

Vinita made another grab for the pages. Ginnevra held them high above her head, out of Vinita's reach. "Jiuseppe left this for me," she said, though she wasn't convinced that was true. For all she knew, the document was intended for someone else and Jiuseppe had died so rapidly he hadn't had time to direct that person to the hidey-hole. But her instincts told her Vinita shouldn't read this, at least not yet, or Jiuseppe would have shown it to her before.

"Everything in this house is my property, including that," Vinita said. "If Jiuseppe made a new will, I demand to see it."

Ginnevra scanned the first page. "It's not a will. It's... actually, nothing to do with you."

"I'll decide that," Vinita said. She held out her hand for the pages.

Ginnevra shook her head. What little she'd read confirmed her instincts. "It's a letter to the king, and Jiuseppe wanted me to deliver it," she said. That was only about three-quarters true, but it was true enough Ginnevra didn't feel bad about lying.

Vinita's eyes narrowed. "*You*, deliver a message to the king?"

"He intended to take it himself, but when he knew he was dying, he had to reach out to the only person who could find that hiding place." Ginnevra let the pages roll back together and thrust the roll into her shirt. "Thank you for your time, Lady Vinita, and we'll be going now."

"You will not." Vinita put herself between Ginnevra and the door. "I think you're lying about what's in those pages. You will hand them over to me this instant, or I'll have the guards on you for theft. You won't trouble me if you're locked up in the justiciary."

Ginnevra took a menacing step forward, and Eodan put a restraining hand on her arm. "You have more pressing matters to attend to, my lady," he said.

Vinita's gaze flicked from Ginnevra to Eodan. "Are you trying to distract me?"

"Lord Jiuseppe was a strong candidate to inherit the kingdom from King Paolo," Eodan said. "House Zuccare is still powerful, and there's no reason the king might not choose to pass the throne to its heir—particularly if the heir has a strong mother for his or her regent."

Vinita's mouth fell open. Eodan continued, "But I'm sure you know better than I what kind of forces are against you, or will be once House Alamanne and House Nazarente figure out that Jiuseppe's death doesn't have to change anything with regard to the succession. I think you have more important things to do than pursue a couple of foreigners who plan to leave this house and never return to bother you or interfere with your business."

"I—" Vinita closed her mouth tightly. Then she stepped aside from the door. "Get out, and don't come back," she said.

Ginnevra brushed past her and headed for the stairs with Eodan close behind. The roll of paper rubbed against her skin, the faintest touch. It was only her imagination it burned with a light anyone could see through her shirt.

The same woman servant who'd greeted them emerged from

the hidden door just as they arrived at the front door. She handed over their cloaks, which for a miracle were barely damp. "Have a nice day," she said, opening the door for them.

Ginnevra hurried outside and toward the gate. She could almost feel the gazes of the guards on her back, burning holes in her shoulders. The rain had stopped, and the clouds had lightened somewhat, but she put up her hood anyway, feeling an absurd desire to avert the guards' gaze. It didn't matter that they couldn't hurt her; what she carried might be figuratively explosive, a secret she didn't want anyone discovering until the time was right.

TWENTY-THREE

T here was no one to open the cherub gates, but Eodan pushed on one until it moved enough to let them both through. Outside, Ginnevra paused to adjust her cloak, which she hadn't donned properly in her desire to get far away from the Zuccare mansion as fast as possible.

"So, what does it really say?" Eodan asked. "I don't know that the king will see us without an appointment."

"We're not going to the king, not yet," Ginnevra said. "I need to read this fully to find out exactly what Jiuseppe learned."

"Ginnevra, stop being cryptic. Curiosity is killing me."

Ginnevra jerked her head in a direction away from the mansion. "Walk, then. Back to the hostel. I don't know much yet, because I'm not a fast reader and I didn't want to stand there examining the pages while Vinita might tear them away from me. But I know Jiuseppe was a damn fool. He confronted Rainaldus last night after we left."

Eodan swore explosively. "Why did he do that? If Rainaldus

was behind all those deaths, he might not care about causing one more death if it meant protecting his secret."

"Jiuseppe was an arrogant bastard who was convinced his status was a protection." Ginnevra dodged a puddle and reflected briefly on how much cleaner city streets were when there weren't a lot of horse-drawn vehicles clogging the roads and dropping waste everywhere. "The first lines of what he wrote are an explanation of what he suspected about Rainaldus' involvement in Dianetta's death. I think he intended to give this to King Paolo, though I don't know why he wouldn't just meet with the king and tell him everything."

"Maybe that was his plan, and this was his security," Eodan said. "Jiuseppe *was* paranoid and suspicious."

"That's possible. Probable, even." Ginnevra shifted her sword so she could steady it better. "At any rate, I'm sure the document was intended for the king, because there's no mention of us or our involvement. He wanted to take all the credit for discovering Dianetta's killer."

"Typical." Eodan made the turn onto the hostel's street and immediately had to step out of the way of another pedestrian coming around the blind corner. He apologized to the woman, then continued, "But we don't care about getting the credit, do we?"

"Only in the sense that I want the king to connect Rainaldus' hiring the mercenaries to the paladins and Captain Ercole being innocent, so I can use that to influence him to stop the religious war." Ginnevra hurried faster to reach the hostel. Her curiosity about what else Jiuseppe had written burned inside her. "It's not about my personal aggrandizement, certainly," she added as she pushed the front door open.

Inside their room, she shed her cloak and pulled the roll of papers out of her shirt. "Jiuseppe has—had good handwriting, at least. I'm not great at reading aloud, but I'll do my best."

Eodan settled into the chair opposite her, leaning forward with an intent look on his face. Ginnevra shifted into a more comfortable position and silently read the first few lines. "It says this is his affidavit—if Quinizelle is like the other city-states of the Lordagne, that means he's swearing to the truth of what he writes in the same way he would if he were testifying before a justicer. That makes this legally binding. But I'm not sure what happens if the testator is dead—it doesn't matter."

She cleared her throat and read, "'I, Jiuseppe Zuccare, discovered evidence that High Priest Rainaldus Mastarcce was responsible for arranging the murder of Lady Dianetta Napolle four years ago using my brother, Lord Jiovanni Zuccare, as his pawn. I further accuse Rainaldus Mastarcce of murdering or causing to be murdered Lord Jiovanni Zuccare to prevent my brother revealing the High Priest's crime.' This is fairly bold of Jiuseppe."

"Keep reading. There has to be more to indicate why he took such a chance," Eodan said.

Ginnevra nodded. "'On this the twenty-second day of Hiraldi, I went to Rainaldus Mastarcce's residence to require him to admit to his crimes. Rainaldus at first denied everything, like the lying deceiver he is, until in the course of our conversation he revealed knowledge of Lady Dianetta's murder that he should not have had were he innocent. When I pressed him further, he freely admitted that he had suborned Lord Jiovanni into hiring mercenaries to attack the caravan Lady Dianetta traveled with and ensure her death in a way that would lay blame on the paladin captain who commanded the caravan, with the intent of blackening the Faith in your eyes.'"

Eodan put a hand over Ginnevra's. "You're crying."

"I know." Ginnevra swiped at her tears. "It's just that seeing it all laid out so starkly makes me angry in a way I wasn't at the time. All those murdered paladins. Poor Captain Ercole. I feel as if I betrayed her in believing the accusations laid against her."

She wiped her eyes again and cleared her throat. "There's more. *'I informed Rainaldus that I would take this story to you, your majesty, upon which Rainaldus boasted that you would not believe me because he has a hold on you. Whether he spoke figuratively or literally, I do not know, but I believe you should know Rainaldus' deceptions and manipulations might extend to an attempt to control the ruler of Quinizelle.'*"

"That's ominous," Eodan said.

"Very. *'I write these words as my sworn testimony, recognizing that I have no evidence beyond my word of Rainaldus' evildoings. However, you will recall, your majesty, the curious behavior of my brother Jiovanni before his death, how he avoided Rainaldus and refused to meet with you at all. At the time, Jiovanni confided in me that he wished to divulge a secret, but he was killed before he spoke with me again. I now believe Jiovanni intended to expose Rainaldus as the mastermind behind the plot to kill Lady Dianetta.'* Damn. Think how much trouble would have been saved if Jiovanni had had a spine."

Eodan shrugged. "It was the High Priest of his religion who suborned him, and Jiovanni wasn't all that bright, as far as we've been told. He might have believed he was doing the right thing to serve his religion."

"Even so, I doubt Jiuseppe would have gone for it even if his lover hadn't been the target. *'Again, I have no proof, but I ask you to recall my many years of faithful service to Quinizelle, my reputation for honesty, and my loyalty to you, your majesty, and further ask that you put your considerable resources toward proving or disproving my claim. I intend this affidavit to serve as written testimony to support what I will tell you in person. Written this twenty-third day of Hiraldi by Lord Jiuseppe Zuccare, his mark.'* And then it's sealed with the same mark as on the wax seal, only in black ink."

Eodan leaned back. "So he really did plan to tell the king. I wonder why Jiuseppe hid this so well?"

"This would be like a match to dry tinder, accusing the highest authority of the Torune religion of murder and conspiracy," Ginnevra said. "He couldn't risk anyone getting their hands on it before he informed the king. Which is probably why, when he was dying, he wrote that message pulling me in. We might have disliked each other, but once Jiuseppe was convinced I was telling the truth, I became his only ally."

"He had more integrity than I believed, if he could set aside his hatred like that." Eodan rubbed his hands together. "Now what? We need to take this to the king, but as I said, I doubt he'll be willing to see you without an appointment."

Ginnevra stood and rolled the pages together again. She stowed them in her shirt again, this time more carefully; she'd chipped the wax seal the first time, and she had a feeling it would provide legitimacy to her claim and to Jiuseppe's affidavit so long as it wasn't destroyed by careless handling. "We're going anyway," she declared. "Jiuseppe's death was no accident. He left Rainaldus' house last night having accused the High Priest of murder, and to me that gave Rainaldus all kinds of motive to kill Jiuseppe, as quickly as possible."

"By magic," Eodan said. "I know it sounds impossible, but I'm convinced it's less impossible than someone sneaking into the Zuccare mansion and suffocating Jiuseppe without leaving any signs of an attack."

"By magic," Ginnevra repeated. "I agree. I don't know how to prove it, but if we can convince the king that Rainaldus was behind Dianetta's death as well as Jiovanni's, that makes the idea that he killed Jiuseppe more plausible."

Eodan stood as well and handed Ginnevra her cloak. "Then we ought to hurry. Rainaldus might have guessed Jiuseppe was paranoid enough not to count on just his spoken word to the king, and if he has some influence over King Paolo, who knows what he might do?"

They hurried out of the hostel and were most of the way down the road when Ginnevra heard Filippa calling her name. The flash of irritation that shot through her and then disappeared embarrassed her, or maybe it was just that she'd forgotten they'd intended to meet later that made her feel guilty. She stopped and turned around.

Filippa ran toward them and stopped, breathing heavily. "Where are you going?"

Her unspoken *without me* deepened Ginnevra's guilt. Before she could let it silence her, she said, "I'm sorry. So much has happened, I forgot we were supposed to meet up here."

Filippa's expression changed from curious to neutral in the space of half a breath. "If you don't want me here, tell me," she said.

"It's not that," Ginnevra said, despairing. Memory struck, and for a moment she was four years in the past, saying *If there's anything left to say, I don't know what it is* and then walking away from her best friend. Her heart constricted, and she was briefly mute, choked with a dozen responses that might change the past. Except that was impossible.

She removed the pages carefully from beneath her shirt and handed them over. "Jiuseppe left me a message that led to finding that," she said. "Read it. You'll see why it made us forget everything else."

Filippa's eyes moved rapidly as she scanned the page. She had always been a better reader than Ginnevra. The memory again tore at Ginnevra's heart. Surely there had to be some middle way —but there was nothing that could bridge that four-year gap that didn't also mean saying Filippa had been right. For a moment, Ginnevra remembered what Eodan had said about forgiveness, and about not seeing Filippa's choice as deliberately meant to hurt her. She watched Filippa's face, so intent on her reading, and something clicked inside her head. "Filippa," she said.

Filippa let the pages roll together. "That changes everything," she said. "Were you going to see the king?"

With that reminder of their mission, Ginnevra changed her mind about what she meant to say. "We were. You should come. If we can get in to see him, you can swear to the truth of Jiuseppe's story, at least as far as the evidence that says Jiovanni was involved."

"I doubt he'll be interested in the word of a disgraced ex-paladin." Filippa didn't sound bitter, just matter of fact.

"If we didn't have this—" Ginnevra took the roll of paper from Filippa and tapped it against her other hand— "I doubt he'd listen to our accusations at all. We have to hope Jiuseppe's word is enough to compel the king to hear the rest of the story."

But Filippa's comment reminded Ginnevra of how precarious their situation was. With King Paolo hating her for what she represented and wanting to see the Faith humbled, there was a good chance they'd never make it as far as showing him Jiuseppe's testimony. She squared her shoulders, testing the position of her sword, and added, "We have to take the chance. And if he won't see us..." Her voice trailed off.

"We'll think of something else," Filippa said. "I haven't come this far to give up before we've failed." She smiled. "Remember Negozente?"

Ginnevra laughed. "I shouldn't have encouraged you, but that singer was so handsome." For once, memory didn't pain her.

"Granted, he wasn't interested in me, but if I hadn't approached him, I wouldn't have met his partner. And *that* was a spectacular night." Filippa's smile faded. "I haven't thought of that night in years."

"Me neither." Ginnevra hesitated, conscious of Eodan standing nearby. It wasn't as if she didn't trust him with all her secrets, but this conversation had taken a decidedly personal turn and she wasn't sure she wanted to continue it in the presence of an outsider. She cleared her throat. "Anyway. We should go."

Filippa nodded. "Do you have a plan for getting into the palace? I've seen those guards. We could take them easily, but that's not the precedent we want to set."

"I have part of a plan," Ginnevra said. "I'm hoping inspiration will provide the other part."

THE ARCHED STREET leading to the gate glistened in the wan sunlight. No water pooled on its curve, but the stones hadn't dried yet, either. A few more months, and a rainfall like that would leave the street icy enough to be dangerous. The four soldiers in their hardened leather armor were unfamiliar to Ginnevra, but then she hadn't paid close attention to them in all the times she'd entered the palace grounds.

No, that wasn't true—one of the guards was a woman with a long scar along the right side of her jaw. Ginnevra did remember her; she was the one who'd spoken to Ginnevra on her first visit, instructing her in where to go. Even if Ginnevra had believed in omens, she didn't think this was necessarily a good one.

"Stop there, paladin," the scarred woman said. She stepped forward and held her halberd crossways in a warding position. "You haven't been summoned."

Ginnevra opened her mouth to say *I haven't*, and a sick chill swept over her, settling in her stomach like a warning. She heard herself say, "We were meant to follow Hallowed Nevante, but I believe she's outpaced us."

The guard raised an eyebrow. "She said nothing about you when she arrived."

Ginnevra's mind tried to make sense of all this and was over-ridden by her instincts, which came out as, "I'm sure she had other things on her mind. Will you allow us to pass?"

The guard examined Ginnevra closely. Ginnevra sent up a short but fervent prayer that the Goddess knew what she was about. She knew how it felt when the Dark Lady influenced her words, but every other time she'd experienced it, it had been accompanied by a warm feeling of rightness, not this sick, stom-ach-churning dread. Something was very wrong, something the Goddess wanted her aware of. She pushed aside her clamoring thoughts and smiled pleasantly at the guard, hoping the sick feeling didn't make her smile look false.

Finally, the guard raised her halberd. "You can pass," she said, "but we don't recognize the other two. They stay here."

"I'm a physician, and I treated Lady Benitta Napolle a few days ago," Eodan said. "This is my assistant. The lady's atten-dants will vouch for me."

Now both the guard's eyebrows rose. "I see," she said. "Then you're free to enter. Wait in the courtyard for a guide."

"Thank you," Ginnevra said, deliberately not responding to the command. She made herself walk casually past the guards and the raised portcullis. Drawing more attention to herself by running was a bad idea. Beside her, Eodan and Filippa kept pace. Ginnevra realized Eodan wasn't carrying his physician's satchel, and the sick, worried feeling deepened. If those guards turned around and noticed, if they were all as suspicious as the scarred woman, that might be the end of Ginnevra's ploy. She hoped the Goddess's intervention extended to distracting the guards.

They walked through the short tunnel that passed beneath the outer wall and entered the courtyard. For once, there were people there, crossing between the walls and descending the stairs from the keep. Their presence reminded Ginnevra that usually the courtyard was empty because it had been cleared in anticipation of her arrival. If they hadn't cleared it for Hallowed Nevante, that might mean she hadn't been expected, either. Ginnevra's stomach churned again, and this time, her dread had a focus. The Hallowed approaching King Paolo uninvited could not mean anything good.

"Hurry," she said, and broke into a run. Far behind her, someone called out a demand for her to stop. She cursed inwardly, but kept running. It wasn't likely the guards could catch up to her before she reached the keep. With Eodan and Filippa flanking her, she sped across the courtyard and up the stairs to the keep, dodging people who stopped to stare and didn't have the wit to move out of her way.

Within the keep, the receiving chamber was empty, its black and white tiles brighter and its ceiling murals more distinct in the wan sunlight. Ginnevra didn't slow to look around. She followed the path Pattero had taken her by the first time she'd visited the palace, deeply grateful that she'd paid attention to the winding passages. Filippa's breath wheezed in and out of her lungs, but she didn't complain or slow her pace. With the plush carpet silencing their footsteps, Filippa's breathing and the sound of Ginnevra's sword slapping against her posterior were all the noise they made. Ginnevra superstitiously wondered if that silence was part of the Goddess's plan, too, though she didn't want to speculate on what that meant about the Goddess's plan. She hoped again that there was one.

They came to the double doors leading to the throne room, one of which was ajar the barest crack. Ginnevra came to a halt there and drew in a deep breath to soothe her tortured lungs. "Listen," she said, mouthing the word so no sound emerged.

She heard Hallowed Nevante speaking in an angry voice. "You have no care for those of your citizens who don't bow the knee to your religion," the woman said. She wasn't shouting—yet—but Ginnevra was sure it was only a matter of time before the conversation became ugly.

"Quinizellans are free to worship however they like," King Paolo said. "But we will not permit them to disrespect their king."

"Then their king ought to be a man worthy of respect," the Hallowed shot back. "Not someone who is nothing but a pawn in the hands of a reprobate."

Eodan pressed his lips nearly to Ginnevra's ear and whispered, "Shouldn't there be guards on this side of the door, too?"

A chill shot through Ginnevra. "Damn it," she whispered. "She's going to be killed." With a shove, she sent both halves of the door flying open. They were heavy enough to swing only as far as the guards positioned inside, and she heard the thump of hands against oak, stopping them from opening further. With a few quick strides, she was inside the throne room, well past the possibility of the doors closing on her again.

She was peripherally aware of Eodan and Filippa taking positions beside her, but most of her attention was focused on Nevante, standing in front of the carved wooden throne at the far side of the room, and on King Paolo, seated before her. Groups of courtiers huddled in perfect silence to either side of the throne, staring at Nevante as if they expected her to attack or burst into flame or begin speaking in tongues or do something equally exotic.

Nevante hadn't turned when the doors opened, but King Paolo sat up, looking past the Hallowed at Ginnevra. His lips peeled back in a snarl. "You dare," he shouted. "Guards!"

Ginnevra immediately unslung her sword and let it fall to hit the carpeted floor with a muffled thud. She held her hands away from her body in a nonthreatening gesture. "Forgive me, your majesty, for entering armed," she said in a loud, carrying voice, "but I was in a hurry. I swear I am no threat to you."

Behind her, the doors slammed shut, and she heard the heavy footsteps of the approaching guards. She kept her eyes fixed on King Paolo, though her paladin's instincts were screaming at her to turn and fight. "Please believe me, your majesty," she said, her shoulders tensing. "I don't want this to turn into a fight. I'm here because—" She swallowed. Her other instincts, the ones that had overridden her at the gate, told her bringing up the Goddess was the wrong move. "I'm here because I want to see this matter resolved peacefully. Please."

A hand closed over her shoulder. Beside her, Eodan growled, but it was a human sound and not the spine-chilling terror of a werewolf's warning. She couldn't stop her muscles from tensing again, but she managed not to turn on the guard and break his wrist.

The king sat back, nodding. The hand was removed. Ginnevra rolled out her shoulders and said, "Thank you, your majesty."

"We choose to overlook this blatant disregard for our person —for now," the king said. He wasn't looking at Ginnevra anymore, but at Nevante, and his glare could have melted steel. "Hallowed Nevante, your complaint has been heard. We invite you and Prime Cassaline to withdraw."

Ginnevra walked forward until she stood at Nevante's side. She hated the feeling of being unarmed in a room full of enemies, even if none of them were capable of giving her a good fight, even the armed guards positioned around the throne room. "Has Hallowed Nevante done as you asked?" she said.

King Paolo's expression soured. "We believe the Hallowed has made her position clear. There will be no apology."

Ginnevra wished the sick feeling would go away. This was clearly what the Goddess had warned her about. "King Paolo, I am certain—"

"Do not abase yourself, prime," Nevante said, her voice tense with fury. "The king chooses to align himself with Torunes and shows no regard for anyone or anything else. I refuse to put myself in Rainaldus Mastarcce's power."

Movement behind the throne drew Ginnevra's attention. She had been so focused on the king and the Hallowed she hadn't noticed Rainaldus standing there. His smile was openly gloating. No wonder Nevante was furious, in the face of that smile.

Ginnevra's gaze flicked from Rainaldus to the smaller yet still ornate chair beside the throne. Benitta Napolle looked calm, far calmer than anyone else in the room, until Ginnevra took in her trembling hands and clenched jaw. Benitta's gaze was locked on something far distant—no, that was wrong, she was looking past Ginnevra, and a quick glance around told Ginnevra it was Eodan Benitta watched.

Rainaldus stepped forward, keeping one hand on the back of the throne. "Your majesty knows I am a loyal subject. I regret that my counterpart cares more for her personal power than for the well-being of ordinary Quinizellans."

Nevante's face contorted in fury. "You smooth-talking *bastard*," she snarled. With one hand, she snatched her jet grace bound in silver from beneath her black robe. With the other, she pointed at Rainaldus. "Your false god has no power, and I will prove it. *By Your grace I bind my foe!*"

CHAPTER

TWENTY-FOUR

ainaldus stiffened, his arms rigid at his sides as if he was bound, and then toppled to the floor. The courtiers screamed and ran for the doors, scattering throughout the room. Amid the chaos, the king shot to his feet. "You dare work your foul magic in our presence?" he shouted. "Guards, stop her!"

"No!" Ginnevra screamed. She grabbed Nevante by the shoulders and shook her. "Stop it! This isn't what the Goddess wants!"

Nevante laughed. "You, telling me what the Goddess wants? That's ridiculous." She wrenched out of Ginnevra's grip, which hadn't been tight because Ginnevra didn't actually want to lay hands on an anointed. "I'm past being patient with these people. They should want to serve a true Goddess, not some made-up god intended to keep them subservient to their false priests. *By Your grace—*"

Ginnevra grabbed her again, this time covering her mouth and peeling her fingers away from her grace. That time, she'd been pointing at the king. For a moment, Ginnevra wondered whether

283

the Hallowed had gone mad. Then she had to snatch the woman's hand away from her grace again.

Nevante pulled away from Ginnevra's hand over her mouth. "You can't stop me doing what's right," she said triumphantly. "Look—"

Her mouth fell open. Ginnevra didn't want to risk losing control over Nevante by looking to see what had startled the woman. "You can't attack—damn it, Hallowed, this isn't right! We have to go!"

"I don't think so," Rainaldus Mastarcce said.

Ginnevra twisted around, not letting go of the Hallowed, and felt as stunned as Nevante looked. Rainaldus was pushing himself to his feet. He was clearly no longer bound by Nevante's grace. "Your Goddess has no power over what Torun protects," he said. "But if you want a fight, Torun will gladly give it to you."

"You shouldn't—why are you not bound?" Nevante whispered. She sounded frightened rather than confused, and she stopped fighting Ginnevra's grip.

Rainaldus grinned. He flung his hands high in the air and began muttering words that sounded like Sezarni. Ginnevra's cold, sick feeling of dread grew. Either Torun was real, or the Goddess had withdrawn Her power from Nevante, but either of those things was enough to frighten her.

She released Nevante, who sank to the floor, still staring at the chanting High Priest. "Your majesty!" Ginnevra shouted. "You have the power to end this. Do you really want full-out religious war to ravage your kingdom?"

She caught sight of Benitta, who was crying, and added, "So many innocents will be hurt, King Paolo. Please, ask the High Priest to stop."

"Hallowed Nevante brought this on herself," King Paolo said.

He, too, was staring at Rainaldus. "Why should I stop the High Priest proving to these witnesses the power of Torun?"

Ginnevra walked forward until she stood between Rainaldus and Nevante. "Because I am still the authorized representative of Abraciabene," she said, "and I am sworn to defend the anointed, regardless of the circumstances. Either you stop him, or I will. And then I will impose sanctions on Quinizelle. You don't want that. Choose, your majesty." She pushed up her sleeves and readied herself for a fight.

King Paolo said nothing. Ginnevra turned her attention on Rainaldus. Based on what she had seen the night of the dedication, the Torune High Priest had to work himself up to performing divine magic, like a ritual. And his chanting certainly looked and sounded like ritual now. So, how long could she give the king to decide before she had to act? Not long, she concluded.

Rainaldus' eyes had rolled up in their sockets until almost nothing but white showed. A thin line of foam extended from one corner of his mouth, which went on moving ceaselessly in a murmured chant. Ginnevra drew in a breath and let it out slowly. Distantly, she heard Eodan say her name. She hoped he wouldn't reveal himself. That was all this debacle needed, a werewolf complicating matters.

She cracked her neck and rolled out her shoulders. "Your majesty," she said.

"Enough," King Paolo said. Rainaldus didn't stop murmuring. "I said *enough*, High Priest," the king repeated, more forcefully.

Ginnevra took a step toward Rainaldus, then another. Whatever magic the High Priest had in mind, she didn't intend for him to release it. That probably meant she was about to die. Silently, she prayed for strength to endure whatever came next.

Then Rainaldus lowered his head and wiped away the foam from his lips. "As you command," he said. Three simple, ordinary words, but Ginnevra was still looking at him, and he was furious. Ginnevra realized she stood between him and the king as well as between him and Nevante and decided not to move. For the first time since entering the palace, she remembered what had actually brought them there and considered how far Rainaldus' loyalties might go.

"Your majesty," she began again.

"Don't speak," the king said furiously. "We choose to spare Hallowed Nevante whatever fate Torun intended. But the fact that one of the Goddess's anointed could attack one sworn to serve this kingdom, as well as threaten the king's person, says that there is no room in Quinizelle for the Faith or its Faithful. Lay whatever doom you choose on this kingdom, prime. We would rather endure hardship than put up with such corruption at our heart."

Ginnevra turned to face him. "I don't understand," she said, but the sinking feeling in her stomach said she did.

"From this moment, we banish the Faith from Quinizelle," King Paolo said. "Every Faithful has seven days to either convert to the true religion or leave the kingdom entirely. We have spoken." He turned and flung himself into the throne.

Ginnevra's gaze automatically fixed on Benitta. Her skin was pale, and she sat with her hands clasped together, though despite this they still trembled. Benitta returned her gaze with a look of agonized indecision.

She heard movement behind her, the sound of Nevante getting to her feet with Eodan's help, but the Hallowed said nothing. Then Eodan said, "That's rather drastic, your majesty. You would condemn innocents to exile? Innocents who trust your capacity for honorable judgment?"

The king leaned forward. "Who is this stranger?"

"That is Eodan, the physician I mentioned," Benitta said. Her voice trembled as much as her hands.

King Paolo turned to face her, and his expression softened. "You need not fear, Benitta," he said. "This is for the best."

"I don't think so," Eodan said. "Your majesty—"

"We honor your calling, and your treatment of our lady wife," King Paolo said, glaring at Eodan. "Do not mistake this for honoring your uninformed opinion."

"Your majesty, surely you won't endure the presence of these Faithful any longer?" Rainaldus said. He sounded sincere, but his smile once again gloated over Ginnevra's defeat. "Have the guards escort them out."

"Of course," the king said, rising from his chair. "Guards—no, dearest, you are clearly overwrought," he added as Benitta rose as well. "Please, sit, and we will have someone see to you."

Benitta shook her head. "I can't stay, Paolo," she said.

The king's brow furrowed in concern. "What do you mean?"

Benitta's trembling stopped, and Ginnevra suddenly had a moment's vision of the immediate future. She thought she might be the only one not surprised when Benitta fished her obsidian grace from within her skirt pocket and extended it so King Paolo could see it. "Because you have just exiled me," she said.

The king took a startled step backward. "Benitta," he said. "Benitta, what game is this?"

"No game, Paolo." Benitta looped the silver chain around her neck and settled the grace openly on her chest. "I am of the Faithful, and I have been since before we were married. I tried—oh, my dear one, you don't know how often I nearly told you. I didn't want to keep secrets from you, but I was afraid. I'm so sorry this is how you found out." She wiped tears from her eyes and curtseyed low before her husband. "A week, you said? I'll gather my things

—don't worry, I won't take anything I didn't bring with me to this marriage."

King Paolo put a hand out to stop her walking away. "Did you think I would hate you? Benitta, what kind of monster do you take me for?"

Benitta shook her head. "It's not that. It's—Paolo, haven't you ever had something in your life that was greater than you? Something that makes you the best version of yourself?"

"I thought I did," the king said, lowering his hand. The corners of his mouth quivered as if he was desperately holding back tears.

Benitta choked on a sob. Ginnevra prayed more fervently than ever that she wouldn't do anything to draw attention to the fact that there were other people in the throne room. Even Rainaldus was perfectly still and silent. "I love you," Benitta said, "and I love the Faith. I thought I could have both, that I wouldn't have to choose. I'd meant to tell you about my religion the night you proposed, but..." She smiled behind her tears. "You remember, don't you? It wasn't the right time."

"There have to have been a thousand right times since then," King Paolo said. "I don't understand."

"I was afraid you wouldn't want me anymore, that you would remember Dianetta's death every time you looked at me." Benitta wiped her eyes again. "I should have trusted you. I'm sorry."

This time, when she walked away, the king didn't stop her.

Ginnevra wished there was some graceful way to grab Eodan and Filippa and Nevante and vanish. King Paolo watched his wife cross the throne room and pass through one of the doors. At least, his head was turned in that direction; Ginnevra suspected he didn't see much of anything just then.

Rainaldus cleared his throat. "Your majesty is saved a terrible fate, being yoked to an unbeliever," he said.

Ginnevra involuntarily took a step away from Rainaldus and

bumped into Nevante, who let out a gasp of pain from Ginnevra stepping on her foot. Ginnevra shushed her. Rainaldus was as oblivious as Nevante if he thought that was something the king wanted to hear right now.

"We will make a proclamation and send it throughout the city," Rainaldus went on, still unaware of the king's clenched fists and unseeing gaze. "You can leave everything to me."

"Get out," the king whispered.

"Excuse me, your majesty? I didn't hear—"

"I said *get out!*" the king roared, turning on him. "Get out, and don't return until I summon you!"

"You don't mean that, your majesty," Rainaldus said.

The king drew a deep breath, preparatory to a monumental shout. Ginnevra quickly said, "Forgive me, your majesty, but I have something that won't wait."

King Paolo rounded on her. "Sanctions? You think I care about sanctions now?"

"Not that, your majesty." Ginnevra withdrew the rolled papers from within her shirt and extended them to the king so the yellow wax seal dangled freely between the two of them. "This is something you should read."

The king glanced at the swinging seal, then took a closer look. "What is this?"

"A message from Jiuseppe Zuccare," Ginnevra said.

The king's brow furrowed. "Lord Jiuseppe is dead."

"Yes, and this is clearly a ploy by this paladin to confuse you," Rainaldus said. He reached for the papers. "Do not allow her to interfere in Quinizellan matters."

Ginnevra moved the roll of papers out of Rainaldus' reach. "I'm just the messenger, your majesty." She again offered the papers to King Paolo.

The king ignored her offering. "Jiuseppe would not have entrusted you with anything important," he said.

"He didn't, really." Ginnevra glanced at Rainaldus. The High Priest looked impassive, far too impassive for someone who'd been in a rage only moments before. "I was just the only one available."

"The woman lies, your majesty," Rainaldus said. "Lord Jiuseppe could not have had anything to commit to paper, because he was a loyal and trusted servant—"

"He wanted the throne, and he would have done anything to achieve it," King Paolo said. He drew himself up to his full height. "All of you, get out before my guards discover the limits of a paladin's martial skill."

"You don't mean me, your majesty," Rainaldus said with a sympathetic smile.

King Paolo glared at him. "I mean *all of you*. Now." He strode away to the door beneath the Zuccare shield and slammed through it.

As the door shut, the guards positioned throughout the room came to life, converging on their little group. Eodan said, "Let's not turn this into a worse disaster than it already is."

Rainaldus was already headed for the main doors, which the guards had opened and now held wide. Ginnevra shoved Jiuseppe's affidavit into her belt and hurried after him, flanked by Eodan and Filippa. She stopped to scoop up her sword by the belt and then gripped it in her left hand, feeling the need for the reassurance the scabbard's smooth leather and the sword's heft gave her.

All of them, including Rainaldus, paused outside the doors as they shut. Rainaldus no longer looked impassive. He glared at Ginnevra. "Whatever you think you know," he said, "you have no proof."

Ginnevra met Rainaldus' gaze. "You've lost," she said. "As soon as the king reads Jiuseppe's testimony, your time is done."

"I think not," Rainaldus said, and he smiled. It was such a terrible, confident expression of triumph Ginnevra had to stop herself taking another step back. "I have the king well in hand. Even if he reads that nonsense, which he obviously never will, he won't believe the written word of a dead man over the testimony of a living priest of Torun. And then I will... encourage... King Paolo to fulfil his word and cast the Faithful out of Quinizelle."

"Don't be so proud," Eodan said. "You can't see the future any more than we can." He held Nevante by the elbow in a way that put her behind him so he stood between the Hallowed and the High Priest, though Nevante looked too stunned to be a threat.

"I have seen the future, by the power of Torun." Rainaldus' smile widened. "It holds nothing but defeat for you."

"You think?" Filippa exclaimed, startling Ginnevra, who'd forgotten she was there. Filippa took two quick strides to face Rainaldus and grabbed the neck of his robe, throwing him off balance. She pulled him close until they were nose to nose. Ginnevra gasped when she saw the wickedly sharp knife in Filippa's other hand. In a flash, Filippa laid the knife against Rainaldus' throat. Rainaldus, who had begun to jerk away, froze.

"You *bastard*," Filippa said in a low, hoarse voice. "You killed Dianetta and my sisters and you might as well have killed Captain Ercole too. And you have the nerve to believe yourself justified in all that. Tell me why I shouldn't end your life right here, right now."

"Filippa," Ginnevra said, then fell silent. Watching the two of them poised on the brink of death, she couldn't think of a single reason to stop Filippa killing Rainaldus.

"Don't try to stop me, Ginna," Filippa said without taking her eyes off Rainaldus. "It's justice."

"It's murder," Eodan said. "It doesn't matter how many lives he got away with taking. Killing him now won't bring them back, and it won't be justice."

Eodan's calm, deep voice brought Ginnevra back to the real world. "He's right," she said. "Killing him will stop him hurting anyone else, true. And maybe that's enough. But we won't have justice for our dead unless he's tried and condemned legitimately. Rainaldus kept a secret the Goddess will punish him for, but only if we do this right. Filippa. Let him go."

Filippa's chest heaved with the force of her breathing. Rainaldus stayed still, his eyes on Ginnevra rather than Filippa. Whether he thought he could look to her for compassion, she didn't know, but he was a fool if he believed she was on his side just because she'd argued for justice over vengeance.

Then Filippa withdrew the knife and released Rainaldus. The High Priest straightened and rubbed his neck. "The king will hear of this," he said.

"No, he won't," Ginnevra said. "You're not stupid. You don't want any more attention on you than you've already got, not while the king might still believe Jiuseppe's words. And I don't think you're as sure of your hold over him as you say." She grabbed Filippa's elbow and tugged. "We're leaving. And you'd better stay out of our way, because I'm not totally convinced your death isn't a necessary outcome." She strode away, dragging Filippa with her.

Eodan followed behind until they reached the courtyard, making Ginnevra grateful she had him to watch her back. They crossed the courtyard side by side in silence. Ginnevra glanced at Filippa once or twice, but the woman stared at her feet rather than her surroundings, and her expression was as bleak as Ginnevra had ever seen her look.

They passed the guards without acknowledging them, though the scar-faced woman followed them a few steps as if she wanted to say something. Ginnevra didn't have anything she wanted to talk to the guard about. Now that they were safely away from the king and the palace, doubt had set in. She should have made the king take Jiuseppe's testimony. She should have insisted on him reading it immediately, and never mind Rainaldus' presence. Now the odds of King Paolo even looking at the papers were so small Ginnevra might as well have lit them on fire right there in the throne room.

"Let go of me," she heard Nevante say. She turned to see the woman wrench free of Eodan's grasp. "You should not lay hands on me."

"Why not?" Filippa said. "It's not as if you're Hallowed anymore."

Nevante turned on her, her face twisted with rage. "I don't know who you are, but I don't let anyone pass judgment on me except the Blessed herself."

"Or the Goddess," Ginnevra said.

Nevante jerked away from Filippa. "I'm not under condemnation. That was..." Her voice trailed off, and she wouldn't meet Ginnevra's eyes.

"So you want to believe Rainaldus' made-up god overpowered the Goddess?" Ginnevra snapped. "What the hell were you thinking, attacking someone unprovoked?"

"He provoked me," Nevante shot back, but she still wouldn't look at Ginnevra. "That smug smile—you know as well as I, prime, that that bastard wanted nothing less than to see me humiliated. I had no choice."

"The Goddess clearly doesn't agree." Ginnevra grabbed Nevante's arm and made the woman look at her. "A paladin isn't meant to judge the anointeds' worthiness, but from what I just saw, that's unnecessary. The Goddess has withdrawn Her blessing from you."

Nevante jerked away. "I refuse to believe that."

"That's what Captain Mennagrande said," Filippa said.

Nevante turned on her. "You dare compare me to that filth?"

Filippa stood her ground. "I know what it's like to lose the Goddess's blessing. You'd do better to beg Her forgiveness than to rage about what ought to be."

"Filippa's right," Ginnevra said. "Go back to the sanctuary and ask Revered Bariatte to contact the Blessed. She can tell you what to do next."

Nevante's chest heaved again with her rapid breathing. Her lips curled in a snarl. "If you'd followed instructions and commanded King Paolo to intervene, none of this would have happened. I'll go back to the sanctuary because, thanks to you, I have to arrange for the evacuation of hundreds of Faithful. And if you think *I'm* condemned, you ought to take a close look at yourself." She turned and strode away through the crowds, shoving aside anyone who didn't get out of her way fast enough.

Numb with sorrow and guilt, Ginnevra watched her go. Nevante was delusional, but she was right about one thing—this was Ginnevra's fault. She'd put so much effort into her own solution she'd forgotten the Blessed's instructions, and—

"No," she said aloud, drawing both Eodan and Filippa's attention. "No. I did the right thing. Nevante was as much at fault as Rainaldus for the violence, and I couldn't force the king to penalize only the Torunes. So maybe this was where things were going, all along."

"It can't have been destiny," Filippa said. "You know that."

"No, not destiny. Just the outcome of every choice I made." Ginnevra sighed and settled her sword more comfortably across her shoulder. "Tomorrow I'll return with the official decree that cuts Quinizelle off from Abraciabene's economic support. I don't think King Paolo will agree to see me again today."

"Did you know Lady Benitta was of the Faithful?" Filippa asked.

"We did. I told her to tell her husband the truth." Ginnevra set off down the street. "Two more lives ruined because of a secret wrongly kept. And Benitta loses her home as well as her marriage."

Eodan put a hand on her arm, stopping her before she could step around another of the blind corners Quinizelle seemed to have so many of. "This isn't the end of the world. What happened to your famous optimism?"

"The Faithful of Quinizelle have to leave their homes," Ginnevra said. "Quinizelle's economy is going to hell. The Hallowed of Quinizelle is under condemnation just when the Faithful need her most. And we can't prove Rainaldus Mastarcce is guilty of more than two dozen murders. I don't see anything to be optimistic about."

Eodan released her. He said nothing. Ginnevra, who despite herself had hoped for reassurance, shook her head and walked on.

TWENTY-FIVE

G innevra woke at dawn, going straight from dream to reality with an abruptness that made the dream dissolve without leaving a trace in memory. She lay blinking at the ceiling, which seemed very far away at first. Beside her, Eodan snored lightly. She almost put a hand on his back to center herself, but realized in time that would wake him. This was not a day when anyone ought to be awake any earlier than absolutely necessary. She wasn't sure what internal signal had roused her, but she resented it.

She knew it was dawn despite the curtains obscuring the window; she recognized the color and texture of the light from hundreds, maybe thousands of mornings as a paladin. Usually, dawn was her favorite time of day, a time when everything was fresh and new and she was the only one awake. Today, with half a dozen unpleasant tasks looming in her future, dawn was something else she resented.

She closed her eyes and tried to fall back asleep, but it only took a minute for her to admit this wasn't going to happen.

Opening her eyes, she once more stared at the ceiling. She had to deliver the official document severing trading ties between Abraciabene and Quinizelle, and then she had to go to the sanctuary and report this action to the Blessed. Whether anyone there could invoke the grace that made the eternity fountain a communications conduit, she didn't know, which meant she might also have to temporarily shut down the sanctuary. A sanctuary wasn't supposed to function without a Hallowed's presence, and a Hallowed had to be anointed by the Blessed herself. With Revered Bariatte being male and Revered Aperrede being rather timid, that meant someone new being appointed to take over.

Then she remembered that thanks to King Paolo's edict, the sanctuary would be shut down regardless. What a nightmare.

Eodan's breathing changed. She rolled onto her side to find him watching her. "I wish I could tell you 'good morning,'" she said.

Eodan smiled, but his eyes were full of sympathy. "Still not optimistic?"

"I've tried. Nothing about this is good." She sighed and put one arm across his chest, hugging him close. "I've about resigned myself to putting this mess behind me, but every time I consider that, I feel guilty, like I'm not doing my best."

"You're the most responsible person I know," Eodan said, "and the most compassionate. It's natural you'd feel the burden of this. But don't consider it your failure. You did everything you could, and you shouldn't bear more of a load than you deserve. King Paolo and High Priest Rainaldus and Hallowed Nevante are at least as much to blame."

"I know. I'm not used to passing off blame to someone else, though. It's not something paladins do." Ginnevra rested her head on Eodan's shoulder and sighed again. "I'm glad you're with me. I don't know if I could bear this alone."

"Let's look forward to moving on, then. Maybe somewhere warm." Eodan kissed her forehead. "Somewhere not quite so wet."

"That's a beautiful dream," Ginnevra said.

A knock sounded at the door. Ginnevra groaned and rolled out of bed, wincing at the chill in the air. She padded to the door bare-foot, not bothering to dress, and flung it open. If her state of undress shocked whoever this was, maybe they'd not bother her at dawn again.

It was the hostel owner. Her gaze took in Ginnevra's loose linen shirt and drawers and returned to Ginnevra's face. "I'm sorry if I woke you," she said, with no indication of discomfort, "but you have guests who insisted on seeing you immediately."

"Who is it?"

"They refuse to give their names, but they are of the Faithful, and they seem very distraught." The hostel owner's hand strayed to touch her obsidian grace, which hung openly around her neck from a silver chain. "I should have sent them on their way, but I had a feeling..."

"I understand," Ginnevra said, though she still felt annoyed. "Will you show them up in five minutes?"

The hostel owner nodded. She turned to go, but then said over her shoulder, "There will be an interruption of service in the coming week as we prepare to leave Quinizelle. I hope you won't mind."

Ginnevra felt like the biggest heel in the history of the world. "Please, don't apologize for that. I feel responsible enough already. I should be asking you if there's any way we can help."

"We don't blame you. I think this expulsion has been coming for a long time, at least as long as Rainaldus Mastarcce has influ-enced the king." The hostel owner smiled, but her eyes were bright with tears. "This is just one step in the journey, after all."

"Still. If we can do anything, anything at all—"

"Thank you for the offer. I'll remember." The hostel owner nodded and turned away.

Ginnevra closed the door and leaned against it, pressing her forehead to the wood, and swore under her breath. "I don't know who to curse first."

"No point in it, beloved." Eodan rose and reached for his trousers. "She's right. All we can do is take the next step."

"That's a lot less satisfying than profanity, but I can accept that."

They were fully dressed and the room tidied when another knock came at the door. Eodan opened it. His body blocked Ginnevra's view of the visitors, but the way Eodan's back tensed told her this wasn't going to be a simple matter.

Then he stepped aside, and Benitta and Pattero entered.

Ginnevra rose from her seat. "I didn't expect to see you. Either of you. Please, sit."

Benitta's face was pale, and her hands shook. She made no move to take the chair Ginnevra offered, but Pattero took her elbow and guided her to it. He didn't sit. "My lady," he said, "I apologize for intruding, but we had nowhere else to go."

"The Alamannes wouldn't take you in," Ginnevra guessed.

Pattero nodded. "I thought they would at least be willing to shelter us for a night or two before we leave Quinizelle. But—well. It wasn't pretty, the scene our father made when we approached him last night. He was extremely displeased at how we'd lied to him about our religious beliefs, and he was furious with Benitta for, as he put it, throwing away her chance at being royalty."

Benitta let out a sobbing breath, but she shook her head at Pattero when he exclaimed. "I'm sorry, I'm being dramatic," she said. "This is how it has to be. But—my lady paladin, we've never been anywhere but Quinizelle. We don't even know what the world looks like beyond the mountains. I know it's a huge imposition, but I hoped you would help us."

Ginnevra and Eodan exchanged glances. Eodan wore the look that said he was deeply grateful this was a paladin's responsibility. Since Ginnevra knew it meant he would support her in whatever she decided, the look made her feel merely weary instead of resentful. "What kind of help did you have in mind?"

"We have distant relations in Devoyenne," Pattero said. "If we could travel with you—we'd be able to pay our way, of course."

Ginnevra had a sudden bleak vision of herself and Eodan leading a train of Faithful through the mountains to Paese and beyond. Fortunately, it was her imagination and not a warning from the Goddess. "I think we could manage that," she said.

Benitta clasped her brother's hand tightly. "Thank you. It's more than we hoped."

"You'll need a place to stay for a few days. We aren't leaving until the end of King Paolo's week," Eodan said.

The look on Benitta's face as Eodan mentioned the king sent a shock through Ginnevra, stealing her breath momentarily and making her skin tingle. "That's not enough," she heard herself say. "Lady Benitta, you need to speak to your husband one last time."

Benitta paled further, and she swayed in her seat before gripping the armrest with her free hand to steady herself. "He doesn't want anything to do with me."

"It's not about him, it's about you," Ginnevra said. She didn't know where any of this was coming from, but she felt the sense of rightness that told her the Goddess approved. "You are the only one who can stop this exile."

"I?" Benitta's eyebrows furrowed in confusion. "What can I do?"

"You can ask King Paolo to rescind his edict for your sake."

Ginnevra sat on the chair next to Benitta so they were eye to eye. "Ask him to show compassion for the innocents who will suffer."

Benitta laughed. It was a mirthless, croaking sound that ended in a raw-voiced rasp. She cleared her throat and said, "You think he'll care? You're mad."

"I think it was one thing for him to banish a bunch of people he's never met," Ginnevra said, "and something completely different to cast out the woman he loves. Benitta, the king received a terrible shock yesterday. He's had all night to think about it. I think he deserves a final chance to change his mind. And you're the only one he's likely to listen to."

"I think she's right, Benitta," Pattero said.

Benitta looked up at him. "You, too? What am I supposed to do—abase myself before him, beg him to rethink his position?"

"Exactly that," Pattero said. "Sister, I've said repeatedly that I didn't think it was a good idea for you to conceal your Faith from Paolo—no, don't, I didn't mean that as a criticism," he hurried to say as Benitta let out another heartrending sob. "My point is that I've always had faith that things would work out for the best if you could just bring yourself to be honest with him. And I don't know that it's too late for that. Please. You might be able to change his mind."

Benitta swiped a hand across her tear-filled eyes. "But what if it doesn't work?"

"Sometimes it's not about the result you get, it's about doing the right thing," Ginnevra said. "And I'll go with you. My presence isn't likely to infuriate King Paolo further, if he's set on expelling the Faithful, and I have to deliver my official ultimatum, anyway."

"I don't—" Benitta swallowed. She looked again at Pattero, whose lips were taut in an expression of steely resolve. "All right. I'll do it."

"Then let's go now," Ginnevra said. "No point waffling when

you've made up your mind. Eodan, will you meet me at the sanctuary in an hour? This shouldn't take long."

"You're going to confront Hallowed Nevante," Eodan said.

"I hope 'confront' turns out to be the wrong word, but yes."

Ginnevra looked at her armor, piled neatly in a corner. For a moment, she considered leaving it off for this errand. If, by some miracle, King Paolo was in a forgiving mood, she didn't want to ruin that by presenting him with a reminder of what he hated. Then she mentally slapped herself. She was a paladin, a prime sworn to the service of the Blessed, and she wasn't going to conceal that for any reason. If the king decided to take offense, that was his business.

Twenty minutes later, she and Benitta walked up the arched street toward the palace portcullis. For once, the sun was shining, not a wan, weak light filtered through storm clouds, but a strong golden glow that warmed the air and made the clear, cloudless sky look as deep as the ocean. The sunlight cheered Ginnevra and put a spring into her step, though it couldn't dispel her knowledge of what was coming next. Benitta didn't seem to feel the same; she kept her hood raised, and she walked with her head bowed as if they were headed for the gallows.

The scar-faced guard met them halfway to the portcullis. "Paladin," she said, then glanced at Benitta and jerked back, her eyes widening. "My lady."

"We have business with the king," Ginnevra said, fixing the woman with a steely glare. "And no, we haven't been summoned. I am not interested in playing dominance games. Either you let us pass unmolested, or I give you the fight I know you're itching for."

The guard's jaw hardened. "I should make you fight me," she said in a low voice that didn't carry farther than the three of them. "It's as much as my job is worth to let unauthorized visitors pass. But..." She looked again at Benitta. "You are in my lady's company, and I choose to consider that authorization enough."

"I'm outcast," Benitta said in a low, rough voice. "I am no longer entitled to your respect."

"We have no orders to prohibit you passing, my lady," the guard said. "And I don't know that that's an oversight." She saluted, bringing her halberd upright. "Go right ahead."

Ginnevra and Benitta hurried past the other guards and into the courtyard. It was busier than Ginnevra had ever seen it. A stillness spread outward from her as the courtiers passing recognized the shining silvered armor of a paladin, one person after another stopping in their tracks until the courtyard was full of motionless, well-dressed men and women. Ginnevra swallowed. She'd never felt so conspicuous.

"Come with me," Benitta murmured, and led Ginnevra to the stairs up to the keep. Instead of entering by the great double doors, they walked briskly along the terrace fronting the keep until they came to a smaller door. It was iron banded and looked as impregnable as the main entrance, but Benitta depressed the latch and it swung inward easily, making no noise.

Lanterns rather than windows lit the hallway beyond, and between the fine, dark red carpet and the warm brown paneling, Ginnevra had the impression of passing from day into night. Even the hall with the stained glass windows didn't feel as opulent as this.

Benitta put back her hood and strode forward, showing no evidence that she felt intimidated by her surroundings. Ginnevra hurried to catch up to her. "Where are we going?" she asked, more to fill the silence than because their destination mattered.

"My chambers," Benitta said. "It's tradition that no one enters the king's private rooms unless they're invited. I'll send one of my

—my former servants with a request that I be allowed to speak to him."

"What if he refuses?"

"Then he refuses, and we leave." Benitta didn't look at Ginnevra.

"Lady Benitta—" Ginnevra began.

"I can't bring myself to impose on Paolo. Not after I hurt him so much." Benitta walked faster. "If the Goddess wills it, then I'll have my chance."

That sounded like a terrible idea to Ginnevra. "Sometimes doing the right thing means discomfort or pain," she said, "not giving up before you've tried."

Benitta stopped and rounded on Ginnevra. "I am *not* giving up. But Paolo—" She rubbed tears from her eyes. "I don't expect you to understand."

Ginnevra said nothing. She wanted to challenge Benitta, but she felt in her heart that would be pointless. "Fine," she said after it was clear Benitta was done talking. "Let's get this over with." She put a hand briefly on the scroll case tucked into her pistol belt. She'd left the pistol behind as she had every time she'd entered the palace, but she needed someplace to put the Blessed's edict so her hands would remain free. The black scroll case, sealed at either end with the silver new moon of Abraciabene, felt bigger than it actually was.

She'd stuck Jiuseppe's roll of papers, now somewhat crushed, beside the scroll case. It wouldn't matter, because the king wasn't any more likely to read it than he had been the previous day, but miracles did happen. It was better to have it and not need it than the other way around.

After a couple of turns, the dark hall led to a door which opened, to Ginnevra's surprise, on the stained glass hallway. She wished she were in a mood to appreciate how the direct sunlight set the glass on fire with color and heated the hall to a degree Ginnevra felt like basking in. Benitta continued to walk rapidly, not raising her head. This was her home, or had been, so it made sense that she wasn't impressed with its grandeur and beauty, but Ginnevra still felt it was a shame that she didn't appreciate the windows. Then she remembered Benitta's grief and was glad she hadn't expressed that thought.

They passed a number of courtiers, all of whom ignored Benitta so ostentatiously it was obvious they saw her. Ginnevra glanced at Benitta's face to see if their shunning bothered her. Her eyes were dry, but her lips were white with tension, and she kept her attention fixed on a point somewhere ahead of them. Ginnevra's earlier irritation with the woman's fear and reluctance vanished. She wished now she hadn't insisted on Benitta speaking to King Paolo—though that hadn't been her insistence, had it? Ginnevra prayed silently for the Goddess's continuing guidance, wherever that guidance led.

They crossed the gray and black courtyard to a hallway Ginnevra hadn't entered before. It was as dim and dour as the others, with more portraits of unhappy people, possibly people who resented spending eternity in a dark hallway. Two armed and armored guards flanked the one door, which was at the far end.

Benitta's steps slowed as she and Ginnevra approached the guards. "If they won't let me pass," she whispered.

"Let's worry about that when we come to it," Ginnevra said.

But before they reached the door, it opened, and King Paolo emerged.

Benitta let out a gasp and stopped. The king's eyes widened when he saw her, and he, too, stood still. Ginnevra, who was a step behind Benitta, considered her options. She'd promised Benitta to stand with her, defend her, but that made a private conversation between her and her husband impossible. On the other hand, King Paolo did not look like someone interested in conversation. His jaw was tense as if he was holding back an outburst, and one hand closed into a fist.

Benitta's breathing had become loud and harsh, and Ginnevra's extraordinary hearing perceived the rapid beating of her heart. "Have faith," Ginnevra whispered, not knowing if it was she or the Goddess who had prompted it.

Benitta shuddered. Then she walked forward, stopping a few feet from the king. Ginnevra couldn't see her expression, but the king's face grew more wooden. "I thought you'd gone," he said. He showed no sign that he was aware of the guards at his back or of Ginnevra.

"I did," Benitta said. "But..."

Her voice trailed off. The king's eyes narrowed. "Come to claim more of your possessions?" he said, his voice harsh and rough.

Benitta shook her head. "I wanted to speak to you."

Again, she went silent. Ginnevra felt as if her head might explode from the tension of waiting for Benitta to gather her courage. She shifted her weight preparatory to taking a step, and an invisible hand closed around her, holding her in place.

"You have something more to say?" King Paolo said in that same harsh voice. "Some other devastating blow?"

Benitta shook her head once more. "No, Paolo," she said. "I came to beg your forgiveness."

"You think you deserve forgiveness?" The king's voice was no more than a whisper now. "You lied to me. You betrayed me—"

"I made a terrible mistake," Benitta said. "I was so afraid of losing you I didn't realize I was on a path that would lead to that very thing. I told myself you didn't ever need to know about my true religion, and then I told myself it would hurt you to learn the truth." She drew in a shuddering breath. "I was such a fool. I love you, and I treated you like a child who wasn't strong enough to face a challenge head-on with me. I can't express how sorry I am."

"Because I cast you out?" King Paolo said.

"Because I hurt you." Benitta clasped her hands in front of her, out of Ginnevra's sight. "I wish I could forget how you looked yesterday when I showed you my grace. I'm going to live with that forever. And I barely dare ask your forgiveness, because I know I don't deserve it."

The king took a step forward. "I don't understand any of this. I don't understand why you thought I would let what happened to Dianetta influence how I felt about you. Does your religion mean more to you than I do?"

"It's not a competition. You are who I love. The Faith is who I am." Benitta's hand flew up to cover her mouth as if that would stop her crying. In a choked voice, she added, "I know it doesn't matter anymore, but I do love you. Nothing that has happened has changed that."

"Then prove it," King Paolo said. "Renounce the Faith, and stay here with me."

Ginnevra let out a startled hiss. Neither King Paolo nor Benitta reacted. They might as well have been alone in the hall. Benitta tilted her head to look directly at the king, and Ginnevra wished she could see the woman's face, because King Paolo's expression froze. "I can't," Benitta whispered. "Even for your sake. And if I did, the woman who stayed with you wouldn't be me anymore."

The king closed his eyes for a moment. Then he reached out slowly, as if he were approaching a frightened animal, and took Benitta's hand. "I hoped you would say that," he said.

"Paolo," Benitta said, sounding startled.

"I spent the night blaming myself for your choice," King Paolo said. "If I'd been less harsh, you wouldn't have feared me. I didn't even care that you'd lied to me. And sometime early this morning, it came to me—you'd told me the truth in the worst, most hurtful way possible, but you *had* told me the truth. You might have gone on lying, stayed here while the rest of the Faithful left Quinizelle, spent the rest of your life pretending. But you didn't." He sighed, and took her other hand in his. "I told myself, if I ever saw you again, I would make that offer. And if you accepted, I would cast you away forever."

"But...you hate the Faith," Benitta said.

"And I love you," King Paolo said. "The Faith failed me, and it failed Dianetta. But I don't know anymore that holding onto that grudge has made me happier, or made life better for my people. I would rather look to the future, and you, dear heart, are my future."

Benitta let out another choked sob. "I truly am sorry," she cried.

"Then let us forgive one another," the king said, and put his arms around her, pulling her close.

Ginnevra couldn't have moved if the entire palace had suddenly uprooted and tumbled down the mountain pass. She carefully watched the carpet instead of the embracing pair and wished she could be elsewhere. But she still had a duty. She hoped the royal couple's reunion meant it wasn't quite so difficult a duty, after all.

TWENTY-SIX

After a little while, during which she did her best not to listen to the whispered endearments that were none of her business, she heard the king say, "Paladin."

"Yes, your majesty," Ginnevra said promptly.

The king and Benitta approached her, hand in hand. Benitta's eyes were all for her husband; the king's attention was entirely on Ginnevra. "There have been many misunderstandings all around," he said, "and I would like that to stop. I intend to revoke my rather hasty decision to banish the Faithful from Quinizelle. But I have a condition."

Ginnevra, who'd begun to feel hopeful, felt her stomach sink. "You may ask," she said. "I can't make any promises."

"I cannot overlook the fact that Hallowed Nevante turned her magic on someone loyal to me, and might have attacked me as well had you not intervened," King Paolo said. "I request that, as a condition of the Faith remaining here, someone else be appointed as Hallowed of the Quinizelle sanctuary in her place."

Ginnevra controlled her first response, which was *You don't get to make demands*. It hadn't been worded as a demand, but Ginnevra observed how tense the king still was and had no doubt that was what it amounted to. She also didn't want to reveal Nevante's fall from grace, for fear the king might take it as more evidence of the superiority of Torunes. He might feel generous now, but she couldn't count on that lasting.

"Your majesty," she said, "what will you do to High Priest Rainaldus? He, too, attempted to use his religious power to attack someone."

The king's lips pursed in thought. "He was defending himself."

"That's true," Ginnevra said, hating that she had to give in even a little bit, "but—"

"Paolo, you know Rainaldus will use this opportunity to further persecute the Faith," Benitta said. "He is utterly committed to seeing Torunes dominate Quinizelle. It's not right to persecute others simply because they are in the minority."

"I can't tell him he's wrong to think that way," King Paolo said. "I've seen him work great miracles in Torun's name. Of course he believes he's right, and he will do whatever it takes to show others the truth of that."

Ginnevra crossed her arms over her chest. Her elbow brushed something soft that rustled. She had completely forgotten Jiuseppe's affidavit. "Your majesty, I think you're unaware of the full extent of Rainaldus' activities," she said, drawing the roll of papers from her belt. "You're right that he's deeply committed to his religion, but that doesn't excuse murder."

"Murder?" The king's eyes narrowed. "That's a strong accusation."

"And I'm not the one who makes it," Ginnevra said. "Lord

Jiuseppe Zuccare learned the truth behind Lady Dianetta's murder, your majesty. He intended to tell you in person, but he was killed before he could do more than commit his testimony to paper. Please read this, your majesty, before you make any more decisions about the High Priest."

The king accepted the roll of paper and flicked the dangling yellow seal. He slid the ribbon off and unrolled the pages. Holding them where Benitta could see as well, he read silently, his eyes flicking back and forth faster than Ginnevra could follow. His expression changed from curious to impassive before he reached the bottom of the first page. Benitta's face was more expressive; she looked utterly stunned by what she read.

When he finished reading the third page, the king let the papers roll back up. "I do not believe this. I have known High Priest Rainaldus for decades. He would never commit treason or murder."

"Even in the name of his god?" Ginnevra said. "You said you know him—is he committed enough to his religion to put its needs above everything else?"

"What does my sister's death have to do with religion?" For once, the king sounded genuinely surprised.

"Your majesty, before Lady Dianetta was murdered, what was your attitude toward the Faith?" Ginnevra shifted into a more relaxed stance she hoped would invite the king to relax as well. "You were content to let the Faithful coexist with Torunes here peacefully, isn't that right? You didn't hate us until we were responsible, as far as you knew, for your sister's death. But High Priest Rainaldus has hated the Faith from the beginning. He didn't like the fact that we were in Quinizelle at all. Is it such a stretch to imagine him doing whatever it took to get rid of the Faith entirely?"

King Paolo opened his mouth to reply. Then he closed it. He appeared to be thinking hard about something. "One man's word is not enough," he said, but he sounded neutral, and Ginnevra recognized the face of a man who wanted to be convinced.

"High Priest Rainaldus confessed his crime to me, as well," she said, "and I know a woman who has spent four years investigating the massacre who can also give evidence."

"And I am not to believe you would say anything to exonerate your captain?" King Paolo's words had little heat behind them, as if it was a rote response.

"You're not familiar with our doctrine, your majesty, or you would know why that's impossible," Ginnevra replied. "There is no point in redeeming the reputations of the dead, because they are gone where such things don't matter anymore. But I am a paladin, sworn to pursue justice, and for four years Lady Dianetta's murderer has walked free. That's unacceptable to me. I'm counting on it being unacceptable to you."

King Paolo nodded once, slowly. "I will investigate," he said. "Jiuseppe wanted the throne, and I believe he would have seen me as an impediment to his rule if I had named him my heir. But he loved his brother, and if he suspected Rainaldus had something to do with Jiovanni's death, that is something worth looking into."

Ginnevra came to a decision. "And I will consult with the Blessed about your request. I'm sure we can come to an agreement that will satisfy the demands of justice and mercy."

The king put Jiuseppe's affidavit away inside his doublet. "Thank you for your service, paladin," he said. "I recognize that you did not need to strive so hard for a fair solution. You could have forced Abraciabene's will on us at any time."

"Technically, yes," Ginnevra said, "but in practice, primes really are encouraged to find the right solution, not just the obvious one." She bowed to the king, and realized to her surprise she meant the respect she showed.

"Please excuse me now to speak with the Blessed," she added, hoping that was still a possibility. "When would you like me to return, your majesty?"

"I think I can bend to Abraciabene's schedule this once," King Paolo said with an uncharacteristic smile. "Return when it's convenient for you, and I will leave word that you are to be admitted to my presence at any time."

"Thank you," Benitta said, extending a hand to Ginnevra. "You were right. About everything. I'm sorry—"

"It's all right," Ginnevra said. "It was my honor to serve."

Since it didn't look like Benitta planned to let go of her husband's hand any time soon, Ginnevra bowed again, more shallowly, and returned the way she'd come.

She took her time in the stained glass hallway, feeling she'd earned a little reward. The sunlight, more direct now, blinded her if she tried to look right at the windows, so instead she closed her eyes and strolled down the hall using her other senses to navigate. This wasn't hard, given the straightness of the way, but it let her pretend she was somewhere warm and sunny far from Quinizelle's chilly rain.

She decided to return by way of the main doors, partly because the memory of that dark corridor depressed her and partly as a sign to the world that she'd succeeded, at least for the moment. True, she might not be able to get agreement for Nevante's ouster even if the eternity fountain worked, and the king might be fooled again by Rainaldus, but when she remembered the joyful look on Benitta's face, she couldn't help feeling victorious.

To her surprise, the great doors stood open, and two guards waited there, their backs to Ginnevra and their halberds held at the ready. Wary, Ginnevra slowed her steps, watching the two men carefully, but neither paid her any attention, even when she walked through the doorway and stopped on the terrace.

Lightning shattered the clear blue sky, followed by screams. Ginnevra threw herself into the lee of the doors, scanning the heavens. No clouds, not even the high white ones incapable of producing lightning.

She leaned out and surveyed the courtyard. Men and women fled in all directions, some of them tripping and falling and being helped up by their neighbors. A few ran up the stairs and rushed past Ginnevra into the keep. Ginnevra ran past them to the rail bordering the terrace. From that perspective, the courtyard looked like a spilled inkwell, with threads of colorful ink pouring away from a point left of center.

Standing at that point was Rainaldus, his hood pushed back and his arms raised above his head. Eodan faced him, as unyielding as a stone. Someone crouched behind Eodan, their hands covering their head. It took Ginnevra a moment to realize the crouching figure was Nevante. Black shards lay scattered before her like slivers of shadow against the paving stones. Nevante's jet grace, broken beyond repair.

"You dare challenge me?" Rainaldus roared. "You, with your puny faith in an upstart Goddess? Torun will endure your disrespect no longer!"

He gestured, a complicated motion involving both hands, and lightning speared from the sky to strike the stone mere feet from where Nevante crouched. A thunderous crack drowned out Nevante's cry as she flung herself away. Eodan followed her, throwing himself between her and Rainaldus. Why he didn't attack Rainaldus, Ginnevra couldn't imagine, but her own duty was clear.

She ran down the stairs to the courtyard, dodging frightened courtiers, and leaped over the last eight steps to the ground. Swiftly, she drew her sword and threw the sheath to one side. "Rainaldus!" she shouted. "Is this your idea of behavior worthy of Torun? Terrorizing a helpless woman?"

Rainaldus lowered his arms and turned slowly to face Ginnevra. "Paladin," he said. "You think you can best me? I have the might of Torun behind me. You can't defeat that." He again gestured, and the air around his body shimmered with golden, glittering light that vanished in half a breath.

Ginnevra strode toward him, her pace deliberate, her sword at the ready. "High Priest Rainaldus, I don't want to attack you. But I've said before that I am obliged to protect the Faithful. Strike Hallowed Nevante, and I will defend her." She regretted instantly calling Nevante Hallowed. A broken grace could mean only that the Goddess had removed Her blessing from Nevante. But that was a problem for another time.

With a cruel smile, Rainaldus gestured, and a narrow shaft of white light shot toward Ginnevra. Ginnevra dodged and felt hot sparks scorch her flesh as the light passed. Someone screamed behind her, but she didn't dare look to see whether the magic, whatever it was, had found a target.

Again Rainaldus cast his white dart at Ginnevra. This time, she deflected it with her sword. It flew back to strike Rainaldus, but again the air around him shimmered gold as the dart neared him, and the white light disappeared like a stone dropping into a dark pool. Rainaldus' smile vanished. "You dare," he snarled.

Ginnevra ran at him and swung her sword, using her momentum to add power to the blow. The sword rebounded off the invisible barrier, throwing her off balance so the next dart sailed harmlessly over her head. Ginnevra went to one knee, spreading her arms wide to keep from falling over. "I dare," she said. "And I don't think much of a god who would let his servant murder in the name of strengthening his religion."

"What I do in Torun's name is holy," Rainaldus spat. "He will not endure the presence of the Faithful."

Ginnevra flung herself backward to avoid another dart. "Torun's not much of a god if he's threatened by the Goddess. Was he the one who told you killing Dianetta would benefit him? Or was it you who benefited?"

"You know nothing," Rainaldus shouted. "Lady Dianetta's death was a necessary sacrifice. She gave her life to bless her faith."

Ginnevra swung again, prepared this time for the rebound. The sword made no more impression on Rainaldus than before. Breathing heavily, she shouted, "I was there, Rainaldus. Dianetta died screaming for someone to help her. That was no holy death. It was you taking matters into your own hands." She sucked in air and swung again. "You wanted power and you were willing to kill a woman to get it."

"One woman's death means nothing in the grand scheme of Torun's plans," Rainaldus said. "I am not ashamed. Whereas *you* are defending someone who has lost her Goddess's favor, so how does that make you anything but a mindless slave?"

Ginnevra got to her feet once more. "Insult me all you like," she said. "It won't change anything. And it won't stop me fighting you." With a roar, she swung the greatsword again, putting all her strength into the blow.

The sword struck the golden barrier, and shattered like ice.

The force of the blow sent shockwaves through Ginnevra's arms. Ginnevra staggered and fell to her knees, off balance again. She stared at the hilt in her hands. Sharp needles of steel, as if the blade had been made of crystal and not metal, were all that was left of her sword.

She heard Rainaldus laughing, a terrible mocking sound that fell heavily on her numb ears. "And you claim to have power over me? The Goddess is nothing but a sham compared to the might of Torun."

Ginnevra looked up at him dully. "You broke my sword," she said.

Rainaldus laughed harder. "It was easy. Nothing stands against Torun's power."

"Is that why you lack faith, Rainaldus?" someone behind them shouted.

The ringing in Ginnevra's ears faded. Now she recognized King Paolo's voice. Without standing, she turned to look past Rainaldus at where the king stood at the terrace rail, looking down at them. Beside him, Benitta still held his hand. She looked frightened, but didn't seem poised to run.

Rainaldus lowered his arms. "Your majesty challenges my faith, here amid so many proofs of it?" he said.

"I heard you admit to arranging my sister's death," King Paolo said, his voice ringing out in the sudden silence. "For the sake of building up the Torune religion, and to weaken the Faith. Why would you have done that if you didn't lack faith in Torun's power?"

"My faith is evident in how Torun works through me," Rainaldus said. "Come, now, your majesty, you don't mean to question me? After everything I've done for you?"

The wheedling sound of his voice broke through Ginnevra's stupor. His fingers flexed, trailing golden light after them. Ginnevra's gaze drifted to the king. His eyes were unfocused, and he slowly released Benitta's hand. "After everything you've done," the king said. His voice sounded normal, lacking the forcefulness it had previously had. "Of course. You are Torun's servant. I have faith in you."

MELISSA MCSHANE

Ginnevra shook her head like a dog coming out of deep water and felt the world snap back into focus. She rose to her feet and said, "You're controlling the king."

"Merely showing him the truth," Rainaldus said in a low voice.

"The hell you are," Ginnevra said. "Let him go."

"You're a broken paladin," Rainaldus said. "You're powerless."

Ginnevra looked at the hilt with its needle-sharp slivers of metal. Then she threw it away so it bounced and skidded across the courtyard. "My sword is broken," she said. "The rest of me isn't." She took a few running steps, closing the distance between them in half a breath, and slammed into Rainaldus, knocking him to the ground.

An explosion of white light nearly carried her off her feet, deafening her again. The light didn't blind her; she saw Rainaldus clearly, if starkly outlined. He rolled onto his back and raised his hands in a now-familiar gesture. Quick as thought, Ginnevra punched him in the face. She felt no resistance, no barrier, just the clean and satisfying power of her fist into his jaw. Rainaldus' head snapped back, and he sagged, unconscious.

Ginnevra drew in a deep breath and let it out slowly. Then she got to her feet, shaking out her hand. The white light was fading, which reassured her; she was too much a paladin not to associate white with the Bright One, even though she didn't believe Torun had anything to do with Her.

A short distance away, Eodan rose, keeping a hand on Nevante's shoulder. The fading white light turned his skin parchment pale, but he didn't look injured. Ginnevra cast one last look at Rainaldus before searching for the king. He was clinging to the railing, his head bowed, and Benitta had her arms around him and was speaking to him in a voice too low for Ginnevra to make out.

"Lady Benitta," Ginnevra called out, "is the king well?"

Benitta looked up. "He's not breathing properly," she said, sounding terrified.

Out of the corner of her eye, Ginnevra saw movement. Eodan raced across the courtyard and up the stairs, shoving past the few courtiers who still remained on the terrace. He took King Paolo by the shoulders and gently helped him lie down, supporting his head. Ginnevra took a few steps toward him, silently praying for Eodan's skills to be enough.

Eodan listened to the king's chest, then rested the king's head on his knee, elevating it slightly. "He just had the wind knocked out of him, or something like that," he called out. Ginnevra's knees trembled in relief. Then Eodan shot to his feet, shouting, "*Watch out!*"

Something struck Ginnevra in the middle of her back, knocking her forward to land on hands and knees. Pain like shattered bones radiated outward from the blow. Shaking, Ginnevra tried to stand and was hit once again by the unseen force. She rolled to the side and saw Rainaldus standing over her, holding a wrist-thick rod as long as his arm. It gleamed with the same golden light his barrier had.

Panting, Ginnevra brought up both arms to block the next attack. Rainaldus slammed the rod down, and Ginnevra screamed from the pain that again felt like it had broken every bone in her arms. She rolled again and found to her relief her arms weren't actually broken when she was able to push herself into a squat. She twisted away from a blow she sensed rather than saw and landed on her shoulder, kicked out with her foot and caught Rainaldus on the shin.

The blow didn't affect Rainaldus at all. He raised the rod again and snarled, "I'll see you dead, and then I will whip every last one of the Faithful out of Quinizelle—"

A howl echoed off the walls of the keep. Rainaldus' head jerked up. His eyes widened, and his mouth fell open in a perfect O of shock and growing horror. Then an enormous black-furred wolf leaped over Ginnevra and hit Rainaldus in the chest, knocking him backward.

Ginnevra sat up. Eodan had both front paws on Rainaldus' shoulders, and his muzzle hovered inches from the High Priest's throat. A low, menacing growl that set off every one of Ginnevra's primal flight instincts issued from Eodan's mouth.

Ginnevra managed to stand after only a couple of tries. She tottered to Eodan's side and knelt. "Thank you."

Eodan's growl intensified. His attention never left Rainaldus' jugular vein. Ginnevra gingerly put a hand on his ruff. "You can let him up," she said. "He's lost, and everyone knows it."

Eodan didn't move at first. Ginnevra looked at Rainaldus. Gone was the arrogant, self-assured expression; Rainaldus looked as stunned as if he'd hit his head too hard, which might have been true, but Ginnevra suspected was at least as much a matter of being attacked by a werewolf. "Eodan, let him up," she repeated.

Eodan backed off. Rainaldus didn't rise. "High Priest, you're going to answer for your crimes," Ginnevra said. "Please don't make this harder than it has to be."

Rainaldus squeezed his eyes shut. Then he spoke, rapidly and urgently, in the liquid polysyllables of the Sezarni tongue.

Eodan growled again, like an inquiry. "I don't know," Ginnevra said. Rainaldus had lost, and without his divine power, he just looked pathetic. But the sound of Sezarni raised the hairs on the back of Ginnevra's neck. "I...think we should move away."

She backed toward the stairs to the keep, her eyes never leaving Rainaldus. Eodan walked with her, pacing back and forth well out of her path. Rainaldus continued to speak without standing up. It was the eeriest thing Ginnevra had seen since Rainaldus' wounds healed at the dedication.

A shadow fell over the courtyard. Ginnevra looked up, but there still wasn't a cloud in the sky. She scanned the courtyard. The shadow came from everywhere and nowhere, as if a film had wrapped itself around the stones, centered on the High Priest. As the shadow grew darker and more solid, *things* moved within it, shapes not quite animal and definitely far from human. Ginnevra looked at her own hands and hissed in shock. The shadow made her skin seem tattooed with alien symbols, but what shocked her was the feeling of almost but not quite understanding them. She rubbed the backs of her hands, but the symbols remained.

Eodan let out a whine, and then in a haze of silver he resumed his human form. "We need to get out of here," he said.

"To where?" Ginnevra gestured at the courtyard. "It's everywhere." She looked over her shoulder. The shadows had reached as far as the terrace and the doors to the keep and shifted over Benitta and the king. "We can't abandon them."

Eodan took another step toward her. "Then what do we do?"

The shadows thickened until they were a solid mass, shifting like animals caught outside in a bad storm that mill about looking for direction. The bulging shadows reared high above Rainaldus' supine body, bearing down on him, though he showed no sign that they hurt him. Then Rainaldus got to his feet. He moved stiffly, one joint at a time, until he stood within the massed shadows. His eyes glowed solid gold with a light that gleamed brighter and warmer than the sun.

"Torun has answered my call," he said. His voice no longer sounded entirely like his own; it rumbled and shook like an earthquake. "You will hear his words, and obey!"

"This is a trick," Ginnevra said, stepping forward. "I challenge you to stop your lying and bow to your king's justice."

The shadows stirred. Still in that deep, rumbling voice, Rainaldus said, "No human justice surpasses a god's. I will not bow. You will kneel." He raised a hand ponderously, as if it were made of stone, and pointed at Ginnevra.

Golden light flashed, striking Ginnevra in the chest and sending her flying.

TWENTY-SEVEN

Ginnevra skidded to a stop along the paving stones and lay on her back, gasping for air. In the next moment, Eodan was at her side. His lips were moving, but she couldn't hear anything but the pounding of her heart and the wheezing of her breath. Across the courtyard, Rainaldus took a heavy, slow step, then another, moving in her direction.

With a snap, sound rushed back into her world. "—eed to get up!" Eodan shouted. "I don't think that was his full power!"

Ginnevra scrambled to her feet. "If that wasn't his full power—"

"Ginnevra, we have to get the king and Lady Benitta out of here," Eodan said. "There's no reason Rainaldus won't turn on them next." He moved to grab her elbow to steady her as she nearly lost her balance, but stopped before touching the silvered mail. "Come with me!"

Ginnevra shook her head. "If we don't stop him, Goddess alone knows what he'll do. And then it won't matter where anyone tries to hide." She steadied herself and touched her grace.

"Maybe Torun is a real god, but I refuse to believe he's more powerful than the Goddess. Take care of the others. I'll keep him from attacking."

"I'm not going to abandon you," Eodan said. In a shimmer of silver, he was the wolf again.

Ginnevra glanced at the oncoming Rainaldus. He continued his ponderous approach, lifting one leg at a time in a jerky motion like pulling his feet free of a mire. "Fine," she said, recognizing when Eodan was done arguing. "Get around behind him while I keep his attention on me."

Eodan bared his teeth in a snarl, but stepped away from her. Ginnevra reflexively went for her pistol, cursed under her breath, and again touched her grace. *"By Your grace I have power!"* she shouted.

Heat surged through her, warming her muscles and filling her with strength. She felt as light as a falling leaf, as agile as a cat. Instantly, she darted forward, gathering speed until she felt like she was flying across the courtyard. Rainaldus waved his hand again, but she was ready for it and dodged the blast. In the next moment, she plowed into the High Priest, knocking him backward.

She'd expected the blow to send him to the ground. Instead, he skidded away, plowing up the paving stones as if his feet were harrows. Ginnevra shoved off him and danced back a few steps. "You don't want this fight, Rainaldus," she said, concealing her dismay at his failure to fall.

Rainaldus smiled. "I will triumph," he said. "Your Goddess is nothing before Torun." He shot another blast of force that Ginnevra again dodged. As he raised his hand for another blast, Ginnevra pounced. She swung her fist at Rainaldus' chest, reveling in the feeling of power the Goddess's grace gave her.

Rainaldus brought his arm around to block the blow, catching

Ginnevra's fist in his open palm. He shoved, and Ginnevra flew backward again, hitting the paving stones with a surprised grunt. She sat up, then flattened herself and rolled to avoid another of Rainaldus' force blasts. Pushing herself to her feet, she crouched, facing Rainaldus. The High Priest's glowing eyes looked like holes into a fiery abyss, burning with terrible power. "So far, I'm not impressed," Ginnevra lied.

Rainaldus took another one of those ponderous steps toward her. He began speaking in Sezarni again, closing his eyes as if his words were a prayer. The golden glow radiated through his eyelids, unsettling Ginnevra. She walked toward him, warily keeping an eye on his hands.

Rainaldus' eyes flashed open, and he pointed at Ginnevra, his arm moving as slowly and heavily as his feet. In the next moment, Ginnevra sagged beneath a terrible, invisible weight that drove her nearly to her knees and bore down on her chest like a boulder. She gasped for air. Rainaldus laughed, a sound like stones rolling down a mountainside. "Feel Torun's presence," he said.

Ginnevra looked past him. She had no breath to spare for a witty rejoinder, but it didn't matter, because she wasn't the only one fighting Rainaldus.

With a terrible howl, Eodan launched himself at Rainaldus' back. Again, Rainaldus staggered, but didn't fall. He turned to face Eodan, and the awful pressure on Ginnevra's chest and limbs eased. As Eodan snapped at Rainaldus' throat, Ginnevra drew in a deep breath and let it sigh out of her, taking the weight with it. Then she charged.

This time, she hit Rainaldus low in the back, putting all her weight and the Goddess's boost of strength behind it. And this time, Rainaldus fell. Eodan was on him instantly, his jaws aimed at Rainaldus' jugular. Rainaldus thrust his arms between Eodan and his throat, crossing them at the wrist, and pushed Eodan away, slowly but steadily. Eodan clawed at the High Priest's chest, tearing his robe but not drawing blood.

Then Rainaldus shifted his arms and got his hands around Eodan's throat, squeezing. Eodan let out a pained, breathless yelp. Ginnevra punched Rainaldus in the chest, but he didn't let go of Eodan, who scrabbled at Rainaldus with all four paws, trying to break free. She punched Rainaldus again, then grabbed his fingers and pried at them to no effect. Silently cursing, she kicked Rainaldus in the side and felt his ribs crack. With a gasp, Rainaldus let go of Eodan, who backed away, shaking his head and breathing heavily.

Rainaldus got to his hands and knees and spat bloody phlegm onto the stones. Ginnevra wound up for another kick and found herself frozen, her feet mired in the paving stones as if glued there. She struggled and managed to free one foot just as Rainaldus stood. "You think you can defeat Torun?" he growled. "You and your dog? No one can stand against Torun's might!"

He threw back his head and spoke, long and loud in Sezarni. Ginnevra wrenched her other foot free and took one step. Her other foot remained stuck fast. Behind Rainaldus, Eodan had recovered and stalked back and forth, looking for an opening. With Rainaldus distracted, they would never have a better opportunity.

She pulled her leg free, took another step, and an invisible hand closed around her, pinning her arms to her side and weighing down her feet so she couldn't move. It didn't feel like the weight Rainaldus had placed on her, or like being stuck to the ground; it felt more like a gentle insistence that she hold still. *Wait*, it told her, and despite her eagerness to defeat Rainaldus, she waited, and watched.

Rainaldus' body convulsed, once, twice, and then he shook violently as if the earth around him was buckling and trembling.

The golden light from his eyes was stronger, two visible beams shooting away from his face into the sky. His speech slowed, then stuttered, no longer the liquid beauty of Sezarni but something harsh and cold that filled Ginnevra with dread.

Then Rainaldus screamed. It sounded like the tortured cry of a storm wind rather than anything human. It rose in pitch until even Ginnevra couldn't hear it anymore, and yet she was convinced the sound continued to rise past anything a mortal creature could perceive and into the range of the gods' hearing.

The tremors stopped, and Ginnevra had only just realized Rainaldus was hovering with his toes a few inches above the paving stones when his head swiftly snapped to the right with an audible pop. For a moment, he continued to hang there, his body limp as if he dangled from a puppet master's strings. Then he fell, making no effort to catch himself, and sprawled lifeless on the ground.

The force restraining Ginnevra disappeared. She stayed where she was, waiting for Rainaldus to move though she was sure no living body could lie that still. She sidled around, not getting closer, until she could see his face. His eyes were open, but the golden light was gone. The shadows continued to move, more erratically than before.

She waved Eodan back. "It could still be a trick," she said. Swiftly she glanced around and saw no one else in the courtyard. Above, Benitta and King Paolo still clung to the railing, staring back at her. She hoped their presence didn't mean one or both of them was too injured to get to safety.

She looked back at Rainaldus' body just as the shadows drew together in a shapeless, towering mass and plunged toward her.

She had time to draw a single breath before the shadows were on her, freezing her to her core. She smelled old, wet stone, a scent that forced its way into her nostrils and mouth so she tasted it, too, like drinking icy well water from a soil-crusted stone cup. Shadows whirled past her eyes, dizzying her until she didn't know if she was still standing.

A deep, resonant voice overlaid with the rustling of dry leaves said: *Release me.*

Ginnevra tried to speak, but her lips and jaw were frozen solid. The shadows changed course, spinning in a new direction. *I will not be held*, the voice said.

Weight settled on Ginnevra, bearing down on her with the implacability of a mountain. She tried to cry out at the pain and succeeded only in producing a muffled squeak. Bone grated against bone, her lungs compressed so she couldn't breathe, and she felt herself lifted off the ground the way Rainaldus had been at the end, with her toes barely brushing the flagstones. She heard Eodan howl, the sound of a challenge, and hoped he wouldn't be fool enough to get himself entangled in this nightmare. Even if it meant letting her die.

Distantly, she heard the sound of spoken Sezarni, and fear spiked through her. She couldn't fight this thing, Torun or whatever it was, and Rainaldus, too. The thought occurred to her that she wasn't really fighting Torun successfully, so what did it matter if Rainaldus had come back from the dead?

Then the pressure eased. Ginnevra drew in a breath, not a deep one, but it dispelled the dizzy, airless sparks from her vision. She struggled to free herself and discovered she was on the ground with Eodan crouched beside her. The shadows had faded, and she could see clearly. She drew in another breath, a deeper one, and coughed as the air hit her abused lungs.

Eodan leaned over her. "Just breathe, Ginnevra. Breathe."

Ginnevra shook her head. "Where is it? What happened?"

Eodan looked past her. Ginnevra turned to face the keep. Her heart thumped once, painfully hard, as she saw the shadow creature climbing the wall to the terrace where Benitta and King Paolo stood. "Run!" she screamed, then burst out coughing again.

Neither of them moved. King Paolo had put himself in front of Benitta, and his lips moved in an endless stream of Sezarni words. The shadow creature pulled itself over the edge of the terrace and towered over the royal couple. Ginnevra pushed herself to her feet and began to run.

The king stopped speaking. His head was tilted back, and he gazed up at the shadow creature with no sign of fear. Ginnevra ran blindly, only barely aware of where her feet landed as she pelted toward the stairs because she didn't dare look away from the creature. It stood as solid as a mountain, its shape now vaguely pyramidal, the shadows that comprised it moving cease-lessly like leaves shaken by the wind. Ginnevra pushed herself harder. The paving stones sent sharp shocks up Ginnevra's legs with every rapid step, and her lungs screamed in agony with every breath, but she refused to give up.

Vaguely, she realized Eodan in wolf shape had outpaced her and was running up the stairs. A new fear shot through her, the memory of being suffocated within the creature now tied to terror at the thought of Eodan suffering the same fate. She reached deep within herself to tap reserves she never thought she'd need and practically flew up the stairs. For a moment, she lost sight of everything but the stone steps before her, and then she was at the top and speeding toward the shadow creature. King Paolo and Benitta were wavery shapes seen dimly through the creature's body. It hadn't attacked them yet.

Roaring a challenge, she flung herself at the creature—and King Paolo said, "That won't be necessary, paladin."

Ginnevra's momentum made stopping impossible. She managed to convert her attack into a tumble that took her past the creature and King Paolo and Benitta to land in a sprawling heap next to the railing. Momentarily stunned, she sucked in a deep breath and stared up at the shadow creature. From that angle, it had an unexpectedly humanoid shape, almost like draw-ings Ginnevra had seen of the mythical monsters called trolls. Despite the constantly shifting shadows, it looked more solid, more mountainous than anything ethereal.

King Paolo extended a hand, palm out, to the creature. Though it didn't have anything recognizable as a head, its upper body shifted, tilting sideways in a gesture Ginnevra couldn't not see as curious. Then it moved again, extending part of its body to mirror King Paolo's movements. Ginnevra rolled to her knees as man and creature touched, prepared to drag the king to safety if he so much as gasped in pain.

Nothing happened. King Paolo said something in Sezarni, paused as if listening to a response, then spoke again. Ginnevra slowly got to her feet and found Eodan pressed hard against her hip. Absently, she put a hand on his ruff and stroked his fur.

The king abruptly turned and pointed at Eodan as if asking the creature's opinion about the werewolf. Although the creature had no face, its attention on Eodan was palpable. Eodan whined briefly and ducked his head in a self-conscious gesture. Ginnevra understood. Even the edges of the thing's attentiveness felt like being ground under a giant thumb.

She dared tear her own attention from the shadow creature to watch King Paolo. Again the king spoke, and again he paused for an unheard response. The pause went on for some time. King Paolo's expression changed from an alert, intent pleasure to confusion and then from confusion to an impassivity Ginnevra didn't understand. Then she saw tears sliding down his cheeks.

Benitta spoke into the silence. "Oh, my dear, it's not..." Her voice trailed off, and she touched her husband's face, wiping away tears.

The king shook his head once. Then, without looking up at the creature, he said one final word in Sezarni, or at least what Ginnevra believed was a single word. The shadows fluttered like a scattering flock of birds, separating, and the creature fell apart in a sound like boulders tumbling over one another. In the next moment, the space it had occupied was empty, and the only shadows were the ones the four of them cast.

No one spoke. Ginnevra pressed her aching shoulder where she'd slammed into Rainaldus. Now that the crisis was over, the Goddess's gift of temporary strength would soon fade, leaving Ginnevra with a host of bruises. Looking at King Paolo's devastated face, Ginnevra felt uncomfortable complaining about anything so mundane as physical pain. The king looked as if he'd lost his best friend.

Benitta laid a hand along King Paolo's cheek and turned his head to face her. "Don't look like that," she said.

The king swallowed, making the knot in his throat bob up and down. "How should I look?" he responded. "My faith is a lie."

Ginnevra, startled, said, "A lie? That was Torun. He's clearly real."

"Real," King Paolo said, "but no god."

"I don't understand." Ginnevra looked out over the courtyard at the body of Rainaldus and the wreck he had made of the paving stones. "The High Priest summoned Torun, didn't he? And Torun responded when you spoke to him. Even I can recognize what that means, and I would have sworn Torun was imaginary until this week."

King Paolo followed the line of her gaze and shook his head slowly. "It is our tradition that any man may speak to Torun if his heart is pure, just as any woman may speak to Marena. I spoke, and the creature answered. It answered to Torun's name, but it demanded I release it from the binding the High Priest laid on it."

"That—" Ginnevra began.

The king held up a hand to silence her. "It was angry at being forced to use its power to Rainaldus' demands. I felt its anger and its fear, and under that, its indifference to me and every other human. It only spoke to me out of curiosity. That is not the god I was taught to worship, the one who watches over us and gives us his blessings."

"Dear heart, surely that doesn't mean..." Benitta's voice trailed off as the king turned his gaze on her.

"We have been lied to," he said. "I don't know when it started, if the priests knew the truth all along or if they were duped as the rest of us were, but that creature is not our god. I asked what it meant that Lopone, Torun's eldest child—" He pointed at Eodan, still in wolf shape— "fought against the High Priest, and it said it had no children but the stones of the mountain." Tears again streaked King Paolo's face. "Then it told me it should not be summoned again, and it left."

A dozen responses went through Ginnevra's head, and she discarded all of them. She imagined how she would feel to learn the Goddess was imaginary, or was some creature whose connection to humanity was built on coercion and lies, and could not bring herself to reassure the king that everything would be all right.

"I lost my Goddess, too," Eodan said, startling Ginnevra. She hadn't noticed him change shape. "It's not the same, because the Bright One is cruel and vindictive, but I grew up not knowing any of that. And then I realized She cared nothing for me but as a tool she could use."

King Paolo didn't react to the appearance of a naked man before him. "We can't go on worshipping something that isn't real. I'll have to tell—no one is going to believe me. They'll think I'm mad."

"We don't have to tell anyone anything," Benitta said. "People do great things in Torun's name. Does it really matter if they don't know the full truth of his nature?"

"It matters to me," King Paolo said. His voice was so bleak Benitta closed her mouth on whatever she would have said next.

Ginnevra became aware of a deep, subtle vibration shaking her bones, fast enough that it felt like her skin was buzzing. "Do you feel that?"

"Feel what?" Eodan said.

King Paolo's head lifted. "It reverberates through me. And it grows stronger."

Now Ginnevra felt as if she were being shaken rapidly and steadily by someone much, much larger than she. "Earthquake," she said. "We have to take shelter." She cast about frantically, but she'd only once experienced an earthquake before, and it had been over before she could react. She had no idea what one did to protect against a big one.

"Into the doorway," King Paolo said.

They all ran for the doorway, where a handful of courtiers crouched, but they had taken only a few steps when the paving stones of the terrace buckled, sending them all to the ground. Benitta cried out in pain. Ginnevra tried to roll on her side to help the woman and found she was once more pinned by an invisible hand, trapping her on her back. From that position, all she could see was the sky. Roiling gray clouds poured across the clear blue expanse, blocking the sun and sending the temperature plummeting. Ginnevra shivered. Her body no longer vibrated; an occasional tremor pulsed through the ground, tossing her and the others about, but even those came less frequently now.

A voice spoke from the air. It had the same quality Ginnevra had heard from Torun, deep and penetrating and overlaid with the sound of rustling leaves, but this one struck her to the heart.

The words were Sezarni, but for the first time Ginnevra felt their meaning was just on the edge of her comprehension.

When the voice finished speaking, no one made a sound. Then, from somewhere behind her, Ginnevra heard King Paolo say, "Forgive me, but I'm no priest. I understand you, but I don't know the right response."

A cold wind brushed Ginnevra's face. She tried again to move and found herself still pinned, not painfully, but with a finality that convinced her fighting this force was impossible even for a paladin.

Then the voice spoke again. *I do not recognize you,* it said in Lordagni. *You have never bound me or mine.*

"No, and I realize you are not a god," the king said. "I'm sorry if we hurt you. We didn't understand."

Am I not? The voice sounded perplexed. *I am what makes the mountain rise to the sky. I know its depths and its heights. I have the power to render you helpless. Is that not God?*

Ginnevra opened her mouth to explain about the Goddess and Her relationship to humanity, and the same gentle force that had restrained her before Rainaldus died stilled her tongue.

"We believed you made us," King Paolo said. He sounded as calm as if this was a normal conversation. "That you wanted us to worship you because we owe you our existence."

I do not expect the stones to bow to me simply because I created them. I made them, and then I set them free. Why should your kind be different?

"I...don't know." Now the king sounded confused. "It's just what we're taught."

And yet your kind impose your will upon me and mine. You know the words that compel us to act. That does not sound like worship as you describe it. The voice's intensity deepened until Ginnevra felt she might explode from the pressure.

"I'm not a priest," the king repeated. "I don't know what priests do. We believed they called upon you to grant us your power. If they forced you to act, that was wrong. I hope you believe me that we really did mean no harm."

I see into your heart to know the truth of your words. The intensity eased. *You will leave us alone in future.*

"I understand," the king said.

"I don't," Ginnevra said—or something said through Ginnevra's lips. "The worshippers of Torun have praised you and yours for centuries, and most of them did not compel you. And now you will abandon them?"

They enslaved us. We owe them nothing.

"It's not about owing. It's about what you give each other." The words poured out of Ginnevra with that feeling of rightness she recognized as the Goddess's inspiration. "In the beginning, you gave your power to humans freely. You felt sorry for them in their weakness. That's why some of them came up with the idea of binding you to give them greater power—because you set the example that you had power you would share."

A heavy weight pressed down on Ginnevra's chest. It was the same pressure she'd felt from the other creature's attention, but this time it was wholly focused on her. She didn't know how Eodan had endured it. *You know this,* the voice said, *but you were not there.*

Ginnevra squirmed under Torun's attention, trying to get away from how it pressed in on her from all sides, and then gave up. "My Goddess remembers, and She grants me her knowledge," she said. "I know you've suffered, but can't you reach deep and remember how it was before?"

Your Goddess supplants us. We are diminished.

"I know. I'm not sorry, because I believe in my Faith and I know the Goddess is good for humanity. But She doesn't force anyone to worship Her. And there are thousands of people who believe you are their God. They shouldn't be abandoned." Part of her mind gibbered in horror. She was sworn to the Goddess. She ought to encourage people to worship Her. And here she was arguing on behalf of a false God when her silence might have meant those thousands of people turning to the Faith.

"I know Torun is a just god," she continued. "He is strong and demanding of strength in his worshippers. Is it possible for him to be a merciful god as well?"

The pressure eased. The voice said, *You. What will you do if I become your God?*

Ginnevra couldn't tell who the voice was talking to, but King Paolo said, "I don't know. Now that I know the truth, I don't know if I can go on worshipping as I did."

Your worship before meant enslaving me and mine. I will not endure it. Therefore, you cannot worship as you did.

"That's true, but everything we've been taught—was all of it a lie?" King Paolo demanded.

Show me what you were taught.

The king cried out in terrible pain. Benitta gasped. Ginnevra strained to reach him, but she was as immobilized as before. Then the king stopped screaming. Ginnevra could hear his breath rasping in and out of his lungs.

I see. The voice sounded puzzled. *Some of what you know is true. Some of it is distorted. But the only lie is that your priests have the right to compel me.*

"But... we have... to have priests," the king panted. "How else... do we... approach you?"

Either all of you are holy, or none are. The voice built in volume until it echoed across the courtyard. *Speak, and we may choose to listen.*

Ginnevra found she could move. She vaulted to her feet,

grateful to still have the Goddess's grace of strength and agility, and hurried to King Paolo's side. Above, the clouds began to disperse, and with one final shock the tremors ceased.

"It's gone," she said. "Are you all right?"

"I'm not hurt," King Paolo said. "I don't know if that makes me all right." He sat up and reached for Benitta. "Dearest?"

"I think my arm is broken," Benitta said. She sat up awkwardly, cradling her arm to her chest. Eodan knelt beside her and gently felt along her arm.

"It's not a bad break, just a fracture," he said, "but it should be treated."

Benitta looked away from him, blushing. "You should... you're rather naked, physician."

King Paolo took Benitta's other hand. "Lopone's child," he said, and frowned. "Or not. Suppose that was one of the untruths?"

"Eodan is a werewolf, which is true enough," Ginnevra said. "I think you'll have to work at learning which else of your beliefs are true. But it sounds like Torun is willing to help."

"Torun," King Paolo breathed. "Paladin, why did you argue on our behalf? You should have let our religion collapse in favor of the Faith."

"It's like I said. The Goddess never compels anyone to worship Her," Ginnevra said. "She lets us decide for ourselves. And I think maybe She didn't like the idea of gaining worshippers at that cost, as if you only came to Her because you had nowhere else to go."

The king stood and helped Benitta to her feet. "You spoke with your Goddess's voice. You almost convince me to change my allegiance."

"Almost?" Ginnevra said with a smile. In the distance, she heard shouting, and she glanced away to see guards running across the devastated courtyard toward them.

"Torun spoke to me," King Paolo said, "and I would be a fool to disregard that. But I think—" He put his arm around Benitta, carefully not jogging her injured arm. "I think perhaps we will be better able to live in harmony now, Torunes and Faithful."

"I hope that's true," Ginnevra said, and meant it.

CHAPTER
TWENTY-EIGHT

The throne room, though it was as poorly lit as before, still felt brighter and less oppressive. What an effect a change in perspective had. Once more Ginnevra stood at the dim mark on the carpet, facing King Paolo, with silent courtiers watching them both, but this time the king's demeanor was relaxed, and he was even slightly smiling. He held Benitta's hand in a tender gesture that made him seem even more human.

"Prime Cassaline," he said, in a resonant voice that filled the throne room. "I thank you for your diligence in resolving the conflict between Torunes and Faithful. You did more than you had to, and Quinizelle is grateful."

Ginnevra bowed in a true gesture of respect. "It was my honor to serve."

"You can tell Abraciabene that I will personally see to it that the persecution on both sides ends now," the king continued. "There will be no more favoring of one religion over another, and any crimes committed in the name of religion will be punished."

"Thank you, your majesty." Ginnevra hesitated, then plunged

341

forward. "Will you instruct the new High Priest and the new Hallowed to guide the members of their religion in better behavior?"

"I expect whoever Abraciabene sends to govern the Faithful's sanctuary will be informed of the situation, but I will be happy to meet with her to discuss the specifics." King Paolo cleared his throat. "As to a new High Priest, we Torunes have yet to agree on whether that position will be filled at all. But I expect every Torune to behave in a way befitting an honorable person."

"I understand." Ginnevra bowed again. "You have an interesting path ahead of you. All of you."

A murmur rose up from the watching courtiers. King Paolo stood, causing the murmurs to fade into silence. "It is certainly a difficult path. But it is a path we walk with confidence."

Ginnevra wasn't so sure about this assessment. She'd spoken to Benitta the day before, and Benitta had said, "It's been a difficult four days since Torun's manifestation. Very few Torunes want to believe what Paolo learned. If not for him being the king, and for the witness of the few people who saw Torun from the gates of the keep, I think they would declare him mad. Mazzeus Alamanne has made noises about Paolo's fitness to rule. I almost wish Paolo had kept his knowledge to himself."

"You know he couldn't do that, not and retain his integrity," Ginnevra had said.

"I know. It's more that I fear for him. But—" Benitta had smiled. "It's as if a light has gone on inside him. He's more confident now. More sure of his words and actions. And we are united in a way I never imagined possible."

She had blushed when she said that, so Ginnevra hadn't pushed for more details. She had only said, "Some experiences are like that. I hope he never forgets how it felt."

"I'm sure he won't," Benitta had said.

Now, looking at the king, Ginnevra still had her doubts. King Paolo was essentially founding a new religion on the ashes of the old. Ginnevra knew the stories of the coming of the Faith to the Lordagne, how amid the tales of miracles were stories of martyrdom. Challenging people's beliefs never went smoothly. But the king's confident demeanor heartened Ginnevra. She sent up a brief but heartfelt prayer for the king's continued courage and for the Torunes' wisdom in hearing his words.

"The Holy City and Quinizelle were once friendly," she said. "I hope that friendship can resume."

King Paolo inclined his head. "Anger and grief can turn even the best relationship sour," he said. "I wish to express my regret for my part in the bad feeling between us."

It wasn't an apology, but in Ginnevra's limited experience, kings never apologized. "Thank you," she said. "And as one of those responsible for Lady Dianetta Napolle's safety, I want to tell you how deeply sorry I am that I failed to save her. I know it can't bring her back, but I grieved with you at her loss."

"High Priest Rainaldus was responsible for the attack, and he has paid for his crimes with his life." Once more the king's words rang out through the room, prompting a response from the courtiers. This time, the murmuring was louder and sounded confused. Ginnevra concealed her surprise at how the king had apparently not spread the word about Rainaldus' deceptions. It was better to look serene and knowing in front of these people.

"And the murder of Jiuseppe Zuccare?" she asked.

"The High Priest's acolytes revealed that Rainaldus used ritual magic to kill Lord Jiuseppe." King Paolo looked grim. The murmuring grew louder. "And one of them confessed to having arranged Lord Jiovanni Zuccare's death at Rainaldus' instigation. Those acolytes are held pending trial—that is *enough!*"

His last three words were directed not at Ginnevra, but at the room at large. The courtiers once more fell silent. The king turned his attention back on Ginnevra. "I have directed a statement be written revealing the truth of the matter and exonerating the paladins who gave their lives defending my sister. I hope that is sufficient." He snapped his fingers, and an attendant dressed in maroon and dark green stepped forward and extended a scroll case to Ginnevra.

"I thank you for the gesture, your majesty." She decided not to say that to the Faithful, the gesture didn't matter. No need to spurn his generosity.

"Is there any other matter you would like to bring to my attention?" King Paolo asked.

Ginnevra shook her head. "No, your majesty. Abraciabene is satisfied."

"Then you have my leave to depart, Prime Cassaline—and, again, my thanks." The king resumed his seat on the throne. Ginnevra bowed and retreated.

Pattero met her at the door. "May I escort you, Prime Cassaline?" he said with a smile.

"Still afraid I might wander and corrupt someone?" Ginnevra replied.

"This time, it is a mark of honor." Pattero bowed and indicated she should walk with him. "And one of my last acts as a courtier."

"Last acts?"

Pattero's smile became rueful. "I'm afraid I am leaving Quinizelle, after all."

Ginnevra stopped. "Surely King Paolo won't exile you? Not if he accepted Benitta's religion?"

"The king has been gracious, but I'm afraid the Alamannes have been less so. My father cast me out. He's still deciding what to do about Benitta, who is also tainted by the Faith, but who remains the king's wife. It's been delightful to watch him struggle with his dilemma." Pattero shrugged. "I confess I'm looking forward to the adventure, and to living in a place where I don't have to conceal my religion. It will be restful."

"I wish you luck," Ginnevra said.

Pattero raised an eyebrow. "Luck, prime?"

Ginnevra smiled. "A figure of speech. Let's just say I appreciate the Torune religion better now."

Pattero left her at the courtyard, where Eodan waited. "Well?" Ginnevra asked.

"King Paolo was surprisingly open to the idea that the fertility issue might be on his side," Eodan said. "I was expecting more masculine resistance. My examination didn't show any gross physical defects, but there are some things my people do to encourage male fertility that I was able to suggest. A change in diet, a change in dress...I hope it's enough. Some things, nobody can help."

"I choose not to anticipate a given future," Ginnevra said. "Whatever comes, they'll face it together."

"As we do," Eodan said with a smile. The smile faded, and he added, "Though you'll have to deal with Nevante alone. I'm afraid that's not something I can help with."

"I know. I'm not happy about it. I wish she was cooperative." Ginnevra cast her gaze on the skies. Another storm was coming after five days of clear weather. It would have felt like an omen if Ginnevra believed in those. Instead, it felt symbolic, as if the gray clouds threatening to dampen the streets intended to dampen her spirits as well.

"Let's see if we can't outrun the storm," she said.

The first fat, freezing raindrops fell when they were a dozen yards from the sanctuary's stables. Ginnevra put on a last burst of speed and came to a halt outside Dauntless's stall. Her horse whickered a greeting, and she petted his nose. "Smell that storm?" she said. "It will keep us here a bit longer, but then I promise you'll have time to stretch your legs."

Dauntless nodded his head, making Ginnevra chuckle. She turned to Eodan and said, "This isn't going to be pretty. I wish you could join me."

Eodan kissed her lightly, avoiding the silvered mail. "It will be over soon," he said, "and all this anticipation will be in the past."

"I wish—" Ginnevra shut her mouth. There was no point wishing for impossibilities.

When she left the back rooms for the sanctuary proper, she found Revered Bariatte and a couple of acolytes she didn't recognize waiting by the front door. The Revered looked somber, like someone with bad news to deliver. "I'm afraid Hal—Madama Nevante refuses to leave her office," he said.

Ginnevra's heart sank. She'd expected problems, but she'd hoped they wouldn't be quite this bad. "I'll speak to her," she said. "If you don't mind, I think I should see her alone."

"Of course." But Bariatte didn't move away from the stairs. "Prime, if I may—what do you intend to do?"

"My duty," Ginnevra said. It came out harsher than she'd intended, but her initial despair had given way to anger. Nevante had abused her position and used her divine gifts to frighten and compel others, all to her own glorification. And now she was fighting against the Blessed's instructions, which meant Ginnevra might have to do the unthinkable: carry a former anointed out of the sanctuary in bonds.

Bariatte stepped away, touching his forehead and saluting Ginnevra with an anointed's salute. Ginnevra climbed the stairs slowly, imagining she could feel the weight of the armor for the first time since becoming a paladin. It clanked lightly as she ascended, musically in tune with the creaks of the steps. At the top of the stairs, she took a moment to examine the paintings of the phases of the moon, circling around from the new moon to the Bright One's full, white orb. Tomorrow was the first day of the full moon, and she and Eodan needed to be out of Quinizelle before that. Ordinarily, she looked forward to those three days. With the burden of Nevante weighing on her, all she felt was weariness.

She crossed the floor, treading on the ritual circles without trying to avoid them, and rapped gently on Nevante's door. No one answered. She pushed the door open anyway.

Nevante sat behind the desk, slumped in her chair. She didn't move when Ginnevra entered. For a moment, fear pulsed through Ginnevra that Nevante had done something drastic, but then the woman raised her head and looked at Ginnevra through eyes dark-circled with pain and dull sorrow. "I'm not leaving," she said.

Ginnevra stood still, watching Nevante. She observed the woman's trembling hands and the faint lines radiating from her lips and furrowing across her forehead. Then she removed her helmet and coif and set them on the desk between them. "I won't make you," she said.

Nevante sat up. "Isn't that your job? Force me to return to Abraciabene in disgrace?"

"My job," Ginnevra said, "is to escort you safely to Paese, where you'll take ship for the holy city. How you go is up to you. But if you refuse, I won't carry you bodily out of here."

"I don't understand. You saw me lose my grace. I'm no longer Hallowed." Nevante clasped her hands in front of her, but they continued to tremble. "But this is my home, prime. I shouldn't have to leave."

"Then stay." Ginnevra shifted to a parade rest position and tilted her head to look down on the former Hallowed. "Stay, and watch some other woman take your place here. Watch her lead in worship the way you used to. Watch her confer with the Revereds and teach the Dedicates and acolytes. If you think that will make you happy, I won't stop you."

Nevante rose, slowly, scooting her wooden chair back so its legs scraped along the floor. "Damn you," she said in a low voice.

Ginnevra said nothing.

Nevante lowered her head. "When do we leave?"

"Depending on how long the storm lasts, this afternoon or tomorrow morning." Ginnevra picked up her helmet and coif, but didn't put them back on. "If you'll have your things ready, we'll meet you here later."

"You're not staying to wait out the storm?"

Ginnevra shook her head. "I have one last important thing to do."

AT THE LAST MINUTE, she decided to get out of her armor before her final errand, which meant she was caught in the rainstorm for the final hundred yards before Filippa's inn. She dodged pedestrians who'd been caught out as well and flung open the door to the tap room with uncharacteristic force. Only a few patrons paid her dramatic entrance any attention; the rest were talking loudly over the sound of the rain beating on the roof and shouting for more drinks. Ginnevra squeezed water out of her short hair and headed for the stairs.

The onion smell was stronger on the dark, narrow stairs than it had been the last time Ginnevra had been there. Maybe the wetness in the air carried the scent farther. She trudged up into the darkness, all the way to the second floor, and then knocked on the third door on the right. No one answered. Ginnevra knocked again.

The door swung open. Filippa looked her over. "You look like a drowned kitten."

"No sane person ought to live where it rains hard enough to wash the thoughts right out of your head," Ginnevra replied. "Can I come in?"

Filippa stepped back in invitation. The room was less well lit than Ginnevra remembered, with rain pattering against the thick, greenish glass, but Ginnevra's paladin's eyes adjusted to bring the narrow bed and small clothespress into clear focus.

Filippa shut the door and leaned against it. "I'd ask you to sit, but…" She gestured at the tiny room and its lack of seating.

"It doesn't matter. I'm not—" Ginnevra pulled the king's scroll case from her waistband. "Here."

With a curious frown, Filippa took the case and worked the cap free of one end. She tipped the paper inside into her palm. "What is this?"

"Read it."

Filippa's eyes moved rapidly as she scanned the paper. Then she read it again. "Is this real?"

"It's the king's seal. Not his own hand, but I don't think it matters so long as his name is on it, attesting to the truth." Ginnevra examined the clothespress and decided it was too small to sit on. She shifted restlessly. "Anyway, yes, it's real."

Filippa let the paper roll up on itself and slid it back into the case. Her eyes were unfocused, staring at some point past Ginnevra's left shoulder. "Justice," she said, her voice faint. "For all of them. For us."

Ginnevra's heart ached with a pain she'd never forgotten. "Filippa—"

"I thought I'd feel something," Filippa said in that same distant voice. "Some kind of release, or vindication. But I just feel cold."

"I thought you'd be happy. It's what you wanted for four years."

Filippa slammed her fist against the wall. "Isn't that rich? I get my heart's desire, and it turns out my heart moved on. Maybe a long while ago. And that means I threw away my life for nothing."

"Filippa—" Ginnevra tried again. "It was what you believed in."

"It was the wrong thing." Filippa let out a deep, harsh breath. "I abandoned my vows and I abandoned you, and for what? Ginna, what was I thinking?"

"That what happened was wrong and unjust," Ginnevra said. "You only wanted the right people to take the blame. There wasn't anything wrong with that."

"That's not what you said before."

Ginnevra closed her eyes so tightly she saw sparks. "I told myself for years that it was your fault we lost our friendship," she said. "I blamed you, said you made me walk away. But you couldn't make me do anything I didn't want to, Filippa. Which means what happened between us was my fault." She opened her eyes. "It was all my fault."

Filippa was staring at her. "I broke my vows."

"And I was young and stupid and terrified that if I didn't repudiate you, it meant I agreed with your choice. I was afraid that made me no longer a paladin, either." Ginnevra wiped her eyes. "I should have listened to what you really wanted instead of what it looked like you intended."

"Ginna, you can't think like that."

Ginnevra wiped her eyes again. "Because it's blasphemy?"

"Because it won't change the past." Filippa put her hand on Ginnevra's shoulder. "I blamed you for a long time, too. Told myself a real friend, a real sister, would have taken my side. But time passed, and the memory of what happened faded, and eventually all I could remember was how close we'd been, and how much I missed that. I'm sorry."

The words struck Ginnevra to the heart. "So am I," she said.

Filippa put her arm around Ginnevra's shoulders and hugged her. Tentatively, Ginnevra hugged her back. The tears fell more freely now, and she didn't have a spare hand to wipe them away, but she found she didn't care.

How long they stood like that, Ginnevra didn't know, but at some point she became aware that the rain had stopped and the room was brighter. She stepped away from Filippa and scrubbed at her eyes. "I'm sorry this took so long."

"I choose to be grateful we had the chance to make amends." Filippa picked up the scroll case and extended it to Ginnevra. "What are you going to do with this?"

"I couldn't exactly tell the king no one in Abraciabene would care." Ginnevra tucked the case into her waistband. "I suppose I'll send it to the holy city as part of my report. Maybe the Blessed will see it as binding the Faith's relationship with Quinizelle."

"But you're not going back."

"Eodan and I are escorting Madama Nevante to Paese. From there, I don't know. Possibly there's an assignment waiting for me in the Paese sanctuary." Ginnevra dipped her hand into her belt pouch and came out with something small. "But I wanted to give you this first."

She dropped Filippa's grace on its leather thong into her friend's hand. Filippa's hand automatically closed over it. "I didn't think I'd see this again," she said. "I thought you'd feel required to keep it. It's not as if I can wear it."

"Maybe not," Ginnevra said. "But I was thinking—at least, it occurred to me later—about Nevante's grace. I wasn't there to see it shatter, so I don't know specifically what she did to earn the Goddess's rejection. But those shards were clear evidence that she'd lost the Goddess's favor. And I remembered that yours is intact. I thought—maybe it means something."

Filippa's eyes filled with tears again. "I'm not a paladin anymore, Ginna. Maybe my grace didn't shatter, but I know I've broken my oaths."

"And maybe being a paladin isn't what you want anymore," Ginnevra said. "I can't tell you what to do. But I think *this*—" She tapped Filippa's closed fist with the leather thong dangling from it— "this means the Goddess isn't done with you yet. Just...think about it, please."

Filippa let out a deep breath. "I will." She cleared her throat, and added in a more normal voice, "Are you leaving soon?"

"Eodan and I need to be out of the city before the full moon," Ginnevra said.

Filippa looked puzzled. "Why the full moon?"

"Because—" Ginnevra stared at her and rapidly thought back over every interaction they'd had since Devoyenne. She *hadn't* mentioned Eodan's race, had she?

She sat on the bed, making the mattress rustle. "There's something I'd like to tell you," she said. "It's not a short story, but for this, I'll make time."

LATER, as she crossed the city headed for the sanctuary, Ginnevra was struck by a memory. She didn't know if she'd forgotten it, or had actively suppressed it, but it brought a smile to her lips now: her first day in her first paladin company, being introduced to the stocky woman with unusually long hair she was told she would ride with. She'd thought *There's no way we'll ever be friends*, because she was nervous and excited and had been certain she was the only one who felt that way, and Filippa had looked so confident. And it had taken less than a day to discover Filippa was as nervous and excited as she.

It hurt, a little, to think that they were going separate ways again, though this time they parted as friends. Primes traveled even more widely than ordinary paladins, and the chances of their paths crossing again by accident were small. But Filippa had said, "I found you once. I can find you again," and in the face of her confidence, Ginnevra discovered a measure of peace.

She splashed through the puddles the downpour had left and breathed in the damp, clean air. True, it was cold, and she was even colder because she'd left her cloak with her gear so it wouldn't get soaked, but there was something beautiful about Quinizelle that even Ginnevra could appreciate.

Eodan waited outside the stables, standing on the porch by the locked front doors of the sanctuary. "You look happy," he remarked. "Like someone who has laid down a great burden."

"You're so insightful." Ginnevra put her arms around him and drew him close. "Is Madama Nevante ready?"

"I assume so. The stable hands all behaved very awkwardly around her, so I came out here to get some fresh air." He sniffed ostentatiously, making Ginnevra laugh. "I'm sure it will be easier once we're on the road."

"That's unexpectedly optimistic of you."

"I always feel optimistic about the beginning of a journey. So many possibilities." He hugged her close and then released her. "Though with Nevante there," he added in a lower voice, "our usual full moon activities will be sadly curtailed."

Ginnevra laughed. She knew now how amorous werewolves became after chasing the full moon all night. "We have self-control. And it's not like we depend on the full moon for that."

"Very true." He kissed her, slow and sweet, making her head spin. "Let's get packed up."

Ginnevra followed him for a few paces, then stopped. "Eodan, you know I love you, right?"

Eodan's eyes narrowed. "That sounds like the prelude to something unpleasant."

"No! It's just—" Filippa's face rose up in memory. "You don't ever talk about your past, and I won't push you to," she said, holding up a hand to stop his protest. "But I've learned recently that the past doesn't always stay in the past. I want you to know that whatever you've experienced, whatever you want to keep secret, if it does ever come out, I'll stand by you. Whatever it is."

Eodan stood still, his whole body tense and his face expressionless as if he was suppressing a powerful emotion. "That's a rash promise. My past might contain things you'll despise me for."

"I don't think so. I trust you. I hope you know you can trust me." Ginnevra squeezed his hand. "For anything."

"Ginnevra—" Eodan closed his hand around hers. When he spoke, Ginnevra was sure it wasn't what he'd originally meant to say. "Thank you. I hope you don't regret that."

"You could always tell me," Ginnevra said with an impish smile, teasing him.

Eodan didn't smile back. "Someday, beloved," he said.

"That's better than all right," Ginnevra said.

About the Author

In addition to the Books of the Dark Goddess, Melissa McShane is the author of many other fantasy novels, including the novels of Tremontane, the first of which is *Servant of the Crown; Burning Bright,* first in The Extraordinaries series; *The Book of Secrets,* first book in The Last Oracle series; and *Hidden Enemy,* first in the follow-up series The Living Oracle

She lives in the shelter of the mountains out West with her family, including two very needy cats. She wrote reviews and critical essays for many years before turning to fiction, which is much more fun than anyone ought to be allowed to have. You can visit her at her website **www.melissamcshanewrites.com** for more information on other books and upcoming releases.

For news on upcoming releases, bonus material, and other fun stuff, sign up for Melissa's newsletter **here.**

If you enjoyed this book, please consider leaving a review at your favorite online bookseller!

ALSO BY MELISSA MCSHANE

www.ingramcontent.com/pod-product-compliance
Lightning Source LLC
Chambersburg PA
CBHW070909260626
47162CB00007B/2614